PAPER STONES

Copyright © 2020 Laurie Ray Hill

Except for the use of short passages for review purposes, no part of this book may be reproduced, in part or in whole, or transmitted in any form or by any means, electronically or mechanically, including photocopying, recording, or any information or storage retrieval system, without prior permission in writing from the publisher or a licence from the Canadian Copyright Collective Agency (Access Copyright).

We gratefully acknowledge the support of the Canada Council for the Arts and the Ontario Arts Council for our publishing program. We also acknowledge the financial support of the Government of Canada.

Cover design: Val Fullard

Paper Stones is a work of fiction. All the characters portrayed in this book are fictitious and any resemblance to persons living or dead is purely coincidental.

Library and Archives Canada Cataloguing in Publication

Title: Paper stones : a novel / Laurie Ray Hill.
Names: Hill, Laurie Ray, 1956– author.
Series: Inanna poetry & fiction series.
Description: Series statement: Inanna poetry & fiction series
Identifiers: Canadiana (print) 20200330160 | Canadiana (ebook) 20200330187 | ISBN 9781771337854 (softcover) | ISBN 9781771337861 (epub) | ISBN 9781771337878 (Kindle) | ISBN 9781771337885 (pdf)
Classification: LCC PS8615.I41725 P37 2020 | DDC C813/.6—dc23

Printed and bound in Canada

Inanna Publications and Education Inc.
210 Founders College, York University
4700 Keele Street, Toronto, Ontario, Canada M3J 1P3
Telephone: (416) 736-5356 Fax: (416) 736-5765
Email: inanna.publications@inanna.ca   Website: www.inanna.ca

PAPER STONES

a novel

Laurie Ray Hill

Inanna Poetry & Fiction Series

INANNA PUBLICATIONS AND EDUCATION INC.
TORONTO, CANADA

1.

HI. I'M ROSE. I don't know if you've thought much about what the point of your life is? The point of mine, ever since I figured out that we're in a rockslide, has been to keep the rockslide from squashing Jenny.

Mind you, I'm no use if I'm like a red splat, under a ton of rocks myself. So I been crawling out from under.

The way I see it, how most of the trouble in the world got started must've been a good-sized rock must have fell from a height onto some cave man. Smacked him. Bullseye in the bald spot. When he stood up, his brain had went haywire. He goes wandering back to the cave and he sees his own little boy running out to him. Hauls off and slugs the kid. Busts his jaw. Then he sees his little girl. Gets her behind a boulder. And he comes on to her, like she was his wife.

Them kids were soon screwed up, eh, living with this nut cake. So screwed up that, when their day come, they turned around and done wrong to their own kids.

And that's the whole history lesson on an awful lot of families. Just over and over again, right on down, more sick-in-the-head people bringing up more and more sick-in-the-head people, whole frigging time the world's been going. It's like that first rock set off an avalanche that's been roaring down the mountain, from then to now, gathering dirt.

My niece, Jenny, she was right in line for it. Knowing her grandfather. Me and my sister, Sandra, we'd got it from that old man. Our father, he "abused us physically and sexually," if you want to sound like a shrink.

And now my sister Sandra, she'd took up with a creep who put me in mind of Dad. And they'd went and had baby Jenny.

I could feel the ground shake. Old avalanche heading for that little tiny baby girl.

She's laying in her basket, learning how to smile, finding out she's got toes, and I'm thinking Christ almighty, what am I going to do?

What I want to tell is how we got things fixed up. I like to think that reading this here will be somebody's first step.

It's quite something. We were wrote up in the newspapers. Good news for a change, human interest. Us losers from the abuse survival group that wound up doing so good. Bunch of Cinderellas getting like a free ride in a magic pumpkin, to hear the paper tell it. They want to talk about our good luck. Never mention that we also worked our brains to the bone (as Dave would say). If yous want to get out from under that rockslide, eh, yous might as well know right now: it's a ton of work. You can do it, though. That's what I want to say to all of yous. If you yourself have been ran over by something like this, there's no need to lay there squashed flat all your life.

That makes me think of a joke Dave tells: "What would you call Batman and Robin if the rockslide had ran over them? *Flatman and Ribbon.*"

Anyways. First good decision I ever made was I joined this therapy group for people like myself that had got abused as youngsters.

Everybody always interrupts me when I get started telling this. They always ask, "What about the fortune teller?" They're talking about the one member of our group, Josie, who seems to know everything ahead of time.

What can I tell yous? Josie's got the second sight. I don't claim to know how she does it. Gives me the goosebumps.

I'll start off by giving some answers to questions about Josie that are asked frequent. Yes, she did see the lost gold that had fell in the lake. Yes, she knew the lake was behind the white church, in the town we had to find. Yes, she seen the house in the valley. Yes, she seen the man at the door with a lucky ticket. The toy cow that come out in the trial too. And, yeah, pretty well everything she says seems to come true, one way or another. Long as you're not too "literal minded," as our group leader, Meredith, would say. Even Sally and her thing with the hardware man come true, sort of. We had a laugh out of that one. So now just sit tight and I'll tell yous more about Josie as we go along.

What got me started was I was back at the women's shelter. That time, I was hiding from I think it was Darrell. The one who managed to bean me with the door of the broom closet. I'm walking by and he reefs on it, eh. Deliberate. Cracks my head open.

He was number I-forget-what. It was what I done in them days. I'd take up with some jerk and get clobbered. Never meant for it to go that way, of course. But that'd be the way she went, every frigging time.

Pam, at the shelter, sits me down in her office.

I always stare at this poster she's got on her wall. Wide river. Dark grey cloud on our side. But, over on the far shore, it's lit up in a patch of gold sparkle. My eyes get pulled to follow these stepping stones across the river. Something about them stepping stones! I can never quit staring at them, the way they lead off into that dark water and right on across to the light.

Wrote underneath the picture: *Take the First Step*.

"Rose," this Pam woman says to me, she says, "I strongly recommend that you join. It starts this coming Tuesday. The leader's name is Meredith."

I drag my eyes off the pinkish stepping stones leading into gold sparkle. Start rubbing my thumbs together. My head's sore as fire. Nine stitches. I says, "I don't need that."

Pam, from the shelter, I can feel her looking at me. She's trying to get me to go to some therapy group.

"Alls they'll do is whine," I says, talking to my thumbs.

I'm fidgeting around in the chair, eh. What if I went to that group and they asked a lot of nosy questions? What if they found out? At that time, I used to think the civilized earth would end if anybody ever knew about me, that I done it with my own dad.

This Pam woman, she's going on about how it's free. It's a great opportunity. I'm so fortunate the Family Services Alliance is providing this. There's not many places you can join a group like this for free. I'll be able to stay in the group as long as I need to.

I don't care if they're offering to pay *me*.

"Would you like to talk about why this feels so scary, Rose?"

"What it feels is useless. I picked a loser. He hit me with a cupboard door. What's some shrink supposed to do about it?"

I was being Defensive. I know the name, now, of every stupid thing you can be.

Back then, I never knew what the frig I was being.

Pam at the shelter, she says, "The therapist will work with you to take a look at some of the events in your past."

"That's over and done," I says.

Which just shows what I knew in them days! Thought I was being smart. Acting practical. Moving on. I says, "I can't do nothing about the past. I got here-and-now to think of. I've missed a week's work. I got the rent to pay. Asshole Darrell's took off."

"It's surprising how much of the past is not over and done, until we have dealt with it." That's what Pam said.

I said I had more important things to think about.

Avoidance. That's the name of when you say you got no time to do whatever it is you know damn well you need to do.

I never went to no group that time.

Never went the next time, neither, after Gary. But I remembered what the woman at the shelter said about the past. The past don't go no place. Sits right where it is, like the garbage under the sink, ripening up, until you deal with it.

That was the year my sister had a baby. Jenny was born.

I held baby Jenny and I wanted the world fixed. I held her head so careful. Just the thoughts of somebody cracking that adorable head some day! That sweet-smelling, warm little head with blonde fuzz hair.

Or worse. Screwing with her. I thought about the jerk my sister was living with. I thought about old Dad, there, dropping in for visits.

A baby is so beautiful, eh. When I changed her, I cleaned the little flower folds between her wee legs. That's when I started to hear the rockslide rumbling, heavy, up there, heading for that baby. And I'm thinking, "No! Nobody's going to mess with this darling little baby! Not while I'm still kicking!"

To do anything about it though, it took me all the way to Donny, who broke my dollhouse and my thumb.

It's three years later. I'm back at the shelter, laying low till they catch Donny.

My sister Sandra is living with a different creep now. No different than her other creeps before, far as I can see. She's putting up with horse shit. Just like I tend to do, and our mother always done, when she was living.

Our poor mother was one of them real nice people, eh. Soft and sweet as candy floss. You felt ashamed to think a thought around her that wasn't just peachy. I used to think she was a saint. The way I see it now, she'd have did better to speak up and say what needed saying. Willing Victim. That'd be the shrinks' name for poor Mom.

Anyways, there I am. I'm back in Pam's same old office at the women's shelter. Nothing's changed. She's still got her same poster up. I'm in the hot seat again. Jenny's three years old. World ain't fixed.

I'm sitting there thinking about my little Jenny. She couldn't quite say, Aunt Rose; christened me "Ann Toes." I'm thinking, ain't that cute!

Pam's talking to me: "Rose, I would strongly encourage you to join a therapy group this time. There happens to be a new group starting two weeks from this coming Tuesday. I don't know if this particular group would interest you?" she says, and she looks me in the eye. "It's for survivors of childhood sexual abuse."

I'm like hit by lightning. *Pam knows! How does she know? Is it wrote all over me? Can anybody see, just looking at me? Am I walking around naked and don't know it?*

I don't know where to look. I want to say No! Nothing like that would be any interest to me! Why would I take an interest in anything as puke gross as child abuse? Nothing to do with me! No!

But nothing come out.

I just sat there. Couldn't rub my thumbs this time because the left one was broke. Felt my eyes getting hauled into that poster. River looked cold. Fast. Dark. Dangerous. But there was the stones to step on, all the way to the other side, where the sun was shining. Solid-looking rocks, big enough for your feet. I'd never saw stones that pinkish colour.

Take the First Step, it says.

I said, "I am worried about my little niece. I want to do something to help her, so she don't ever get diddled with." I'm hoping Pam will think I'm just taking an interest for Jenny's sake.

"Sexually abused, do you mean?"

I give a nod.

"Do you suspect anyone of abusing her?"

"Not yet. No. But I can see where it could happen. I want to help her. I want to teach her so she knows to look out for herself."

Just like my mother. I was trying to look like a saint. Help somebody else when I was the one needed help the worst right then. This Pam woman told me. Said I had to help myself first. She talked to me about the oxygen masks on an airplane. In an emergency you got to put your own mask on first, she said. Make sure you're breathing first, and then help the next person.

That made some sense. You're no use to nobody if you're passed out with your tongue on the rug.

"You have to help yourself, Rose, before you can help anyone else." She said that again. Could she really know about my father? How in the world would she? Was it all over town? Did everybody and their aunt know that about me? Did the shrinks have some secret file on me?

I was dying to get away and hide. Could've ran out, dove into the first compost bucket I come to, pulled the squash skins and dead tomatoes over me, and rotted, for shame.

I'm staring at the poster. If I could just get away, get myself to someplace else, like on the far side of that river. And take Jenny with me!

Jenny playing on that sunny shore, where the sand's warm! Jenny safe! Out of the danger. Both of us away from here. Out of the disgusting stuff. Over there in the sparkle!

I surprised myself. I said, "Okay," I said, "sign me up, would you mind."

Pam, she's been trained not to faint. She don't shout, "Well, it's about freaking time!" or nothing.

It's funny to think of going to that building by the park, finding the side door, like they'd told me, and climbing them stairs for the very first time.

I'm climbing and I'm thinking, okay, I'm going. But I'm not talking. I'm just doing this to find out what I need to do to make Jenny safe.

Even if they did somehow know something about my father, they weren't going to dig no dirty particulars out of me. They could think what they liked. I wasn't telling them nothing. I figured one or two meetings should about do it.

What do you do to make sure a kid don't get abused? Maybe there was some way to warn her without scaring her. I could teach her. Like they talk about street proofing. Only in her own home. It wasn't no strangers in the street I was worried about. It was my own dad and these prize winners my sister shacks up with.

There was three women in this waiting room, memorizing their shoes. They looked up.

Fattest one give me a smile and a little soft hand. Aunt Marg, the lionheart. That's what Jenny calls her now.

The pretty one with the long, blonde hair said she was Sally and this was Tammy.

So there I am, seeing Marg, Sally, and Tammy for the first time! Not planning on talking to them.

Tammy, she had her collar buttoned up, but you could still see the top of a dark blood bruise on her neck.

I sat on an orange plastic chair.

Then we all froze. There was this out-of-the-old-horror-movies, slow *clunk* ... *clunk* ... *clunk* in the downstairs hall. Then it was coming up the stairs. We looked at each other.

Sound kept coming. *Clunk ... clunk ... clunk*. Up the stairs. We heard it cross the first-floor landing. It kept on coming. It was in the hall. Coming along towards us. We stood up.

Black-and-blue face peeked in.

Tammy yelped.

Marg laughed.

Gleaming out of that beat-up face was the brightest eyes I ever seen.

Josie's eyes are even more like high-beam headlights, the way she is now. But even then, with her bruises, first thing anybody seen was them halogen eyes.

Josie, she gets pissed off if you call her a fortune teller. But she must have *saw* something about this group. She took in solid Marg. She took in wide-eyes Sally. She took in Tammy with the bruises on her neck. She looked me through and through.

Them eyes of Josie's, running over us one by one, put me in mind of the sun through a magnifying glass. Seemed like if she stared at a piece of paper, it would catch on fire.

Josie's a little shrimp. Looks something like a lawn gnome. Had her left leg and foot in a cast, which is what made her sound like *The Mummy Returns*, eh, dragging herself upstairs.

Well that broke the ice. Sally (the pretty one, with the long blonde hair), she dragged an extra chair over and got Josie set there, with her foot up.

We told the whole thing over to Darlene, when she showed up. They take six in a group. Darlene was number six to show up.

Pretty good joke. *Josie Returns*, sequel to *Josie and the Swamp Thing*.

Marg says, in a spooky voice, "It's turning on to your street."

Sally says, "It's coming up your stairs."

"It's going to suck your blood."

We were laughing when the leader, Meredith, showed up with her helper. They stopped in the door. I don't think they'd ever saw a bunch of the losers that they work on having a good time like that, before a first meeting. We were supposed to be still all nervous there, picking lint.

What went through my mind was that this leader lady, Meredith, did not like us sitting back, laughing. Frances, the helper, she just smiled like a human. But something weird went over Meredith's face before she thought to smile.

Me and Josie hung around for a smoke afterwards. It was a nice cool night in the fall. We went across to the park. She sat on a bench sideways. Put her bad foot up. I stood around.

I says, "I don't think the leader there was too happy to see us all laughing when she first walked in."

Josie, she stopped with her cigarette hand halfways to her mouth. "If I say something like that," she says, "everybody's ready to burn me for a witch." Josie was grinning, with her head on a tilt. Them eyes of hers, glittering under the street light, give me the shivers.

"A witch?" I says.

Josie shrugs and takes a drag. "You seen," she says, blowing out the smoke. "Alls I ever do is tell what I've saw, but people freak out."

I could guess why, the way she give me the shivers.

I says, "Well, anybody could've saw that. It was wrote all over that Meredith's face. She walked in, give us a look like she'd bit a lemon. Then on, she never quit smiling."

Josie, she pointed her cigarette fingers at me. "Not everybody would see that. Or know enough to worry about it," she says.

"Don't know that I'm worrying about it." But I guess I was. Didn't trust that group leader.

Josie started staring at a leaf that was floating down through the air. It went through the bright part, where the streetlight was shining. Landed in the dark.

That come back to me a long time later, when it was important. I could see Josie, sideways on the park bench, forehead scrunched, thinking over the group leader, Meredith. Them eyes of hers watching that yellow leaf miss the patch of light. First time I ever seen anybody look at an omen.

Once you're out there in the middle of the river on your stepping stones—and they can be slippery buggers—you want to feel like you can trust your leader.

I never thought about nothing like that till a long time later. Josie being Josie, I bet she thought of it way back then. Josie seen that we'd have to keep an eye on this leader, see just how she was missing the patch of light, find out what kind of dark she was landed in, that made her sour to see us laugh.

It got so I looked forwards to Group every week. Got to know them girls. We'd talk about things we were going to do someday.

Josie got this idea that she never shut up about. Said we were going to have a hotel and serve dinner. And, in the back, there was going to be this room—"Lost Gold Room," she got calling it.

I asked her how she come up with that. Josie wouldn't say. She didn't like to talk about her second sight. Back then, we all had our secrets.

Josie said this room was going to be just for people like us.

Marg says how are we going to know who's like us? Marg's one of these people who's got to have every detail of everything planned out ahead. (Sally used to tease her. Said Marg never done nothing on faith. "Marg, I bet you wouldn't start out on a trip until every traffic light was already turned green.")

Tammy says, "What would we do when men come into the hotel?" Tammy, she spent her time worrying about all men except the one she needed to worry about, which was the one give her that blood bruise on her neck. She was scared of the men that were going to come into our daydream hotel.

Josie says, "They'll keep their hands to themself in our hotel!"

Marg laughs. (Marg laughs like a jug of milk getting shook. Kills me.)

Darlene rolls her eyes. She was the last one that got there the first night. That's Darlene. Always last, lagging behind, missing out. Somebody must have told Darlene, when she was about four years old, that that was cute on her, rolling her eyes like that. Maybe it was, thirty years ago.

One Tuesday, Josie come clunking up the stairs and she digs this picture out of her purse. "Look at this!" The picture is some little back-north town. There's maybe a dozen frame houses and a few storefronts, gas station with the shell hanging crooked, old white church. But Josie's wound up.

"Look at the colour of the stones!" She points to the pinkish rocks in the picture and she takes this sideways look at me.

It's something you got to get used to with Josie, that like cold touch on your neck. She's showing me pink rocks like stepping stones, and she's looking at me.

She won't even pass the picture around. She's got to hold onto it while everybody takes a turn looking. It's just some picture she's cut out of a magazine. I said, "Where is it?"

That took the wind out of her sail because she couldn't remember where she cut it out of. She'd went and cut the name off too, and all the information.

Sally said, "It's nice, Josie. Look at the pretty little white church." Sally believes in God.

Josie, she loved that picture. Even dreamed about it. She was telling us the next Tuesday. Said there was water behind that white church—deep, clear water that looked blue, silver, or green, depending.

I says, "Depending on what?"

Josie sucks you in, eh. You hear yourself asking a question on the stuff she's talking about, as if you took it serious. So I'm asking her what the colour of the water behind the church depends on. (The water ain't even in the picture, remember. She dreamed the water.)

"It depends," she says, with this spooky look on her like she just seen a spaceship.

And you've got to ask her, "Depends on what?"

She'll tell you, too.

It got to be this funny thing. We'd sit there and talk about it every week when we were waiting. We started getting there early. We'd all (except Darlene) show up at seven on the nose just to have the time to talk. And we'd get excited and we'd talk about the hotel and the town. Like a bunch of kids with a secret game.

Marg, she's got this nice calm way with her. Sensible, steady. Says she would have liked to be a nurse, if things had been different. I liked Marg, right off. She's the one that's fat, friendly, laughs funny, plans ahead, and, in an emergency, turns out to be lionhearted.

One night, Josie'd managed to haul ass upstairs even earlier than usual. Sally dragged a chair for her to put her foot on. (Sally is as sweet as she looks. Youngest one here but she's everybody's little mother.) Josie's all happy. She bends forwards. "I've been thinking!"

Josie never quits thinking. When she'd lower her voice like that and lean in, you knew you were going to hear something nuttier than peanut brittle and just as much of a treat.

"This woman will make pies for the dining room."

She takes out that picture in her purse.

Sally asks how we know that there's a woman to make pies.

Josie holds her little magazine clipping picture under the light. We're all crowded around looking, and you can just see where there's a sign on the fence in front of a faded yellow house. It's a teeny tiny sign but she didn't dream it.

"What's it say?" I need longer arms.

Tammy, the one with the bruise on her neck, who worries about all the men except the asshole who tried to strangle her, she reads it out: *Home-Made Pies Fresh Picked Local Blueberries.*

"People are going to drive a long way for them pies," Josie says. "And we'll get our eggs, fresh, off of these people here. The homemade pie will be just for people like us."

If I squint at the picture, I can make out a chicken scratching in the dirt outside the place next to the garage.

Josie says that is what they call a free-range chicken and we're going to charge extra for its eggs. Except people like us, who are going to get them regular price.

Sally says, "We should make the dining room so it looks out over the lake."

That's the water behind the church. It's a lake now.

I can see it: People taking it easy, eating their high-price eggs beside a shining lake. Us all in summer dresses, with our hair done, running the place. Wouldn't Sally be right in her glory, looking after everybody! We'd put Marg at the front desk. No baloney from the public would phase solid Marg. She'd be out there, calm and steady, friendly look on her, setting everybody straight.

Josie says she knows what type of furniture we're getting. She's got it figured out that the guy in the blue house made the two-seater swing and octagon picnic table in his yard. She likes his style, she says. It goes with our hotel. Back-north style, pine logs.

I said, "How can you see what style it is?"

She's got a magnifying glass! Takes it out of her purse.

Marg's still laughing at that, glugging like a jug of two-percent, when Meredith, the leader, prances in. We quit laughing, file in like good kids, and sit where we always sit.

Everybody takes a turn to talk about their week. Our week is generally crap, when you get right down to it. We talk about our anxiety attacks. We tell how we binged on beer or double chocolate with sugar sprinkles doughnuts or whatever, on Monday night, to feel better. And felt like shit afterwards. We say things like that we let some jerk move in on Wednesday and he got drunk Friday and broke the handle off the stove so now we're using the dog leash to get the oven door open. Somebody's normally lost whatever dumb job they were doing and can't get their welfare cheque for three weeks. Whoever's got a car, it's usually broke down and their boyfriend's took off and won't fix it. Or he's got the car and he says it's his because he made the last three payments on it, only that's bull, usually. The money he put in was supposed to be for rent and he's been eating off us too.

The leader, Meredith, she sits and plays with her diamond bracelet. She wants to know if we recognize any pattern in the way we keep letting a different man move in and break something else or whatever each stupid one of us just done for the tenth time.

Pattern. That's a word Meredith likes. She's trying to get us to see our pattern.

We all got different problems. But if you stand back and look at what we keep doing it is just as clear to see as footprints in snow. We're going right around in circles. Guess that's a pattern.

We get a fifteen-minute break. Josie hops downstairs. Got to have her smoke. We stand outside, smoking, and we're back to the hotel. I say the mosquitoes will eat you. We'd better screen in the patio.

Sally says we could grow flowers on it.

Just to see her smile, I get Sally to tell me what kind of flowers she is going to grow on our patio.

Sally lights up. "Pink!"

We boost Josie back upstairs. You can pretty near lift her with one hand.

Her and Sally are slim. Everybody else here is fairly fat, including Meredith the leader and her helper.

If yous want to know what I look like, I can tell yous I got a different opinion on that now myself. I'm short and stocky, kind of flat. Rear end on the larger side. My hair likes to stick out. Old Donny there, that broke my thumb, he used to tell me I was so ugly I'd make a train take a dirt road.

But self-image is something you make progress on in Group. And now I try to think about what Dave said. (I'll tell yous all about Dave in a minute.) What Dave said was, he said there's nothing wrong with how I look. I'm straightforward looking, he said. The lines around my mouth and eyes, he said, they just show that I like a good laugh. He said something nice about my hands too. My hands are broad and plain. But Dave, he looked at me stroking Jenny's hair one night when she was falling asleep on the couch. I got a kindly touch, is what he said.

Meredith, she helped me out a lot with the self-image problem too. Always called me on it if she heard any Negative Self-Talk out of me.

This week Tammy's the one with the biggest disaster. Tammy is married. Two kids. Little boy nine, girl eleven. Their father has what Meredith calls "an anger problem." He's a goddamn menace that tried to strangle her, in other words, and Tammy needs to get those kids the hell out of that house. He caught the little boy, Matthew, in the head last Sunday night. Matthew bled from his ear and couldn't hear on that side until this morning. That's what Tammy told us on the way upstairs. Alls she said to Meredith was that part about him choking her. Didn't say nothing about what happened to the little boy.

Meredith is sitting there asking Tammy how it makes her feel to relate the incident.

The kid has been bleeding from his ear! I never even heard of bleeding from your ear. Don't sound good. I want Tammy to tell Meredith what happened. And I want Meredith to tell Tammy to kick the jerk out of the house.

Tammy ain't telling and Meredith ain't doing nothing.

Meredith never tells us what to do. Not her job description. (She don't have kids, herself. My Jenny, she's changed the way I look at everything, like she was my own.)

Josie's fed up. She's hunkered there, arms crossed. Eyebrows stiff. Eyes like a couple of blow torches. Marg's had it too. She's studying a crack in the table, chewing on her lip to keep her mouth shut. Darlene's curled into her fuzzy jacket, keeping to herself like a cat. Sally can't sit still. Gets up to reach a box of Kleenex for Tammy.

Nobody's supposed to talk out of turn. We're to let Tammy get through expressing herself. Tammy is supposed to make her own decisions. Nobody's allowed to hand out advice.

She's got to get those kids out! She's got to get those kids out. She's got to get those kids out. I'm squeezing every muscle I got, to keep my trap shut. *Why don't Tammy tell Meredith what happened to that poor little kid? Why don't Meredith tell Tammy to get out of that house? Leaving her sitting there getting choked!*

Tammy says that her husband got mad because the front room was a mess.

Meredith wants to know if Tammy feels that it's her responsibility to keep the house tidy.

Tammy breaks down. Says she tries but she's no good at

keeping house. Meredith can't get Tammy to see that that's not what she was driving at, and they go around in circles over housekeeping.

Meredith asks Tammy if she has considered contacting the police. Tammy won't. Don't want to rat on her husband.

Couldn't Meredith call the cops? How can we just sit here?

Meredith asks if Tammy would like to talk about her feelings of loyalty to her husband.

I can't take this shit. I'm going to scream.

I shut my ears and go into a picture in my head. Tammy's two kids swinging in the two-seater, north-style, pine-log swing that the guy in the blue house is going to make for the lawn of the dream hotel. Standing up, facing each other, laughing, pushing with one foot and then the other to make the swing fly. I pictured that so hard I could hear the swing creak. I could hear the kids laughing their two different laughs. I could smell the fresh cut grass. I could see the little girl's skinny legs pumping that swing. One polka dot sock falling down. I had the little boy in a sky-blue T-shirt. Dirty little fingers gripping the swing. Bright grin on him. I went there so I didn't have to listen about Tammy getting choked, nobody doing nothing.

Nobody even talking about what the hell is happening to the kids.

Meredith leaves Tammy with a Question to Think About until next week: "Who is responsible for your husband's anger?"

I know the idea is for Tammy to see that the asshole himself is responsible. Tammy is not going to figure that out.

Meredith's got a PhD degree, but I don't think she knows what it's like to be Tammy. I bet I got more of a clue myself.

Afterwards, soon as the door is shut on Meredith and her helper, we all mob Tammy. "Why didn't you tell about Matthew's ear?"

Tammy hangs her head.

"What the frig are you waiting for? You've got to get those kids out!"

Marg's calm voice says, "How about you go home right now, get Matthew and Meghan and head for the women's shelter."

Josie says, "Asshole's out tonight."

Tammy looks at her and nods.

Good. Marg tells her: get a bag. Collect the kids' baby pictures, pyjamas, school clothes for tomorrow, school books. And if they've got like a favourite Spider-Man or teddy bear or anything to hang on to.

"That's alls you need," Josie says. "Get your three toothbrushes. Hop in the car."

Tammy's car is working, for a wonder. We go over the plan with her on the way downstairs. We make her repeat what she's going to do.

"Do it tonight," I tell her. "Don't sit around there another minute."

Tammy says, "What about Harold?"

"Who?"

Matthew's gecko, that he loves. Tammy says she'd better put him in a jar and bring him along. We say, "Well punch holes in the lid."

On top of everything else, we don't need Harold the gecko suffocated.

"Call me when you're there," Sally tells her.

"Hurry," Marg says.

Tammy tends to fiddle and fart around. Takes her forever to do anything. I can picture her trying to think whether to leave the meat out of the freezer that she got out this morning or if it's okay to put it back or if she should throw it out. She could be standing there worrying about that when the Asshole comes home.

I tell Tammy. I say, "Don't diddle with nothing. Okay? Just get the kids and go."

Tammy says, "Now what were the things I have to pack? The baby albums, school clothes, Harold." She counts them off on her fingers, and I have a sinking feeling.

I say, "Just get the kids and drive. That's the only thing. Get the kids. Go to the shelter."

Tammy says, "Would they have toothbrushes there?"

"Oh sure." That's what I say.

Marg says, "Hurry Tammy. You want to be out of there before Asshole comes home."

Tammy says, "But they'll need their school clothes tomorrow. That was right."

"Not as much as they need to sleep safe tonight!" I says.

Tammy says, "What about the babysitter?"

We tell her: drop the babysitter off on the way to the shelter. Her husband always takes the babysitter home. Well tonight Tammy's got to. Tammy don't know where the babysitter lives.

The babysitter knows.

Marg says, "Hurry."

So Tammy drives off. She knows where the shelter is. She's been there before. Most of us has.

2.

I GOT A LITTLE BUSY with my own stuff that week. I was working at this carpet-cleaning place. Doing telemarketing. You got your dryer vent sucked out, free, that month with our hall and two rooms special.

The owner, Ken, he decides he wants something else sucked, free. I couldn't just tell him to go to hell because it's a job, right? But I wasn't doing that for him if I could help it. He's this big fat older guy that stinks.

I had to watch myself every minute. Went to a lot of trouble over it. I come in and left with the other girls. Got somebody to come to the bathroom with me so he never had a chance to hit on me.

Every day, in the back of my mind, there's little Jenny. The ground feels like it's rumbling. I got to hurry up and do something. Like we told Tammy.

Hurry. Hurry. Do something before the kids get hurt.

I talked to Pam at the shelter about it one day. Called her up in a panic.

I said, "They're not doing nothing at that group you sent me to! Time's going by! They haven't said one word about how to help a kid so she don't get abused."

Pam asked me again if I had any evidence that Jenny was getting hurt or abused.

"Not yet. But my sister keeps picking up these frigging jerks and she has Dad over there all the time playing with Jenny. It's making me crazy!"

"The best thing you can do right now, Rose, is keep on going to Group. You've got to give it some time for the group to get established. Soon you'll be working on your own healing. Remember the oxygen mask. You need to help yourself before you can help anyone else."

I was fighting off a panic feeling half the time. It would pop into my head. Some dirty man beckoning to little toddling Jenny. "Come in here. See what I got to show you."

And I'm like, NO! *Jenny, no!*

When Friday finally come, I went down to The Pig & Whistle to play bingo. They're giving away a fridge at the end of this month, and you get your name entered just for showing up. I could sure use a new fridge. Mine's been temperamental ever since Darrell.

Josie's there with her old boyfriend, I'm sorry to see. Last I heard, she kicked that guy out and it was high time by the sounds of it. He's got a pal with him. Name of Dave. (This is the part where I meet Dave!)

I won twenty bucks at the bingo so we were all having a beer.

Then who struts in but Ken, my boss. He's been playing pool in the back room and having a few. Starts hitting on me.

This Dave fellow, he can see I want Ken to bugger off. Dave asks me to dance.

Dave stands up. Ken don't come up to his chin.

Ken fades away and I get up and dance with Dave.

That's all right. Dave don't smell bad or nothing. Around my age. God, it's been a while! And it's been a long week.

I just let my breath out slow as I let my face settle into where it fits against Dave's chest. There's a dent in him there under the collarbone where my face comes to rest. He pulls me in a little closer. It feels so blessed good to relax like this, rest in somebody's arms.

I don't know the guy. I don't even care. A hug can feel good, eh. The music was loud but not to hurt your ears, just big, like this guy. We're dancing slow, holding each other. I think he's liking it too, the simple fact of somebody's arms around him. Not personal. Not even what I called "sexy" at that time—no big rush. Good, warm hug on this cold night, like you wanted all the time you were a kid. I've got a buzz from the beer.

Josie's there beside me, her foot in the cast, trying to dance. She's got one crutch and her boyfriend. I can hear her yelling in his ear, over the music, telling him there's going to be dancing every Friday at this hotel she's thinking of building.

He laughs at her and rubs her curly head, kind of rough. "What do you use for brains?" he says.

Something I remember, clear, from the night I met Dave was his clean jokes. He kept telling us these corny, harmless jokes like an eight-year-old tells and then he'd grin, sheepish.

He said, "Two guys walk into a bar. Third one ducks." And he grinned.

Took me a minute.

Well, anyways, I wound up letting this Dave guy come home with me.

So there's me the next Tuesday. I'm trotting up the stairs, cheerful. I run into Marg on her way to the washroom. I tell her, "Guess what! I've met someone!"

Marg gets this look on her like, *Here we go again. Rose and some guy.*

I said, "It's not like you're thinking. There's no big buzz. It's just plain nice."

Dave could've been a daddy long-legs crawling out of the hole in Marg's chocolate sprinkles doughnut, to judge by the look on her.

Back then, I couldn't explain about Dave. If I had to put it into words now, I'd say he was not injured like any of the men I'd knew before. Old rockslide had passed him by.

Getting to know him had a friendly sort of a feel to it. No head rush or fireworks. None of what Meredith calls "drama" or "heightened intensity." I was not walking on any clouds.

"Are you going slow?" Marg knows I don't tend to go slow. But I says, "You know, Marg, maybe I am, for once."

Tammy shows up. We jump on her. "So? Are you moved into the shelter? How's the kids? Lizard make it?"

She says not yet. She's going to do it soon, she says. She's getting organized, she says.

We all start screaming at her.

Tammy says, "Next week for sure. I need to do a few things first, to get ready. I cleaned house this week."

We're sitting there in the waiting room, checking out the ceiling tiles, picking at our fingernails, chewing gum. How long till Tammy and those kids get beat up again? Why the frig won't she get out? How come Meredith don't do nothing?

After a while, for something else to think of, Sally starts telling us how she saw these cans of paint cheap at Liquidation World. "We could start buying things like that," she says, "a step at a time until we've got everything we need. How else could you build a hotel?" Sally says. "You couldn't get everything at once. It's a pretty, soft shade of pink, like the inside of a shell. They got eight cans left."

Sally always buys stuff on sale and saves it up. Half the tomatoes and brown beans that ever were put in a can were now at Sally's place. The linen closet, she had that stuffed with lima beans. Must've came across a lima bean blow-out. Far as toilet paper went, Sal had stockpiled enough already to start a hotel. (All them beans and all that poop paper, she could get ten counties rooting and tooting and wipe their ass afterward, according to Dave.)

Josie's not so sure she wants the hotel to be pink.

I say, "Just a minute!" Spending money is a different thing from daydreaming.

I get interrupted by the leader, Meredith, and the helper,

Frances, showing up. We troop in and Meredith wants to go around the circle to check in with everybody, see how their week has went.

Tammy says she had a nice week. She cleaned out the rec room, she says. Me, Marg, and Josie, we got steam coming out our ears, listening to this bullshit. Why don't Meredith tell her to get the frig out of that house? Never mind farting around cleaning it!

Meredith just moves on to Sally. How was Sally's week?

Now the thing with Sally is: her mother slept all the time. Saved her the trouble of living. And Sally'd been doing the same. Sleep calling to her every day. Just to pull the blankets back up after breakfast and know nothing. But Sally, she's trying to fight it off.

It would be a lot easier for her to shut her eyes, with some of the things she's looking at. Sally had a little daughter that died.

To meet Sally, you'd take her for the softest soul, so gentle, kind. Wanting to like everybody, help everybody. But Sally's got grit, too. She runs up and down the stairs of her apartment building for getting out stress and rides her bike to the country, which is why she's looking so good. And she prays to God every day for what it takes to keep her eyes open.

Meredith says she's doing very well.

The way Meredith says that don't hit the right note, far as I'm concerned. It's the voice that's pissing me off. It's like Meredith thinks she's better than Sally. Not at keeping in shape, she sure ain't. But she uses that "good for you, dear" voice. She can't hand it to Sally in a regular voice.

Everybody's better at something and worse at something else. That's the way I see it. There's no like *Best Over All* the way there is at a frigging dog show.

Meredith's in a red chair. Her hair is frizzy. I get a picture of her as one of them thousand-dollar poodles, sitting on a red pillow. Her necklace is the sparkly dog collar.

Meredith says I look happy today.

It's her at the dog show that's making me smile. But she's got me cornered, so I tell about Dave.

I have not been looking forwards to telling Meredith about Dave. I had sort of a deal with Meredith. Weren't supposed to be no more men until after Christmas. Give myself a break, was the way she put it.

We all were doing some damn thing, and I was doing men. Meredith said we done it to distract ourselves from our problems and numb ourselves from our pain. Avoidance. We'd be farther ahead to face our past and our pain, she said. But, in them days, none of us were doing much facing up. Sally slept. Marg ate. Tammy pretended like nothing was wrong. Darlene hid in her apartment. Josie drank.

Me, I was famous for the no-good men. I'd get such a buzz off any new thing with a man, I'd lose my brains. I'd feel like a million bucks for a few weeks. It was so good not to feel like shit that I just couldn't resist it, in them days. Then, of course, it would all blow apart and I'd be ashamed for not knowing better. Then I'd feel so low and stupid that I'd be desperate for something to make me feel better, all over again. So the next guy that come along, there I'd go again.

It was the same with all of us. Going in circles. Whatever we were doing, we were doing it to try to blank out from feeling our pain and our shame. Anything rather than admit that, or take a look at it. And every time we looped around again, we knew that alls we'd did was make it worse.

But I told Meredith. I said, "Like I was telling Marg, I wonder if it's something different with Dave because I'm not getting no big buzz off it?"

Meredith says I'm in "the honeymoon phase."

I tell her Dave hasn't broke nothing.

She wants to know if he's eating off me.

I say, "Well all right, but he's going to put in for the rent money." It'll help, if he does.

Every face around that table has got some type of a look

on it. Meredith has her lips squashed together. Sally's all wide eyes and worry. Tammy, she looks like she wants to loan me her mace spray to squirt on Dave. Marg's a cement block.

This ticks me off. I'm not allowed to be happy for fifteen minutes. They sit there with them faces. Dave's getting kicked out the first time he acts up. For now, he's kind spoken, he smells good, his feet and hands are warm, he tells grade-four jokes, and he's got a place on his chest where I like to rest my face. It's not like I think I've got all my problems worked out. I'm still coming to Group, ain't I? I'm still waiting, patient, to find out what I come here to find out.

These nosy bitches can back off.

Meredith's got this exercise for us today. She hands out crayons and pale pink paper. We're to draw pictures of our stepping stones.

I raise my head. Stepping stones? Is there like an echo? I look at Josie, who sees omens. I look at Sally, who thinks God leads us by the hand.

Stepping stones?

I'm sitting there staring at my sheets of paper. Everybody else is going at it with the crayons. I sneak a look at what Josie's doing.

Meredith says, "Rose, do you need help to get started?"

I admit I got no clue what to do.

I feel weird.

Pinkish stepping stones. Does she know about the poster? She could, maybe. But not the rocks in Josie's town. What is it with all these pink rocks?

Meredith's repeating the instructions over. She says I'm supposed to make pictures of the steps I need to go through, for my healing, like we've been discussing, she says.

I'm still blank as the paper. The steps I need to go through? I don't know what even the first one would be.

"Or could Rose start with a picture of where she'd like to

get to and then maybe work back?" The helper puts that in. As soon as she says that, I'm set. I start trying to draw our hotel. Stick people at a table. Big smiles on them. Purple triangles for blueberry pie. Wavy water. There's glue and sparkles. I stick sparkles on my lake. Looks like hope.

I'm just getting started. I grab another sheet of paper. Tammy's two kids on the swing. Quick lines for the girl's hair flying. Now the pie lady's yellow house. Music notes floating out her chimney. Singing while she bakes.

When I look up, everybody else is done and waiting on me. Well, it turns out we've all did the hotel or the town.

Josie's just got one picture she worked on the whole hour. Josie's a real good drawer. Maybe because she can see things so clear in her mind. Her picture looks like it was drew by an artist. Real 3D. A resort lodge. Stone, wood, and windows. Stone path leading up to glass doors. Tall pine trees in the yard. In the middle of the building, there's a high part, built of stone. Yellow flag flying. Letter *J* on it.

Sally, of course, she took it that *J* stood for Jesus, like at the Flying J gas station.

I says, "Duh. Sal. Her name's Josie."

Josie, she held up her picture under her chin. I can see that to this day. Our hotel getting held there in the air under Josie's smile.

We had fun, everybody showing their hotels and towns. Sally's was all pink, with a fountain, flowers, butterflies. Rainbow over the roof.

Meredith let us go on for a while before she said, "You've done very well in evoking a picture of the kind of life you would like to have. But the idea here this evening is to think about how you can move toward that better life. What are the steps between here and there?"

We all shut up like we'd been shot. I mean, frig, if we knew the answer to that, would we be sitting here?

It's time to go home. Meredith says we'll come back to the stepping stone business.

I'm the one left with a Question to Think About this week. What am I avoiding by getting involved with another new man?

Meredith never let me off the hook, after all. I give her a dirty look for that. She smiled at me like I was four years old.

In the hall, Marg says to me, she says, "You get the rent money off this guy, up front."

Darlene says, "Watch out. He's twice the size of you."

Tammy's crowding up to me. "Oh Rose," she says, "you haven't gave him a key, have you?"

Sally said I was in her prayers.

They went on at me all the way downstairs. They wanted to know how much rent I'm paying and how much of my food Dave's eating and what he does and whether he ever helps out.

I say I'll only keep him till the weather warms up. I'm using him to save on heat.

When I'm hurrying away up the street to get away from them, I can hear Josie in her cast, clunking after me. I speed up. I don't want to hear it. But she yells.

I turn around. "All right. What?"

She's puffing. She smokes too much. "Rose," she says, "I don't know this for a fact. I didn't see no omens. But we heard that guy's hooked up with some bad ones."

"I thought he was supposed to be a friend of your boyfriend."

"They've knew each other since they were kids. But that don't mean nothing. Brent's not so much good himself. Plus he runs with some that's worse."

I says, "Why did you take him back?"

"Why did you take this Dave guy in?"

There was Christmas lights in the store window beside us there. Josie was lit up green. I'm sure I was too. We stood there, shivering, pale green.

How do you quit doing the same stupid thing over and over your whole life? Or even know if that's what you're doing?

God, it beat Josie and me, at that time!

I had this thought that Dave was better because I wasn't getting a buzz off him. But I didn't know if that made sense. I wanted to ask somebody. I wanted to say, *How can I know if this is any better than the other times?* I don't feel so sure, even, as I usually do. (Normally, at this stage with a guy, I'm sure he's the missing half of my heart.)

What are the stepping stones? Where do you put your foot so as to take a forward step? I wanted to say, *I'm like in a bad dream where you can't get no place.*

All that come out was, "What's wrong with us?"

We stood there in the cold, our cheeks on fire. Pale green tears.

I says, real unsure of myself, I says, "I think maybe this time is going to be different?"

Josie, she just put her arms out. Give me a tight hug. Then she brightened up. Dabbed her eyes with a used Kleenex and said, "In the town, I seen this house with blue curtains."

I let out a sigh. Her and her frigging daydreams! There's a time and a place. And this was not.... But then I blinked because I was looking at blue velvet curtains. Did the night clouds ever look like that, swagged over the dollar store roof, with three stars hanging in the window of sky between them! It lifted up my mood. I wiped my eyes with my sleeve.

Walked her back to Marg's car, holding her arm so she wouldn't slip and kill herself. Her little red toes sticking out, freezing.

"How come you don't have that cast off by now?"

"Slipped again."

"What and wrecked it all over again?"

"It was pretty near healed, too."

"Just slipped, did you?"

"Yeah." She said it firm.

"Where?"

"On some ice."

I wondered. But alls I said was, "Why didn't you let somebody else chase after me?"

Marg had drove her. She was sitting there in the parking lot, waiting. Marg can't walk around for fear of her father, who's been threatening her.

She didn't have the car running. Marg thinks about the air. Don't pollute the air, she says, or what are the grandchildren going to breathe? Marg, she's had breathing problems since she was a kid and she knows what it feels like when you can't breathe.

When Josie was getting in, I could hear Marg asking, "Did you tell her?"

No answer.

So Marg cranks down the window. She says it in that voice that would have been good for a nurse. Just like she was saying, *Now, here's your medicine. You're going to have to swallow it.*

"Rose," she says, "that new man of yours, Dave Smith, eh. We heard he traffics."

3.

THE NEXT TUESDAY, we're all up there in the waiting room. Darlene's been at it all week long, drawing her notion of the hotel. Every picture has a cat in it. Josie's laughing, "A cat house!"

I said, "Why don't you put no people in it?"

Darlene, she just rolls her eyes, like it's cute to be so scared to death of people you got nobody in your life besides a white cat. Shy don't half cover it, where Darlene's concerned. She gets so she's too scared to go to the store.

Darlene was the only one I didn't feel close friends with, by that point. I was trying. But it wasn't happening.

Tammy still hasn't got her kids or herself out of the house. Dave's still at my place. Josie's not looking forwards to telling Meredith what happened to her this week. Her face is lit up black and blue again, so she's going to have to say something.

"Fall down drunk?" Sally asks her.

Josie shrugs.

I give her a sideways look. I'm really starting to wonder about all this falling down of hers. She won't look at me.

Sally is still on about pink paint. Wants to buy it on faith.

Marg says, "For frig's sakes, Sally, you've got to have a wall first, before you go and spend money on paint to paint it pink."

Meredith and her helper lumber in. I wonder where you get a jacket like what Meredith's got on. How much would that cost to buy? Too bad she strains it at the seams. Even green shoes to match! Look like they'd punish your toes, though.

(I asked Frances, the helper, once, where Meredith had grew up. To look at her, I thought she must be from the big city. But Frances said, no, actually, Meredith was a local girl. Did that ever surprise me! We only had one school in that town. Thought I knew most of the kids to see them. She could've been a few years before my time, though.)

Anyways, I seen Meredith take a look at Josie's new bruises.

Of course she don't say nothing. Squashes her lips together. Josie's going to get a Question to Think About this week, for sure.

I want to hear more about them stepping stones. I'm thinking, all right, Meredith, teach me something. It's not like I keep screwing up on purpose. You show me, step by step, how to get from here to Happy Hotel. Show me step one.

I could see that we needed a bit of time at first, to get to know each other. But by now it was high time we started getting some place. I was always thinking of the clock ticking. Jenny getting older. How old was I when my dad started?

Meredith's got glue and scissors and a stack of magazines. We're to do a "collage of fear."

Don't like the sounds of that.

She's going on. I'm sitting there with my ears shut.

Looking at it now, I'd say I was being Defensive again. Shutting down when somebody was trying to get at my problems.

I'm looking at my blank cardboard and stack of magazines. What in the world is a collage of fear? Everybody else is snipping away. It bugs me that even Tammy knows what to do. Tammy's good-hearted, eh, but I think it's fair to say that she is quite dumb.

And me, apparently, I'm dumber.

The leader's helper, Frances, she leans over me in a cloud of deodorant. Wants to know if she could help me get started. Do I remember what I was afraid of when I was a child?

"No." (Shut right down.)

"Maybe some of the pictures in these magazines might help you to remember."

I'm thinking, you can't make me. *You can't make me go there. Leave me alone.*

The shadow that moved along the wall of the mop closet at school, under the little, high, wire-screened window of the boiler room. The shadow slid along to the mop closet. The floor-cleaner smell and the smell of the other thing, my father's....

I tell the helper I'm sorry but there ain't going to be a picture in a magazine of what I'm thinking of.

There's nothing special about the magazines, eh. They're just the ones you see every place.

Frances, the helper, says, "It's surprising sometimes."

She opens the first magazine. Lets the pictures flip by, in front of me. And there it is, an open closet! It's too bright for the mop closet but I seen the shadow of a tall man on another page. I could cut it out and paste it on.

It's strange to make a picture of them long ago hours. The tall shadow with the bumpy jaw. The way it used to slide along the wall, coming for me.

I trimmed the shadow. My hand knew the shape to make it. Funny it was right there in the magazine!

All right. I get it. I'm started now.

I can put in my present fears too, Frances says. She says if I just look at a picture and feel it could be scary, okay, put it in. I don't have to know why.

If I don't have to know what the frig I'm doing, I'm good to go. I find a paved school yard. Like if there was no water behind the church.

Where did that come from? No water behind the church? Stupid thing to think of.

Good job I don't have to know what I'm doing. I put that grey school yard in the middle. It takes up a lot of the room on my bristol board. All grey, cracked pavement. Nothing living. I find a guy that looks a little bit like my father. Glue him on to the pavement school yard. Give him a floor mop in his hand. I find a big, long, green jungle snake. Glue it on his crotch. I cut out instant mashed potatoes. Glue a lump of potatoes on Dad for his lumpy jaw and little sucked-in mouth. The shapes were right there in the mashed potatoes, the mouth and everything. I find floor polish. I can just smell that biting my airways! I find pictures of two little girls in blue dresses. Bit like me and my sister. I put us in the closet. Rip our heads in half. Look a lot like us now. Snake coming at us with its green, devil's fork tongue.

Turns out half the pictures in all the magazines are about stuff that can scare me, one way or another. You try that sometime. I'm telling you: don't laugh till you tried it.

How I felt when I was doing it—I felt like, wow, it's all here! Boy, I was right back there! Three feet tall, dirty little blue plaid dress, down at the hem on one side. Ashamed of my chubby thighs.

You can be so scared when you're a kid, eh. That nightmare feeling. No way to wake up. Little heart just banging. Something coming to get you.

The next minute, I snapped out of it. My brain kicked in and it starts thinking, what the frig was the point of that? I'm grown up. I'm not wearing no dirty dress. I don't have to be scared of no mop closet at this time of day.

I asked Meredith, "When are we going to start doing the thing about the stepping stones?"

She said that was a stepping stone we just done.

What?

"I meant like the steps to get someplace in our life," I says. I was thinking of little Jenny. How long could I fool around like this?

Meredith says, "Recognizing our early traumas and fears is an important step toward healing."

This didn't make no sense. I thought she was going to tell me something practical. Do Step A and get to Step B. I was dying to go forwards. This here was going backwards if it was going anyplace.

I told her I wanted to help my niece.

She asked if my niece was being abused.

"Not yet. That's what I come here for. To find out what's wrong with my family, how I can fix it up in time so my niece don't ever get abused."

Meredith told me healing was a process. It was going to take some time. And she give me one of them smiles of hers, like she was smiling at a kid.

What was the use in grown-up people sitting here playing with scissors and glue? How the frig was this supposed to get me out of the hole I was in at work? How was this supposed to help me with my men issues? How was I getting any closer to protecting my little sweetheart?

I raised my voice. "I got serious problems!"

"I know you do, Rose."

"How's this playing around going to fix anything?"

"It's a process. You need to be patient."

"I come here for somebody to tell me what the hell to do about some big problems."

"No one here is going to tell you what to do. We're here to help you with your healing."

I got burning hot. "I come here to get sensible help! Yous are not doing nothing! I already passed kindergarten!"

Meredith told Frances, the helper, to go out to the other room and discuss it with me, one on one.

I stomped out. Ready to quit.

I'm tired, eh. Worked all day. Spending my evening over here to get some frigging help. I don't need this horse shit.

Frances, she don't talk to you like you're retarded. She listened to what was pissing me off. I told her I was wasting my time there, cutting out pictures. Meredith was treating me like a baby.

"It's hard to see any point in these exercises at first, I know," she says, "but, if you can just hold on and give it some time, Rose, you might come to look at it in a different way."

"I don't think I got much time. My niece is growing so quick. How can this look like anything but fooling around with crayons and glue? What I want is to quit screwing up. And help my sister quit screwing up so her daughter don't get hurt like her and I did!"

"This work we're doing could help you to make good decisions, in time."

"Oh BS! We're just playing around. How is that supposed to help me or my family? My niece is in danger. How is me sitting in my diapers cutting up magazines going to do anything for her?"

Frances, she listened to me, patient. Asked some questions about Jenny and her mom. Told me my concern was wise. Told me it took time to heal. I'd start to see where this was all going, soon, if I could hang on, stay with it, give it a try. I remember she warned me, too, that I wasn't going to be able to fix my sister.

"Your sister would have to work on her own healing before she could ever change."

"You don't know my sister Sandra. She's never going to go to no group or nothing like that. She won't even go to the shelter. She don't believe in shrinks."

"Well," Frances said to me, she said, "that's her decision. The decision to heal is very personal. I know."

I looked at Frances. She'd said that last remark so quiet and ordinary.

What I want to say to any of yous that are leaders, is: You got to see to it that you're patched up good enough yourself, before you go trying to help somebody else. Oh, you might know all the steps. Meredith, she knew them. And the fancy names for them. But she could not have got me to take the first one. The just-lips smile. The high-horse voice. Fiddling with her bracelet. Pinchy little shoes shuffling around under the table. Weird face expressions. People like us are going to pick that right up, eh.

I can see now that I was scared. Making that picture of my father in the old boiler room cupboard had shook me up. It's like I opened the door a crack and this slimy, cold hand whipped out. Grabbed me hard, by the ankle. Tried to pull me in. Cold slime grabbing all up my leg, right up me, pulling me in, ready to screw me. I had to kick it off. Slammed the door back shut. Jesus! That thing was still right there!

When you first peek behind that door you've been leaning against, when you draw them bolts and open up a bad past the first bit, that is so scary!

Things that could make you shit for fear when you were four years old, they still can. We lock them things away, but they are still right there. When I found that out, I was shaking, shocked. Cold right up to the crotch. Just the thought of that boiler room!

Meredith, she wasn't no help. Seemed like she was scared too. Sending me out of the room so quick.

Whereas Frances, here, even though she was just the helper, she didn't seem to be scared. She didn't have no big degree. But her voice was normal.

I looked her up and down as she sat there. Face was normal. Shoulders relaxed. Hands resting easy on her thighs. Her feet there, comfortable-looking, in her brown socks and loafers, steady on the floor. That's what calmed me down.

Frances said she'd saw a lot of people take these steps and go forward with their life and go on to help others.

Then she told me, in the same kind of an ordinary voice, with her hands relaxed and her feet still, that these same steps we were going through were how she got where she was, herself. Didn't make no secret of the fact that she was a sex abuse survivor herself.

Frances was the first person who ever come right out and said that to me. I'll never forget how she done that. Sitting there like an ordinary person. Not making no big deal out of it. Just telling me the information.

I stayed with Frances for some time, thinking about taking a step off the riverbank. Could I put my foot on that first slippery step? Both feet? Stand right in the middle of what scared me so bad when I was a little girl at Ferry Street Public School? What if I lost my balance? Fell in with the monster? Got sucked down into that bad old dream and drowned? I'd go crazy. Have to hide under a bed all day to keep that cold slime from running up my leg and getting in my underpants.

Frances sat there listening.

Jesus. I could see this wasn't going to be no picnic. But, whatever we were in for, Frances'd been through it all before. It sure hadn't made her nuts, so I figured it wasn't going to kill me neither.

I crawled back into the meeting room.

Now, at that time, I never took my hunches serious. Started saying to myself, why did I think Meredith was scared? She gets paid for this. She's got the big degree there. Nice enough. Seems to know what she's talking about. I should trust her. Come on, Rose, I says to myself, don't be foolish.

I've learned better, since. If I get a hunch, now, that somebody's scared, I figure they're scared. That just goes to show yous how far I've came.

They were going around the circle, telling about their week. I come in on the end of Tammy's. Asshole has been getting moody again.

You don't need a calendar with Tammy's asshole husband. Week one, he blows up. Week two, sweet as candy. Week three, hold your breath. Then *kaboom!* And it starts over. Perfect circle.

Marg, she talks about it like he was a woman. "Asshole's got PMS." Or, "Asshole's on the rag."

Meredith wants to know if Tammy has noticed any pattern

in her husband's behaviour. That's too hard of a question for Tammy. She says he's been touchy, the past week. Rest of us groan.

Josie's a breath of fresh air at the break with her eyes twinkling there in her little black-and-blue face. Says she's saw something else about the town. She gets out the picture of the little town and we're under the light, hunched over Josie, trying to see the house she's talking about. You can only see half of it at the near end of the street, but Josie, she's hopping up and down.

"Let Rose look. This is for Rose."

I'm sucked in as usual, squinting through the magnifying glass, steaming it up with my breath. Alls I can see at the near end of the street in the picture is one half of a fairly clapped-out clapboard house. Looks to be apartments.

Then it hits me. Blue curtains. And, hanging in the window to catch the light, stars! Three of them.

Josie's sparkling them good-witch eyes on me.

The way I seen her blue velvet curtains up in the night clouds over the Dollarama, with a window of sky and three pretty stars.

I told her, I said, "You're scary."

Josie grins.

"You are!" I says. "You're right scary. I should have put you in the scary collage."

The rest of them's all chirping to know what's up. But Josie just smiles at me. With them two black eyes, she looks like a raccoon, a raccoon that's friends with like elfs.

We get started again, after the break.

Darlene's heading into one of her times. Hasn't picked up her mail now for so long that her box will be full and she'll have to ask the lady at the post office. Darlene's getting too scared of people to do that.

Meredith gets Darlene to hold up her collage. Tries to help her dig into the root of the fears.

Darlene's got three men pasted on her bristol board, that she says all look like her cousin, and pins and knives and matches.

Little girl about seven. Darlene's ripped the top off her head. Couple of bathrooms. Kid's nightgown ripped in half.

Darlene's holding up all this. She says things that happened to her weren't so bad. Lots of people have had worse, she says. If you ever think you're bad off, she says, go take a look around a blind school. She'd saw a blind school once, little kids running into stuff.

"Now that's real trouble," she says. What happened to her was small potatoes compared to something like that.

Darlene was Minimizing. That's the name of when you refuse to take a look at your own problems by saying they ain't much. Start yapping about somebody else's that's worse. Learned that in Group. My mother was a minimizer. And my sister Sandra sounds just like her. I was too, at that time. It's another way to get out of looking at whatever you're too scared to look at. You sound like you're a saint because you care so much about somebody else's dilemma. Everybody's supposed to think, Ah, ain't she or he nice, feeling bad for the blind kids or whoever. But alls you're doing is you're making sure you don't have to open the scary door.

Meredith says, "Can you tell us about the matches, Darlene?"

Darlene rolls her eyes like she's cute (which, believe me, she ain't). She says she don't know why she went and glued them on. She never got burnt like a kid she heard of who—

"Were you burned, Darlene?"

"Nothing like this one kid who—"

"Can you tell us about the knife, Darlene?"

"I never got cut bad like some people. Some people—"

"Were you cut with a knife?"

"Not really bad or nothing. Not like this poor guy I seen on the news who—"

"Where were you cut, Darlene?"

Meredith tried for a long time. Couldn't drag nothing out of Darlene. Couldn't get her to say boo about her fears collage or her past.

I'm so fed up I shut my ears and start thinking hard about blue curtains clouds. Velvet, open. Silver stars. We could make the curtains that night blue colour at the hotel.

I won't quit that until Darlene's done talking. Sally hands her the Kleenex box, and she goes out with Frances. Bawling. Knows she's heading into a time when she won't be able to go out of the apartment. She's saying there's people that can never come out at all.

Josie gets hit with a Question to Think About. Meredith tells her to think if there's anything going on in her life that tends to be associated with drinking.

"Pardon me?"

"Is there anything happening now that was also happening around the last time you were drinking heavily?"

Josie promised to give it a thought.

Then she lit out of there. She's fast, even with that foot.

We all took off after her. Caught her on the stairs.

Marg says, "All right, level with us. What in the world happened to your face this time?"

Josie, she didn't want to say nothing, but we pretty well had her there, trapped in the stairwell. Said she fell down drunk. She was drinking because she didn't like Christmas.

And she slipped through our fingers.

Me and Tammy hung around for a smoke. Sally stayed to preach us a sermon on wrecking our God-given health.

I says to Tammy, I says, "You know your husband's due to take a fit this week, eh? Next week at the latest."

Tammy says no. Things haven't been too bad. He took the family out for pizza on the weekend. He told her she was a good wife. Said he was sorry for the last time. He's going to be better from now on.

Sally says ah, isn't that nice, but I have to look up at the moon. Blow smoke at it.

I try it again. I say, "Tammy, there's a pattern to it. After he's took a fit and beat yous up, he's always nice for a while.

Then he gets touchy. Then he blows up again."

Tammy looks straight in front of her.

I don't get it. Why can't she leave this guy?

Sally says maybe if Tammy goes real, real careful this time and don't do nothing to piss him off—

"You can't do it," I says. "You can turn cartwheels to try and please him. He's going to still get mad. He gets mad. It's what he does. It's him. You heard Meredith. He's got an anger problem. *His* problem. Nothing to do with you. He'll get mad because you're breathing in and out!"

All Tammy can do is look in front of her and tell us he's buying a ping pong table for Matthew and Meghan this Christmas. That's supposed to mean he's changed. He's going to be nice from now on.

I stepped on my cigarette butt a lot harder than what it needed and left.

4.

DAVE'S TRUCK WAS PARKED in front of my place. I smiled. He was pretty well moved in. As soon as I opened the downstairs door, I could hear he had country on up there in my place (second floor of an old house). *All my exes live in Texas.* I dance up the stairs and as I open the door, I'm singing along, "Baby, that's why I live in Tennessee!"

We laugh.

I gotta throw him out before he brings the cops, but I keep putting it off. I was thinking, if it wasn't for he's a dealer (if he was), Dave was way the best guy I ever had. He hadn't broke nothing. He put in for the food, even, on top of putting in for the rent. He fixed the shelf where Hal busted it. He was fun around the place.

He snapped the dish cloth at me. Made sure he didn't touch me with it though. And, see, that's Dave too. Not rough with me. Not at all.

We wind up dancing in the kitchen. He's pulling me in close, not coming on, just holding me that way he does. He's got these big solid arms. He smells good. He's warm, like a friendly bear. I can't help it. I rest against Dave. I'm starting to get a new idea on what sexy is. This safe feeling melts me like ice cream in August. Bertie downstairs is banging on the air duct for us to turn the music down.

We made popcorn. Cuddled up to eat it. We're always hugging. It's like Dave's the only way I know how to get warm these days. And he's the same. He's got to pull me up close all the time.

I curled up there, with his arm around me, feeling good, and I thought to myself, I thought, "I'm as bad as Tammy. I got a guy I can't leave." To act as dumb as Tammy, now that's depressing.

It's easy to see what everybody else should do, eh. But yourself, that's different.

Wednesday, I went out to the storeroom to get a new cartridge for the photocopy machine. I turn around and there's Ken, my boss, blocking the door. He closes it behind him and I can hear that he's locking it.

I think, Shit, I'm even worse off than Tammy. She's always got her mace spray for strange men.

He's lugging out his equipment there, telling me if I want to keep my job, I'd better give him what he's looking for. It made me want to puke, but I done it. He sat on three boxes of carpet-cleaning fluid, stacked up. I needed my job.

I didn't say nothing about it. Just went and washed out my mouth in the sink after. The girls were still coming to the bathroom with me. I didn't have the heart to tell them not to bother no more.

Have I got a neon sign on my forehead or what? Every jerk always figures he can hit on me.

Anyways, it'll be the easy way to get rid of Dave. I'll tell him this. He'll call me a whore and take off. I won't have to say I want him to leave, which, face it, I don't.

Me and Dave went for a beer, and to get our names in again for the fridge draw, on Friday.

I never phoned Josie because she's drinking heavy. Last thing she needs is some so-called friend to phone her up and ask her out to the bar. She was there anyways, ripped, singing karaoke. She's up there, leaning on one crutch, yelling along. For such a little squirt of a thing, Josie's got quite the voice. Belts her right out. Last week's bruises are toned down to the yellow stage, and she's got them covered up pretty good with her makeup.

Dave and Josie's boyfriend Brent take off. For a game of pool, Dave tells me. There's a lot of people that want to play pool, all of a sudden. Four of them stand up and follow Dave and Brent into the back room.

I'm sitting there by myself, thinking maybe I'll tell Josie what's going on with the boss at work, if she's not too drunk to listen.

But the first thing I know she's up there saying my name into the mic. "Ladies and gentlemen, this one's for my good friend, Rose Underhill."

Then here comes the boss, Ken, himself. Thanks a lot, Josie. Now he knows I'm here. Wants me to dance with him.

I say I'm waiting for somebody. I'm praying that Dave will come back soon. I know what's going to happen if I try to leave. Ken will catch me outside and try to haul me into the alley.

I don't want to go into the pool room and see that Dave's not there. Then I'd have to quit letting on to myself that I don't know nothing about the dealing. Or maybe he's in there playing pool like he said.

I should go find out, once and for all.

Don't have the nerve. Don't want to know. Avoidance.

I looked up at Josie, wishing she wasn't so hammered, so maybe she could stand by me here.

Hammered or not, Josie seen what was going on. And it's all over the bar, she's yelling into the mic. "Hey, everybody! Look at this jerk over here in the front corner, trying to hit on this lady here who don't welcome his attention." People laugh, eh, and look at Ken. He's trying to ease away from my booth.

It was pretty good.

Dave, he must have heard. There he was, coming through the door with a pool cue in his hand.

Just the outline of him and I thought, I've got it bad! I'm feeling all this relief, just looking at the shape of him there, like a nice big bear in the doorway. Just the sight of him across the room, with the light behind him, and this warm flood come over me like, I'm safe, I'm safe!

I sat there after Ken buggered off, looking at the bubbles in my Coke and thinking, this is worse than ever. I gotta watch I don't fall right in stupid love with this guy. I gotta think about where he's getting this rent money he gives me. The cops are maybe going to bust him one of these days. I'd have to let him go anyways. I'd be better off to let him go now, so I don't get attached to him any worse.

When you're talking like that, it's too late, eh. And he did have that pool cue. Maybe that's really alls he was doing. Maybe the girls are wrong.

Dave come and sat with me. Ordered a beer and he says, "Are you hungry, Ann Toes?" He gets a kick out of little Jenny calling me that.

I never buy food out. It's too dear. But Dave wants to know what I'd like. I can have whatever, he says. I was hungry. Said I guessed I'd have a small fries.

"Come on. You're hungry. Get something more."

He had me talked into the banquet burger before he would quit. A banquet burger with large fries and coleslaw costs more than I make in a hour on the phone trying to sell the "hall and two rooms" carpet-cleaning special, with people insulting me and hanging up and frigging Ken looking for chances. Dave said he was paying. He did, too.

And he bought me a beer. When it come, we noticed that the glass wasn't clean. Smear of lipstick on it that hadn't got washed off. I just turned the glass around to drink out of the other side.

"For Pete's sakes!" Dave says. He says, "Ask for a clean one." He calls the waitress over.

I didn't like to make a nuisance of myself.

"Sorry," I said, "but it looks like this glass didn't get cleaned. Sorry to bug you."

I ate all the food right up. When he paid, I said I was sorry that I'd been so hungry.

"You know something, Rosie? You apologize way too much."

When we were done, he says, "I'd kind of like to get out of here, what about you?"

He asks me what *I* want to do! I says, "Fine by me."

It was so cold out and so quiet, after all the music and carrying on, all that heat and noise. Me and Dave, we walked over toward the park. They had a lot of the trees lit up for Christmas. I like when they do all the same colour on one tree and a different colour on another one. They had it like that. Red tree. Blue tree. Yellow tree. Green tree. Like Jenny has in her book, something about fish. I felt happy. Red tree, blue tree, shining in the dark.

Dave asked me which colour I liked the best! I never would've thought about it. I looked at each one and said maybe the blue. What about him? He liked the red.

Some guys don't want you to hold their hand, so I wasn't sure. Dave's big hand was hanging there in his mitt, curled a bit. His touch surprises you. How can he touch that gentle with them big hands? I didn't want to do nothing wrong. I wanted things to keep shining. I kept looking at that hand, swinging there, empty. It made me think of that dent he has in him, under his collarbone, where my face fits. I felt like my hand would just fit in his. He wouldn't even have to move his fingers, just the way they were curled, I could slide mine right in there. I wasn't sure. Didn't want to screw up. I kept my hand to myself.

It was good and cold out, I'll tell you, but no wind. We were dressed warm enough. Stars were out. It was real quiet.

Dave says, "What should we do for Christmas?"

Like we're family! The coloured trees went blurry. I never met a harder guy to kick out.

"We can go to my sister's place and see Jenny open her stocking."

Dave says okay and he says how about we go up and see his dad in the afternoon. His dad lives back north. Dave wants me to meet a bunch of his cousins. His aunt's cooking turkey, over at his dad's. He thinks I'll like his cousin Jan, particular. Jan will like me, too.

Dave don't seem to know he's just another guy I met in the bar. He don't know I don't expect nothing like this. He's acting like it's for real. Like he means it. Like I'm something to him.

He don't know the type of trash I am. If he knew what I was like, he'd never want me to meet his dad or his cousin or nobody. What happened in the supply room at work, if he knew that, he'd never want me to eat his aunt's turkey with this mouth. That's what I was thinking.

We planned it all out, to go spend Christmas morning with Jenny and my sister and this guy, Ian, she's with (who I don't take to, myself). Then we'd get in the truck and go up to Dave's dad's.

It was clear I wasn't getting nowhere with kicking him out.

On the way back up through the park, he reached over and he held my hand.

5.

TUESDAY NIGHT, Sally was the first one there. When I come in, her face lit up brighter than the lights at a baseball diamond. Tells me she hasn't slept one day this week.

I says, "Well, you're doing good! What are you keeping busy at?"

Sally sits forward. "I'll show you!" She whips open a bag. Pulls out a stack of big and small squares in blue, pink, and yellow fabric. This is about the nuttiest thing I've ever saw. What these must be are tablecloths and napkins. For the daydream hotel?

"They had remnants on special at Fabric Kingdom!"

There's Sally, petting her stack of folded linen, beaming like it's Kingdom Come she's been shopping at. She's lived with how it feels to be awake, threading her old Singer sewing machine with her favourites (soft blue, yellow, and especially pink), folding the cloth, ironing it smooth, sewing the remnants together, trying to believe in better times to come. Trying to make them come. Acting on faith, as she says.

She's shining that pretty face of hers at me, anxious to hear what I'll say.

What am I going to say? The obvious? Sally, you're coo-coo? We'll never have tables to put those on?

I says, "How did you sew these edges so straight?"

Marg come in and I watched the different looks go acrost her face: *What's this? Oh, jeeze! Poor Sal—bless her heart!*

Marg run a piece of the cloth through her fingers. "Good weight to it," she says.

Tammy come in and we told her what she was looking at. "You mean we're really going to do it?" she says. Poor dumb Tammy.

Josie limps in. Looking rough. But, as soon as she sees Sally's project, the sun busts through. She's hopping, quick as a squirrel, all over that waiting room, spreading out the different coloured cloths, trying the napkins on them.

"Yellow ones on the blue tables and blue on the pink. Or we can mix and match!" She whisks away a stack of magazines. Grabs a bunch of fake flowers off the bookshelf. Plunks them in the middle.

"Can I get yous some blueberry pie? We have it made right here in town."

"I believe," says Marg, "I will have it warm, with ice cream on the side."

"The ice cream is going to cost yous extra. But you'll agree with me that it's worth your dollar. Alls we serve is this homemade, super premium ice cream a guy makes special for the hotel. Hundred percent free range milk."

Sally's flamingo pink and giggling. She's so tickled.

I'm laughing. "Free range milk! Who ever heard of that? Cows running loose!"

Tammy's tapping on the other little table by where she's sitting. "Can we have service over here?"

Josie says, "Wait your turn. If you want to come to a famous hotel for people like us that's wrote up in the paper, you gotta expect they'll be others ahead of you." To me, she says, "The cows is fenced in, for God's sakes, but they're out in the air."

I was laughing but could I ever see that dining room! Just the way Josie'd drew it. Wood, glass, and stone. View of the sparkling lake out every window. Water reflections jiggling all over the ceiling.

I thought that Sally, starting to sew, was not stupid so much as brave. Well, stupid and brave. Maybe that's what acting on faith is.

When we heard Meredith and Frances coming, we bundled up the cloths in a flash and tucked them back in Sally's bag. It's funny how quick we done that, like we were afraid of getting caught. We filed in. No Darlene.

Went around the circle and checked on everyone's week. Tammy's husband ain't blew up yet. We can hear him ticking like a bomb. Except Tammy. She still thinks things are going good. He's a little touchier this week. He did kick the dog's teeth in. But he hasn't laid a hand on Tammy or the kids. He promised her last time that he would never do that again.

Oh right. I'm sure. I'd like to know what's changed since last time.

I wish to God Meredith would tell her to get out while the getting's good. Of course she won't. Alls Meredith does is ask Tammy if the incident with the dog seems acceptable to her.

Tammy says the poor dog was only barking at a rabbit.

Josie pipes up. Says even her dog, who was a Chinese philosopher in his last life, will bark at a rabbit.

(Meredith gives Josie the look. Josie's a bad girl for speaking out of turn.)

The Asshole broke one and a half of the dog's teeth. Tammy wanted to take it to the vet, but he says he's not paying for that. Tammy, she's got a bit of money coming in, of her own, from a disability pension she has on account of her bipolar disorder. But Asshole grabs the cheque every month, makes her sign it over, and Tammy never has a penny of her own to spend. Has to get his royal permission if she wants to buy Matthew or Meghan a new-to-you winter coat from the second-hand store. I'm so sure he's going to pay for a doggie dentist.

Tammy's feeding it aspirin and wondering what to do about the half tooth. She tried pliers, the way her dad used to do on them at home. (He'd put his knee on their chest and twist.) She got bit. Zippy won't eat.

Meredith steers back around to the point about whether this behaviour on the part of her husband is acceptable.

How is Tammy supposed to know about "acceptable"? Her dad didn't believe in dentists. Stuck his knee on her chest and twisted with the dirty pliers out of the shed.

As usual, I'm working on not hearing too much. I think about the hotel dining room. All them pretty tablecloths. Soft pink, blue, yellow. Fresh and clean and smooth. Water reflections from the lake rippling over the silverware.

I was what Meredith calls "Escaping into Fantasy." But I still say you got *to* do that sometimes.

Josie makes light of things, when it's her turn. Says she's doing great.

Meredith looks at her bruises. But Josie sticks to her guns. Nope, she's doing awesome.

Meredith says (not to nobody in particular), she says that admitting we have a problem can be the first step toward healing.

Josie knows damn well that Meredith's talking to her. But she won't admit a thing. She's having a hunky dory Christmas season. Everything's dandy.

Meredith gives up. Moves on to me. I want to tell about the boss, but I don't want them to know I'm a dirty whore so I say I had a good week.

Meredith asks a couple of questions about the man who is living with me.

"Dave," I say. (I told her ten times already.) "His name's Dave Smith."

"And has this Mr. Smith been contributing money for expenses?"

I can see she thinks that's a made-up name, like nobody's really called Smith.

"He puts in more than his share."

"Oh." That surprised her. "Good. And his behaviour is acceptable?"

I told her Dave's behaviour was fine.

"And how do you feel about this man living in your space?"

"I feel ... safe."

That hit a nerve! I'm telling you, there was a sigh went around that table. Leaders and all, they looked at me like I was waving a million-dollar lottery ticket. A man who makes me feel safe!

Meredith breathed in short like I'd socked her in the gut. She might just as well have told me that whatever big shot she's with don't make her feel that way.

Meredith would never look twice at a guy like Dave in his ball hat and his plaid coat from Zellers and his worn-down work boots. And Dave, he'd be scared to talk to a woman like Meredith. Just even her manicure fingernails would make him nervous. The way she talks, he'd be afraid to sound stupid.

Dave is not stupid, mind you. He asked the landlord if he could take a try at fixing the old fireplace in my apartment.

Landlord says, "That thing'll never draw worth a tinker's dam."

Dave, though, he got her going. Brought home wood, and piled it neat in the mud room. He lit a fire in the evenings. I put up our Christmas cards on the mantelpiece. Jenny made us a card with cotton wool glued on for snow. You can bet that was front and centre.

Dave says, "Look at how good she drew that tree! That kid could grow up to be an artist."

How was Sally's week?

Sally said it was good. Meredith wanted to know what she'd been doing.

"Not much." Sally was mumbling, talking to her lap. So Meredith got the idea that Sally was having trouble and back to sleeping all day.

Sally was doing excellent. She just didn't want to tell Meredith about the tablecloths. That was the first time anybody in Group ever lied to hide how *good* they were doing.

We all sat there, trying not to laugh, listening to Meredith asking Sally if she could identify what she was Avoiding. Sal went red in the face. Didn't know what to say. She wasn't going to tell Meredith she was sewing dining room linen for a hotel that was all in our crazy heads.

Meredith moved on to Marg. Now Marg, she's got her hands full with a court case. Her cousin's finally charged Marg's father with molesting them all when they were kids. About time they shut down that old man. Marg's got to go and testify in court. She's scared to death he's going to do something in the meantime. He's out on bail, mad as hell, threatening everybody that's got anything to do with it. He's twisted. Set a fire before. He's got a gun.

Then we got to this week's exercise. We got a sheet to fill in. *Childhood Guilt*, it says at the top, and they've got all these boxes to check. You're supposed to put a checkmark for people you feel guilty about. (Think what you'd put, if somebody give you a sheet about your guilt to fill in.)

MOM. Jeeze. I checked that. (My saint of a mom, sneaking me jars of ointment for where my cunt was tore, even though it was her husband I was having sex with. Also I broke her heart when I quit school and left home.)

DAD. I checked that. (I never go see him.)

SISTER (Name). I wrote in Sandra. (Should've took her with me when I left home.)

There was room for guilt about three more sisters, if I had've had them. There was room for guilt about four brothers. Seven blanks. Thank God no more of us was ever born!

Okay, next section: *Check responses that describe what happened when you felt guilty.*

When I felt guilty, my mother usually:
• *Never knew*
• *Reinforced my guilt by blaming me for things I did not do*
• *Made me feel even more guilty*
• *Other.*

I sat and bit my pencil. Started picking out a carpet for the hotel. How about dark blue to match the drapes? The girls from where I work would call up and offer to clean it. I'd treat them kind.

Meredith says, "Rose, do you need help?"

I say, "Sorry. No."

I try to think about my mom. What did she do when I felt guilty? The fact is that I always felt guilty. That was the basic feeling of being me. And Mom did make it worse. One time she walked into the kitchen and she heard what my father was telling me about my little hairless pussy. I can see it yet, the hurt look on Mom's face as she's reaching up for her pill bottle in the cupboard. Then she turned around and walked out without a word.

I checked off: *Made me feel more guilty.*

But then I felt guilty for putting that checkmark. I was screwing Mom's husband and she never said a word. She looked so hurt. But not on purpose to make me feel bad.

We had to fill in the same questions about Dad. Poor old man. He's up in years now. All alone. I should ask him over sometime or go see him. I should forgive and forget like my sister does. She'll have him over, see that he's fed. I never do.

I used the *Other* space for him. I wrote, "It's not his fault."

Then I wondered why I'd put that. Tried to rub it out.

Looking at it now, I'd say I was Deeply Confused. (That's what the shrinks are kind enough to call it when you don't know your ass from a hole in the ground.)

We had to read this next part called, *Accepting Powerlessness as a Child*:

> *Because children have limited mental, physical, and emotional resources, a major part of parenting involves physically and psychologically protecting the children—allowing them to be safe. As children, we need security, love, happiness, and honesty in order to grow and feel good about ourselves. Yet in many homes we find parents who are not able to provide for these*

> needs. ... Not only do parents often ask children to take responsibility for things for which adults should normally be responsible, they often insinuate that their children are the cause of their (the adults') problems. Children oftentimes become confused. They have a distorted view of their own power and believe they can affect far more than they truly can.

I read that over again. Did you ever hear a living person open their mouth and say "oftentimes"?

...*Children are the cause of their (the adults') problems.*

I'm not a fast reader. I don't get it. I underline *to be safe*.

The next page wants you to write something you feel guilty about that wasn't your fault.

Meredith says to do that for homework.

Sally gets a Question to Think About. She's to figure out what she's avoiding by sleeping so much.

Marg glugged. A Marg laugh, eh, but she tried to let on it was a belch. Josie laughed right out. Which started Tammy giggling. Sally goes stop-sign red, glaring at them all to shut up. It was the look on her that set me off.

In the hall, Sally scolds us, "Do yous want Meredith to find out about the tablecloths?"

Marg's still grinning. "It's a crying shame how bad you're doing, Sal," she says. She give Sally a pat on the shoulder.

We all walked Marg to her car, kept her in the middle of the huddle in case her old man was hanging around anyplace there behind the post office or the Dollarama.

Josie jumps back out of Marg's car and gives Sally a big hug, made-on-faith tablecloths and all.

6.

I COULDN'T GET JOSIE on the phone Friday night. Saturday morning, I hiked through the snow, over to her place. Her philosopher-in-its-last-life dog went nuts. Jumping up, yapping, clawing. Ripped her curtain that she's got in the window beside the door. There's Josie, twisted funny, on the floor! I call Dave. He come quick and broke the lock. We seen she wasn't just sleeping. Got her to the hospital.

I'm sitting with her the next day, eh. After they'd pumped her stomach and gave her an IV. She's dehydrated. Alcohol poisoning. Rib broke that they figure is from where she hit the table and a goose egg from where she hit the floor.

She was trying to whisper something. Her mouth was all dry and cracked so I went and got a lip balm for her from the volunteer shop. I greased up her lips.

"What lights?" I says. I couldn't hear her.

"Northern," she whispers. "And elks."

"What are you talking about?"

Took me five minutes, with my ear to her mouth, to figure out that it's this new angle she's got for the hotel. People from the States and like Europe and Japan are going to come to see the northern lights and the birds and the big game.

I didn't know whether to laugh or cry. Messy, short hair out in all directions, she's white as a sheet, except where she's still yellow from last time. Skin and bones, lump sticking out of the side of her head. Foot in a cast. Needle in her skinny arm with the skin purple all around it. She can't hardly breathe. But eyes like the blue part of a fire.

I says, "There's a lot, is there, that will go that far out of their way to see a elk?"

She's sure. People that are made of money. Nothing better to do than fly around looking at things they never seen yet. They are going to beat a path to our hotel.

I felt like talking sense. Told her Dave had to break her lock but he was going over today to put a new one in.

"He can be the handyman," Josie says. For the dream hotel.

"You watch," she tells me. I'm leaning my ear down to hear her. "He's going to be a handyman. It'll be a new start." She got hold of my arm. "Dave will be okay then, Rose. I seen it. He'll build things. He'll be a wonderful man for you."

She'll never explain it to you, this stuff she "sees." I don't think she knows, herself.

Sure seems to be something to it, though.

That Sunday afternoon, when Josie had fell asleep, I left my number with the nurse and went on home.

Dave, he was back from fixing Josie's door. He had a fire going. Josie's dog was flopped in front of it, snoring. Hind foot going. Chasing after Plato in his last life, I guess.

I'm telling Dave what Josie said. He gets a kick out of her and her hotel. He laughed when I told him she's got him picked out for the handyman.

I said, "She tells me it'll be a new start for you. You're going to fix things. She can see it in the air. Says you're going to do wonderful."

Dave was in the middle of chuckling at that when the phone rung. It's the landlord. Says he's impressed with how Dave fixed the chimney. Would Dave like to come over tomorrow morning, take a look at a couple of handyman jobs he wants done?

Dave, he sets the phone down and looks at it. He's by a window. Where the sunlight's catching his left forearm, I see the skin raised up in gooseflesh.

"Ain't Josie weird?" I says.

"Just seen me today, starting in to be a handyman, did she?" Dave give his head a shake, like to shake off the weirdness.

We took our time making Hamburger Helper—and love—that Sunday afternoon. It was snowing outside.

When it quit, we took Josie's dog for a walk. Everything looked like little Jenny's Christmas card, fluffy and white. Bike racks, newspaper boxes, garbage cans, fences, roofs, all white as if some sweet kid had been playing at making them pretty.

Dave was feeling great. "Even that's nice." He was pointing out a garbage can. It had a big white hat on it and daubs of fluff up one side, and a smooth drift swirled around behind it like a wedding dress.

I thought about Ken at work in the supply room. Felt like I was the trash can. I might look nice to Dave right now, but there was garbage froze inside.

Monday, Ken caught me again. There was nobody in the kitchenette at work. I put my pea soup in the microwave. I turn around and there he is with the door locked and his pants open. He tells me again that I better not give him trouble, if I want my job. I think about giving him hot soup where it would do the most good. But, shit, if I can't pay the rent next month, what am I going to do? I went off welfare when I got this job. I don't know how long it would take to get back on. The landlord would be pissed and Dave wouldn't get to do his handyman work.

I did Ken fast.

Didn't want my lunch after that! Even just the smell of pea soup, ever since! Threw it down the toilet.

I sold five carpet-cleaning specials that afternoon, which ain't bad. A lot of people, they like their place cleaned up nice for Christmas. Ken was happy. Said something must have got me pepped up on my lunch break. Thinks he's funny.

You know, the boss there, Ken, he truly don't get it. It's no big deal, the way he sees it. He gives me a job. He wants a little job done for him. No clue that his behaviour is what Meredith would call unacceptable. It's the way his own dad carried on, most likely, and everybody in his family since cavemen days. He knows that women make a fuss about it, but, the way Ken sees it, you can't worry about the women. He thinks like what my father always said: "Women should have their mouth shut and their legs open."

On the way home, I was thinking, Ken's the only kind of guy I deserve. Knows what I am. Don't say nothing about me being a good person, the way Dave does. Ken, he already knows I'm a piece of garbage.

This thing with Dave was too good to be true. He was going to find out about me. Or he was going to get busted. Or maybe he was just going to snap someday. I hadn't saw much wrong with him yet. Kept wondering when he was going to beat me up or break something or take off with another woman. He had never even swore at me.

I was so sure I didn't deserve such good treatment that I kept thinking, every time I was on my way home, he'd have took off. Coming around the corner, I'd brace myself every day for no truck.

Truck was there.

Dave's by the fire, reading one of his adventure stories, some guys climbing a mountain, that he tells me what's going on in. "They're at a chasm," he says. "They maybe could rig a bridge but they.... What's wrong?" He put his book down. Took me on his knee.

I grabbed his soft plaid shirt in two handfuls and held on. How was I going to tell him, when he was so good to me, how bad I was being to him?

We made supper and he brung me up to date. He was excited because the work the landlord had for him wasn't just some half-a-day job. He's got at least three weeks of solid work for Dave, and he knows a guy that's looking for somebody after that. "If I do good, he says it could lead to something steady. They've got a couple of lots and they're going to put up houses."

After supper, I got around to the homework for Group tomorrow. Sat at the kitchen table.

Homework sheet said, *Now write about anything you might feel guilty about that was not your fault.*

Rest of the paper blank. Room for piles of guilt. Fault? Was I ever mixed up about whose fault was what!

I had wrote beside Dad's name, and then tried to rub it out, "It wasn't his fault."

Whose fault was it, then? His dad's? His dad was bad to him. Broke his jaw. Give him that chin that looks like a lump of mashed potatoes. I thought, Grandpa. All the trouble in our family must've been his fault. But then I thought Grandpa's own dad could've twisted him, for all I know. So maybe it wasn't his fault neither. Maybe it was my grandfather's father's fault. But maybe his father....

So who was the first sick-in-the-head father? How did it ever get started? That was the first time I got that idea of a rock dropping, smack, on some caveman's head.

"Rose, do you need help to get started?" I could just hear Meredith asking me. Tried to get back on the track.

Write about anything that you might feel guilty about that wasn't your fault.

I felt guilty about my mom. But that was my own fault. I screwed with her husband. I quit school and left home at fifteen. Dad told me I broke her heart.

I felt guilty about my sister. That was my own fault too. Should have stopped what Dad done to her. Should've took her with me when I got out. Should've never left her there.

I felt guilty I dropped out of school. I felt guilty about all the guys I'd been through. I felt guilty Dave was there wasting his time with me, when I was doing Ken. I felt sick guilty that I hadn't did a thing yet for Jenny. But, the way I seen it at that time, it was all my fault.

I see it different now, thank God. But I remember—at this same table I'm sitting at now—trying so hard. And I could not, for the life of me, think of one thing that didn't seem to be my own fault.

Few months later, it was simple.

Back at the start, though, I didn't have a clear picture of how the rockslide goes roaring down through time. Parents to kids. I had her bass ackwards. Blaming myself for my parents' faults. As if a rockslide could slide up hill.

Think that over, careful. See if yous do that too. Whatever you feel guilty over, are you sure it's really your fault?

I put the pencil down. Went and called Marg. Told her about Josie.

"Poor Josie just don't like Christmas," she says.

I says, "Guess what she's laying there thinking!"

"Don't tell me!" I can hear, over the phone, that Marg's grinning. "Don't tell me she's laying in hospital, going on about that hotel!"

Just the thoughts of Josie and her hotel, and you had to smile. Me and Marg got a laugh out of the elks.

7.

TUESDAY WE HAD A SMALL GROUP, what with Josie in the hospital and Darlene stuck at home. Darlene just lives across the park there in one of them apartments by the old dockyard. But she never showed up. So it's me, Marg, Sally, and Tammy.

Tammy looks bad. Moving stiff. We're going to hear something. Marg don't look good neither. She's nervous over her old man's trial coming up. When Marg's nervous, she eats. She's awful overweight as it is. Puffed up and white. Not getting much sleep, neither, by the looks of her. Sally hadn't heard about Josie. She took it bad.

I says, "Josie's going to be all right, Sal."

"You just keep sewing," Marg says.

Sally had her bag there, but she never opened it. Said she'd show us the new stuff when Josie got better.

Sally looked so let down that there was no Josie this week to show her work to. Alls I could think to do was I started in about the people coming from all over the place to look at northern lights and wild animals. I didn't tell it for a laugh though, this time. Told it so Sally could hang on.

Marg said she'd saw the northern lights once, back in Pickerel Lake, and was it a sight to see! Green and deep rose, she said it was, sheets and ribbons, all lit up, slow dancing. She said it's like the way sheets on a line will flap and blow. "Picture deep rose sheets made of light."

It was singing to my insides. Sheets of light, flapping on the sky line. Maybe it wasn't so nuts to think that people would go a long way to see that.

Meredith and the helper come in, and we went around the table.

How was Sally's week? Sally shocked us. Come right out and said she was sewing tablecloths for a hotel. (Never said nothing about it being an air hotel made out of daydreams, but it wasn't no lie, so her Christian morals was happy.)

Rest of us are looking at each other, wondering what she's going to say if Meredith asks any questions. But Meredith just says isn't that great. Glad Sally's got work. (Shifty-eyed smiles shoot around the table.)

How was Marg's week? Marg's old man keeps phoning to say he's going to set her building on fire if she don't call off the court case. (Which ain't even up to Marg anyways. She's only one witness.)

How was Rose's week? I didn't say nothing about Ken at work.

Meredith can see I've got some problem. Thinks it's Dave.

How was Tammy's week? Asshole had blew up. Pounded the shit out of Tammy.

At break, we talked about how far north you've got to go to get a good look at northern lights.

After break, we got another one of them sheets: *Accepting Powerlessness As An Adult.*

Today, I'm not responsible for...

Meredith's looking at me. Can I share with the group something that I'm not responsible for?

"Free range cows?"

"All kidding aside, Rose." Meredith's fidgeting her tight shoes and giving me her lip-twist smile imitation.

"Sorry." I says, "How Dave makes a living?"

"That's very true. You are not responsible for that man in any way." I had my doubts on that.

Tammy gets her same old Question to Think About. Who is responsible for her husband's anger?

Just before we're to go home, Frances, Meredith's helper, pipes up. Would we like to try a relaxation exercise?

M-m-m-m! Those are my favourite. Frances gets you to notice if your toes are warm or cool, comfortable or tight, tells you to relax the muscles in your toes and then in your feet. She works her way up. Relax your calf muscles. How are your knees today? Thighs comfy? She gives you time to think of each part of yourself.

If your body's been hurt, your body's going to need help to heal. Not just your brains. I recommend yous try that.

By the time we're feeling our eyes sink back, heavy and letting the tension float up out of our foreheads, I'm just like I'm laying on a pile of feathers.

As I was coasting out, I said thanks to Frances.

Meredith give me one of them sour Meredith glances. Like, what was I thanking her helper for? Why not her? Worse than a five-year-old.

In the hall, they were on Tammy. Had her backed up against the wall, crying. How many times was she going to take this shit? How many times was she going to let them kids see this?

Marg says, "Tammy, I'd like to drive you home right now, get your kids, and drop yous all at the shelter. How would that be? Is your husband out tonight?"

Tammy nods.

I says, "Will I come with you?"

I'm real relaxed, eh. Not thinking too clear about what I'm volunteering for.

Tammy, she nods. Sally is fishing in her purse for tissues. Can't find none, so she gives Tammy one of her table napkins, a pink one. "Go ahead. We got lots."

So Tammy's there blowing her nose and wiping her tears and that's the first use that got made of Sally's dining room linen.

We all went. Marg's got an '86 Chevy Caprice you could fit

the whole town into. We left Tammy's car where it was and drove out to Tammy's place.

Tammy, she lives in the country. She's got the nicest place of any of us. Her husband is some kind of car factory worker, and they own their own house. He must be nervous letting Tammy join this group, for fear she'll tell on him. But, see, Tammy tried to commit suicide the year before. Wound up in hospital. And the shrink there said she had to go to a therapy group for her childhood abuse. They followed up on it. Asshole had to let her. Of course, he's gave her the technicolour picture of what he'll do to her and the kids if she ever tells about him and his little anger problem there.

Anyways, there we are, heading out to their place, that cold night in December. I've forgot there's such a thing as relaxed.

Tammy lets out a gasp when we turn a curve where you can see the house, because Asshole's truck is there. She wants Marg to turn around, go get her car, don't say nothing.

Marg, though, she won't even slow down. Keeps going steady until we get to a clump of bushes, just by where you turn into Tammy's long driveway.

Tammy goes nuts. Starts crying and begging Marg, pulling on her arm. "Stop! Marg! Stop! He's there! He'll strangle me! He'll break my arm. He'll hurt the kids! He'll hurt Matthew's ear again. Stop! I don't want his head hit no more. Meghan's still sore. It'll hurt more! Stop!"

Marg finally brakes. Puts it in park. Turns it off. Marg won't leave a car running. Don't care if it's thirty below.

Tammy's screaming, she's so scared, tearing at everybody, trying to jump out of the car. Me and Sally are hanging over from the back seat, fighting to keep hold of her. She'd jump out and run into the woods, freeze to death, sooner than face her husband. I got accidentally smacked in the mouth.

"Tammy," Marg says, like a kind nurse, who's saying, *we've got to jab you now*. She says, "Tammy. Tammy. Tammy. Listen to me. There's four of us here. Tammy. He won't do nothing in front of the rest of us." Marg keeps talking, and Tammy, she finally stops screaming and flailing. Marg gets her to where she's just crying.

Marg's so awful fat it ain't easy, but she turns herself and takes Tammy in her arms. Tammy bawls her heart out and Marg gives her time, holds her in a nice soft Marg hug.

Me and Sally sit tight.

It's getting cold in there. The windows are steamed up. Sally gets out another one of her napkins, a blue one. Starts wiping the windows. Marg takes it and does the windshield.

"All right now, Tammy," Marg says, "This is what we'll do. I'm going to drive up there. You're going to go in and get your kids to introduce them to me and Sally and Rose. If he asks, say you're just bringing them out to say hello. Okay?"

We practised that over a few times. Your car wouldn't start in this cold. Your friends give you a lift home. Your friends want to meet the kids. Asshole don't want us asking no questions. He'll let the kids come out and say hello.

Tammy says, "Three friends of mine from the therapy group want to say hello to the kids. My car broke down. Three friends of mine want to say hello to the kids."

It seems pretty thin to me. I can see a lot that could go wrong with this plan. But I don't have a better one, so I don't say nothing. Me and Sally, we just squeeze each other's hands. Marg starts the car.

Tammy's in the front seat, talking to herself: "He don't want them asking questions."

We pulled up to the house, didn't see nobody. Tammy let herself in by the side door. Marg done a three point, turned that boat of hers around. And she left it running.

I never sat through a longer five minutes. Rolled the window down, cold as that night was, so I could hear if there was anything to hear.

Marg says, "If they don't come, we'll go call the cops. I'm not sitting still, letting that Asshole beat her no more."

In them days, nobody had a cell phone.

But Sally says, "The police can't do nothing unless she's ready to tell on him."

We know she won't tell. Cops could drive up this lane right now and Tammy'd send them away, say nothing was wrong.

We didn't hear nothing and we didn't hear nothing. We didn't see nothing and we didn't see nothing.

Then the front door opens and there's two kids walking down the steps. Dark little shapes, there, against the light from the house. *Where's Tammy? Where's Tammy? Where's Tammy?*

I'm ready to scream. But good old Marg stays calm.

"Open your door there, Rose." She rolls her window right down.

The little boy comes up to us. Snow crunching under his feet. Big wide eyes. He's holding something in his coat. He just looks at us. His sister comes up behind. Whispers, "Mom said to say hello."

"Well, hello!" Marg says. I don't know how she can keep her voice like that. She's got one eye on the house, but she says, "This here is Sally and Rose and I'm Marg. We're friends of your mom's. Did she tell yous to get in the car with us?"

The kids stand there staring. Their breath coming out of their mouth and going up like smoke.

Marg says, "What have you got there, son?"

The little boy opens his coat. He's got a margarine tub. Lifts the lid up at one side.

Marg peeks in and says, "Wished I had green toes like that, and could stick to a wall. Somebody give you a hard time, you could walk right up the wall and look down at them from the ceiling."

The little boy stands there, watching Marg talk to him.

Sally puts in, she said she wasn't sure if geckos were the ones could do that. "Can Harold there climb up a wall?" she asks the little boy.

I know I'm ready to climb the wall.

Where's Tammy? Come on Tammy!
Sally says, "Ain't yous cold? Did yous want to do your coats up?"
Marg whispers to me and Sally, "Grab them if he comes."
The next thing we seen, dark against the yellow light from the doorway, was Tammy and a man. He makes a grab for her. She dodges him. He's a fair-sized son of a gun. He grabs again. Gets her by the coat.
Marg says, in this cheerful voice, like we're going out for candy apples, she says, "Okay, kids, here comes Mom. We're going for a ride. Hop in!"
Tammy's struggling to get loose. Asshole hanging on.
I crank up the window. I'm ready to haul the kids into the car. But they scramble in. I smile at them the best I can, trying to copy the way Marg's acting. I slide over. They're on the seat between me and Sally. I reach over them. Slam the car door, lock it. Fast as I can. Sally's standing up, reaching over to open the front door for Tammy.
Tammy sheds her coat. He makes a grab for her. Gets her sweater. I seen something flying catch the light. Button shooting off. She runs right out of that sweater, chest stuck out in front, arms trailing, leaves the sweater in his hands. Makes a run for it. She's sprinting across the yard. Chest out. Arms working. T-shirt and pants. No shoes. Sock feet in deep snow. Asshole right behind her.
I don't know how the next things happened. Tammy took a leap and a scramble over a snow pile and made a dive for that open car. Asshole come roaring after her like a snowplow, made a grab for her hair. Door slammed. Hunk of hair in his hand. Marg gunned her. We were screaming out on to County Road 63. Back end sliding wide on the turn. Me and Sally scrambling for to get the kids in the seat belts.
I guess Asshole had to go get his truck keys. That's likely what give us the head start. We took the long way. He might not think of going that way. Took a side road. It was icy, twisty,

hilly. What if we go in the ditch? Marg's gunning that old V-8. Then we could hear a car or truck behind us, far off. But we couldn't see it, the road was so twisty. Marg, she thought she knew another back way into town. She come around a bend. The one behind was getting closer. Marg jerked onto the next side road. Fish-tailing on the turn.

"God, let's not get lost!"

The guy behind makes the second turn too. Still after us.

I'm saying, "Tammy, watch! See if it's him!"

Tammy's froze solid, staring forwards.

Sally's praying out loud to Jesus, who said for the little children to come unto Him. She's got the little girl huddled against her. I'm hugging Matthew. Skinny little fellow. Hid his face against my ski jacket.

We were running up a steep hill. As we come over the top, we could hear the guy behind starting to climb after us. We went flying down the other side. At the foot of the hill, Marg slammed on the brakes. Took a sliding left turn, run right inside a farm shed that was standing open there. Shut the lights off. Truck come sailing down the grade.

We held our breath.

It roared on by.

We breathed out.

I got my hand on Marg's shoulder, thinking of her weak heart. Marg put her forehead down on the steering wheel.

I can hear us all breathing. Sally squeezing Tammy's daughter and mumbling her thanks to the Lord.

I'm saying, "Was that your dad, kids? Was that him that went by?"

It's dark and the two of them is crouched down. Didn't see nothing. Shrug their shoulders.

We're trying to think it through. If that was him just went by, we should turn and go back the way we come. If not, that would be no good. We could meet him.

Then Tammy says, "Oh! Melissa!"

"Who?"

"The babysitter!"

Marg looks over her shoulder at me.

Shit. Shit. .

At least that decides us on which way to go.

Marg does more deep breathing. Then we back out of the shed on to the road and head back up the hill towards Tammy's.

The moon comes up, shining on the white fields, like as if there was peace on earth. What now? What if Asshole's still there? How are we going to get the babysitter out of the house? Can't leave her.

We try to think of a plan. If he's there, Marg says she's going to honk the horn and keep the doors locked.

"Don't get out of this car, whatever yous do," she tells Tammy and the kids.

We turn back onto 63. We're getting close to Tammy's. I'm not religious, myself, but I'm praying louder than Sally. "Oh God. Oh Jesus Christ."

We come around the last bend before their place. I can see the house looking dark on the white land. Not many lights. I'm trying to see if his truck's gone.

Something moves in the laneway. Somebody walking. Weird hump on their back. I'm in that state of mind where you expect to meet something out of a nightmare. The deformed frog that lives in Tammy's basement and gets beat every day and just crawled out now because the door was standing open.

Oh! It's a youngster with a backpack hiking out of the lane. *Thank you, Jesus!*

Tammy cranks the window down. "Melissa!"

Lights behind us show up in the mirror.

Melissa the babysitter's in. And Marg, she's gunning it again, going straight for the main way into town this time. Leaving whoever it was way behind.

Melissa says, "Everybody left. What's going on? I called my mom but my brother said she went to the store."

At the town limits, Marg's old car starts coughing. Marg shoves her foot down. "Come on, baby, sweetheart! You can do it! Frigging Piece of Crap! You can do it, Old Lady!"

Ten-fifteen, we come rattling up to the front of the women's shelter, thank God for it!

Tammy and the kids were took upstairs. Tammy in her bare, red feet, carrying her wet socks. Matthew with his lizard margarine tub in both hands. Young Meghan hadn't never said one word the whole ride. I watched her walking upstairs. Small for her age. Coat too big on her. Long dark hair.

Rest of us slumped in the kitchen while the kettle boiled. The one woman asked Marg for her keys. She'd go put the car out of sight.

Marg said, "Keep your foot right to the floor while you crank her." Then she looks at us two and her voice goes quavery. "Can't believe we done that!"

Sally went and found a blanket. Draped it around Marg's shoulders. Marg's brave as bears when she has to be. We sure seen that. But it takes a toll afterwards.

Melissa got a hold of her mom and she come to pick her up. We could hear the shelter woman (my old friend, Pam) out in the hall, telling her not to let her daughter go to that house again, ever.

We got thinking about what Josie was going to make of this when she heard about it.

"Never mind hotelkeepers," I says, "she'll be telling us we're going to be like a SWAT team! Call us for your hostage incidents."

Marg's voice is shaky but she says to Sally, she says, "Better get sewing parachutes!"

I phoned Dave. Could have stayed where I was. Didn't like to bring him out in the cold, this time of night. But he says no problem.

Sally and Marg, they didn't say nothing but I could see them wondering what man is anybody's first choice over a nice cozy women's shelter? The two of them sat there warming their hands around their tea mugs, looking at the steam. They wished they believed in my little fairytale lasting.

Driving home, I told Dave our night's adventure. He kept saying, "Holy jeeze!"

At home, coming up the stairs behind me, he says, "I don't want you taking them type of chances no more, okay?" He says. "And don't you go trying to play the sheriff with that old man of Marg's, neither, will you? He's a bad bugger, from what I hear."

Dave wanting me safe, caring about me. It was like floating me up the stairs.

I tried to picture any one of my old boyfriends talking like that. Could hear what old Donny would've said: "What did you want to put your nose in that shit for? You're stupid as a box of rocks."

That's the type of compliment he liked to pay me. Gary would've just laughed. Darrell would've got mad. Wouldn't have liked me interfering in another man's home. A home was a man's, the way he seen it. And so was everything in there: woman, lawnmower, kids, chairs.

That's going through my mind, and at the same time I can hear Dave behind me on the stairs, saying, in this worried voice, like it really mattered, "You could've got hurt, Rosie."

That right there was the minute I become sure that Dave was different. With him, I was somewheres I never been in my life before. I was with somebody that would care if I got hurt.

First time! Think about that. First time you're with somebody that would care if you got hurt is supposed to be the day you're born. That's what your frigging parents are for. Right? *The parents are supposed to provide physical and emotional safety*. It said that on the paper.

I turned around to face him at the top of the stairs. He was a couple of steps down so his honey brown eyes come right level with my own eyes. I had a strong feeling in my chest and throat. Aching. Wanting to cry. It was good. But it hurt. At that time, I did not know the name for what that feeling is. Brand new to me. I put my hand on his warm, sandpaper face.

He says, "Promise me you won't go messing in nothing dangerous like that again."

I wanted to say, "And you promise you'll stick to fixing chimneys and never mind selling dope." That subject hadn't came up yet, though. And this didn't feel like the time to start in on it.

I says, "Okay, Dave."

When I went to draw the blind, I could see snow coming down again, making a clean, white, cotton-batting wonder out of this dirty old world.

8.

WENT TO THE HOSPITAL to see Josie the next day after work. Took down a Santa that was bugging her. She was glad to see me. Said nobody'd been in or phoned since Monday.

"That's good about Tammy," she says.

I wasn't used to Josie yet. I stared at the white bed cover. It had lines wove into it, white on white. If she didn't talk to nobody yesterday...

"How do you know about Tammy?" I said.

Josie, she shrugged.

Friday night, I went to get Jenny, to stay over. Jenny, she was four by that time. Little spark of pure sunshine. She got a big kick out of Josie's dog that was still at our place. Wanted to brush it. I give her an old hairbrush. She worked away. Dog laying there patient.

I says, "Well, don't he look good!" The dog gets up, walks over and puts his feet up on the window ledge.

Jenny says, "He wants to see the reflection of his hairdo."

I laughed, said a dog don't understand. But I hadn't got to know that dog yet.

Jenny loves to cook. We were getting out the bowls and spoons, bags of flour and sugar to make Christmas cookies, when Dave come in. I figure Dave will turn around and go out with the guys, but Jenny says he's to help with the baking.

I says, "No, now, sweetie. Dave's been working hard all day

putting up drywall. He wants to sit down with his friends, take it easy."

But Dave, he gives me a wink. Says he's right ready to make him some cookies. That's what he was hoping to do tonight, he says. He rolls up his sleeves, washes his hands, and lets Jenny boss him.

Cutest thing you ever seen, that man taking orders from short-ribs there. She's standing on a chair, my apron tied around her neck, telling him, "Mix it thoroughly." She gets all these words off the cooking shows. Jenny loves cooking shows. And big words.

Dave, he mixes away and he says, "How 'bout that there? Is that about mixed thoroughly now, would you say?"

"It needs to have a thinner consistency," she tells him. "Add milk."

Dave's face is all concentrating while he pours in another little dribble of milk. "How's that look?"

"Ann Toes, we need eyes, noses, and buttons."

"We're good for all that. Look." I show her the little bags of dried fruit and candy that I got for her at the bulk food. She lights up.

"We're making gingerbread men," I fill Dave in.

He gives my shoulders a squeeze. Says, "You know what, Miss Jenny? Ann Toes takes pretty good care of us, don't she?"

Jenny thought so too.

What I thought was that her and Dave just didn't know what a piece of shit I really was.

Well we rolled our dough and cut our gingerbread people.

Jenny says, "They're not all men."

"How can you tell?"

Dave's grinning but nothing like my father would. Not at all sexual.

Jenny, she tells him. She says, "The girls are going to have silver buttons."

"What?" says Dave. "No fair!"

"It's fair," Jenny tells him. "The boys get raisins."
"Raisins!" Dave lets on that he can't live with that. "The guys get raisins and the girls get silver!"
"Because the girls are princesses."
"Well, then how come the boys ain't kings?"
"They're princes," says Jenny. "Princes get raisins."
You can't win an argument with Jenny.

So there's Dave with these tiny little silver ball candies in his great big fingers, trying his level best to put buttons on the gingerbread princesses. He's trying not to dent them in with his fingerprints. And there's Jenny, with this look on her like she's doing the final exam in brain surgery, putting chocolate sprinkles on the gingerbread people for hair.

I can hardly stand what I'm feeling. I almost want to kick Dave out so I won't have this feeling no more.

That feeling like last Tuesday on the stairs. So good but pretty near too strong for me, aching in my chest, scaring me, making me want to cry. And I didn't even have a word for it, back then. Which is pitiful when you come to see that the word for it would just be *love*.

I kept a hold of myself, looking at the two of them, out of the corner of my eye, while I peeled the carrots.

I can still walk past a bakery now, get a whiff of ginger cookies baking and I'm right back there, when Jenny was little and the feeling for Dave was new.

Later, when Jenny was sleeping, face on her like an angel, I went and sat by the fire. Dave's there, munching a gingerbread prince, reading his adventure book. He tells me, "They're out of food. They can't shoot nothing or they'll start an avalanche. Plus it's forty below and, see, up where they are, the air gets thin...."

I start crying.

Dave's getting good at this. He marks his place with a screwdriver that's laying there, puts his book down. He hugs me and tells me, "It's okay."

I have to just shake my head when I think about where I was at that time. Nothing wrong with me but love. And it's so new and so weird that I'm bawling. Needing somebody to tell me that it's okay.

In the morning, we didn't get to sleep in, the way we normally did on a Saturday. Little miss, she's up wanting to know when we're going out shopping. I told her we'd go get presents for her mommy and Ian today.

Dave wasn't allowed to come. He says, "I don't get to hang out with Ann Toes, eh? Just you get to have her?"

"I had her first," Jenny tells him.

Dave winks at me as if to say, she's so quick!

Jenny's holding my hand and we're looking in all the store windows, picking out what we're going to buy each other when we're rich. I says, "Look at them royal blue ones. They'd look good in your castle."

"My castle is going to have yellow towels in its bathroom and a yellow flag on its tower," she says, "with a hand-writing *J* on it for my name. Not a printing *J*."

I get feeling how precious she is and squeeze too tight on her hand. She wiggles it free. I say, louder than what I mean to, "Hold my hand."

She holds her hand, in the little fuzzy mitten, out to me again. "Don't crush my bones," she says.

I can't even hold somebody's hand right. I tell myself that I'm not meant to be happy. What am I doing walking around holding hands with a good guy or a sweet little girl? He's not my husband. She's not my kid. I'm a wannabe.

We got green bath beads for Jenny's mom.

For her mom's boyfriend, Ian, Jenny wanted to get a doll with blonde pigtails.

I says, "I don't know, sweetie. I don't think most grown-up guys play with dolls so much. What about a nice pair of warm socks?"

She said something then, I wished to God I'd've paid more attention to. She said, "Ian would play with her. She looks like me."

That was a clue. Plain as day. But back then I was not clued in. When we were done shopping, I was in the Christmas spirit. Made up my mind to go over to Darlene's place. Cheer her up with the sight of Jenny. Figured I should try harder to make friends with Darlene.

There's her little green eye peeking out between the vertical blinds. She let us in and Jenny petted the cat.

I says, "Darlene," I says, "how are you doing? Have you got food left?"

"At least I'm not starved the way they are some places. I seen on the news..."

Her cat was meowing, circling around.

"What's that cat want?" I says. "Give me your mailbox key. Your cheque should be there. We can get you some food."

In that town where we lived, back then, there was no mail delivery door to door, see. You had to go get your mail at the post office. So me and Jenny went and got Darlene's mail. She signed over the cheque, and we got her some groceries and cat food.

I asked her why the frig she hadn't came to Group for so long. Darlene said that Group wasn't doing nothing for her.

We're carting the grocery bags through to the kitchen. I says, "Well, how can it, if you won't go? And even when you did go, you didn't do the work?"

Darlene said Meredith ought to get her some pills. I asked her what was wrong with her that she needed a pill for. She's in pain, she says. She wasn't talking about a pain in the elbow or nothing. She meant emotional pain, like what we all got. She's already on a lot of stuff for that.

I says, "You don't need no more pills. You need to get out to Group and do some of this work they got us doing. They say that's how you get to feel better. I think it might be starting to work on me." Very first time I ever said it. Group might be starting to work.

But Darlene, she just kept whining. She was in pain. Somebody should up her dose. Her dose, I heard Darlene say before, is already high as the doctor would let her have.

I says, "Darlene," I says, "they will try and help you, if you let them. You got to do something for yourself. You got to come out to Group. And try."

"Them exercises are for babies."

"You got to try them for a while before you make your mind up."

"I done their stupid fear pictures."

"You wouldn't let Meredith fish out of you what it was all about. And you never done another thing since. We're on some question sheets now that are not for no babies."

"I'm having a bad day, Rose." She pulls back away from me like I'm going to jab her or something.

"How come that lady's scared?" Jenny asks me when we're walking away from Darlene's place.

"Something happened to her a long time ago that scared her bad."

Jenny says, "Why is she still scared now?"

I took my time on that one.

The sun's shining, eh. It's a real nice, sparkling blue-and-white winter day. The dockyards across the way are all quiet, and the ice is froze way out so it's this pure white, level. There's Christmas decorations on the balconies. And Jenny's waiting for me to tell her what a grown-up person is scared of right here and now.

"She don't see today," I says. "She's looking at some other day."

Jenny didn't say nothing else. Skipped along beside me halfway across town before she says, "We should go back and tell her."

"Tell who what?"

"Tell the lady with the white kitty that it's today."

"I will," I says. "Next time I see her, I'll tell her that from you."

"She'll be scared all the rest of today and at night when she goes to sleep and when she wakes up in the morning, if she thinks it's a scary day."

Nothing would do but I had to promise to tell Darlene, today, that it was today. And that today was not a scary day. I said I'd phone.

I did, too. After my sister come and picked Jenny up, I called Darlene and tried talking to her. I says, "Look Darlene," I says, "you and me both, it's high time we were taking some steps, here. Face our pain so we can go forwards."

"I don't know how you call that going forwards. What they want us to do in Group, it's more like going backwards. Digging back down into all that shit from the past."

"That's what I said too, when we were starting out. But that's the thing of it, eh. You got to go backwards first. So you can turn around and go forwards. That's what I hear them say."

She says, "It's upsetting, Rose. Thinking about that old stuff."

"You're telling me!"

She says, "I don't see a point in it."

"Well, I can't say that I do neither. But I think we got to trust them people and give it a try. There's no bullshit to the helper there, Frances, anyways. Have you tried talking to her?"

"I don't want to talk to nobody."

"Look, what else are you going to do?"

"I want some more of them pills that makes you feel better," Darlene says.

"We been over this. You got all the pills you can use. They can't give you no more."

"I want enough so I don't feel nothing."

I tried to get her to say that she'd come out to Group. Darlene wouldn't promise nothing. She just told me, before she finally hung up on me, that I was a good person.

Maybe that's what she thought.

Monday, Ken at work got me in a corner outside when I went out for a smoke towards the end of the day. He tells me he wants me to move in with him.

"Get in the car," he says. He'll show me the nice place he's got. He took a hold of my arm, tight, and there wasn't nothing I could think to do. Now, I'd know something to do, but back then I'm in his car before I know it and he's driving through town with the radio on loud. What was that song what's her name was always yelling? It's quite a few years back, now. Something about getting it good.

Radio was blasting and I was trying to think. It's pitiful how mixed up I was. I remember thinking that Ken didn't give me that weird ache in my chest like Dave done. (No clue, eh, what that weird feeling is. Duh.)

I'm thinking, maybe I should move in with Ken. He knows me. He knows what I'll do to keep a job. I'm not no fake or wannabe with him. I'm just my fair-and-square shit self. Dave thinks I'm something special. Dave must be crazy. I remember striking on that idea and thinking, Dave's nuts. Yeah, that explains it! That's why he's treating me so good. He thinks I'm somebody else who's worth caring about.

Just past the hospital, Ken turns up a side street. Stops the car. "Did you ever live in a detached house?"

We're in front of a white bungalow on a decent enough street. Shrubs in front, covered in snow. Green front door. Wreath on it.

I'm all mixed up. Trying to figure out if it would be better to go live with Ken. I tell him I want to see inside.

He says, "Whoa, baby! All right!"

He unlocks the car doors, heaves his heavy-set ass out. I follow him a few steps up his driveway. He's got his back turned. He's picking out his house key.

My head clears.

I take off. Run across the road. Right through the people's yard. Bust through their back hedge. Snow down my neck.

Rip my pantyhose. Don't quit running till I'm in the hospital emergency waiting room. Lock myself in the can, lean on the sink and catch my breath.

I look at the puffing person in the mirror and pant out, "Dave's way better than Ken."

The mirror woman looks me in the eye like, well, shit, genius, no kidding!

Then I go see Josie. She's sitting up in bed looking better. Shines them eyes of hers on me. I let out a long breath as I sit down.

Josie, she waits a while, looking at me. Then she says, "I seen something."

I'm thinking, not now, for pity's sakes.

But she starts in, telling me this daydream she had. She seen me holding a candle. And a man come to my door with a winning lottery ticket. Snow falling on his ball cap.

"I wouldn't laugh, Rose," she says. "Once in a while, somebody wins. Why couldn't it be you?"

"I don't buy them tickets. They're nothing but a tax on stupidness."

But Josie, she put her head to one side and sat there, looking at me, smiling, like, in her mind, I've already had some lucky ticket handed to me.

"Oh, and..." she says and stops. She rummages around in her bedside table drawer there, and hasn't she still got that magazine picture! She gets me to look careful at the space between two houses. I look through her magnifying glass. There's her finger, big, pointing. Fingernail looks like a new moon.

In front of that moon, you can just see somebody. I never noticed no one before. But there's a person in the picture alright, a man in a plaid shirt. It gives me a jolt because, jeeze, under the magnifying glass, he looks a lot like Dave.

I toss the picture like it's caught fire. "You're scary!"

She says, "Maybe that guy's your winning ticket."

I says, "Who was running after me in their cast a few weeks

ago, telling me Dave was no good, telling me to kick him out?"

"I told you it was just what I heard," she says. "That's what Marg and them were saying. I told you I never seen nothing, then. It's just since I been laying here I seen him as a handyman. Then I seen the man at the door with a lucky ticket. Then I seen him in the town. Those are omens."

I says, "You're cracked. You're right nuts."

She says, "The more you look, the more you see, right?"

I let out a big sigh and slumped down. Ken would be steaming pissed now. He might fire me. Or he might be hanging around wanting to beat me up. I didn't know if he seen where I went.

I wanted to tell Josie. I just wanted so bad to spit it all out to her about Ken. But she'd think I was a disgusting bitch. After what she just said about Dave, too, I figured I'd better keep quiet.

"Seen Darlene yesterday. Didn't have nothing in the place, not a kibble left to feed her cat. Peeking out of her blinds there, like there's a war in the street."

And I told how Sally was backsliding without her. "Never gets out of bed but to shit, pee, or open another can of lima beans."

Josie says, "There's just the one person in Group whose story I ain't heard lately."

But I just couldn't tell her my story. What if Josie lost all respect for me? Stopped giving me them icy little fingers of hope on the back of my neck? Stopped making me smile and wonder?

Ken wasn't anywheres that I could see out the window.

I went out a back door of the hospital, slipped along the back way, and got home.

When Dave come in, I was sitting at the kitchen table staring at my sheet of homework for tomorrow. It's a blank sheet that just says at the top, *Today, it's not my fault when....*

9.

JOSIE'S DOG WAS STILL AT OUR PLACE and taking up a lot of the floor. When Dave went to go around it, he caught his leg on the edge of my TV stand. I says, "Oh! Sorry! That thing's sticking out."

He says, "I walk into the furniture and you apologize." He says, "I ought to go where I'm looking."

"Well," I says, "I could put some tape or something over that corner so nobody dings themself."

"If I go in the kitchen and sit on a knife, what are you going to do? Run and tape up all the knives? Apologize to my butt?"

He sees my paper there that I'm trying to work on. Asks if it's okay if he looks at it. (He asks me!)

I says, "Sure." Slide it over to him.

"*Today, it's not my fault when....* Boy, they got your number! Put down, *It's not my fault when Dave Smith walks into the furniture!*"

I laugh, eh, but he's serious. Thinks it's a good example.

I says, "I'd feel foolish writing that."

He hangs around and bugs me. "What are they after, then?"

I don't know. More important stuff.

Dave won't quit. It's the tip of the iceberg, according to him. He says I apologize for breathing. "Write that, about the TV stand, and see what the shrink says. I bet she's going to say you're right on to something."

I sat there trying to think of some more important kind of

thing that isn't my fault. "Rose, do you need help to get started?" That's Meredith's voice in my head.
 Okay. Sorry. I'm starting. I'm trying to think. This is just the same as what I didn't know last week. What, in my life, is not my fault? Ken?
 No. I do something to make men hit on me. I must. It's not like I was good-looking. Ken must be my fault. Besides, I run away when I was fifteen. If I hadn't did that, maybe I would have finished school and gotten a decent job. So I'm poor and hate my job and have to put up with shit at work, but that's all my fault because I quit school and run off.
 I sit there, chewing the pencil, thinking, the whole mess of my life is my own fault.
 Half hour later, Dave wants to know if I've put down about the TV stand. To shut him up, and because I can't think of nothing else to put, I write that down.
 "See there," he says, "now you're started. Put down about the dirty glass at The Pig. Remember when you got the dirty glass and you were saying, 'Sorry to mention it. Sorry to bug you!' Sorry, sorry, like as if it's your fault they didn't wash it right."
 I wrote on my homework, "It's not my fault if they don't wash a glass correct at The Pig & Whistle Pub."
 "Don't that feel good?" Dave says. "What about the sidewalk? You should hear yourself. You say to every person that walks into this place, you say, 'Watch out for the bump there. It's heaved up. Sorry.'"
 "Do I?"
 "Every time. 'Sorry,' you say, like it's your fault. Like you're in the public works crew and it's your job to patch the sidewalk."
 So I wrote that down. "It's not my fault the sidewalk outside of here is heaved up."
 I said I could put down stuff out of the news. Blood, fires, crazy religions, floods, which was, none of it, my fault. Dave didn't think I should run off at the mouth with all of that.
 He says, "You never apologize for none of that anyways."

"What else do I apologize for?"

Dave says, "You know, Toes, the first time I pulled up your sweater and seen your little body there, you know what you said?"

According to Dave, what I did then was I apologized for the size of my boobs. (I never got an A in school, eh. Only in underwear.)

"You want me to write, *It's not my fault I'm flat?*"

He says, "You're the shape the good Lord made you and it's cute. I don't know how you're going to say that on the sheet. But that's the whole thing, right there. There's nothing wrong with you, Rosie. You're good the way you are. Your body's nice and you're nice. You're fun. You're straightforward. You're quick to catch on. You got a heart of gold. You look fine. You don't have to be sorry for nothing about the way you are."

I says, "You are a lucky ticket!"

Then of course I had to explain to him about Josie's dream of me and some lucky ticket. And I told him he's in her picture, there, kind of shadowy, coming out from between two houses.

He laughed. He says, "That girl has fell on her head once or twice too often."

Josie's dog opens its eyes, lifts its nose off the floor and gives him this look, as if to say, watch what you say about Josie.

"Even her dog's spooky," he says. "Ain't you?" he says, running his sock foot, gentle, over the dog.

Then he went and monkeyed with my old dollhouse. He's repairing it for Jenny. Landlord lets him use the garage to do his sawing in.

I wrote down everything else I could think of that I'm always apologizing for.

"At least you done your homework," Dave says, when we're getting into bed. "Have you heard the one about the student who says to his teacher, he says, 'Would you punish me for something I didn't do?' Teacher says, 'Of course not.' Kid says, 'Good. Because I didn't do my homework.'"

Dave never went too far in school. His dad wanted him to go to work in his uncle's garage but he never did.

"That work don't suit me," he says. "I like to take and build things. I'd like to build a house again some day soon. That's what I like doing. My cousin Tom's doing real good, contracting back north. They put up the big summer homes for rich people, eh. Or, you know what I've been dreaming of this fall?" he says when we're cuddled down. "I could get into a bigger challenge. Someday I want to build something bigger than a house."

I opened my eyes wide and looked at the dark. Couldn't even croak out, what, for instance, did you have in mind to build, that's bigger than a house?

Dave was asleep, that night, long time before I was. I looked into the dark and seen Josie's drawing like it was shining on the wall from a projector. Stone and wood and glass. Standing out on a fine, waterfront lot. I could smell the fresh water and feel the breeze off it. Dave in a hard hat and tool belt.

Yellow flag snapping. It's got a *J* on it. Not a printed *J*. Handwriting *J*. It was Josie who drew that, wasn't it? But didn't Jenny say it? My mind snagged on that question a second before it let go and washed along the river to sleep.

Ken never did nothing to me at work on Tuesday. Didn't say nothing about yesterday.

When I got to Group, Marg and Sally were sitting in the waiting room with Tammy, talking about what's the best colour to paint hotel bedrooms. Marg, she likes a butter yellow. Perks her right up, she says. Of course Sally is pushing for pink. Tammy wasn't saying much.

We didn't expect to hear no clunking cast on the stairs this week, but there it was.

We all stampeded to see Josie and help her out. She comes limping up the stairs with her overnight bag, wearing reindeer antlers. Says they're not reindeer. They're elk antlers.

She was so light and weak. Just got out of hospital. Took a cab straight to here.

Tammy grabbed Josie's little case. Sally had to know if Josie was warm enough or too warm or if she wanted a drink of water. She was propping Josie's bad leg up and asking if she'd had any supper.

"Ladies!" Josie says, when she's all set up there like the queen. "We got no further problems!"

Marg, she busts out with her funny laugh. Like a three-litre jug getting shook.

We are like your one-stop shopping for any problem you might care to name. But Josie's Josie. She'll tell you the sky is purple polka dots. We got no further problems, she says.

Josie's been laying in the hospital just doing her best work, there, with the daydreams. The hotel is going to have these canvas deck chair items like they have on an ocean liner, eh, and you can open them out flat for to look at the sky. Our screen porch is going to have a clear ceiling, so you can lay on your deck chair and take in the stars and the northern lights. There's going to be maps of all the stars, with low red lights to see by, because Josie heard somewheres that red light don't wreck your night vision. And there's going to be experts come to see the caves.

"What caves?" I says.

Josie gives me a glance and she says that, on the far side of the point, there's secret caves. She seen them, she says.

"What point?"

Hotel's going to be on a point of land sticking out into the lake. So you can see the water on three sides.

And there's a man coming out of the cave, holding a rabbit by the ears. Josie seen him up against a clear blue sky. A crow flew past his head. Nobody knows about these caves except they're in old legends that the Native people tells.

My niece Jenny's going to find them. The man in the cave will show her. He's not good news, the cave man. But he's going to be the last of the bad news. She seen him up against the sky, holding a rabbit by the ears.

Everybody's dazed, listening.

I figure it's whatever they got her on for pain, except I wouldn't put it past her to know that I have been thinking about that brain-injured caveman father. (Humans, eh? Far as I know, nothing else is twisted like us. The father robin, out in the trees, he don't try to mate with his little birds, does he? A rock must have never fell on no cave bird.)

That's what Josie's doing making up these caves, I bet. This here man with a rabbit, he's going to turn out to be a dream of our first bad ancestor.

The rabbit put me in mind of my sister Sandra's stuffed rabbit that she had when she was a little girl. She held it in her hand when Dad held her down in the boiler room at school.

Tammy says, "Will we take red lights into the caves to look at the pictures by?"

Sally says that they've got a good deal on flashlights now, over at the Canadian Tire. We could put red plastic over them.

"No, we'll need real burning torches," Josie says. "The firelight is going to flicker and it'll make the old pictures come to life. Them old stories will be like alive on the walls. They'll tell us the secrets that are under the world."

Meredith heard that. She stopped in the doorway. Frances bumped into her. Like two out of the three stooges.

We're the toys in the toyshop, and they just caught us, off the shelf, alive, playing.

Meredith never said nothing. Squashed her lips together and walked on into the meeting room. We filed in behind her. The weirdness, it followed us.

There was a new pot of red geraniums sitting on the windowsill. Were them flowers ever bright red!

We all kept on looking at Josie. Heads full of secret caves and firelight. Icy fun tickling up and down our spines.

We went around and heard everybody's week. Sally'd slept

every day. Meredith tried to get her to talk about what it was that she was avoiding by going to sleep. Rest of us weren't worried. Sally'd be okay now that Josie was back.

But Sally answered the question. She's got all these thoughts that goes through her all day like hot needles. "If I'm awake, I remember things."

Meredith was on that like a tiger. "What things do you remember?"

"Bad things. A radio."

"Is a radio bad?"

"That's where I went."

"When did you go into the radio?"

"When bad things were happening."

"You're safe here, Sally. Do you want to tell us what bad things happened, that made you dissociate yourself from your body and pretend to be one of the people in the radio? Is that what you did?"

Sally looks around at us. Big blue eyes wild. Like she's getting ready to jump off a bridge.

"What was happening when you needed to go into the radio, Sally?"

Sally's breathing quick. God, I can feel it right with her. She wants to take the jump and tell. But she's scared what we'll think of her.

Now, Marg moved. Just shifted her weight, so that Sally glanced over at her. Sally looked at Marg for about a week. Breathing scared. Everybody was froze, waiting. Marg looked back at her steady, like, okay Sally, we're here for you.

Sally busted out with it. "When I was a little kid, Mr. Mullen used to do it to me in the back room of his auto shop!"

When she said it, the world did not end. "He seemed like he liked me. I used to go over there. He was the only person who seemed like he liked me."

Meredith said, "So Mr. Mullen abused you, but yet he provided your only source of affection?"

Sally nodded.

"That must have been very confusing for you."

Sally nodded, staring at Meredith.

Meredith told her that telling the group about Mr. Mullen was a very important new step in Sally's healing. And to have this out in the open was a step forward for the whole group, she said.

Sally, she sat there, blinking.

You carry a memory for years and then finally spit it out? Wow!

I could see what Meredith meant by a new phase for the whole group. I mean we all knew already that Childhood Sexual Abuse was what we were here about, but nobody hadn't told the particulars about their own case before. It's the particulars that's real.

We looked at each other. Wow. You could say a thing like that! Not some shrink words like Abuse, but the real thing of your own. The auto shop and who it was and everything. You could say it right in front of the whole group, and it would go on just like normal. Nobody was calling her a piece of garbage. Meredith wasn't falling off her chair. Meredith's helper, Frances, was looking at Sally with a satisfied face like she'd did good on her homework.

Josie and Tammy, sitting on either side of Sally, were letting her squeeze their hands.

Sweet Sally's soft and gentle. But she's been the bravest out of all of us, more than once, along the way. See, Sal is strong on hope. She can sometimes take them leaps of faith forwards, long time before anybody else.

It was plain that nobody thought any less of her for coming out with the facts on Mr. Mullen in the auto shop.

Meredith moved on, normal. Wanted to know how Tammy's week had went.

Well, Tammy, she told about our little adventure there, last Tuesday night. Asshole, he's been making a nuisance of himself on the phone to the shelter ever since. But the workers, they won't tell him if they have anyone by the name of Tammy staying there or not. That's the policy. Meanwhile Tammy's trying to get used to the idea that nobody's going to slug her when she walks into the kitchen or pound the shit out of her kids.

She's scared that Asshole's going to grab the kids on their way to school. The people from the shelter are helping Tammy get to a lawyer next week. She's hoping she can get a court order.

Josie just give us all a grin and said it was too bad she missed the high-speed car chase. Wouldn't talk about how it was that she ended up in hospital.

Marg's old man hasn't burnt her place down yet. Keeps showing his ugly face where Marg don't expect it. He's got Marg good and jumpy, so I guess he's happy. Marg's got to go to court over him first week in January. Maybe he still figures he can scare her out of it. Good luck, buster.

I said what I knew about Darlene.

Sally had saw her too. Won't come out for nothing. Darlene's talking to some man on the internet, though, according to Sally. Just what Darlene needs, eh—some guy from someplace in what used to be Russia there wants to come over and marry her. I wish I could say for sure that she was going to be careful on this. But Darlene, she's only careful where you don't need to be. She's careful picking up her junk flyers off her stoop for fear somebody's in the bushes. She's scared to talk to the lady at the post office. But she'll do the damnedest things. Darlene's the dumbest one out of all of us, I'd say, even counting Tammy.

Dumb is what dumb does, eh. Tammy don't sound too swift when you talk to her. But look at her going forwards there, staying at the shelter, working on getting a court order to keep Asshole away from the kids. And then look at Darlene. She can sound real well-informed. Tell you what's going on in the third world, who's worse off than we are and all that. But there don't seem to be any way to get a new crack of light into Darlene's head. Meredith's getting paid a bundle to make

Darlene feel better. Darlene don't feel no better. Meredith must be screwing up. That's the way Darlene looks at it. Won't lift a finger for her own healing. Pisses me off.

It got around to my turn. If Sally could tell about Mr. Mullen there, maybe I could tell about Ken?

But no, Sally was a little kid when that happened. Here I was, a grown woman. Mine was way more shameful.

After she give up trying to pry stuff out of me, Meredith went on to what she calls our focus for tonight.

She said we were going to talk about smells.

Smells?

"Yes," she says. "What are some good smells?"

We come up with a bunch. Frances the helper, she was up there with a marker and a white board, writing them down. She can't spell to save her life, Frances can't. But you know what she does about that? She just says she can't spell and gets Marg to help her. Marg's a real good speller.

Who knows if Meredith can spell? She'd never let on. She sits tight, making sure to look wise and not risking no comment as to how many Ns might be in the word *cinnamon*.

Can we name some good smells? Roast turkey, air-dried clothes, baking bread, cut grass, clean babies, carnations, new leather, the beach, oranges, cinnamon, talcum powder, chocolate, summer rain. I wanted to say Dave, but I said lilacs. (My second favourite.)

"Okay. Great. And now, What are some bad smells?"

Sally says, right off, "Motor oil, grease, rusty metal."

I seen where this was going!

We had our break then. We're outside, freezing, having a smoke. The rest of them are talking about where Josie's town probably is. They're cooking up the idea that we're going to go looking for it next summer. The Abuse Group road trip.

There's a rock cut where the road goes off the edge of the picture. That tells you that it's the north, where they'll blast through a hundred foot of rock and put a road in. Josie's pointing out a crown on the highway sign sticking up over a bush, so it's Canada, not the States.

Marg laughs. "Oh, well good," she says. "Somewheres in north Canada. Narrows it right down so we shouldn't have no trouble finding it."

Me, I'm quiet, smoking, thinking about the flash that just come into my head. I'm on to Meredith! I know what she's driving at with this smells business. She's tricked Sally already into coming out with details on the place she was abused. Motor oil and rust. Sally don't like them smells because of that Mr. Mullen and what he done to her in the back of his auto shop.

I get Defensive. Meredith's not getting nothing out of me.

I know what bad smell comes into my mind. Smell of my own cunt. But I'm sure not saying that!

When it's her turn to say bad smells, Marg says, "Tide laundry detergent, Old Spice after shave."

It's like she might just as well have told me, right out, that her old man, that's trying to burn her place down, wears Old Spice and that he done it to her in a laundry room.

Tammy says, "Vegetable soup, garlic, pepperoni, wet wool rugs."

All right. So she must have got it on the floor, out in the back room of some Italian restaurant or Italian relatives.

I wonder if this is what it's like to be Meredith and sneak secrets out of people. I wonder what all she's guessed about me?

I thought Josie'd make some smart answer when it come her turn, but she never did. She said, "Alcohol on people's breath—rye, beer, rum—and pine trees and men's sweat."

I thought to myself, shit, I'm seeing through this! I can quit telemarketing right now and be a shrink!

So then everybody's looking at me and it's my turn to say a bad smell and there's only one bad smell in my mind. I blurted it right out!

Didn't talk to nobody afterwards. Ran straight home. When I got there, I rubbed my face in Dave's good smelling shirt and hid. "I can't believe I said that!" I kept saying to him in a whisper. I was feeling so ashamed and low I could've walked under a snake's belly, wearing a top hat.

The minute it had came out of my mouth, I couldn't believe I said it. All the way home, alls I could hear was me saying, "Women's smell, from like the vagina."

I don't know what I was expecting Dave to say. Guess I figured he'd tell me it was okay to name a bad smell when they asked me to.

What Dave actually come out with, blew me away. Got me to what Meredith would call "a new stage in my healing."

"That," he says and he nuzzles me, "to me," he says, "that's a good smell. I'd put that smell in the first list you had there, along with the line-dried clothes and the fresh cut grass, and the baking bread," he says.

10.

THERE WAS REASONS behind Meredith's little exercises. Now that I was starting to get a notion how to see what they were, I couldn't wait for next Tuesday.

I'm Sherlock Holmes all week. Figuring stuff out and piecing it all together. I'm walking around thinking things like, Josie said pine trees has a bad smell. Funny smell to not like. Most people like pine. Five minutes later, I'm thinking, ah-ha! When she was a kid, somebody must have did it to her under a Christmas tree! And then I'd get it. Oh ho! So that's why she don't like Christmas!

Dave, he got to hear a lot of this, and he says he's happy for me that I'm getting into it.

Haven't found out the downside of Dave yet. I can't hardly believe he's for real. Jenny's sweet and she's for real. But how could a grown person wind up still being as much of a sweetheart as Dave seems to be?

I mean, he ain't perfect. He's bad to belch. He don't clean house. He'll leave his shirt on the floor. He don't notice what way I've got my hair or what I've got on, or nothing like that. He's not the type to go out anywheres fancy. He likes the Pig & Whistle on a Friday and he'll go out with Josie's Brent and some of the others once in a while. He likes a game of pool. They play hockey on Thursdays. He's not one to get dressed up.

But, Jesus, I don't have a problem with none of that. I've got this even-tempered, fun, kind-spoken guy here, paying more than his share, fixing everything, making improvements around the place, treating me like I'm one of them princesses of Jenny's, made out of sugar and spice, that he was so careful not to dent.

We took Josie's dog back to her in the truck Wednesday night and sat with her and this Brent fellow of hers. There wasn't one scrap of a Christmas decoration no place in there. Josie's on the wagon, so we had a Coke with her while Brent drank whiskey.

Brent, he never done nothing but boast about what he shot out of season and how many games he'd won at cards off of some mentally slow guy. He's laughing at how the poor bugger never caught on he was cheating. And even, right in front of Josie, he starts talking about some woman who is stacked and he figures likes him.

I asked Dave on the way home why it is that he puts up with Brent.

Dave says, "Me and him go way back. He was a good kid."

"Well, what happened to him? He's a piss poor grown-up."

"His old man was awful rough on him. Beat him down."

That story again. "Is there nobody that lays down and makes a kid that can stand back up again and raise one?"

Dave says, "Wait till you meet my dad."

Christmas morning, we went and seen Jenny and my sister Sandra. Dad was there too, which Sandra never told me he was going to be. I hadn't saw him in a long time and I was none too happy to see him now.

Me and Dave are sitting on the couch, Ian and Dad in two chairs. Dad's got Jenny on his knee. I don't like it.

Jenny, she wiggles down off of Dad's knee and comes over to me and Dave. I put my arm around her. She leans against me.

There's Dave, trying to be friendly to my folks, eh. He takes the odd glance at me. I can see he's wondering why I'm so clammed up and cranky.

Dave says to my father, "So, Albert," he says, "what line of work you in?"

Dad says he's a janitor.

I'm stiff as a chunk of froze fish.

"Oh yeah?" Dave says. "Where do you work?"

I hear Dad telling him the name of the school. Ferry Street Public School. Right here in town. Just the thoughts of him still at it over there, more little kids coming in every year! Including Jenny. He likes them young, eh. The mop closet and the boiler room. And him never getting caught once in all this time. He's held that job for twenty-eight years, he says.

Dave's saying, "Ain't that something." I'm feeling sick. Sun's coming in, and I can see my father's shadow on Sandra's wall. Same lumpy-chin shadow used to slide along the pale green boiler room wall. The windows in there were little, dirty, high-up things, with wire over them on the outsides. This very same shadow slid along under them windows when I was a little girl.

I wish they hadn't made me remember that, in Group. But then again, it's no use forgetting them shadows neither, is it? If I blank that out, what am I? I'm like a shadow on the wall myself.

My sister's boyfriend, Ian, he calls Jenny over to him. Starts playing a game with her where he tries to grab her with his feet and legs. She's kind of laughing. I'm not.

Me and my sister Sandra had a low-voice fight in the kitchen.

I says, "What did you have to ask the old man for?"

Sandra said, "Did I have to be so mean on Christmas Day?"

I says, "Mean?" I says, "I don't want to see him, but that's besides the point," I says. "You shouldn't have him around Jenny. You know what he's like."

This is the closest I've ever came to talking about it to my sister. Up to now, it's been like the boiler room never happened.

But she just says, "How is Dad going to do anything to Jenny with us all sitting there?" (Which shows you that she did remember.)

I says, "Even the way he talks to her, asking her if she's got a boyfriend at junior kindergarten. Makes my skin crawl."

"He's just joking."

"And the way he gets her on his knee. It's inappropriate, Sandra."

"You and your big words you're picking up from that shrink. A grandfather can hold a kid on his knee."

"But did you see the way he done it? He was pulling her back against him! He was rubbing on her."

Sandra just made a snort, like I was disgusting, and poured the frozen peas out, rattling, into the pot.

"And another thing," I says. "I hope you're watching that Ian around her."

I wasn't crazy about that game he was playing with Jenny, grabbing her with his legs.

My sister gets mad. She says, "Jenny's a good girl."

"Of course she is," I says. "I'm not talking about Jenny. I'm talking about Ian. How long have you knew him?"

"Long enough."

"Long enough so you know for sure everything he might and might not do? Do you keep an eye on him with Jenny?"

"Jenny's a good girl. Or I'm teaching her, anyways."

"Don't keep saying that! Who's talking about Jenny!"

"Well, I thought we were."

"Jenny's four years old," I says.

"Well, what are you talking about?"

"Ian."

"What about him?"

"Do you leave him alone with Jenny?"

"So what? Do you think she's a slut?" Sandra says.

"I think she's three feet tall. What's she supposed to do if some hockey-playing—?"

"This Dave guy of yours plays hockey too."

"Alls I'm just saying is Ian's a great big grown man."

"Rose, what is your problem with Ian?"

"I don't happen to like the way he plays with Jenny. And I'm just saying promise me you won't leave her alone with him."

"Open this, would you mind." Sandra whips a can of cranberries out of the basket the church sent her and bangs it on the counter in front of me.

A change was starting to come over me. Yous will find that yourself, too, once yous start your healing. You get a good deal more mouthier. I would have never paid attention to my own hunch about Ian before, and I sure wouldn't have came out and talked about it. Now I'm in there, cranking Sandra's can opener, putting out my views pretty definite.

I says, "Don't leave Jenny alone with Ian or Dad."

Sandra, she didn't know what to make of me. The two of us wound up good and pissed at each other. She told me to mind my own business.

I was making up my mind that, the next time I seen her, we were going to have a long talk about Dad and the boiler room.

In the afternoon, we drove up to Dave's dad's place. Took about three hours. By the second hour, I'm thinking of Josie's picture. We were starting to drive through rock cuts, eh. All that pink stone they got back north. First time I'd saw it for real.

I start checking every little one-horse town we drive through as if I'm going to see Josie's magazine town. I seen a gas station sign that could've been hanging a tiny bit crooked and yelled for Dave to stop.

"What?" he says. He's sitting with the truck running, looking around.

Me, I'm staring at the row of old frame houses along the main street there, trying to see if they're the right ones. There's a little white church all right, with bush behind it but no lake, so I let Dave go on.

Dave's dad's place was a plain-looking little tarpaper house on what had tried to be a farm once. Three rusted out cars were sitting in the front yard, covered in snow.

In the house, there was like a whole clan of Daves, with their families. Most of them's built similar, on the big side. Their eyes runs to honey-brown and tends to be fair-sized and spaced apart good. They look at you humourous and friendly, same as Dave does. And, when you get talking to these people, they make you think of Dave even more. Kind-spoken, easy-going. Tell corny jokes.

Dave's dad put me right at ease.

After dinner, he got out his accordion. Started playing "Rudolph." Kids knew smart-Alec words to holler out between the lines. They went on to a bunch more Christmas songs. Everybody sang. Funny words, that they all knew.

"We three kings of glory and tar
Tried to smoke a rubber cigar
It was loaded and exploded
Now we're on yonder star."

They had a bunch of them. "*While shepherds washed their socks by night...*" You could see they done this every year.

One guy, Tom, he says to his niece, he says, "Want to hear a goofy knock-knock joke?"

Kid grins up at him, waiting to hear it. I see she's got the family look to her. Big, warm, honey-brown eyes, spaced wide apart, lit up with fun.

I get tight in the stomach, waiting for the kind of a joke my dad would tell a little girl.

Cousin Tom says, "You start."

Kid says, "Knock-knock."

"Who's there?" Tom says.

And then he sits there, laughing at the look on her when she sees she walked into it. She stamps her foot and swats him.

"You start!" he says again, laughing at her.

I met Dave's cousin Jan (Tom's wife), who Dave knew I'd like. They've got a little baby she's nursing. She says he don't need no formula. Guess he must not. He's got fat feet and foldy rubber wrists. Just from her breast milk. Cute little tinker.

I like the way Jan takes an interest in her baby's mind. She read a book about babies, how they learn. She says little Alexander there, he's got no way to know, if she walks out of the room, if she's ever coming back. He hasn't learned that yet about the world, that what you can't see is still here.

Like how do I know, when you walk out that door, that you don't blink out like a light? That's why baby Alexander cries, Jan says. He don't know but what his mother just blinked out like a light.

I told Jan I was just learning something like that about the world, myself, how the past disappears and we can't see it no more. But it's still here. Like as if my dead mother's just gone into another room.

That was an interesting conversation.

I sat and thought about my sister Sandra afterwards. She's got a crush on this Ian of hers and she don't even want to think about whether that's okay for Jenny or whether it's not.

Sandra would've never thought about why Jenny was crying, like the way Jan's thinking here. Jan, she's a real good mother. And that's something, I'll tell you!

I don't give a care what else you do or you don't do in your life. What you look like. How much money you got. If you're a good mother or a good father, I'm thankful you're on the earth.

That Christmas Day with Dave was the first I ever spent time with a family where there was no abuse. I watched three little girls, safe as could be, twirling to make themselves dizzy. Uncle Al (Dave's dad) moved a chair back to make room but, when they fell over, he never even looked up their little velvet Christmas dresses.

It wasn't like nobody touched the kids. Dave and his folks, they bounced tots on their knees. They arm-wrestled teens for loonies. They hugged and shoved and carried on. But, boy, was it different to what I'd grew up with! Nobody grabbed a youngster in a way to make you queasy. There just wasn't none of that in the air. Not at all!

I watched the snow blowing against the window and I wished I had Jenny in here with these people, safe.

Best Christmas Day I'd ever had. Or would've been, if I hadn't of had that feeling about Jenny. Worrying about her was like a cold I was coming down with. I could feel it heavy in my head and sore in my throat.

Well, I can tell yous, in the new year, Group had gotten to be a different story. I was like the star pupil there. Instead of dragging my homework out last thing on Monday nights, and sitting, stupid, sweating over what to write, I'd be right at her. I'd sit up late, soon as I got home. Just ate them sheets now. And, in Group, instead of trying to keep Meredith and the others from finding out my stuff, I was the motor mouth. Remember how we worked on smells? Well, we done the same with taste, touch, hearing and sight, one a week, right through January.

I liked the night we done hearing. For the pleasant sounds list, we come up with dry leaves, the sound they'll make on a sidewalk, snow crunching, happy laughing, bells, wild geese, wind, rain, creek water, far-off train whistles, humming, and silence. Yous should try it. Shut your eyes and see what good sounds come to mind.

Of course, on the unpleasant list, which is what Meredith was working up to, we got about what you'd expect out of people with what she calls our "background." Women who got screwed by grown men when we were kids, if you want to come right out with it. We don't like the sounds of yelling, slapping, screaming, door slamming, children crying, guns, bangs, or kissing, moaning, or panting. None of us.

There were also weird certain things for each person. Sally don't like to hear welding. Tammy, she don't like the sound of a cappuccino machine. Marg can't listen to a spin cycle.

It's getting so plain that it's almost comical.

Myself, there's a certain sort of a wet chewing sound some

people make with their mouth if they have anything wrong with their jaw. Meredith looked at me funny when I mentioned that.

I says to Josie, that night when we were going downstairs, "Did you see the way Meredith looked at me?"

Josie says, she says, "When Meredith done that, I seen a little red-brown toy cow with its tail broke off."

"What the frig are you talking about?"

"What I seen when Meredith give you that look."

"What's a toy cow got to do with anything?"

Josie shrugged.

By the time we got to eyesight and we were making collages of bad sights, nobody was trying to hide nothing. We had Worked through our Defences, Meredith said.

We were right at them magazines. There wasn't a picture of a dirty-looking old man left in them. Every man that looked like any father or older brother or out-of-line restaurant guy or Mr. Mullen at the auto shop or whoever, his face was pasted on to our collages. Or his nose was, or his finger-missing hand was, or his puffy chin, or the hairy wrinkles of his neck or whatever part of him we could find and glue on.

Josie had a Santa hat glued on to some underpants-ad fellow that she said looked like her brother when he was twenty and she was five.

Tammy, she cut out every silky shirt. Some old bastard used to buy silky shirts for her and her little sister when they were ten and eight. She had pictures of the Italian food there too, and the wool rug. Sally, of course, she was cutting out wheels and fenders out of the car ads, making like a regular auto shop out of her bristol board. She found a radio that looked about right for the one she used to pretend she was in when Mr. Mullen was doing it to her. (She was one of the happy people who lived in the radio and never got mad or cried.) All she could get of Mr. Mullen was his wristwatch and his two eyes out of two different heads. He had one squinty. Marg, she found a washing machine and she's got a hand getting shut under the lid. That shows how trapped she felt at that time, Meredith says.

Darlene just come back to Group the end of January there so she was way behind. Didn't do nothing but cut out kitty cats.

Me, I could see my life on just about any page of any magazine you could show me. There was the window in our public school. There was the terrazzo floor, the black stairs, and there was the bulletin board full of kids' art, next to the janitor's closet. There was my sister Sandra's green rabbit that she called Sour Bunny and held in her hand. There were the pussy willows that we dunked in the creek on Easter, to make them clean. I seen two hearts and I tore them in pieces, for my sister Sandra's and my own.

Marg said to me, she says, "Remember when you used to always have trouble getting started?"

"I'm started now," I says. And boy, was I!

One big night, Frances, the helper, says, "Rose," she says, "I wonder which of the events in that picture were your fault?"

I said, "No, I was just a little g—"

I choked.

Everybody else had bawled in Group. That there was the first time for me.

Meredith said it was a significant shift and a step in my healing.

Frances said to me on the way out, she said she was glad I felt comfortable enough in Group, now, that I was able to cry.

"I cried in Group," I says to Dave when I got home.

"What over?"

"Because nothing in my whole picture was my fault!"

Dave don't expect nobody to make sense all the time. So he just give me a pat.

I curled up in bed feeling about the best I ever felt yet in my life, up to then. Sheets so smooth and happy feeling.

Sleep's coming and I feel like I'm floating up. *Not my fault. Not my fault. Not the terrazzo floor or the broom closet or the boiler room. Mom not my fault. Sandra not my fault, not my fault*.... It was like the mattress was floating up, out the window between the blue velvet curtain clouds, with all that weight lifted off me.

I'm in a courtroom and the judge, God the Father, in a long white beard, is booming a shining gold hammer on a kettle drum, rumbling, in a voice like far off thunder, when the storm is over, "Not guilty! NOT guilty!" Sally and all the angels chiming in with the high notes. We fly over the drum and it's a shining lake. The sand on the bottom of it is gold.

Of course, I had to wake up the next morning when I got to work. Ken, he had settled down after I took off that day through the neighbours' yard to get away from him. I don't know whether maybe somebody seen and said something to him, or what. Anyways, he'd backed off. And I been thinking, thank God.

But I guess his New Year's resolution had wore off by around about the first of February there. Day after I got to the bawling stage of my healing and had my dream of flying over the lake where the gold was, Ken got back to his old tricks.

So that set me back. Put something right back in the picture that was, as far as I could make out, my own fault.

Mind you, I now had about one eighth of a doubt on that. I was nowheres near to saying what I learned to say later, that what Ken does is Ken's responsibility. But I had my first little start of a question. If nothing in that picture was my fault, if my father wasn't my fault, then, about this situation here...?

But I still had this voice in my head that kept saying, you're grown up now. What happens now is your own fault.

I went to dump the trash. Ken caught me in the back room. Twisted my arm up to my shoulder blades and yanked my face down. Shoved it in my mouth. It did go through my mind to wonder if possibly this might not be all completely my fault.

Stupid, eh? I'm gagging and I'm still sort of assuming it's my own fault this is going on.

But it did go through my mind to wonder if there was any question about that. Just the faint question. But, see, for me, at the time, that was a start. To have that much of a question in my mind. Like just possibly him doing this did maybe not mean I was a born whore who deserved it? Could it by any chance be partly Ken's own fault how Ken acts?

Don't laugh at me. That's alls I could do that day.

You've got to take it easy on yourself when you're getting started with anything. You'll likely be stupid at it. That don't matter. Long as you're getting started.

Josie's generally good in the new year, she says. She quit drinking. Kicked out Brent. Got herself a waitress job at the Queen's Hotel there, in the dining room. Of course she was always talking about the Queen's Hotel on Tuesdays now, telling us that she was picking up a lot that would come in handy, when we had our own hotel to run.

She was looking better. Got her hair curled cute. She'd been out of her cast for a long time. Limp was gone. No new bruises on her. She gained a few pounds so she didn't look like a starvation victim.

The next good thing that happened was she got Sally a job there too. That's the first job Sally had since her daughter died. Sally's daughter died when she was two. Sally was seventeen at the time. Fell asleep on a beach and the little girl drowned.

The waitress thing worked out good. Sally being tall, slim and blonde, that and the way she loves to look after everybody, means she got good tips.

It was fun for her and Josie to work together. They were playing our game all the time, pretending they were just there to look into running a hotel. Dreaming their heads off.

They couldn't usually come to Group the same nights. But whichever one could show up reported in for the two of them. Took back the homework. So we all kept in touch and kept on going.

We were doing different education topics now in Group. We learned about our Human Value. Everyone's got Human Value. We had to write down some things we like about ourself. That was hard, at first. Try that. Write down fifteen things you like about yourself.

I come out with: reliable, work hard, don't get in flap in emergencies. Felt a bit sheepish doing it, but I also put down some of them things Dave says. That I'm straightforward, fun, got a kindly touch.

It wasn't fifteen. But I was started.

One night, we learned about sexual harassment in the workplace. My ears was sticking out like a couple of satellite dishes, I can tell yous! Sticking out and flapping. Meredith was saying, there, that a person can go to jail for what sounded like a lot less than what Ken gets up to!

Another night, I remember we learned all about men and women. Did yous know men and women was evolved different? Women are set up for multi-tasking, Meredith said. And the men, they're set up for thinking of one thing at a time. I thought that was interesting.

Marg had her court case back in January, and her old man was in jail. That was a relief except, of course, she couldn't get it out of her head that it was her fault somebody's in jail. He's an old man. His health is not so hot. She was always asking Meredith about what it's like in jail. Do they feed them good? (Marg's got to know about food.) Would he get beat up?

I'm at my new stage, so I'm sitting there wanting to say to her, "Marg, it's not your fault. If he hadn't abused kids, he wouldn't be eating jail food, would he?"

But you can't just go and tell somebody. I knew that because every time I tried to tell my sister what I was getting out of Group, I hit a wall.

"I can't believe you want to sit there and talk to a bunch of people about such personal shit," my sister says.

"It's not like I love talking about it."

"Nobody's making you."

"But it's doing me good. I'm feeling better. I'm telling you, Sandra, I never felt this good in my life. I wish you'd try something like this. You could—"

"I don't see where you're any better off."

"I can understand things different. Some of the guilt's getting lifted off me. And I've got such good friends now. Feel like they're connected with me real deep. And I'm so close with Dave."

"You're just plain lucky there."

"No. I mean I am lucky. But there's more to it. I'm keeping Dave on purpose because I like how he treats me. I'm learning how to know real love when I see it and when I feel it. And there's not so many frigging secrets hiding in my closets like a bunch of dragons with green teeth. I'm healing, Sandra."

"You're starting to talk weird, and you have a lot to say about what other people should do. That's all I know."

That's the way it ended up every time I tried to talk to my sister. She would not talk about the boiler room. Didn't remember any such a thing. That's what she always said, with her eyes zipping sideways, up, down, like a couple of panicking little grey bugs in a jar.

Marg's saying, "They wouldn't have locked him up if I hadn't of testified. The lawyer said my evidence tipped the scale." Marg sounds more like a patient than a nurse.

Sally was there that night. In the hall afterwards, she says to Marg, "I see they got the paint on sale at Colour Your World. Why don't we do your front room? I'll help you."

Marg says oh no, she wouldn't trouble Sally. But she gets this little smile, so they done that the next week. Marg picked the type of butter yellow that perks her up.

Marg's trying to get used to the fact that she's not in danger around town. She went out and got the paint, her and Sally.

Tammy, she's still scared to go out, too. With good reason. Asshole's on the hunt. Even with the court order, Tammy don't feel safe about herself or the kids. Marg and Sally picked her up from the shelter, though, and she went and pitched in with the painting. Said it done her good to get out.

The shelter people are telling Tammy she has to try to get out more now. They want her to look for an apartment. The lawyer tells her she can stay in the house and kick Asshole out. She don't want to. Wouldn't be safe there. Wants to live where they lock a door downstairs.

Little Jenny was over at our place one Saturday. I had some crayons there for her, and she's sitting at the kitchen table making pictures. I was cutting up an onion for stew.

And Jenny's saying, "Are you crying about my picture, Ann Toes?"

I says, "No, sweetie. It's just the onions. They're stinging my eyes."

She says, "Because it's a sad picture."

Something must've told me what that picture was going to show. I dumped the onion in the pot. It took a long time falling. I scraped the cutting board with the knife. I put the knife in a bowl of water that was in the sink. I washed my hands with soap. I dried my hands on the dish towel. I turned around. I bent over the table. And seen Jenny's picture.

I said, "Who's that there?"

"Ian."

Jenny's mom's boyfriend laying on a bed with this sticking-up dick on him that's as big as the bedroom door.

"Whose bed is that?"

"Mine."

"Is this what you seen in your bed?"

Jenny, she looks up at me. When she sees I'm not mad at her, she nods.

"Did you tell your mommy this went on?"

"Mommy says it's bad to talk about."

I says, "It's something that needs talking about!"

"Mommy said I'm a bad, bad slut girl."

"You? No! You're not bad!"

I'm squeezing Jenny, smelling that little child smell of her hair, feeling her arms tight around my neck, telling her, "You're not bad!"

I must have told her thirty times. "Oh sweetheart, it's not your fault! You're good as gold. Honey, listen to me. It's not your fault. Okay? It is not your fault. Ian's a grown-up. He's the one that ought to know. Not you. You're just little. The grown people are supposed to look after you. They're the ones that did bad. Ian wasn't looking after you when he done that. He was thinking of himself, not you. Oh, it's not your fault!"

I was sitting with her on my lap. She held on tight to me. She's asking me, "I'm not bad?"

"No, Jenny."

"Ann Toes, what's a slut?"

"Something bad, but you're not."

"Mommy said I'm a slut girl."

"She made a mistake."

"Ian said not to tell."

"He shouldn't have said that. It's good to tell."

I could see that little soul was all mixed up. Jesus. I thought, see? This is how you wind up what they call Deeply Confused.

When Dave come home, I put a movie on for Jenny and I told him.

Dave hit the roof. He's got the phone book out, whipping through the blue pages. Says he's calling Children's Aid. I'm trying to pull the phone book out of his hands. I'm saying my sister would never forgive me if I told.

I says, "This is private stuff!"

"Keep it secret? That's just what the dickhead wants!"

"Dave! Wait!"

He slaps the phone down. Looks at me. "Okay," he says, "what do you think we should do?"

Well, that shut me up. What did I think we should do?

My dead mother was right in front of me, her embarrassed face not looking at me when she'd sneak me a tube of ointment, both of us knowing what it was for. My sores down there. Not a word spoke. The world would end if we ever breathed a word.

But then I thought about Sally coming out with it in Group. And how calm the shrinks reacted. I thought of Frances coming out with it to me. How matter of fact she told me. The world don't end when you tell. I knew that much by now.

I put my hand on the counter to help me stand steady and I says to Dave, I says, "I changed my mind. You're right. We got to tell."

Children's Aid made Sandra kick out Ian. She's all like, "I miss him. We're in love."

I says, "Fuck that," I says. So she quit speaking to me.

11.

At group, I yelled, "I knew something like this was bound to happen! I seen it coming since my niece was born. I told yous all. I said, 'That kid is in danger,' I said. But alls yous could do was make me diddle around filling in frigging questionnaires on thirty years ago. Cutting out magazines. Doing blank all."

"Rose," Meredith says, she says, "you could not have prevented this."

"So why didn't you tell me? If there's no hope, there's no hope! What am I wasting time here for?"

"There is hope, Rose."

I took a fit and shouted at them all that hope was done now. There was no use talking to me about hope. The worst thing had already happened. It was over and done with. Jenny'd be screwed up now forever. Sitting here when she was our age, messed up like us, all mixed up, ashamed of her life.

"Thanks for nothing!" I'm yelling at them. "Thanks for wasting my time, sitting here! I told yous what was going to happen to my niece! I seen it coming! Yous wouldn't lift a finger!"

Frances, of course, she got the job of trying to cool me down. I don't know how long I screamed at the poor woman, out in the other room, before she finally got through to me with the idea that all the hope in the world was not gone.

She worked on me, patient. It was not time to give up on this journey. Jenny was going to need my understanding now, more than ever. Jenny was going to need me healed up and well-informed. Jenny needed me to learn all I could. Jenny needed me to keep working on my own healing to be strong for her.

Hadn't I learned a lot already? Didn't I have some new perspectives? Couldn't I see a glimmer of light at the end of this tunnel, for myself? Hadn't I done the right thing phoning Children's Aid? Would I have done that before?

That got me to think. Would I?

No. I wouldn't. I would've just did like what Mom always done.

Frances kept on at me. Wasn't I going to be able to offer a lot more to Jenny if I could keep learning and healing myself so that I could make right decisions like that in the future also?

I troop back in. Dump myself in a chair. Slam my homework on the table. I'm still in the frigging Group.

Sally's apartment was so jammed with stuff she was rescuing from the Queen's Hotel that Dave started calling her "the Sally Ann." She had a box full of guest satisfaction questionnaires in the old colour scheme. (New paint job's a sick grey. Josie calls it "Morning After.")

"They should have left the decorating to you, Sal," Marg says. Because Sally likes everything dolled up pretty.

Josie says, "Leave it up to Sally and the whole place'd be Pepto-Bismol Pink."

"*The Milk of Magnesia*," Marg says, like it's the name of the hotel.

Josie says, "I seen the lake behind the church again last night."

We all shut up and leaned in. I could feel the goosebumps spreading over me. Like it was time for the campfire ghost story.

Josie says, "That's one deep lake. And, in the olden days, when there was a lot of mining back north, a girl was crossing it in a canoe. Grey blue shawl around her. Late in the fall of the year, paddling over from the bush side, towards the church.

She was gliding past the point there, where the secret cave is, that they call the Cave of Time. The woods, they were down to nothing but the last of the yellow leaves fluttering at the tops, and it was cold.

"Then, when the girl's way out in the lake, the wind comes up sudden. It starts belting down icy rain. Waves start going in two directions at once so the canoe was getting it from both sides. There's great big waves coming at the girl east and west, just throwing that canoe, crashing and roaring, and the spray is flying. The girl kneeling down, hanging on to the cross-piece. Shawl, it takes off in the wind, turns into a great blue heron. Paddle jumps out, slaps the water and dives like a beaver. Girl is choked with rain and wind.

"And then one almighty pair of waves comes together underneath her. Canoe goes flying one way, girl goes the other.

"Something else goes flying up out of the rib cage of the canoe. It flies way up into that grey sky. It tries to sprout wings and fly away. But it's too solid. It falls back down and hits the water—smack—and it sinks down and down. It's a bag of gold. And gold can't change into nothing else than what it is. Alls it did was it sank down out of sight while the storm kept roaring up above. And that gold rested, quiet, at the bottom of the lake."

We're all limp, listening to Josie, following the pictures through the air.

It was March by this time, not so frigging cold or dark. The water was running under the ice in every creek and ditch. Bay was full of ducks coming through on their way north. The wind was warm and it smelled like good black topsoil. Hope was back. There was Dave to walk through the park with, holding hands, down to the bay. He can tell you the name of every different kind of a duck.

And there was Group. They were doing work about having compassion for the child you used to be.

And there was Jenny, with her life a long, long ways from over, squatting down by the ditches. "Listen, Ann Toes," she says, "the water is back to life!"

My own life, it was the same as them ditches. Still froze over, as far as anybody could see. I was still working for Ken there, telemarketing his "Spring into Spring" special. But there was something moving in me like the water running under ice.

Me and Josie and Sally all say we're doing real good. Meredith takes a close look at us to see if we're lying. We're not supposed to be doing this good yet. That's the feeling I get from the way she looks at us.

But then, of course, I think, that's dumb, Rose. Why wouldn't she want us healed up quick as possible?

"Are you still with the same man?" she asks me.

"Dave. Yeah."

I can see this is the wrong answer. He's supposed to have busted my nose by now.

I says, "Dave's a true nice guy. Comes from good people. I figure I've finally drew the lucky ticket this time."

A dark look come over Meredith. She swelled up and started in on a speech. Nobody but ourselves could be responsible for our own healing. Nobody could rescue us!

She slaps her hand on the table. "Do you expect some man to make your life into a fairy tale?"

(What's the matter with Meredith? I don't expect nothing like that.)

Dave can't fix my life, she says. The work I do in Group is what's going to help me! Meredith's all excited. Pretty near yelling. Fidgeting around like there's ants in her pants.

"We can't expect some shining knight to come galloping over the hill and save us!" she says. "You may think that this Dave person is safe for you. He's not! He's dangerous to your healing process if you think that any man is going to be the solution to problems that stem from issues in your own childhood!"

She's red in the face, leaning her big boobs over the table at me. "It's no good clinging to some man," she says. "It's as bad as expecting alcohol to solve your problems. You have to do the work yourselves. There's no short cut. Nobody's going to do it for you or miraculously make you feel better."

I've been bawled out. I don't know what for. I catch Josie in the washroom at break, and I ask her, through the partition, "What's Meredith got against Dave?"

Josie says, "Ah, don't mind her."

I says, "I'm doing the work! It's not like I'm sitting back waiting for Dave to do it for me." I flush and go out to wash my hands.

"You're doing good, Rose," Josie says.

"What's she want?" I says. "I bust my butt trying to figure out everything we're supposed to. I'm trying my hardest. I'm here every week. I take part. I do my homework. I feel like I'm getting someplace, too. She sounds like I'm the way Darlene is—just sitting there whining for pills. What does Meredith want out of me?"

Josie flushes her toilet. She comes out and looks at me in the mirror while she's washing her hands. I'm dabbing at my eyes.

She says, "Don't forget I seen that broken toy cow."

"What?"

Josie says, "Alls I know is I seen that toy cow that was broke."

"What are you talking about?"

"That's what I seen."

I stand there looking at her in the mirror.

Josie shrugs. "It comes when I'm thinking of Meredith. Something to do with her is broke, maybe. And once I seen that leaf land in the dark."

"Oh, for crying out loud," I says.

"You're doing good with Dave for two reasons, okay?" Josie tells me while she's shaking the water off her hands. "One is that Dave's a decent guy."

"That's the whole thing right there," I says. "I'm just damn lucky."

But Josie, she says, "No. You know better. The other part of it is something about yourself."

"I'm not doing nothing different." I dab a bit of makeup over the red, to hide from Meredith that I've been crying.

"Yes, you are." Josie tosses her paper towel.

"Tell me what I'm doing different." I stand there with my makeup tube open.

"Like you said. You're doing your work here in Group. It's like with the lake behind the church."

That's how Josie thinks. Alls she can ever tell you is the picture she's got. I have to laugh at her the way she figures she's explained everything. Meredith's a broke toy cow or a leaf, and I'm the lake behind the church. So that's all cleared up nice.

On the way back to the meeting room, I says, "I woulda liked to seen your tests in school. I bet they asked you how many people live in Hong Kong. You put down *bugs in the woods* or *sand on the beach*. And figured you'd answered the question."

Josie says, "Better than sixteen million or whatever it's supposed to be. Bugs in the woods, you can picture. Same as a broke toy cow."

Meredith walks in. Now, you sit and stare at a big woman you're mad at lumbering in and you try your damnedest not to picture a cow.

Tammy's still at the shelter. But trying to find someplace else to live. Every day she wants to just go back home and make up with her husband and not have to think for herself and do all this hard stuff with lawyers and social workers and landlords and the bank. Tammy gets all mixed up. She don't understand what they tell her and she has to ask over again.

Josie, she's serving alcohol at the Queen's Hotel, thinking of how it would be to just get drunk and forget about everything. Her ex-boyfriend Brent's bugging her to take him back. But she hasn't caved.

Sally's working as a waitress, keeping her eyes open, doing

her homework, running up and down the stairs to get out stress, sewing.

Meredith turns to Darlene and she starts asking her about her week. Of course, Darlene's no farther ahead. She's not stuck indoors now. But she's running all over town getting drunk, going home with strange men, taking drugs she don't even know what they are that make her fear and pain go away for a while. With Darlene, it's the one extreme or the other.

"What do you think you are Avoiding by getting stoned?"

But Darlene won't think about it, won't do nothing for herself. Still just wants to get sent for more medication. Whines about it every meeting. "Oh, Meredith, I just want the pain to stop!"

She's the one that needs a lecture, as far as I can make out. She's the one in this group that needs to hear that nobody else is going to fix this for her.

Pain? Jesus. There's no getting away from that, is there? Walking home, I was thinking about that. If you do like Darlene and refuse to stand any pain, if you just want to run away from pain all the time and never stop and feel it, you're no place.

Meredith, she's long forgot about the stepping stone thing, I guess. But, when I got home, I got out some construction paper and markers that I keep in a drawer for Jenny.

I take a red paper. Cut me out a stepping stone, big enough to put my both feet on. I write on it: *I can stand pain*. Put it down on the floor.

I'm standing there on my stone when Dave comes in. I'm embarrassed, but I show him what I've wrote.

He just took it in, shaking his head sympathetic.

To me, just about everything Dave does has the right feel to it.

He learned how to be from them people in that tarpaper house back north, where we sang on Christmas Day and I wished I could've took Jenny.

I says, "Is that what they do back home when somebody's got pain? Just keep quiet and show by their face that they care?"

Of course, he never thought about where he learned how to be or what was showing on his face. He loves them people. But he's got no idea.

"Your folks are so good, Dave. Lots of people aren't like that. You got no idea—no idea!"

He says, "What do you call a deer if it can't see? No-eye deer."

I wasn't in a mood for jokes. So Dave shut up

He paid attention to what I was trying to say, too. Dave's smart, eh. He listened to me explain about the solid gold that's gotten handed down in his family, through the times that's past, parents to kids, all the way to lucky him.

Got a thoughtful look on him. And he said, "The human race, it must be a relay race."

I like the way Dave puts things. I told him how some people don't want to deal with their own problems. Like my sister Sandra and Darlene. Won't try to fix their own problems. Always change the subject to the problems of somebody else who's worse off. Start yapping about Sick Children's Hospital or Africa or somewheres.

Dave says, "That's like saying you don't have to fix a flat tire because it ain't a busted gasket. Standing there by the side of the road in the rain, eh, doing nothing, talking about worse things that are wrong with somebody else's car. Instead of getting at her and changing the tire on your own."

The next day at breakfast, I says to Dave, "I don't like working where I am now."

Nothing's overly complicated in Dave's world. If something's broke, you look at fixing it.

He says, through his half-chewed Shreddies, "Had you thought about looking for somewheres else?"

I go down to the employment office first thing Saturday. I read the notices. I phone for a job at McIlveen's Plumbing and Heating.

I tell them I'm good with people. Good on the phone. I'm reliable. I work hard. I can keep track of things.

"And I don't get in a flap in emergencies. I really want this job, and yous won't be sorry if you hire me."

I never said half so much in my own praise before. But it was true, and I knew it. I relaxed my shoulders, and I told it to them straight out, thinking of how Frances, the helper at Group, is, how straightforward she tells you the truth about herself.

They phone me at work Monday morning. Tell me I can have the job.

I get up. Walk into Ken's office. Shut the door. Say I'm quitting. I don't want no more bullshit out of him or I'm telling the police and they're going to charge his ass with sexual harassment in the workplace. I tell him what that is and that he could go to jail for it. I'm talking to every other girl here, too, and telling them what to do if he tries it with any of them. So he better watch himself from now on.

I walk back to my desk and the phone rings again. It's Josie telling me the colour of the lake behind the church is changed. The sun's bust through, she says. The water's shining like a field of diamonds.

I sit there and I've got a few tears. I'm telling you, it's sunnier right here.

I tell Josie. I lower my voice but I tell her, over the phone, right there from my desk, the Ken story.

"So that's it!" she says.

She's been scared I was going to die in a German restaurant because she daydreamed I was choking on a bratwurst sausage.

"Must've been just his sausage! It's about time he found out that *harass* is one word."

Feels strange to be sitting at that desk, laughing. I gab on. I tell her me and Dave have just painted our kitchen blue. Paint's on the dark side, but we like it with the white trim. Red tea towels and cookie jar to set it off. Looks smart.

Josie says Dave's going to be the builder for our hotel.

"Got promoted up from handyman, did he?"

"He's earned it," she says.

I says, "This looking for a new job was Dave's idea. But I'm the one did it. He never done it for me. I don't get why Meredith thinks I'm trying to get rescued by Dave."

"Ah, she's just landed in the dark," Josie says. "Dave's nice to have around, like what my dog here is, but you're rescuing yourself." She lets on that there ain't nobody in the world better to have around than her hound, which was a philosopher in another life.

I ask her how come he got busted down from thinker to beagle mix. Taking my time, having a personal conversation instead of trying to sell hall and two frigging rooms carpet cleaning.

She says her dog thinks about the universe. Lays on the floor with his ears out flat and wonders why things is so weird.

On the way home, I know what other stepping stones I want to make.

I get out four sheets of paper, sunny bright orange and yellow, and I write, *I'm good with people*, *I'm reliable*, *I work hard*, and *I don't panic*. All my golden Human Value stuff that I said on the phone to McIlveen's Plumbing.

Nobody's looking so I put them down on the floor and stand on them one at a time. I'd recommend that to yous. Feels great.

12.

"WHAT ARE SOME of the good things about you?" I says to Jenny the next day she was over. I was thinking I'd let her try that thing with the stepping stones, teach her about the solid gold of her Human Value.

She says, "I've got a tight pussy."

A voice that don't sound like me says to her, "Is Ian back living with you and mommy?"

She says, "No."

"But does he come over sometimes?"

She nods.

"Does mommy leave you with him?"

"So she can have some peace and quiet."

"And does he tell you that about yourself?" I'm breathing between everything I say. Holy jumping, I'm mad! But I don't want her to think that it's her I'm mad at.

I say, "Okay. What are some other things you like about being you?"

I'm going to settle with my sister! If she can't see this child is looked after right! God dammit.

Jenny says she likes being pretty.

Shit. Shit. Shit. I thought this with Ian was at least over and done with! I say, "Okay. And what about some things you like to do?"

"I like cooking with you and Dave, Ann Toes. I like when Dave tells me the name of the ducks. I like talking to Timothy (that's her stuffed rabbit). I like Ashley in my class. She can count over fifty-five."

"Wow," I says, "that's pretty high counting." *I'm going to fucking kill my sister.*

"So," I says, "do you want to see a game I learned? We make like stepping stones out of paper here, and we take and write things on them that you're good at. And we pretend we're crossing a big, fast, dark river, standing on our Human Value, going over to a sunny shore." *I'm going to get you to a better place, Jenny.*

I wrote, *I can cook cookies*, *I know about ducks*, and *I'm a good friend*. We talked about Timothy the rabbit, and we figured out that she likes to talk to him because she's got more thoughts in her head and more love in her heart than she knows what to do with.

"I say my extra self in his ears."

So I wrote for her, *I think a lot* and *I have lots of love*.

I got out my own stepping stones too, and we made two paths, side by side there, across the kitchen floor. Then we stepped from stone to stone, holding hands.

I'm squeezing that little soft hand, and I'm standing on the paper that says *I'm reliable*, and I'm thinking, I'm going to be reliable for this kid if it's the last thing I do on earth. I'm going to haul her out of the frigging rockslide or I'm going to die trying.

My sister come after dinner to pick Jenny up. Walks into my kitchen and tells me she don't like the new colour. It's too dark, she says.

I says, "Sandra," I says, "we got to talk."

We haven't said a word beyond the stripped-down basics since me and Dave first called the Children's Aid on that Ian piece of shit.

Jenny's watching a movie. I light into Sandra, whispering so Jenny don't hear.

"What the fuck's going on with Ian?"

"Oh," she says, and she gets this little smile so I want to slug her, and she goes, "It's working out good now." She looks at her toe, wiggles it around.

"There's a court order against that creep. He is not supposed to be anyplace near Jenny."

"That's all over with," she says. "He's apologized to me for all that. He treats me real good now. Guess what he bought me?" Sandra's not talking in a whisper at all, but I still am.

"We got to talk about Jenny."

Sandra gets this cold look on her. "What about Jenny?"

"Shhh. She'll hear you."

"So?"

I whisper, "You have to keep him away from her. He's been fooling with her again."

"He wouldn't do that to me."

"He is."

"You're shitting me."

"Why would I? Even ask Jenny."

"The little slut! I'll tan her good. Are you sure?"

"Yeah."

"How do you know? What did she say?"

I told her.

Sandra says, "Jenny!"

My darling gets up from Barney and walks to the kitchen door and stands there. Barney's still singing away. I've got the idea that Sandra's going to do something good. She shouted "Jenny" awful loud, but I don't get it. I think she's just upset, same as I am myself.

Jenny knows better. She freezes there, scared, in the doorway, with the happy kid song in the dark room behind her. She's been laying on the couch. Her blonde hair is all messed up in a soft-looking way, standing out around her face. She's holding Timothy the rabbit, who takes in the overflow of her thinking and love.

Sandra grabs her little arm, jerks her into the kitchen so that

Timothy goes flying, and backhands her—smack—across the face. "That's for fooling with Ian, you slut! You stay away from him, you hear? Dirty sleaze!" Sandra whacks her head again before I can get to her. I can see that little head yet, the way it jerked sideways and back. Sandra wrenched her arm so I was scared she was going to dislocate the shoulder. Why was it taking me so long to get over there to Jenny?

Jenny looks at me as her eyes fill and the red welt comes out on her face. I told on her. She thinks I told on her to get her into trouble. I finally make it to her, grab her to me. My body feels so slow. I heave it like a sand bag between her and Sandra. I tell her I didn't mean to get her in trouble. I wrench Sandra's hand off Jenny's little arm.

Sandra's yelling at her that she's got to the count of three to get her coat on. She's not done with her, she says.

"I'm going to whale you black and blue, you filthy little slut!"

"You're not taking her back there!" I scream at Sandra.

Sandra makes a grab for Jenny. "She's my kid. She's my problem. You can keep your nose out of it."

"Sandra!" I'm hanging on to Jenny, hunching over her to try and keep her from getting hit. I yell, "Listen to me! It's not her fault!"

Sandra takes another swipe at her. Misses. Hits me instead. She's hitting hard.

"Whose fault is it supposed to be if she acts like a whore? My fault, I guess, eh? Everything's the mother's fault? You don't know her. She's a born whore!"

Sandra's pounding me. Out of control. Makes a dive at Jenny. Gets her by the hair. Shakes her.

Screams at her, "Dirty bitch! Every time I take my eyes off you, you're fooling with my man! He's my man, do you hear me? My man, not yours!"

I'm trying to undo my sister's fists off Jenny's hair.

I cover Jenny as much as I can with my arms, yelling over her at her mother, "I'm learning whose fault things is!"

"You don't even have any kids. Trying to tell me what to do with mine!" Sandra's red, panting.

Jenny's flailing like she's in white water, going under, trying to grab on to me.

I scream at Sandra, I can feel my lips hauled back off my teeth like a jungle animal. "You're going to listen to me!"

I must have said that so ferocious that she stops, drops Jenny, and shouts at me, "What bullshit have I got to listen to? Slut, get your boots on."

Jenny grabs me and stays bolted to me.

I want to tell Sandra my whole thing about a rock beaning a caveman, screwing his head. And now this mental trouble, it's built up power till it's this free-for-all rockslide, roaring down the slippery slope of time, balling up dirt and more dirt, bashing thousands and thousands of people, so you can barely make out arms and legs and heads in the commotion. Jenny's in there! It's smacking her, twisting her, shoving her, rolling her head over heels. And it's not her fault or Sandra's or nobody's but the fault of whoever pushed that first big rock. If anybody did. I want to tell Sandra she has to help me. We have to get Jenny out!

How am I going to say all that to my sister who is so pissed off she can hardly get air?

She's jealous of that poor kid because jerk Ian likes her four-year-old tight box! My sister is so starving for a hug, any hug, she'll fight her own child to get one.

All I can think to do is I pry Jenny off me and put my arms out to her mother.

Sandra don't know what to make of this. Stands there and then sort of falls against me.

I says, "Jenny, sweetheart. Hug Timothy. You're this good, darling." I wave my arms out wide around Sandra to show Jenny how good she is. "This good!"

Sandra never offered to let go of me. Once she had my arms around her, she stuck like a bloodsucker. So I hug my poor sister, eh, and I do my best to tell her that one thing that it's taking me so long to learn myself.

"It's not your fault!"

Sandra starts to breathe a bit easier.

"But it's sure not Jenny's neither and it's not even all damned Ian's fault."

I keep hugging her, kind of rocking back and forth. It's the shape the human race is in. My friend Sally calls it "the sin of the world." God knows. But it's sure not Jenny's fault.

"You got to tell her that," I says. I'm still holding Sandra. "It's not Jenny's fault. Tell Jenny it's not her fault."

Alls Sandra can hear is about herself.

"It's not the mother's fault?" she keeps saying, with her face to the floor, her forehead against my shoulder, and her arms around my back like a pair of vice grips.

I pull away and try to get her to look me in the face. I says, "It's not like you can sit back and do nothing. You got to make this kid safe."

Sandra says, "But it's not my fault what happened?"

"Why would it be your fault?" I says.

Sandra whispers into the floor, "I thought she got it from me, being, you know, that kind."

I push Sandra out from me, try to get her to look at me.

She's thinking what I used to think. I'm *that kind*. Men pick on me because I'm *that kind*. No. No. I know better now.

I say, "There is no *that kind*!"

"Well, so why do I always end up with jerks?" Sandra moans to the floor.

I says, "Because you've got no stepping stones to stand on. No gold hasn't sunk into you yet. You don't know your own Human Value."

Of course, Sandra don't know what I'm talking about. Steps back. Gets mad again. Stamps across to the sink for water. Takes a gulp. Bangs the cup down. "So you do blame me!"

Jenny is a slut, the way Sandra wants to see it. Needs to get taught a lesson. She's going to fix it by whacking Jenny. She's going to teach her not to be a slut.

"It's for her own good. So she don't turn out like me."

"Jenny is just caught in this. She hasn't got no power to do nothing about it! You're trying to hold her responsible for things that are the adults' responsibility."

"See it is my fault! That's what you're saying. You sound like a frigging shrink. You should see the way she'll sidle up to a man!"

There's little Jenny in the corner, squeezing her rabbit, watching us with big eyes, taking in all this horse shit about herself from her mother. I picked Jenny up. She wrapped her arms and legs around me tight.

"She's looking for love, Sandra, same as what you are yourself. The two of yous are both mixed up."

"She's not going to steal Ian."

"She's a little kid!"

"She wants it with my man!"

Sandra made a dive at Jenny.

I swung around to protect her, and we had another wrestle. Had to drop Jenny to grapple with Sandra.

"These here are the choices, Sandra." I wind up yelling at her, when I've got her pinned to the fridge. (Thank God I'm stronger than her!) My pictures and magnets and clippings are all getting knocked on the floor. Not on purpose, but her heel come down on a picture of Jenny with Santa.

"You leave Jenny with me until you get that man out of the house, permanent. Or else I am taking her and I am going to the shelter, right now."

Sandra finally wrenched loose. Says she don't want to take the filthy slut home with her anyhow.

Jenny didn't make no fuss about getting left behind.

Dave's on the stairs, coming back from his last hockey game of the season. He flattens his gear and himself up against the wall. Lets Sandra go sailing by.

She's a little bit of a thing, dark haired and tiny there in her dark green coat, running down the stairs with her arms wrapped around herself like that's the only hug she can ever hope to get.

"What's eating her?" he says, hanging up his skates. "Ain't she taking Jenny?"

When I tell him, Dave goes up in a sheet of flames. Shouts that it's high time this Ian piece of shit was took care of. Goes for the phone.

I says, "Who you calling now?"

"Children's Aid."

"What do you think they'll do this time? They already got that order before and that didn't work."

Jenny's like welded to my ribs.

"I don't know," Dave says. "Throw the prick in jail. Or they'll take Somebody away from your sister."

I give him a *watch it, she's smart* look. "Jesus," I says. "Shouldn't we take some time and think this through?"

"There's no more thinking to do," he says. "There's a goddamn limit!"

Now, you see, I never even knew that. I never knew there was any particular limit. The way Dave explains it, he says you can let people do whatever they see fit to do, up to a goddamn limit.

"There's things you don't let no one do. Especially to a little kid."

You should've felt the strength of that child's grip, hanging on to me! Looking back, I know that was adrenaline. Right then, Jenny could've lifted a truck.

I thought about Ken at work, how I'd finally told him where the limit was. I was slow but I was learning. And every single thing I could learn for myself, I could turn right around and use to help Jenny.

So I tried to get this limit thing through my head quick.

I walk around the apartment with Jenny in my arms, give Sandra time to get home. Then I says, "Will you go to Dave for a minute, honey?"

"Is that okay?" he says to her. (He asks her.)

Jenny goes to Dave, no problem. Sucking her thumb and squeezing her rabbit, she puts her face against Dave's shirt.

He holds her in an appropriate way. There's ways for a decent grown man to hold a child, eh. And there's the way my father will hold a child. The difference is plain as day, once you see it.

I called my sister. Told her we had to call Children's Aid again, report that Ian was back.

Sandra was mad as hell. Said she was in love with Ian. They want to get married, she says. And I can keep my nose the fuck out of her life.

"Married?" My voice come out like a fire alarm.

Jenny and Dave were looking at a cartoon together.

I tried to choke myself down to a whisper. "Are you crazy? You want to marry this guy who is screwing your daughter?! What kind of a man is that to pick out?"

Sandra's screaming at me. She says, "Just because the kid is a sleaze, I'm never supposed to have a husband?"

I finally just hang up.

Dave comes into the kitchen. Asks me under his breath, "What's this about marrying?"

I tell him the latest.

He shakes his head in wonder.

I get it, though. I can figure this out now. Sandra blames herself for what she done with our father. Same as I used to. That's what's at the bottom of this. That's how come she's blaming Jenny. If Sandra could see that it wasn't her own fault with Dad, she'd see that it's not Jenny's fault with Ian. It's never the little kid's fault.

I could see now why Meredith was so keen on getting us to figure out whose fault was what.

I made the call to Children's Aid.

Ian, he got arrested for breaking his restraining order, and Jenny, she got took away from Sandra.

They said her mother was not fit. Put Jenny in a foster home.

I was there every day they'd let me visit her.
Jenny had the idea that she was being punished. Poor little soul! She was away from home, staying with these people she didn't know because she was bad. That's what she thought. I couldn't convince her different.
She waited for me. Little white face looking out of the window as soon as I turned on to Shourds Street.
I used to sit in the people's rocking chair in their front room there and rock Jenny. I told her she was not a bad girl. She was a good girl, good as gold, good as gold, good as gold.
"Timothy Rabbit, you tell her."
When it was time to go, the foster mother had to pry Jenny off of my leg. She used to stand there in the window, her and Timothy. Didn't even cry. I'd wave. Blow kisses. But she just stood there, holding her rabbit, like her mother used to.

Tuesday, I'm about ready for therapy. Marg's already there. She says, "How you doing, Rose?"
"Oh, Marg," I says.
Tammy and Sally come in together. They sit down, quiet.
"Rose's upset over her niece," Marg says. She fills them in.
Was I ever glad of them women! Being in a group's a good thing, eh. There's nothing like people that know about a mixed-up life when you're in one yourself.
Tammy says that, someday, her kids and Jenny are all going to be playing together, safe, in the back room of our hotel. The "Lost Gold Room," as Josie calls it. The special room in the back for people like us.
It makes me cry, for some reason. I've gotten through this week without much tears. But that does it. These three sad women in the beige waiting room, sitting on plastic chairs. Their faces lit up so soft and bright, daydreaming of happy times ahead for the kids in some sweet, safe golden room.
Darlene crawls in after the meeting starts, heaving out big sighs so Meredith has to stop the whole thing and ask her what's

wrong. Nothing particular. She tells us about the Russian guy she met on the internet.

Hope to Christ she don't marry him, sight unseen, and let him set up his eastern bloc organized crime headquarters in her apartment, or whatever he's got in mind to do. I wouldn't put it past her.

We check in around the circle.

Tammy's got her own place for next month. Her and the kids are moving out of the shelter. The people there have been helping her get her disability payments so she figures she can manage. She's used to living humble. Don't need a car.

We're all holding our breath because the big thing is: can she stop herself from going back to Asshole the first time she runs into any problems? She's so used to him telling her what to do. It's all right while she's at the shelter with other people to look after her. We'll see.

Sally says her and Josie are doing good over at the Queen's Hotel there.

Marg says she can't sleep sometimes, thinking about her old man being in jail.

Meredith tells Marg that her father, being rather elderly, and being convicted of a sex-related crime, will be held separately from the more dangerous inmates.

Then it's my turn, and I tell about my new job at McIlveen's. There's just me in the office, looking after all the stock and the appointments and the billing and the emergencies. I like it there. People are nice. The guys come in and eat lunch and kid with me. Nobody's hitting on me.

They can't believe how calm I am, talking to people who the water's pouring through their dining room ceilings onto their china cabinets or there's fire shooting out of their hot water heaters.

Me, I'm right at home in them situations. You could say I've been living in fire and flood my whole life. So I'm on the phone there, and I tell people to go get the baking soda or the bucket, talk them through shutting off the power or the tap. I locate our nearest guys and get them over to the address. There's no word you can say to me that ain't been said before, and I don't panic.

They tell me I'm doing good.

"This is all very encouraging," Meredith says. But she gives me a look. She seen that I'd been bawling in the waiting room. Likely figures Dave has finally heaved a hammer through my window.

I tell what I was crying about.

Meredith says that it's very common for women such as my sister who have been sexually abused, themselves, as children, to allow their own children to be abused.

"What? Why?"

You'd think we'd be the ones would know better.

"It's to do with boundaries," Meredith says. (What Dave would call "goddamn limits.")

I was pleased I could follow her. I'm getting better at translating shrink talk into English.

Sandra needed to work on her boundaries (which in regular English means set some goddamn limits on what kind of horse shit she'll put up with).

Meredith says that the issue is rooted in self-worth problems.

What ain't?

By this point in Group, most of them had said something about how their self-worth problems got started. Sally said about her Mr. Mullen. Marg had told about her father in the laundry room. Josie had told about her brother, who looked like the underpants ad guy, when he was twenty and she was five. Tammy had said about the restaurant man that bought see-through shirts for her and her little sister. I hadn't said nothing yet.

Nobody was pushing me, though. In Group, you take a step to the next stepping stone when you're good and ready.

Marg got the Question of the Week. It's getting so I could

make up them questions myself. Marg could too.

Her brains are going, my father's in jail because that's where he needs to be.

But her shoulders are still beside her ears.

We carry our problems in our bodies, they tell us at Group. We got to wake up to what our body's telling us, help it let go of troubles. That's why Frances sometimes will talk right to your body. She'll ask your toes to relax. Then the balls of your feet. Then the arches. And she works her way right up you. Did yous try that yet? Where are you sitting reading this? Are you hanging off the couch sideways, hurting your back? Is your shoulders tight? Did yous need a stretch break? How's the old butt doing?

I just wish Jenny wasn't going to have to go through all this, step by step.

Walking home, that night in March, with the wind a bit warm and smelling like good, black earth, I thought about her all the way. I was going to help her. She would not have to wait till she was my age to take the first step. I'd see she got healed up long before she ever had a kid of her own.

I says to Dave when I got home, I says, "Me and Jenny are going to stop that stinking horse shit getting passed down through time."

I told him my plans. I was never going to quit now. I was going to find out every single bit of information anybody needs to know on this topic. I was going to do every frigging step and sheet and exercise. I was going to get so patched up and sewed back together I'd be like a new quilt. I was bound and bent that Jenny was going to, too.

And you know what Dave says to that?

He says, "Rose," he says, "I love you."

13.

JOSIE COME IN THAT WEEK to see me at my new work. It's just around the corner from Main, but it's the last business on the street. All houses as you go on south from here. I got a big window looking out on the driveway, where the guys are coming and going with their vans. There's a door next to the window, where they come in with their paperwork for me, and a friendly word. There's a window in the south wall too that looks out at the neighbours' yard. They got a bird feeder and some trees. Makes it nice, eh. The old lady there tells me the names of the different birds. I'm starting to learn them. I talk to her over the fence, coming and going. On the north side is the door going into the shop. They can back the vans right in there. Where I work is a plain room, concrete floor. Nothing fancy. But I like it. It's roomy. Roof's high. There's a good amount of daylight. You don't feel boxed in, like what I always done in my little corner at the old job.

You just take abuse out of a situation, eh. And it's a different world.

Josie takes a look around. Says it's just like the plumbing and heating place in the town.

"What town?"

The daydream town. Okay.

I show her around the shop. We got inventory in here, parts and supplies, on shelves. Rolls of different hose, copper pipe, eight grades of black pipe, welding rods. There's a smell of new things. I'm in charge of making sure we keep everything in stock. There's Fred in there getting ready to go out on a call. He's mainly going to check a furnace, but I remind him to take sump pump hose because the people said theirs might've sprung a pinhole leak. They're not sure if it's that or their basement's leaking. They're in one of them old houses with a cellar like Count Dracula's, by the sounds of it. That's another thing I know all about, from my "background." Cellars.

Fred, the plumber there, he grins at Josie. Tells her he don't know how the place ever run before they had Rose.

It's lunchtime. Me and Josie go to the Times Square Restaurant. Josie tells me there really is a plumbing and heating place in the picture.

I says, "Quit it."

But there's Josie digging in her purse, and I'm looking at the light orange slice of tomato laying beside my grilled cheese. I'm thinking, please, I don't want to see a plumbing and heating place show up by magic in that picture, where there never was one before.

Of course there it is. Josie puts her finger on it. It's one of the store fronts if you look careful.

I says, "Why don't I just sit here and you tell me everything that's going to happen, the rest of our life! Just read it off your magic picture there. Tell me what to do and I'll do it."

Josie says, "Why are you mad?"

I says, "Because, if you're some kind of a frigging fortune teller and you've got the whole future right handy there in your macramé purse, why don't you never tell me what's going to happen next? I worked for fucking Ken for two and a half years! I never knew there was a plumbing and heating place in this town where I could go to. Or in that town. Or wherever the hell we are."

Josie, she just sits and looks at her burger. She's sorry I'm pissed off, but there's nothing she could've did different.

She says, "I don't usually know what a picture means until

after, when I see it real. It wouldn't have did no good if I had of said to you, 'Beware of bratwurst.' I didn't know what the big sausage was till you told me about the boss."

I said, "Ken wasn't your fault."

She said, "I wish you'd have told me what you were going through."

"Too ashamed."

Josie nods. She knows what that's about. She sits and nibbles at a couple of crumbs on the edge of her food.

"Darlene's got that guy coming from overseas, eh?"

"Did she tell you that or did you dream it?"

Josie's not sure.

I says, "You still off the booze?"

Yup. She's going out to AA. Her and Marg.

"Marg? I never knew Marg drank."

"She don't," Josie says, "but she likes to go to the meetings. Loves them little chocolate doughnut centres they get in."

"Marg goes to AA for the doughnut holes?"

"Yeah, well, more for the company. She says it's more interesting conversation than what you hear at the Lions' bingo."

"Marg's got nothing to put in."

"She says she drinks. How are they going to know different?"

I had to laugh.

Josie says, "It's fun for her. She makes stuff up just to try how it sounds."

"You get everybody making stuff up!"

I had rice pudding and a tea. Then I had to go back to work, see whose toilet was shooting sludge now.

Josie, she didn't have to go in to work at the Queen's till four o'clock so she walked me back to work. We'd stepped out to cross the corner before she finally told me. "I've took Brent back."

I stopped in the road to look at her. I point my finger at her. "Is he treating you all right?"

"Oh, yeah," she says. But it don't sound so convincing.

"Is he treating you good in this here real town where we're living and breathing? Or is that in some made-up happy town that's all in your head?"

We're still standing on the yellow line. Cars sailing by on either side.

"Josie!" I'm fed up. She won't answer me.

I grab her arm, and we run for the sidewalk. It's time I was back. "Give me a straight answer! Is that man treating you good or is he not?"

No answer.

"Are you nuts? What did you take him back for, when you had him all nice and kicked out?"

"He come around whining so pitiful."

"There should be a dog catcher!"

Josie half smiled. "Shut him in the mud room? Give him a dish of water?"

There's Darlene the next Tuesday telling us about Ivan who's coming over. Ivan, he's "handsome for looking," according to himself on the email. He "admires womans." He "has much exciting" to meet Darlene. Wants to come over here and get married.

Of course Meredith, she's sweating, trying to get Darlene to think about how good of an idea it's likely to turn out, if you go and marry some guy you never seen in your life, that you don't know nothing about.

Darlene gets this shy smile like a six-year-old. Rolls her eyes at Meredith. Says she's very happy. She's in love. Her life is going to be happy now. Why don't Meredith yell at her?

Darlene's never filled out one sheet. Don't know shit about her own life. She's where the people in Dave's adventure books are normally at. Out of food, out of fuel, one foot hanging out in space over a hole in the mountain. Wall of fire on one side, flood on the other. Only difference is the people in Dave's books don't seem to run out of brains.

I used to be just as bad. All them guys I went through? I was generally waltzing over the edge of some cliff.

Your life changes when you take a look at it. You feel yourself smarten up. It quits seeming like just some bad luck used to make you act like a frigging idiot.

See, when I think about it careful, I know I never used judgement about no man before Dave. When I used to get mixed up with one after another, I was like what Sandra's like. And Darlene. I never asked myself one sensible question such as "How does this guy treat people (including me)?"

I was off somewheres else, desperate for anything that could numb my pain and—in a dim light—look like love.

Everybody yaps about following your heart. I'm here to say: use your brains, too.

Tammy, she moved into her own place. Sally went and measured for to make drapes. She can see a nice soft shade of salmon for the front room, Sally says, and she's going to help Tammy sew café style curtains, in maybe a raspberry colour, for the kitchen.

I says, "Look out, Tammy! Sal's trying to make the whole place pink on you."

Meredith walks in. Asks Tammy what her own favourite colour is.

Tammy, she looks blank. So that's her Question for the Week: "What's your favourite colour, Tammy?"

Back before Christmas, I would've turned up my nose at that question. Hasn't Tammy got more important things to figure out? But now I see Meredith's trying to get her to listen to herself. For a change. You can bet Asshole don't care what Tammy's favourite colour is! If she can start listening to herself about what colour in a drape looks good to her, there's a hope she can start listening to herself about what else feels good to her. And what don't.

I can see that that's what helped me out where Dave's concerned. I started noticing them little things like when he asked me my opinion, asked permission to look at my paper, asked what I wanted to do. It felt so nice.

Me taking notice of them things, taking notice how I felt about them, that was all new. That was how I started to have any judgement.

Darlene says her and Ivan just fixed it up today.

"Josie told me last week," I says.

"Did she say if it's going to turn out lucky?"

I lost my temper. "Use your frigging brain! How lucky does it look like it's going to turn out?"

Later, I got what Dave calls a "stairs idea" (what you think of, on your way downstairs, that you should've said). I should've said Josie seen a Russian wolfhound eating her alive. Fangs dripping blood.

The exercise that night was about what Meredith calls Coping Mechanisms. What that is, is it's whatever you done to survive your traumas. And whatever you done ever since, to keep from feeling the pain of your traumas.

Everybody put in ideas. We made a list. I still got it. I'll copy it out for yous and yous can see if your own shit is here:

COPING MECHANISMS:

Taking care of people—focusing on other people's pain (Sally, Marg, me)
Isolating self (me before we started Group, Darlene)
Eating (Marg)
Not eating (Josie)
Falling in love (Darlene, me before)
Being too trustful and/or taking extreme risks (Darlene—both)
Conforming to others' demands (Tammy)
Not conforming (Darlene)
Drinking (Josie, Darlene)
Sleeping (Sally—not now so much)

"Didn't you want your name down for that second-last one, Marg? You with your drinking problem?"

Marg, she looks at me blank, then laughs.

Of course, Meredith goes, "Marg? Is this something you would like to share with us?"

I haven't heard this good of a glug-glugging Marg laugh in a while.

I sing out, "Marg joined the AA!"

Marg can't quit laughing, red in the face, glugging, sticking her soft elbow in me to shut me up.

Tammy says, "You joined AA?"

Everybody's looking at her.

Marg says, "No! I'm going to kill you!" she says to me.

"She only goes for the free doughnuts," I says, and Marg starts hitting me over the head with a piece of paper, laughing.

You got to stir the pot, once in a while at Group, eh, or you feel like you're at your own funeral.

"It's a joke," I says.

Meredith gives us one of her lips-only smiles. Then we go back to listing down our Dysfunctional Coping Mechanisms.

> *Being too cautious* (Darlene, Marg)
> *Compulsive collecting* (Sally)
> *Pretending things are okay when they're not* (Tammy, all of us sometimes)
> *Accepting undue shame* (everyone)
> *Fantasy* (everyone)

I had a question about that last one there. "Can I ask what's wrong with fantasy?"

"Well," Meredith tells me, "we have to live in reality, don't we? It's not healthy to escape into fantasy worlds. It's an Avoidance of Reality."

"Is that what it is?" I says.

"Oh yes. Fantasy is a Coping Mechanism. Abused children

often invent fantasy worlds where everything is good. It's a way of surviving the pain of their real situation. But of course, when we grow up, we have to set that aside or else it becomes a negative force in our lives. As adults we have to come to terms with things as they really are. Fantasy, used as a coping mechanism in adult life, can be very destructive."

That's what Meredith said.

Everything went chilly and dim in our fantasy town. A shadow come over the hotel and over the house where the lady was singing, baking her blueberry pies. The fellow next door who was sanding a garden bench for our hotel—it's like I seen him shiver and look up, wondering how come he couldn't feel the warmth of the sun on the back of his neck. A cloud shadow fell on the white church. Turned it grey. The sparkle died out of the pink stones. The deep water with the bright gold drifting down went dark. The house with blue curtains come under a cloud, and the glass stars in the window quit catching sunshine and casting coloured shadows.

But then I thought, no, dammit. I'm going to use my own judgement! I took and scratched *fantasy* off the bad list with a bold line. Warm sun lit the town up beautiful again.

I called Josie the next morning to bitch about Meredith.

"She don't see the point in fantasy, using your imagination. Wants to nail everything down to what's real and what makes sense," I says.

Josie says. "Sense?" She says, "The world is a ball of dirt sailing through outer space hanging on to us by the feet."

I wasn't to the purple blue stepping stone yet, the spirit stone, which, when you stand on it, means you know you're standing on a world in space and every single thing, yourself included, is beyond belief.

I was a long way from that yet, but I must've had some notion along them lines. Enough to make me stick up for daydreams.

I says, "I gotta go. They've got a dishwasher plugged, up in Snob Hill. Yelling it's a frigging emergency."

Josie laughs.

Dishwasher! They were lucky if they had anything to put in a dish, when Josie was growing up. That's why she can't hardly eat. A whole burger scares her. She's waiting for her brother to grab it or her father to take and cut it in four. Or for her mother to hit her in the side of the head, call her a hog for being so hungry.

Doing her homework for Group, Josie had to sit and write, *I do not need to be ashamed of normal hunger. Being hungry is nobody's fault.*

Just like when I had to write, *It is not my fault the sidewalk's heaved.*

You gotta do it. Write her down. Dumb or not. That's how you yank out the weeds of shame, the way Frances the helper puts it.

And then you work on thinking of what your good points are. Planting the garden of self-worth, Frances says.

Josie says, "Eating out with you at the restaurant? I ate the whole half of a burger?"

"Yeah?"

"Well," Josie says, "that was the first time I ever ate food in front of anybody in twenty-one years."

14.

THE NEXT TUESDAY, Sally come trotting upstairs. Tammy lumbering behind. Both of them happy. Lugging two big bags. They'd went to the fabric store together. Sally was to hold up bolts of material and Tammy was going to say which colour she liked.

Sally held the bag. Tammy, she stuck her hands in deep and pulled the midnight blue up out of there like a magic trick. Tammy's beaming like a sunny day. "I like this colour the best!"

It was a dark colour, real deep. Sure would not have been Sally's pick. But Sally knew enough to keep her mouth shut.

You can like whatever colour you happen to like. You get a handful of them paint chips. And you say to yourself, which of these here do I myself like the looks of? And if it so happens that what's calling to you is some out-of-style colour your sister calls "Slime Green" or you like the kind of red that your mother calls "Whore's Drawers," nuts to them.

What you like is you. And there's nothing wrong with you yourself. That's the message, see? That's the point of writing all this down.

Tammy give me a leftover piece of the blue cloth. I took it home. Spread it out on the table. It was thick, soft, with a bumpy weave. I never knew it was the colour to make my spirit stone, eh, or a clue for how to get to that. I'm just running my hand over it, thinking, this here is a colour that I myself also happen to like. Me and Tammy have that in common.

It felt brand new. Permission to like this dark colour. Somebody else saying it was their favourite too. Mom never would have a dark colour around. Wouldn't let me wear nothing dark. Didn't want to look at nothing dark. Look at the bright side. That was her. Don't look at nothing depressing. Don't talk about nothing bad. Here's the ointment, but we just won't say nothing about the fact your father screws you because that ain't a nice topic.

My stepping stones were getting to reach halfway across that little kitchen by now. Each one stood for some kind of what Meredith called a "shift." Changes. Stuff I come to see different.

I was fired up about favourite colours. Couldn't wait to see Jenny.

When I go over there the next day after work, I take her a big box of new crayons and we dump them all over the table in the foster home. Jenny starts to peel the paper off her sunshine yellow crayon. Now, you know, it was on the tip of my tongue to tell her not to wreck the crayon. But, "I want to see it more. Yellow is my favourite."

So I shut my mouth. I can barely learn quick enough to keep up with being Jenny's aunt.

Friday, I give Josie a call. Boyfriend Brent answered. I don't know if it was the way he was breathing, but I got a feeling off of him. I wish I'd have got it through my head, at that time, that you have to listen to hunches. I thought, something's funny. But then I thought, or maybe I'm nuts.

Brent, he goes, "She can't come to the phone."

I says, "Why not?"

"Christ, you're nosy."

"Well, get her to call me."

"Will do," he says, just like that. Casual.

"Will she call me right back?"

"She'll call," he says, and he hangs up.

I said to Dave, I says, "I wonder if something's up with Brent and Josie."

He said, "Want to go see?"

But no. There's me, still down-playing my own hunch.

An hour later when she hadn't called me back, I says, "I'm wondering."

Dave says, "We can drive over there. Think we should?"

Two hours later, I'm pacing.

Dave, he put a shoelace in his book and shut it.

It was a good thing we went. Brent was nowheres to be seen, and we had to get Josie to the hospital again. The story was she'd got drunk and fell over.

"How'd she ever manage to get a goose egg like that on the back of her head if she fell face first?" That's what Dave was wondering while we're sitting there waiting to hear if she's going to have to stay the night. "Or, if she went down backwards, what the hell happened to her face?"

We looked at each other.

She was home the next day, and you can bet I wanted to talk to her. I showed up on her doorstep late afternoon.

I looked in the window and I seen Josie. She was laying on the couch, looking out the window at the pink twilight. Little smile on her. I bet she was thinking something like what Jenny might be thinking, like about angels or fairy people that live in them soft spring clouds. I took a glance up, myself.

Tapped on the door gentle, not to make her jump.

She waved, and I let myself in. I says, "Jesus, Josie!" Went and gave her a hug. Took it easy, not to hurt her. But she drew in her breath, sharp, when I touched her back.

Josie looks up at the sky. It's turned a deep rose.

She says, "Poor Sally, her and her pink. We give her such a hard time over it. But look at that! It's beautiful."

"Nothing wrong with any colour," I says.

We sat there for a while, watching the sky go through its show. It does that twice a day. How often do I even raise my eyes to see it? There's something about Josie that makes you see more.

Finally she says, in a low voice, "You're right, eh."

"What am I right about?"

"Brent done it."

I says, "I wished you'd have told me before now."

"Too ashamed."

Two of the sweetest people I know, Jenny and Josie. Both so ashamed of stuff that's not their faults!

I started in about Brent. Had a lot to say. Told her I hoped this meant that she was finally going to kick him the hell out. What the frig was he doing back here anyway?

"It was him all the times before, too, wasn't it?" I says. "What did you ever let him back for, after last time? You were in the hospital for a week!"

Finally Josie got sick of me nagging her. She says, "Rose," she says, "I'm sorry for all the trouble I've put you to in the past, and I'm sorry for the future too, because I'll never change."

That got me steaming pissed. I told her she had to get up her gumption and hope for better. She didn't need to have a sorry future. She was going to have a good future. I says, "Look at me working at McIlveen's now and how much better off I am. Did I sit down and say, 'Oh, well, I guess I have to do stinking Ken in the supply room the rest of my life? Oh well. Nothing I can do?'

I says, "No." I says, "Look how I'm learning every day and helping Jenny. My stepping stones are halfway across the kitchen, and when they reach all the way from the door to the stove, me and Dave are getting married!"

I shouldn't have told it to her that night, her all bruised and shamed and the two of us bickering over Brent, with so much to talk about there. But that's the way it come out.

Josie jumped up. Spread out her shawl like wings to hug me.

"When your what reaches from the door to the stove?" she says.

Josie settled back in the couch, smiling out the window, up at the first star, and she planned out the wedding. She was right in her glory. Had me waltzing down the aisle in the church beside the lake. Jenny dressed up like a princess. Josie give me a wedding gown of Tammy's dark blue drapes and a veil of the silver stars.

"You crazy nut." I can't help smiling at her, with tears coming. And at the same time, I am still very pissed off.

I says, "We got something else to talk about tonight besides what I'm going to wear to my wedding."

Josie breezed right on. Marg's a great cook. Marg will cater the buffet. Her and Sally. They'll run the whole thing.

I says, "Josie, we can talk about that later. Where is Brent right now?"

She didn't know.

"What if me and Dave take you to the shelter?"

She wouldn't.

"He won't do nothing more tonight," she says. "There's going to be northern lights on your wedding night."

Dave come for me in the truck about ten o'clock. I was fed right up by that time. Hadn't had no luck trying to get through to Josie. She would not talk serious.

I told Dave about it on the way home. We didn't know what to do. It's not like with Jenny where we could step in, eh. Josie's technically a grown-up.

We're tramping up the stairs to our place. "She's got to just smarten up and kick him out," Dave says.

"But she won't," I says. "Look at how many times things like this has went on already. And she come right out and told me she's never going to change! Oh, Dave, you should've saw her back! I helped her on with her night gown."

Dave can't take it in.

While I'm turning the key in the lock, he's saying, "If you'd knew Brent growing up, he was just like what Josie is now. He was the one getting hurt all the time. We used to feel real sorry for him. Mom and Dad tried to get the police into it. I can't believe he's the one dishing it out now."

"That's the way it goes, I think. One generation to the next." I open the door.

"Are you sure it was him done it?"

"Who else?"

We're hanging up our jackets, taking off our boots.

"Can't be Brent."

"It is."

"Can't be. He'd never want nobody to suffer like what he suffered himself."

I went and poured water in the kettle for tea.

I says, "Maybe he can't stop himself. Maybe he needs help. Needs to go to a group, like me, only for men. And get some help for his trouble. What he's got there is what Meredith would call an Anger Problem. Like the husband of our friend Tammy. Meredith said if Tammy's Asshole wanted, he could join a group and get help for how he acts. Think Brent would? You could talk to him. Anger Management Group, I think they call it."

Me and Dave felt like our hands were tied. What could we do if Josie wouldn't do nothing?

Dave said if it was anybody but Brent, he'd punch his lights out. But he'd try talking to him, he said.

"I could never lay a hand on Brent," he says. "All the times I seen him beat black and blue by his old man. And burned, Rosie! Old bastard used to burn him, when he was just a little kid."

"Jesus. Why didn't somebody call Children's Aid?"

"Like I said, Mom and Dad did. More than once. Couldn't get nobody to do nothing. I don't know why. It was different in them days. Back north, too. You had to pretty near murder a kid to get them to make a move. Plus, Brent's old man had a bit of money. See if you can get Josie to tell your shrink woman," Dave says. "Maybe she'll have a thought. Maybe there's some way to make him go into that men's group."

In bed, alls I could think of was Josie's little bony white back with the flaming red welt across it. Odd shape to it. Like she was hit with a straight thing that had something else sticking out the side.

You can blank out a lot you've heard tell of, but what you've saw yourself is right there. That's why Meredith spent all them weeks on the five senses.

Dave, he rocked me back and forth. Don't fix nothing, but it makes you feel better. I always sit and rock Jenny. Bet cave people done that too. The decent ones that hadn't had their heads squashed.

"You're a sweet girl, Rosie, crying for your friend," he says. "You're my sweet girl."

I says, "You want to cry for your friend right now, too, don't you?"

I knew Dave felt all mixed up. Thinking Brent didn't deserve no sympathy. Sick sorry for him all the same.

"Don't seem right to keep on feeling sorry for him, after what he's did. I should just be sorry for her. Not him."

"The both of them," I says.

I told Dave about the rockslide, how it had took out Brent when he was a poor little kid and now Brent was roaring on downhill with no brakes, in his own day, smashing up the next person.

I put my face where it fits against Dave's chest, and Dave, he rested his cheek on the top of my head.

15.

DAVE, HE COULD SOMETIMES be like the dad and mom I wish I'd've had. But then again too, the more we got to know each other, the more he let out what a kid he could be. He don't like sitting in a tub when the water's draining out, eh. Hops out quick so nothing important's going to wash down the hole. He won't eat a cookie if it's broke. Only eats cheese if it's orange. Hates new clothes. He'll layer two pair of pants, if the holes don't line up, sooner than wear a new pair.

And Jell-O! Him and Jenny is right about the same age when there's a bowl of Jell-O. They mostly don't eat it. What they want it for is to play with. They'll bounce their spoons on it. Try sucking it through straws. They'll stare at what all you can make it do, wrinkle up in little folds and bulge up in mounds. Get rude sucking noises out of it. Red is Dave's favourite. Jenny likes pineapple. I often made them some on the weekends, and they had a grand old time.

Our days with Jenny seemed to go by too fast.

"Time flies like an arrow," Dave says to her. "Mind you, fruit flies like a banana."

She laughed. She got it. She's real smart.

Dave goes down to the hardware store one day for sandpaper and comes home with sandpaper and a fish mould thing to make Jell-O in.

"Look at this here," he says, and he's happy, taking it out of the wrapper. He can't wait to see what Jenny thinks of a pineapple goldfish. He figures we should try it out ahead to make sure it works. Where the tail joins on looks like it might be too skinny and not come out. He don't want her disappointed. He's boiling water and mixing up the stuff, hollering in when I'm taking a shower to ask if he should grease the mould. He keeps checking it in the fridge, giving it a wiggle, poking it with his finger to see if it's set, wondering if he should've made it orange like a real goldfish. The next morning it's set nice. After work he's playing at it again, getting ready to turn it out. I show him to soak it in warm water first, and it comes out in one piece. It's smiling up at us off of the blue plate. Nothing will do for Dave but I have to take it to Jenny today when I go over.

"How am I going to walk six blocks with a plate of Jell-O?"

I usually walk, eh, for the exercise.

But he's out there fixing up a box so it don't slide around in the back of the truck, and then he drives me over to Shourds Street, slow, not to wreck his fish.

There's Jenny standing at the window. Only certain family's allowed into the foster home. But Dave sits out in the truck and watches. Jenny likes the fish. She waves and waves. He keeps waving back. Her and him, they give each other the thumbs up.

I seen Dave cry a few times. He'd get thinking about his mother, who died three years before. She had a real rough time with cancer, eh. Went in her mouth and throat. Cruel way to go. It comes over him once in a while. He'll put his face against me in bed. Then it's my turn to be the grown person, and he takes a turn getting rocked.

We talked about Jenny, and we talked about Josie and Brent. We talked about ourselves and the plans we were making. We could talk about anything.

It was new to me at that time, all this being close to somebody, all this sweetness. I was waiting for it to turn sour some way. But, at least, now, I wasn't thinking every five minutes that I'm a piece of garbage ripening up in the can, just waiting till Dave gets a whiff. At least I'd quit doing Ken. And it was slowly starting to sink into me that I might have a few good points. Maybe just because he loved me didn't prove that Dave would have to be altogether crazy.

I was living like a decent woman now.

The quiet was weird. Going to work, liking it fine. Coming home, liking it more than fine. Working on personal growth in Group with my friends. Rocking Jenny. Reading to her. Knowing she was at least safe, there with the nice foster people. Colouring with her. Walking down through the park to the beach with Dave in the evenings. Sometimes we'd pack a picnic and eat it by the water, with the birds singing for spring and kids playing in the grass. Dave was working real steady, house building for the landlord's friend. Dave loves building a new house, eh. So he's happy. McIlveen's give me a raise. Everything was working so smooth I couldn't get used to it.

I was normally worried about Josie and one or two of the others. But they all had a lull there that spring. Nothing blew up for weeks. It got real quiet.

Once or twice I almost called my sister Sandra. I'm looking at the phone, itching to call her up and scream. I tried thinking I wanted to set her straight about that Ian creep of hers. I sure as hell did want to, as far as that went. But I knew that nothing I could say was going to help.

No, I just plain wanted a fight. Never knew myself to want to go looking for a fight before.

A funny thing started happening to me about that time. It was the next stepping stone, as it turned out. So I'll tell yous all about it. But, frig, it scared me at the time. Didn't know what was going on.

Dave was asleep. I got up to pee and, on the way back, I stood and looked out the window. It was all quiet. Nice spring night. Moon full, sitting up there in a clear sky. And all of a sudden I couldn't stand it. I was ready to howl. All this frigging peace and quiet! I wanted to put a brick through that happy little bedroom window. I would've gave anything to be doing warp speed in Marg's car on an icy road again, maniac roaring after us. The quiet now was making me crazy! Nothing going on! The bedside lamp caught my eye. Fair-sized, black, china lamp, square metal base. Quite the corners to it. The moon was weird bright on it. I got the idea of taking that thing and smashing it over Dave's head.

That would stir up some action, wouldn't it? Then he'd see what I was like. Wouldn't take me for no good, kind, straightforward person.

That black lamp with the silver edge of moonlight gleaming at me like an evil eye! Winking at me to do something strange and wild. I could feel my hands wanting to reach out for it. Like desire.

Had to run out of the room.

I'm charging up and down in the living room. Couldn't tell what was wrong with me. Needed something wild, something bad, something to break up the quiet.

Grabbed a magazine. Twisted it in my hands. Started ripping it. Threw the pieces all over the floor. Went at it with my teeth. Ripped it. Growled. Shook it like a dog.

Then I cleaned it up and went back to bed. Lay there and thought, now what in the world was that?

Dave rolled over and put his arm around me. I cuddled my back up against his nice warm belly and fell asleep feeling damn foolish.

Two nights later, same thing all over again. This time I broke a bottle of mouthwash and poured it on the toilet. Not down the toilet. All over the place, the blue stuff flying around, that mint smell sharp, biting my airways. Splattering the walls. I was berserk in there. I seen my teeth in the mirror. I seen my blood running off my hand. It felt good to be bad. I liked the sting of the cut.

Afterward, I thought, Jesus, I'm mental!

Was I ever glad when Tuesday come! Knew enough by then to open my mouth.

One thing I will say for Meredith. You can't shock her. She has Heard It All.

She told me that I probably had an adrenaline addiction.

What? I wasn't on nothing.

"In a crisis, the body produces adrenaline. It floods the entire person. It affects digestion, heart rate, muscles. It affects the functioning of the brain.

"You've had a lot of crises in your life, Rose. You've spent a great deal of time with a high level of adrenaline in your system. In the process of healing, as your life quiets down and the adrenaline level comes down, it's normal to go through a period of craving and withdrawal."

I looked at her. "You're telling me this is normal?"

"Perfectly," she says. "It's a sign of how well you are doing."

"I threw Listerine all over the towels, deliberate."

"Towels are washable."

"I liked the way a cut felt. I bit a *People* magazine."

"There is no law against that."

"I'm not going nuts?"

"You're going sane. The two things can feel similar." (She got that out of a book. I come across it myself, long time later.)

Sally comes up to me in the break. Looks around to see that nobody's listening and she says to me, she says, "I jumped up and down on a laundry hamper. Had to buy a new one. Nobody'd pissed me off. Nothing. I just took it into my head."

Marg joined the huddle. Told us that she'd been smashing jam jars with a hammer. Mind you, being Marg, she's got it all planned out ahead. Only uses empties. Keeps them in the corner cupboard, with the hammer, all neat and ready for when the urge strikes. Stout box so the glass don't fly around. Wears a snorkel mask.

Tammy, she heard us hooting. (Just to picture that, eh! Marg, berserk, in a hot polka-dot pink little kids' snorkel mask!)

Tammy told us, with a red face, that she tore up her phone book. Can't call nobody.

After break, they all told Meredith.

"When it's happening," Meredith says, "just hang on to the idea that this is normal and that it won't last. It's a shift. Something's moving."

I made a stepping stone about it. I wrote, *I don't need to live in fire and flood*. Wrote it on a green piece of paper. Tore it up once, in one of my times and threw it out of the mud room window. But I made it again. Soft green for calm and quiet. *I can live in peace.*

I would've never thought that peace and quiet would be such a job to get used to!

One day I looked at Dave. He had the window open, feet up on the windowsill, reading one of his books, and I'm telling you I needed so bad to rip that book out of his hands, hit him over the head with it, throw it out that window. I needed to hit him.

Now, I could say it was for different reasons. His pyjamas was on the floor. Flies were getting in the window. Time was, I would've yelled the first thing that come handy. But I stand there, eh, and I know it's this thing I'm going through. Nothing to do with Dave. I know that and I try to hold on, like Meredith said.

Okay, this is normal. It ain't going to last.

Dave raises his head. Stands up. Takes a step towards me.

I yell, "No!"

He stops. I've told him all about this. He takes a pillow off the couch and tosses it to me, looking me in the eye like he's a lion tamer.

I caught that pillow, and then I let go like a stick of dynamite. Threw it down. Pounded it with both fists. Screamed at it every foul word I ever heard of. Bashed my head into it. Over and over. I was on my knees just beating on that thing, yelling that it had pretty near wrecked my fucking life.

"You're not my whole life! There is more to me. I'm going

to have a decent life. I'm going to have a good life just to spite you!" *Whack. Whack. Punch. Pound.*

By the time I got that out of me, and I'm laying there with my face on the floor, listening to the neighbour, Bertie, yelling up from downstairs, I knew this was another new step. Something had shifted again. That pillow had became my father.

So of course, I'm over there, Tuesday, telling them that I found out I got this red-hot fury in me at my father. I could've frigging killed him. Bastard! Treating me the way he done when I was a helpless little kid!

Meredith reminded me how I used to say he was just a poor old man who I ought to forgive now. "This is a major step forward, Rose. You've really made a shift. You're in touch with your anger at your father."

"You're sure this is going forwards? Wouldn't I be farther ahead to forgive him?"

"The time for that may come. But we're not there yet. You see, Rose, as long as you were not able to feel angry at him for what happened when you were young, the anger inside you had to go somewhere else."

"I don't know that I was mad at anybody, back then."

"You may not have been aware of it. But when people are being wronged, there is anger. If we are not allowed to express that anger to the person who is causing it, we divert the anger. We blame someone else. Where do you think your anger has been directed? Whom have you blamed all your life, Rose?"

That was my Question to Think About.

I said, "Smacking that pillow, I seen my father's lump that he has in his jaw. His chin stuck out on one side of it. It was right in that pillow. I was pounding his face in."

Meredith got a look I couldn't read.

Frances looked at me steady, encouraging.

Everybody waited.

You could hear yourself breathe in that room.

Not that it was going to be news to nobody. They all knew

my dad was the one screwed me up. But I hadn't came out with no details yet. That's hard, eh. Saying them gross details.

Okay. I figure I'm ready.

Started fooling with me in the tub when I was a tiny little girl, pushing things up me, playing dirty with me. He had this metal thing. Couldn't even tell yous what it was. Some silver-coloured thing he used to shove up me. Too big for me. He said it was to open me up. He said he was doing me a favour for when I got married. "There'd be nothing worse," he used to say, "than if you got married and you didn't know what to do on your wedding night."

I could tell I was different than other kids.

When I said that, agreement sounds come out of most of them girls. There was heads nodded.

That was them too, in the corner of their schoolyard, standing by themself against the fence. Not knowing that another person alive ever had to do that with their dad. Not knowing another soul ever felt so dirty and ashamed.

I shut my eyes. Hot tears. I was seeing us poor little kids so plain. The coat too short or too long. Wet mitts. Nose running. Shoulders hunched. I seen us all clumping along in our schooldays rubber boots, trudging footsore, lonesome little girls on our long, long way to this table.

Marg was sitting on one side of me and Josie on the other. I felt for Josie's hand.

The old shame took a twist inside me like a cramp. I twisted sideways towards Marg. With her nice baby powder smell. Her arm went around my shoulders. Josie gripped, firm, on my right hand.

I said, "As soon as Dad could fit it in, he done that. It hurt. I wasn't big enough. Ripped me. I was always bleeding. I never knew till I was grown up that it's not supposed to hurt when you pee, let alone when you.... But if I tried to get away—"

I choked. Marg's arm got tighter.

I says, "If I tried to get away.... In the boiler room. He got my sister Sandra if I wouldn't. He used to make me help, to teach me not to run away. I had to hold her hands from scratching and cover her mouth from biting him. I helped him."

The way it hurt to come out with them words! Like I swallowed a fishhook. This was ripping it back up my throat. I must have been crushing Josie's hand, but she never flinched away.

I needed to come out with some more words. I hadn't said it all yet. Like when you know you're not done up-chucking.

I hear Marg's voice, "Did your mom know?"

I let out a gasp from her touching on that sore spot.

"Yeah."

After that was just Kleenex and Meredith's questions.

"Did I understand you to say that your mother was aware of what was taking place?"

I says, "Yes. She was aware."

"And do you feel angry with her for not having protected you?"

"Oh, no. My mom was real nice. I always felt guilty."

"What did you feel guilty for?"

"Being a slut. Doing it with her husband." I hung my head and mumbled that.

"But," Meredith says, "that was not your doing, Rose. You were a tiny child when your father started to condition you to abuse. Do you believe that it was your responsibility to look after your mother in that situation?"

See? Bass ackwards again.

Why was I so mixed up? Where did I ever get the idea that I was to blame because I didn't take better care of my mother? How come I never once thought about the idea that she could've took better care of me?

Meredith said that's a normal type of confusion. Because it's far too frightening for a little child to blame the mom and dad.

I tried to put myself in the place of a kid and think it through. What if your own mommy is crazy? And your dad's twisted?

Jesus, what would you do? They're in charge. You can't get away. It give me a whiff of a nightmare panic feeling in my chest just to think of it. So apparently, kids always choose to blame theirself.

"Blaming one's self is extremely painful but it's not so terrifying as the alternative," Meredith said. "Considering one's parents evil or insane is too frightening. No young child will ever do that."

"Learning to see them in that light and to put the blame where it's due," she said, "is a major shift, a giant step toward a mature perspective."

I walked home in a haze. Lot to think about.

I was still thinking about it when I was sitting at the table in the foster home, two days later, doing a puzzle with Jenny.

She's saying, "No. It needs to have some of the bear's ear. Mommy is good at doing puzzles."

"Yeah," I says, "she always was."

"How do you know?"

"Well, your mom's my sister, eh. When we were little girls, we done things like this together."

"Do you love my mommy?"

"Yes, I do."

"You don't play with her now."

"Well, I'm mad at her right now, but that don't mean I don't love her."

"Why are you mad at my mommy?"

Jenny's got the same knack as Meredith for putting her finger on the Question of the Week. Jenny sits there looking at me with her clear eyes. Her pigtails make me think of two big question marks, like as if you could see the questions popping out the sides of her head.

"Why am I mad at your mommy? Why do you think?"

"I don't know."

"Well, I don't believe you should have to live here, sweetheart.

I think your mommy should make it so you can live with her."

"Mommy says you made me come here."

"She does, eh?"

"But I told her Mrs. B. made me."

That's the social worker on Jenny's case.

"But honey, Mrs. B. and I only want you here to keep you safe. Right? Because Mommy wasn't doing her job keeping you safe. That's a Mommy and Daddy's job, to keep their little kids safe."

"I don't have a Daddy."

"Well we don't know where he is. He's not doing his job, neither. Jenny, your mom shouldn't let Ian in the house, when she knows that Ian is bad to you. Your mom made a big mistake doing that. Okay? She has no business having anything to do with a man that's bad to our Jenny. I'm mad at her for making such a big mistake as that."

Jenny took the puzzle piece that I was holding and turned it around. She snapped it into place.

"You're good!" I says.

She smiles but then the trouble is right back. "Mommy says I'm bad."

I says, calm as I could, "Well, see, I'm mad at her for that too. The way I see it, she's wrong there. You're doing fine on being a little girl. She's screwing up on being a mother. She shouldn't put the blame on you!"

"Is Mommy bad?" Jenny can hardly breathe. She's looking at me with her blonde question marks jumping out of her head.

"Now, Jenny, I never said your mommy was a bad person. What I said was she made some bad mistakes."

God, it's hard work trying to say the right thing to an abused kid, eh. I was thinking about what Meredith said, that it's way too scary for a child to think the mom and dad are bad. But what can she think if she don't think that?

"I miss Ian." Jenny tells that to her rabbit, Timothy, in a low voice.

I pick up the rabbit and talk for him. "Life's pretty mixed up, ain't it?" says the rabbit.

"Ann Toes doesn't like Ian," Jenny tells rabbit, "but Ian likes me. Mommy doesn't like me, but Ian does."

I wiggle the rabbit's ear for him. "I hear everything with my big ears here, and alls I ever heard Auntie say about Ian was she don't like what he done to our Jenny."

I found out that talking in the rabbit voice kind of suited me. So I kept it up.

"Auntie don't really know Ian," the rabbit says. "Maybe he's got a lot of good in him." I made the rabbit point up to the sky with his paw and say, "Maybe God, up in heaven, knows what's inside of Ian." The rabbit, he waves his paw around the room. "Alls we know, here on the ground, is we can't let nobody do wrong things to our Jenny."

She just took my hand and brought me over to the rocking chair. "You smell good," was all she says to me. She put her warm head against my shoulder and snuggled in, with her thumb in her mouth and her rabbit in the crook of her arm.

Sitting rocking her, alls I could feel was boiling mad at my sister. I wanted Jenny to be mad at her too. It was Sandra's frigging selfish stupid needy wanting this Ian idiot so bad she can't even see straight. Still says she's going to frigging marry him. Blaming his child abuse on the kid....

I guess I got that old rocking chair going pretty good.

Jenny says to me, she says, "You're speeding!"

I reined in, rocked slower.

I'm thinking, Jenny, Jenny, who are you mad at? You've got to be mad at somebody for what's going on here. You're not mad at Ian and you're not mad at your mom.

"Are you mad at Mrs. B.?"

Jenny shakes her head, and then she takes her thumb out of her mouth to say, "Mrs. B.'s nice."

"Are you mad at the people here?"

Jenny shakes her head.

"Are you mad at me?"

"No."

"You don't think," I says to the rabbit, "that Jenny's mad at Jenny?"

Rabbit, he got his head nodded for him.

I says, "Oh, Timothy Rabbit! Why would our dear girl be mad at herself?"

And the rabbit, he says, "For liking Ian to touch."

"Well, you tell Jenny that she's good as gold."

I rocked her, talking into her soft hair. "You're a good, good, good girl. None of this is your fault."

It come to me, walking home, what the answer was to Meredith's Question of the Week for me. Where was my anger directed? Who have I been mad at all my life? Duh. Me.

16.

THE MAY LONG WEEKEND, we went back north for Dave to hunt turkey with his dad and the cousins. I was looking forwards to seeing them people again. We were going to tell them about our plans for getting married.

Dave says, "Only maybe don't say nothing about getting across the kitchen floor with your papers there." He don't think the folks at home are ready for the stepping stones. My sister, Sandra, wouldn't know what to make of that neither, so I hear what he's saying.

The country looked beautiful, driving up. We took what Dave called the scenic tour. First we went through farm hills. It was all that green like what you knit a baby sweater out of. I was thinking that mother nature was knitting a soft green blanket for her spring babies. Birdies hatching in the woods. Bunnies in their burrows under the trees, nursing from their soft mothers. I'd tell Jenny about the babies born in the spring. We should bring her out here for a drive. She'd love to see the clean little big-eyed calves and colts in the fields.

Later in the morning, I noticed that the little ones had played themselves out. They were mostly sleeping now, curled in the grass with their big mothers standing over them.

In the past, I would've called myself stupid if I ever cried over a bunch of cows. But I know now I'm crying because that calf we just went by has a mother that stands guard. It has a mother that would moo her lungs out and fight and kick before she'd let harm come to that red calf. It's pretty sad, you've got to admit, when you look at the fact that a Hereford cow makes a better mother than what your sister Sandra does. Or your own mom ever done.

Now there was starting to be rocks sticking out of the fields. Dave, he smiled when he seen that. He loves it back north. We passed the top edge of the farm country in a few minutes. And then the world was all different. Pine trees, little green lakes sparkling, white birch just coming out in leaf. That must have been rough country for to make a road through. They'd blasted it through walls of rock and laid it across swamps. It had to twist and turn to go around the lakes.

I says, "You'd wonder what they ever went to the trouble of building roads up here for."

"For getting to Dad's!" Dave was just a-grinning. Hugging the corners.

"No, but serious. What is there up here? What brought anybody in the first place?"

"Well, of course the first folks was up here, getting around in canoes, hunting. It's good for all that."

"Yeah, but our people. What did they come up here for?"

"Oh, there was timber. Bit of mining. Some thought they were going to find a lot of gold. Some of them tried to farm. Poor buggers. Irish. Scottish. Some give up. Lots of them probably died trying. And then there's a few," he says, "that wouldn't live noplace else."

I asked him, "Why did you ever leave?"

He's smiling at everything in sight, but then I see like a shadow go over his face. "Well, my mom was sick, eh. And I wanted.... Rosie, I should tell you. I thought if I could make enough.... Never mind. Tell you later."

I couldn't drag nothing more out of him.

He's smiling again. He smiles at the tires on the front lawns with daffodils sprouting out of them. He smiles at the trees and at the rocks.

He says, "Are you hungry? We can stop at the Lucky Duck."

We soon come to a Chinese restaurant at the edge of a town. It's got a clump of pine trees in the front, with an old sign nailed to one of them. *Good Luck Restaurant.*

That struck me hilarious, like "good luck with eating here." But Dave, he's been used to it all his life. Says it's great. Pulls into the bumpy parking lot. Jumps out of the truck. Takes off up the old wooden stairs, two at a time.

They had the chicken balls in that glow-in-the-dark sauce and all that kind of Chinese stuff. But they served Canadian food too, which tasted real good. We had the turkey soup. Turkey was shot across the road from here, according to Jinping. She's one of the sisters that runs the place. Her and Hong. Their grandma sits at the till and don't miss nothing, by the looks of her. Jinping tells Dave that their older brother is coming soon from China. A half brother, I gather, that she's never seen. She's all excited about it.

I like to watch Dave with anybody. He's got such a way with him. He calls to grandma there, "You got your boy coming from over home, eh? Your grandson?"

Jinping, she tells grandma what he's talking about, and her old face lights up like morning. She's nodding, smiling, talking away to Dave in Chinese. The gist would be plain enough to anyone. She's happy. Ready to love her grandson.

Good grandmas and good grandpas. Yous might think that yous've pretty well did what yous can do in this world, eh. But maybe your best is still to be gave. Your love to the younger folks.

That's what's going to carry on down the mountain like what Sally calls "a stream of living water."

Better than a frigging rockslide.

At the Good Luck Restaurant, it was noon. The people that come in, they mostly said hello to grandma. And called out to each other.

"Look what gets in when you haven't got a gun!" one old guy

in the corner hollers to another who's coming in with the paper.

"What's new and exciting in Strone?"

"Rained yesterday."

"How's Frank making out with the well?" That was awful funny. There was a roar went up on all sides of the room over that.

I said to Dave, "Who's Frank?"

"Oh, this lawyer fellow, has a summer place up here. There's always some Frank joke every spring. Him trying to fix something."

A woman in her forties come in, and the old guy, Elmer, he calls to her, "I'm looking for a woman that can chop wood."

"You could hire every stick of your wood chopped," she says, "and you still wouldn't find nobody to put up with you."

They all laugh, eh. Kidding back and forth.

They talked to us too. Most of them knew Dave. A youngish guy come in for a coffee. Him and Dave talked over where people was getting turkey this year. The guy sat down with us. Dave asked him if he was still making the log furniture.

I look up from the soup.

I have to say, "Like garden swings and that?"

Yeah, outdoor furniture.

"With logs, you say?"

Yeah, he said, it was mostly pine log, cottage style.

Then I could hear Dave, like as if he was far away, telling John that we might want to look at some furniture.

John, he starts moving stuff on the table to show us a map of where he lives.

"You know the white church," he says to Dave, and he sets the vinegar bottle out to be the church, "you go past that."

I'm froze with my soup spoon halfways to my mouth.

I'm trying to think that there's lots of white churches and people that make log furniture. But a feeling's come over me so strong I can hardly manage to croak out, "What's behind the church?"

Dave and this John, they look at me. I put the spoon back in the bowl.

"Behind the church? Nothing," John says and I feel like I've made an ass of myself. But then it's a jolt because he adds on, "Nothing but water."

"There is water?"

It seemed like the biggest deal—whether, behind that church, there was or there wasn't water. I think I clutched on to the edge of the table and leaned forwards, like a maniac.

"There's a bay there, off of Lost Gold Lake. Good for ducks in the fall."

Lost Gold Lake. Oh my God! Oh, Josie. I slumped back.

I said, in like a whisper, "How come they call it that?"

"What? The lake? Beats me. Uncle Elmer?" he says to the old guy that wants a woman who chops wood, he says, "What was the story about Lost Gold Lake, why they call it that? This young lady wants to hear you tell it."

Uncle Elmer's happy. Brings his chair and his friend, with his chair and his paper. He takes his time and adds in a few things of his own, but he tells it pretty much the way Josie told it. The girl who drowned and the canoe and the storm is all there. The gold that was lost.

"They say it's down there yet," he says.

There was more. John, he takes the metal napkin holder and he says, "There's a Shell station here on the corner. I'm right acrost from that. You'll see my stuff in the yard, lawn swings and chairs."

I can hardly get air, and Dave's starting to look at me with his face one big question, like the way Jenny will.

I ask John, I say, "The sign on the gas station, does it hang crooked?"

"No," he says.

So I can breathe.

"They finally fixed her up. You must have been through here a few years back."

Dave says his girlfriend never come up this way before. "We come straight up 19 last time. We're taking the long way today," he says, "seeing it's so nice out."

Dave peters out and sits there looking at me. I can see John thinks I'm a few sticks shy of a load. And Dave's starting to wonder.

John's done his coffee. He stands up.

"Well, nice meeting you," he says to me. "Don't leave without a piece of Sue's pie."

Sue's pie. I don't even want to know this. But I can hear Dave asking Jinping, "Who's Sue?"

"Lady in the town makes very good pie for serving here."

A lady in the town makes the pie.

"What kind you got today?"

"Is her house yellow?" That's what I bust in with.

Now everybody in the place knows I'm a mental patient that Dave's kind enough to take out for a drive.

Jinping looks at me and she says, "House of Sue is green."

Elmer says, "Used to be yella." He sits there looking at me. He says, "I thought you never been here before."

"I seen a picture." I said that to the vinegar and the napkin thing, that were the church and the gas station.

Dave said he didn't have room for pie, which will show yous how embarrassed I was making him.

"Are you sure?" I says. "It's blueberry." Because that's his favourite.

Jinping, she took a step back away from me, and it wasn't till I seen her do that, with this spooked look coming over her, that I realized nobody'd said it was blueberry.

"Is it?" That was all Dave could say, looking back and forth between her and I.

It was blueberry.

Everybody was turned around looking at me.

Dave, he didn't say nothing after we left that place. Waiting for me to tell him what the hell just happened.

I'm hanging out the truck window. "There's the church!" was alls I could say.

There it was. Sun on the pure white steeple. Water behind it shining like a field full of diamonds.

I'm yelling, "There's the gas station! There's John's! That must be the pie woman's! It's green now. Oh look, Davey! She's still got her pie sign on the fence. There's the plumbing and heating place! Oh! There's a chicken running loose! There's the hardware store! That's the man Sally is going to marry."

After we come out the other side, I told Dave, the best I could, what was up. It sounded lame to just say, "Josie's got a picture of this place." I couldn't think how to really tell him. Wanted to let him know the whole year's worth, how she started, way last fall, seeing this place in like her crystal ball.

"This is the town!" I kept on saying. "This is the town!"

Dave, he was trying. There was wrinkles in his forehead from concentrating, looking at the road and listening to me. But he couldn't make out what was the matter.

"You been weird ever since we went in for lunch."

I talked all the way to his dad's. By the time we were bumping up the driveway, past the three cars that were rusting in the yard, Dave had some kind of an idea what it meant to me to find that town.

"I knew we were close last Christmas," I says. It seemed to make sense to say so, anyways.

Dave's old dad come out on the stoop in his undershirt, it was that warm. He was waving, happy. Dave threw her in park and jumped out, grinning at his father.

You get to be going on thirty years old and you've got a happy face like that when you see your father, that tells me a whole book's worth.

I was awful emotional at that time. Yous will find that, once you're started. You once take the lid off your feelings, and out they all comes. You're mad and you're crying and all the rest of it.

I'm here to say it's all right. Let it all come. Go ahead and cry. Go ahead and pound something. It won't kill yous. And yous will find, too, that the other thing yous can feel is happy.

Don't want to shut yourself down so yous can't feel nothing, the way Darlene's always asking for! Do that and you'll miss out on happy. Which, in view of the fact that it's why we're here, living on the earth, yous wouldn't want to miss.

Dave and his father give each other a hug. I watched the old man's hand patting Dave's shoulder.

This flood come. Tears and tears. Just to see that good father and his son.

The old man put the pot on, that he boils water in. He don't buy tea, though. Uses peppermint out of the garden. He don't use the indoor bathroom neither, except for letting guests use it in the winter. That saves him on the getting the septic tank pumped. But he offers, polite, for me to use it.

When we're all sitting down, Dave's dad says, "I got one for yous." He says, "What comes once in a minute, twice in a moment, but not once in a thousand years?"

I'm thinking maybe the answer is something to do with good fathers.

But Dave says, "The letter *M*?" And he gives me a wink, as much as to say, ain't Dad a funny old buzzard!

"Dad's pretty slick with the crossword puzzles too."

Dave's dad grins, modest. He's swirling the mint sprigs around in the pot. They give off a strong mint smell. Puts me in mind of the night I went nuts with the mouthwash, which seems like another lifetime. You talk about shifts! Was I ever shifted from back there when the peace and quiet used to irk me so bad! Now I was loving it.

We drank our peppermint tea. Window looks out over Lost Gold Lake. There's an island out there, covered in pine, maple, and birch. Big smooth rocks along the shore. Look as if you could dive off of them into that deep, clear water.

"I bet you kids used to jump off of them rocks, eh?"

"Sure, they did," says the old man. "Remember the tires, son?"

Dave sits forwards, pointing with his spoon. "See them four big maples hanging out over the edge of the water there? Now a lot of dads will hang up a tire swing in the yard for the kids, eh. But my dad here, what did he do? He rows out there, pretty near kills himself, standing up in the duck boat (yes, you did). Lassos not one branch or two—was it six, Dad?—seven different branches out there. Puts up tires on all of them. Oh, we had fun on them things! Me and my cousins and our friends bumping into each other, falling into the lake. Brent, he was always up here. God he loved that, swinging on them tires! You could hear him across the lake. Remember that, Dad, how Brent used to whoop?"

Dave's dad nods. The smile fades off of his face. "How is that boy doing?"

"Oh," Dave says, and looks down.

Dave's dad shakes his head. "I used to think it'd do my heart good to take and kill that old man of his with a shovel."

Dave and his dad look out at the water.

Dave's dad—his name's Al—he says, "Your mother talked about that, right up to pretty near the end. She'd sit right here where I'm sitting now and look out, thinking of the bunch of yous playing. She was on morphine and everything, her arms swollen up. Smile on her face, thinking of you kids. She'd say, 'I can see Davey yet, flying back and forth on them tire swings.' Even when she couldn't talk no more, I'd see her looking out there."

The two of them are sitting looking at the lake and the island, drinking their tea.

I'm looking out, too. Trying to get used to the idea that what I'm looking at is Josie's magic lake, where the gold is that was lost by the girl in the storm. The water that's behind the church.

Al, he grins at me. He says, "We used to say if Dave here would ever settle down and give us grandchildren, why we'd hang up the tires again. Lots of old tires in the shed," he says.

I'm thinking of Tammy's kids, Meghan and little Matthew. I can see them yet, that night we rescued them from their father. Their white breath in the freezing cold. Their mixed-up faces wanting to say, *Go away,* and at the same time, *Don't leave us here.*

I try to picture them swinging on tires.

Well, we had a nice long weekend up there. Sprang our news on the family. Bunch come over Saturday night, and there was music. Made me feel real welcome.

It was good to see Dave's cousin, Jan, again. She come and got me while the men were out hunting on Sunday. Took me over to her and Tom's nice new place they got. Screen porch off the living room. There's a thirty-foot rock right there in the back yard, covered in lichen and moss, with blackberry canes and blueberry bushes growing out of it wherever they can get a toehold. I sat on the shiny pine floor and played with her one-year-old son while Jan made lunch.

Jan was telling me some of the family thinks Dave's dad shouldn't live all alone up where he does, no neighbour nearby. Some say leave him to it. That's where he's got his memories and his dignity.

I could see that's what camp Jan was in.

"There's a big fight going on in the family over it," Jan says. "Some feels pretty strong, on both sides."

And I think to myself, nah. You guys, all wanting the best for old Al there, all loving him for the kindness he showed you all your lives? Yous don't know the first thing about having a fight in a family!

I was dying to ask Jan all about the town and the lake. But I didn't want her to start looking at me like they done at the restaurant there. So I sat on the floor, piling up blocks for her little Alexander to knock over. He wanted the pile "huge." That's his new word today, *huge.* He liked to hunker down, wind up good, and send the blocks flying. He liked the pow, the action, things sailing to pieces. I could see what type of movies he was going to be into when he got older.

"Alexander, help Aunt Rose pick those up," Jan says.

I was "Aunt" already. Made me feel good. "My niece calls me Ann Toes," I says.

Alexander, he knew "toes." He tugs my sock off. Grabs my big toe. "Huge!" he says.

I says, "Glad I washed my feet today."

"Uncle Al make you wash under the pump?"

"No."

"Let you use the bathtub?" Jan's impressed. "He's giving you the royal treatment up there, I hope you know. Want mayo on yours? Letting you use the indoor plumbing, in the third week of May? That's a sign he really likes you. Alexander, get down from there. Last woman Dave went out with, Uncle Al used to tell her he didn't have a working john. Made her traipse out in all weather—January, black fly season, thunder and lightning—"

"What, and Dave put up with that?" I would've thought that would be over Dave's famous goddamn limit.

"It just so happened that the bathroom wasn't ever working when Dave and Sharon came."

Jan, she scoops up Alexander and puts him in his high chair. Washes his wee hands for him, gentle, while she spells it out. She says, "Uncle Al's a sneaky old b-u-g-g-e-r. I caught him, redhanded, one day. I went up to take him some applesauce when Dave and her were coming to visit. And there he is, crawled in under the back porch, just his boots sticking out. He's shutting off the water!'"

"Dave'd figure that out pretty quick."

"Got to be a game between the two of them. Uncle Al did something different to the plumbing every time, seen how long it would take Dave to find the trouble. We'd all laugh. Dave couldn't walk into the Lucky Duck without some joker kidding him about it. They'd be sniffing at the air, letting on he stank, saying too bad he couldn't never get a bath."

Dave got a ride out hunting with Jan's Tom on Monday. Left me the truck so I could go into town.

I parked the truck in the grocery store lot and got out. I was standing in the town, with my two feet on the ground. I was standing in Josie's town!

I wondered if something would happen to me. I'd get sucked into Josie's picture, never be heard from again. Josie'd see me with her magnifying glass, froze here in the parking lot. She'd smile that smile of hers, as if to say she knows more about the weird things in the world than she can tell you. I was in such a condition there that I even wondered if, when I was flattened into the picture, I'd be able to see out.

Shook that stupidness off as much as I could and walked out on to the sidewalk.

Found the stone bench. There's a sparkle to that pink stone up north, eh, when you look at it close. Sparkles all through it. Of course, the mood I was in, that hit me as magic-looking. The stone as full of diamonds as the lake. A royal throne, Jenny would call it. I sat there, looking down at the stone, moving my head back and forth to make the sparkles in it shimmer like water.

When I stood up, I didn't have the sense to know I was embarrassing myself, walking around dizzy. I stand there, eh, gawping at a plumbing and heating business like it's Buckingham Palace. The guy finally stuck his head out the door and asked if he could help me.

I said there was no help for me.

He laughed and I wandered off.

Everything I seen struck me like it was famous.

I stood and stared at the pie lady's place.

Seemed funny there was people walking around and driving their cars down the street, like it was a regular little town.

A woman pushing a baby stroller had to say, "Excuse me," to get around me. I'm blocking the way, staring at the hardware, trying to guess which man in there Sally was going to marry.

Sally always had the opposite trouble of mine with men, eh. She'd run away from them all. Never give no guy a chance. But Josie told her a hardware man in the town, he was going to be a different story.

I go over to the church, like a sleepwalker. I'm in the picture that kept us going all winter. I'm walking along with all these sparklies coming up around my feet.

I could hear the lake water lapping before I come around the building. And then I was right on the shore of Lost Gold Lake. It was washing and slapping the rock that church was built on. Shining in the sunshine. Fresh breeze and a clean smell of water coming off it just as if it was a real lake. It dropped right off from the big smooth rocks, clear and real deep. Had to put my fingers in it, feel the bite of that icy spring water, before I could believe it was real.

Went back to the street and walked up to the other end.

There was the stone fountain. In the little park. It was still shut off for winter. I thought about making a wish, anyhow, throwing a new penny into the dry pool.

Now, you can say it was just a coincidence. I'm standing there thinking about whether there would be any luck in a dry fountain. And the township works truck pulls up.

"You guys working today?"'

Seemed weird on a holiday Monday. Said they were putting in today and going hunting tomorrow.

I watch them turn on the water for spring. I see the year's first water jump up out of that fountain, and I hear it rain down on the stones. The dry stone is pale, eh. But once the water hits, you can see how nice the colours are. I watch the water running over them dusty stones, and I look at the colours all waking up. I like the splashing sound.

I seen Jenny do that at the shore, pouring water over the stones with her yellow plastic bucket. "Look, I'm waking up the colours!"

My first wish was for her.

Remember back then we used to have one cent coins? Shows how long ago this is now. I picked out the shiniest penny in my purse and wished for dear life.

Then I picked out another nice one.

"This is for all of yous." I pictured each one of the girls in Group. Wished real hard. It was an awful load of wishing to put on one penny. Probably should've dumped out my whole wallet, for that bunch.

But I felt like I was in a fairy story where I only had three wishes.

And I'd learned enough by that time to know that I wasn't doing no good to nobody unless I had a wish left for myself.

So I take a third bright new penny in my hand and make a wish that I can keep learning.

I watched it settling down through the water. Sun caught it nice.

17.

"Do you think it'll be too late to go see Josie when we get home?" I says to Dave as we're driving home that night.

"Should be in by ten," he says.

Dave's getting a kick out of me this weekend. I'm so excited. I didn't talk about the town in front of his family, but there hasn't hardly been one minute we were alone that I didn't keep on about it. I told him every single thing that was in the picture that I found in the town. He don't get what the big deal is. But he can see I'm happy. So he smiles at me the way you do at a six-year-old who can't sit still on the way to the fun fair. He says maybe we'll get there in time to see Josie tonight. He's already tried saying we could call her. But that won't do for me. I want to see her face when I tell her.

I'm happy it's already Monday and I only have to wait till tomorrow night to see the rest of them. As we leave the north country and we're rolling through the wide fields again, I'm thinking of how it will be.

Marg's usually there early. Maybe I'll tell her separate.

Or maybe Sally will come in first! Won't Sally go nuts! Jumping off her chair with all that blonde hair flying. "Praise the Lord!" she'll say. "Praise the merciful Father!" I get a kick out of Sal the way she talks churchy when she's happy and jumps up and down like a kid at the same time.

Or maybe they'll all be sitting there. I'll light off the fireworks

news right in the middle of them, set them all off at once.
What will Meredith make of us? We'll stifle ourself when she walks in. Bunch of prisoners that just finished digging the tunnel. She'll be the suspicious warden there, trying to figure out our lit-up eyes.

Josie cut a picture of the main street of a little tiny town out of an old magazine once. I found the town. So what? Really, so what?

But I was just a-fizzing. Kept telling Dave stuff that didn't make no sense to him.

"I always believed there was water behind the church!"

"You did, did you?"

"You can't see it in the picture, but it was in Josie's dream."

"The dream where she found out where they got the name for the lake?" Dave's trying.

"I wonder if she cheats," I says. "Maybe she heard that story somewheres. Maybe she read it in the magazine where she cut the picture out of and only thought she dreamed it. Oh Dave! It's so deep and so clear! I knew it would be. I could just picture it, right the exact way it is, when I used to shut my eyes and Josie'd be talking about it. One godawful thing or another would be going on last winter and I'd be just like washing my mind in that beautiful water. Same with Sally. She's been saying all along she's going to be 'like a tree that is near planted by the water, that in season bears its fruit.' That's out of the Bible."

"The bunch of yous are all looney tunes, you know that eh?" he says, smiling at the road.

We put on the radio after a while and sung along, holding hands, rolling over them easy farm hills, all the way home.

Five after ten I run in the door. Make straight for the phone and call Josie. It's funny, now I get telling this story, to see how cell phones have changed things. Them days, you never had a phone with you. You had to wait to get to home to make a phone call. I'm dancing up and down, all set to go tell Josie that we found her town. I'll tell her I just have to drop by for a minute tonight. Can't wait to hear what she's going to say!

No answer.

Dave says, "Could be the urge struck them."

That shows yous what was on his mind right then. We hadn't got up to much at his dad's, what with the thin partitions and Dave being tired out every night from running after turkeys all day. They only had one turkey to show for all their trying.

Dave's putting his gun away. He keeps it locked up good because of Jenny. I'm making us a pot of tea. I got this picture in my mind of them and the turkeys trying to outsmart each other, tiptoeing in and out of the bushes, matched about equal.

I says, "Which of yous was the biggest turkeys?"

He told me a story about talking to a Native guy once, telling him why we call them Indians, because, when we first come across them, we were looking for India. The Native guy said, "Well, then, I'm just glad yous weren't looking for Turkey."

I remember we were laughing at that when the phone rung. I jumped for it, hoping it was Josie.

The hospital. They had my number on the file from before. Josie was admitted. We should come.

The kettle was about to boil. I was ready for that cup of tea. I could picture us sitting around the hospital for hours. I says to the woman on the phone, "Can you tell her we'll be there in a half hour?"

"I think you should come right now," she says. It's that certain type of emergency-calm voice.

So then, me and Dave, we're running down the stairs and gunning it over there to the hospital and running up the stairs and going the wrong place and running down more stairs and up some other stairs before we can get to Josie.

"Holy Christ," Dave whispers when we open the door.

He catches me to stop me, the way you catch a kid that's going to run out on the road. There's a doctor there and two nurses.

I pull loose and barge right up.

The medical people step back for me. I don't waste time thinking that's odd. I lean down to her poor ear. I says, "Josie!"
"Rose?"
"Yeah. Jesus! Was it—?"
Josie whispers, "Your three wishes..."
"Is this the last frigging time that bastard is going to put you in the hospital? Because I am about fed up with—"
The doctor, she put her hand on my arm and give the smallest little shake of her head. I never forgot that doctor giving her head that little tiny shake.
This is the type of time we're good at, us survivors, eh. We can go all to hell after. But there's nobody like us when the avalanche is on.
I said, "Josie," I said, "there is water behind the church."
Josie's dry mouth tried for a smile. I put my ear close to hear what she was trying to say.
Josie whispered, "Dave?"
He bent over her. "Right here, Josie," he says.
"Rose."
Dave, he's got tears. I don't. Not yet. "Don't worry, Josie," he says, "I'll always be with Rose."
I says, "God, Josie, are you dying?"
Josie was thirsty. She kept licking her dried-out lips, but they wouldn't give her nothing, just an ice cube to suck. Something about taking her into surgery. They needed her stomach empty. She moaned.
We stayed with her until they were ready to take her in.
A cop come in. They were looking for Brent. Josie turned her face away.

18.

MEETING WITH EVERYBODY Tuesday sure was not the way I'd been planning on! That holiday Monday (only the day before) seemed like a hundred years ago, me and Dave driving home, singing. Me all happy, wound up to tell the girls about the town!

If you'd've told me then that it would be months before I ever bothered to say a word to them about it!

It was way in the last hours of night when we got home from the hospital. Thought about calling Marg or Sally. Couldn't see waking them up. Josie couldn't talk to them anyways.

Dave says, "What about her family? Where the hell are they?"

I had no idea.

Dave said he had a thought on where to look for Brent. He went out.

Josie had a mother living someplace and that frigging brother of hers that's a lot older. The cops was trying to trace them down too, to notify them.

Marg and Sally were in my kitchen by eight o'clock in the morning. It looked like Josie's family was us. I called in to work. Told them I couldn't come in, I had an emergency.

The call from Dave come around eight-thirty. "I found Brent," he says. "I'm going to tell the cops."

I says, "Good."

"Only, Rosie, when I do, it could go bad for me."

I didn't think I could pump any more adrenaline than what

I was already. New spurt shot through me like whiskey.

"Why would it go bad for you?"

"I don't want to talk about it on the phone."

"Well, Jesus...!"

"I love you, Rosie."

"Dave! What's going on? Why will it go bad for you?"

He wouldn't say.

I come all over frozen calm. Head crystal clear. I says, "Look," I says, "Brent can't do nothing more to her right now so there's no tearing hurry to turn him in. Why don't you come home here and tell me what is going on?"

Took me a while to convince him.

But he did come home. And then, of all times, finally, in the mud room, we had our talk about what the hell, exactly, Dave had to do with drug dealing. The girls were in the kitchen. Sally was working on the coffee and bacon. Breakfast smells were mixing with the coats and shoes smells in the mud room. We kept the door into the kitchen shut and talked low. Dave told me he'd got mixed up in trafficking—just weed—three years ago, when his mother was dying.

He was getting his act together again now, he said. He was making enough in construction now. He hadn't never been into it heavy. Hardly used at all. Just dealt. He come down here to this area, he said, when his mother was so sick. He'd got the idea that, if he could make some money, he could take her to the States for a new treatment he heard of. And that's when he run into his old friend Brent again. And Brent had got him in on some stuff that he never should've, trying for the quick buck.

Brent was always into it way more than what Dave was, and Brent was hiding now in a sugar shack way out behind a wood lot off of County Road 48.

"So?"

Well, so, on the way to this sugar shack where they sometimes hung out, there was a clearing in the woods and that was where the weed was growing. The young plants was just set out.

"Maybe Brent won't tell about you."

Dave didn't have much hope on that.

"Don't tell them while he's there. Wait till he's somewheres else," I says. I sound like I'm at work, talking to somebody with their furnace shooting fire.

Dave's in a state because he never done nothing about Brent before. He's all in a hurry to run to the police. "I knew he was hitting her," he says, "and I never done nothing! I've been sitting on my ass."

"Dave, you've been trying to talk him into going for help. What else could you have did?"

"This never would've happened if I'd have only just blew the whistle on him a long time ago. We knew what he was doing to Josie lots of times before. I should have did something and this never would've happened!"

"Dave, listen to me. What Brent went and done is not your fault. Josie would've had to charge him. Not you. I asked Frances at Group. That's what she said. There wasn't nothing you and me could do if Josie wouldn't back us up. And she wouldn't. I tried to get her to charge him lots of times. So did Frances and Meredith. She would not. The shrinks have some word for it."

"He's been my friend so long, eh, and I always felt sorry for him. I felt too sorry for him, every time I thought about getting him in trouble over Josie. He's had so much trouble. But now look. If I'd have did something sooner, none of this would've happened. I knew it and I done nothing."

"Would you listen to me? There was nothing you could've did!" I leaned my back against the kitchen doorframe. I'm with my face in my hands, trying to think.

"I got to turn Brent in before he takes off. He needs locking up before he bashes the next woman."

"He's not going to bash nobody else for a few minutes. We got to think this through."

"Did you see the way her arm was? It's all my fault."

"Jesus Christ! Will you stop that! It's not your fault! It's not!"

"I'm going to call now."

I can't think no more. I says, "Please, can we just talk it over with Marg and Sally?"

He don't want to talk to them about none of it.

I says, "Dave," I says, "I can't think. You can't think. We need them to help us think. We got to think. They're my only family I got. They're my Intentional Sisters. Come and talk to them! Please! Come and talk to them."

He finally caved and we went into the kitchen.

Sally sits us down at the table and tries to make us eat breakfast.

Marg listens careful and comes up with the plan. "What we've got to do, we've got to go out there and clean that place up, and then you can call the cops," she says. Marg got Dave calmed down a bit, talking to him in that even voice of hers that I love so dear in times of trouble.

He was to go out to the patch. He wasn't to even talk to Brent unless he come out of the shack. And if he did have to talk, say nothing about Josie. Not let on he knew nothing about that. He was just to tell Brent that he thought the growing was suspected. They had to rip out all the plants right away. We'd come with him and help.

No. Dave didn't want us around there.

Okay. The rest of us were to drive out to a place Dave told us to meet him.

So there's Dave, no sleep, heading out to race the clock. Strip that place clean before Brent went anywhere and then get out of there and call.

"But I'll still be in shit because there's this other guy in on it," Dave says.

We look at him.

"Bad bugger."

So then it's Marg figures out how to sweeten the bad bugger. She says for Dave to not just rip out the plants. He's to dig them up, pack them in boxes and we'll put them somewheres the guy can get them back from.

"That'd take too long."

"We'll help you."

He didn't like it, but we didn't see a choice.

"And then," Marg says, she says, "you tell the bad bugger where the stuff is hid like you're the hero savin' the day, and you tell him you seen a helicopter flying over that place yesterday and you risked your skin to go rescue all the plants and they're all his now since this is making you nervous. 'Nice knowing you,' you says to him, and you get the frig away from him and hope for the best. See, and this way it'll make sense to him when the cops show up today and you won't get blamed for that neither."

We collected three shovels from two of our places.

Marg shoves her foot down. "Giddy up," she says. Old Chev takes off. Funny kind of a serious smile on Marg. She likes it when she's got a plan.

We took off out of town, found the corner Dave said, and were there waiting for him when he come roaring up, truck full of boxes from the LCBO. We let another truck go by and then, when nobody was around, followed Dave up a mud lane.

We went at her. Step on the shovel with your foot, pull the little plant out easy with some dirt, lay it in a box, hop to the next one, do it again quick, drag the box along.

"Where's the shack?"

"Over there."

"What's he going to do if he sees us?"

Marg can't dig but she climbed up into the truck bed somehow, fat as she is, and we handed her the full boxes.

That's good soil, back in them hills, nice deep black earth. It ain't hard to dig.

A car come along, out on the county road. You don't usually notice what a noise and commotion one car makes. But out there you sure do. You can hear it a long ways off. Gets louder and louder. Coming towards us. What if it's the farmer who owns this woods? What are we going to do? We run into the woods except poor Marg, who only managed to heave down off of the truck and hide behind it. Awful lame hiding place. The car, out on the county road there, makes this burst and swish and pops from coming to going. Then you hear it a long time after, rumbling away. I stood up. Grabbed the shovel. Adrenaline just a-buzzing. Run back to the patch. I was digging like in fast forward.

When we had it all dug out, we threw leaves and branches around, trying to make the patch look a bit more like nothing hadn't went on around there.

So Dave's truck is full of that shit and he tells us to go get in Marg's car and go home.

"What are you going to do?"

"Call the cops and then I'll take this stuff to a place. Meet you back home."

"I'll come with you."

But there was no way he'll let me. So I go back to our apartment with Marg. I'm leaning over biting my knuckles, prayin' worse than Sally.

Takes four hundred years before Dave finally walks in. The other girls are asking him questions. I can't talk. I'm trying to read the news off his face.

He says he seen Ryan (the bad bugger). "I told him like you said, Marg."

"Did he go for it?"

"Wanted to know why I was stupid enough to screw around out there if the cops were on their way. I let on I never thought of that and just wanted to save the plants. He thinks I'm retarded but I guess he believes me. Told him I didn't want nothing more to do with it."

I'm like with relief pouring over me, but Dave sits down miserable. He don't care nothing about all that commotion with the pot or whether the guy believes him or don't.

He says, "What if Josie don't make it?"

I can think but not feel. I says, "Well, if Brent's went and murdered somebody…"

Dave says, "You should've saw the way he was sitting there in a corner of that shack, leaned against the wall, looking at nothing. Didn't care what I was doing out there today. He don't care about nothing. He's just sick sorry about what he done."

I could see Dave was thinking of Brent as a kid who used to whoop, swinging on the tires that Al put up for them, back on Lost Gold Lake. I knew it had took everything Dave had to call the cops on that poor kid, even though he'd grew up so rotten.

"Do you know what that old jackass used to do to him?"

"I don't want to hear it."

But Dave has to say it anyways. He tells me exactly what Brent's father used to do to the poor kid when him and Dave were boys back north. He come over to Dave's just covered in—

I says, "Dave! I'm sorry. I can't listen to that! It's too close to home." Dave asked me exactly what I meant by that.

After the others had went home, I finally told Dave how I got the scars I have. The boiler, eh, it got real hot. I told him my father held me against it. I didn't say what for. Hadn't never told Dave yet about the sex abuse part of the story.

Josie come through her operation. But she wasn't right. Just lay there all the time, saying hardly a word.

Sally started sleeping all day. No new tablecloths.

Marg was worried over how low Sally was. She went by the Queen's Hotel one day and seen a blue box full of never-been-used housekeeping time sheets out for the garbage. They were even pink.

Marg trots in and says, "Sally, you're falling down on the job. Give me a bag till I go get them time sheets they're throwing out."

Sally says, "Ah, Marg, who are we kidding?"

Marg, she fished them out anyhow.

Marg's funny. Said she didn't believe in this hotel nonsense. But she'd do a thing like that.

I'm sitting by Josie's bed the next week. Josie hasn't said a word for days. All of a sudden Josie says to me, "Act hopeful."

I jump, like as if her dog said something.

Marg and Tammy, they had somewheres to go on their walk every day now. The hospital.

We got in trouble, before, over keeping Josie's dog at our place. Darlene was the only one allowed pets in her building, so she was looking after Josie's dog. (Her cat didn't think too much of that.) Darlene tied up Josie's dog to the bike rack, where Josie could see him and then went and wound up Josie's bed so she could look at him.

That dog give us some hope for Darlene because it made it so she had to go out every day. Like it or not. And get home every night too. And feel something.

Summer come along. It got hot. Josie was just laying there. I used to go over after work and talk to her. What didn't I tell Josie that summer, sitting by her bed? I told her all about my little Jenny, every cute thing she said, how she called the fireflies "star people" and claimed to know that they were visiting our world to get perfume from the milkweed plants in the ditch.

I told her when Dave found a frog jelly mould. Him and Jenny made a lemon-lime frog and sat there poking it to make it quiver. Jenny says it's the opposite of a poison dart frog that he's been reading to her about in an Amazon adventure story. It's an "antidote dart frog," she says. It will heal you instead of killing you. It's going to heal up Aunt Josie.

Josie lay and listened to that, and her poor skin-and-bones face would get the softest smile.

One day she said, "There's hope."

I says, "Do you feel better?"

But not another word out of her.

Josie was weird enough before she got hurt so bad. But after that, Josie was something else. She'd lay there and lay there and never say a word. Then she'd come out with this stuff like, "There's hope." I wondered what hope she was thinking of. Maybe us helping Jenny.

Josie lay right on the edges between life and death, looking down the long path of the times to come, where the kids will walk when we're gone. And I'd sit with her by the hour and look at the slow summer dusk. I was growing, sitting there, just as sure as, out in the farm country, the corn was growing.

The rest still didn't even know I'd found Josie's town. But to Josie, I never shut up about it. Told her how the stone in her town sparkles in the sun like it's full of diamonds. Told her about running into the man who makes the furniture which is the right style for our hotel. I told her it was all bright and pretty in the picture-town in springtime, with the plants coming on. Told her about the fountain getting turned on and me making my three wishes. I talked to Josie like I was wandering through a dream, while she was laying there at the edge.

I could hear myself starting to talk about plans. Told her I was thinking of talking to Al, see what he thought about the chances of a hotel up there. And Jan's husband Tom, who runs a construction company. I told her that me and Sally were going to go up there one of these days and check things out, make a first step.

"You got to get better," I says to Josie one day, not expecting no answer. "You get better and we'll take you to see your town. Oh, Josie, are you ever going to get better?"

She opens mad eyes. "I'm not no fortune teller!"

I had to laugh and give her a kiss.

It was so great to see she had that much spunk back. I said to her what she'd been saying to me. I said, "There's hope!"

The cops called each one of us friends of Josie's, looking for information on Brent. Tammy, she calls me up in a panic. "The police called me!"

"They called here too."

Tammy says, "I hung up."

"You did?" I says. "What for?"

"They asked me a lot of questions. I didn't know what to tell them. I just hung up and called you."

I tried to tell her it was all right. Just answer whatever she knew. "And whatever you don't know, just say you don't know."

But Tammy said she'd better let her husband do the talking.

"Your husband?" I says, "Tammy! You haven't got him back?!"

Oh no. But she was thinking she'd better, if the cops were going to be calling.

I got hold of Marg and we went steaming over to Tammy's and sat her down.

Marg says, "Now look here," she says, "you talked to the bank, right? You talked to the lawyer. Now you can talk to the police. You can do it," Marg says, calm. "They just want to hear whatever you know about Josie's Brent."

"I don't know nothing about him!"

"So then that's what you tell them."

It took us till seven o'clock at night to get her to plug her phone back in. Then we sat there with her till it rang. And we sat there while she said her three word answers to the cops.

When it was all done, Tammy was weak in the knees. But she hadn't took back Asshole. So we toasted her for a brave woman. Clinked our plastic Diet Sprite bottles.

Tuesday, she was still thinking about it, though. It was painful to sit there and listen to her.

Meredith kept on at her, steady. "Tammy, do you think that it would be good for your children to take them back into an abusive situation?"

Matthew's ear, Meghan's right to girlhood innocence, Tammy's own neck.

Poor Tammy. She needed it said over to her. Over and over. And Meredith, she said it over, patient, every Tuesday.

Sally would fuss around her in the hall. "Oh, Tammy, you wouldn't, would you?"

"You'd have to be nuts." That was me put that in.

Marg, she said she wasn't up for no more race car driving.

So far, Tammy hadn't caved. She was in her apartment, keeping her kids safe, clean, and fed. Every day they all went for a walk with Marg.

Darlene and the dog sometimes went with them. Tammy's kids took turns holding his leash.

I kept on working at McIlveen's, talking calmer than ever to people whose biggest trouble in the world was their backed-up drain.

Meredith worked us over with her questions every week.

She drags it out of Marg that Marg is terrified of going to court again. We all have to go to Brent's hearing. For Marg, the idea of doing that is bringing up everything from her father and the court case with him. Marg sits there, solid, though. She's going to court for Josie. But it's not good for Marg to be anxious like this. She's taken to sleeping on the couch. Bed makes her too nervous. With Marg, you can pretty well tell how things are by whether she's sleeping in her own bed. When she's doing good, she can. When she's upset, all the old stuff about bed comes back to haunt her.

Tammy is managing to feel guilty about Josie's trouble. Tammy hasn't got past that step where you figure everything's your own fault.

Like me and the frigging bump in the sidewalk that Dave won't let me apologize for no more. ("What are you, in the public works department? Did they send you to fix this sidewalk and you never done it?" He'll say that now about anything that I'm trying to apologize for, that is not my fault—"You in the public works department?")

Meredith drills away on us like a dentist.

And the worst of it is the breaks. We sit there on rainy nights. That stupid hotel of Josie's is like it's right in the room with us. You pretty near have to put your feet under the chair not to stub your toe against the concrete foundation. But now nobody says a word about it. What's the use of talking about something that dumb now? It's high time we got over that and grew up. That's fantasy, not reality.

Who believes a bunch of broke losers like us are going to run their own hotel? How foolish is that? A room in the back for people like us! What would we do with a bunch more screwed up people?

We were mad at Josie. Nobody said it. But Josie'd got us worked up over nothing, took us in. And then she'd stranded us there with air. Nothing. Josie's dumb daydream. Too stupid to mention. Right there in that plain waiting room, glowing like a rainbow so that alls we could do was stare into space and see it. God, could I see it! Stone on stone. Pine trees waving beside it. Bright lake dancing in front. We didn't know enough at that time to tell each other. Sat quiet, like we were alone.

Josie laying there week after week. Doctor couldn't seem to tell us much. You had to wonder what she'd be like when and if she ever come out.

The first good thing that happened in three months was Darlene broke up with the internet overseas guy. Said she didn't need him now she had Josie's dog.

Meredith's trying to keep a sober face to respect Darlene's feelings about breaking up. "Well, Darlene," Meredith says. But it's past what a human can do, eh, not to be smiling at this piece of news.

None of the rest of us are bothering to look polite. We're all sitting there with our teeth hanging out, grinning.

Tammy says, "When I moved out, I should've took our dog."

Darlene trading up from this guy she's never seen to Josie's dog. Meredith trying to figure out what to say about it other than hooray. Tammy wondering if we'd all have been better off with dogs instead of men. Me and Marg had to laugh at the bunch of them. Felt good to have a belly laugh. It had sure been a while.

Dave was doing great. Took his losses and got himself clear of them drug dealers, finally. Told them they could have the whole works. Said he didn't want no more to do with it.

He was doing good at work. He was talking about going for this training course he heard about, to get some skills with metal construction the builder was into. Wood was old fashioned he said. Wood wouldn't even be allowed for a building material if it wasn't tradition. That's what he said. Wood warps. It rots. It burns. There's serious problems with supply. Takes fifty years to get a new stick of it. You invent a building material like that and you wouldn't be allowed to sell it. No, this metal was the thing. I never seen Dave so keen. Done my heart good, sore as it was, to listen to him.

"And," he said, "you know I've always had that idea I'd like to get into heavier construction some time."

McIlveen's give me a week off in August, and I took Jenny out every day for the whole week. We went bike riding. I had my old coaster there I had since I was fourteen. Bought her a little bike that fit her. Dave put training wheels on it for her. We pedalled, not too fast, but we done it, out into the country, exploring. Jenny said that we were looking for the doors that go into the hills, where the elf people have their homes. She loves being read to, eh. They were reading her fairy stories at the foster home.

Sally come with us one time. We rode all along by the water and found a nice spot to eat our picnic. Me and Sally sat on the sand, and Jenny, in her little red bathing suit, ran in and out of the turquoise waves, scooping with her yellow pail.

It's funny how something can happen that's so bad and you think the colour's gone out of everything and it'll never come back. But it does. It creeps up on you. I'm sitting there with Sally and Jenny and all of a sudden I notice the red and green and yellow. I look up and the sky is blue.

I turn to Sally. I says, "Hey!" I says, "I found the town!"

Well, Sally's face!

She turns towards me, slow. Little bits of light are coming through her straw sunhat. She is working on taking in what I just said.

Pretty soon there's more light under that hat than what there is shining down on the top of it.

19.

THE NEXT WEEKEND, me and Sally were leaving the farm country heading north in Sally's old T-Bird. It hit me that months ago, when Josie was laying at death's door and I was talking away to her, talking and talking about the hotel and the town, that what always come out of my mouth was "me and Sally." "Me and Sally are going to go up there," I said. "Me and Sally will check it out." How did I figure it had to be Sally first?

Well, Sally works on faith. Not like Marg who's got more sense.

Myself, I'm somewheres in between the two of them. But I had a hunch that what we could use right then was not being careful or planning but just a crazy burst. Some kind of a forward leap that nobody'd be wide-eyed silly enough to take but Sally.

Me and Sally got to Strone at eleven o'clock in the morning. Our idea was to eat lunch at the Good Luck Restaurant there and fool around town for the afternoon. We thought we might find someplace to take a swim. We were supposed to be at Dave's dad's by five. He was cooking supper. We were going to stay over.

We pulled up to the restaurant and the car bottomed out on a pothole in the parking lot. "Got to fix that!" Those there were the first words that come out of Sally's mouth in Strone. Like it was her pothole.

That's how it happened for her. No discussion.

The young woman there, Jinping, remembered me. When she give us our coffees, she said, "You will marry with Al's nice boy."

"You got a good memory," I says.

"Last time spring, you know what kind of pie."

"Listen, that's a long story. I'm not a fortune teller or nothing. This is my friend, Sally."

"Hi. Good morning."

"Hi there," Sally says. "Yous wouldn't be looking for an experienced waitress, would yous?"

Jinping says to me, "Your friend is also fortune teller!"

It turns out that Jinping, just this minute, walked out here from the kitchen wondering what in the world she was going to do about the weekend lunch crowd that's right ready to stampede through that door because her girl just quit with no notice. They get tourists here in summer.

"In kitchen," she says, "I am one arm paper hanger in high wind, and now this girl quit and it's very suddenly, but if you want start right now, seem like it is good luck. Do you wish to do so? Maybe had other plan?"

Sally, she says this fits in with her plans amazing. She stands up. But Jinping says, "Oh finish coffee. Have lunch, no charge. You save my life!"

Me and Sally look at each other.

"You don't mind, do you?" Sally says. "We can look around the town when I'm done my shift."

I can't keep up with the pace here.

I says, "Shift? What did you just go and do, take a job up here? You got nowheres to live! Are you quitting Group? Don't you want to think this over?"

"It's the will of God," Sally says, smiling at me, churchy, with the steam from her soup curling past her pretty face. She eats down the soup, tells me about fishermen that left their nets laying on the sand and took off after Jesus Christ. And then she gets up and walks to the kitchen, carrying our two spoons and empty bowls. Just like that.

"Rose," she turns and says, just before she disappears, "I have set my hand to the plough."

Five minutes later there's Sally in an orange apron, all that blonde hair tied up cute with an elastic band. She's running back and forth with dishes of soup and plates of egg rolls. The old guys sitting around in there are all perked up something wonderful.

I recognize the one they call Uncle Elmer. He tells Sally he's looking for a woman that can fix a tractor.

Sally tells him, good-natured, that she'll fix him if he don't watch it. She looks like she was born here.

I have to smile at the talk. From what I can make out this Frank fellow, that they all talk about in there, seems to be keeping the whole town entertained as usual. Today, he's got a forklift stuck up on a hill. Three of them's going over after lunch to see what they can do. He's up here from Toronto. Has a big summer place on high ground looking over the lake. He won't pay none of the local guys to do nothing around the place. Always figures he can do it himself. They just wait till he screws up, and then they go and repair his repairs. They were saying they make more getting him out of the holes he digs for himself than if he paid them to do a job right in the first place.

"If I had his money, I'd burn mine," Uncle Elmer says.

Sally is really going to do this! She hands me her keys, says take her car. So I walked out, dazed, into the bright August day. I drove over and stopped in on Jan.

Little Alexander was busy learning new words a mile a minute. Jan's interested to hear about Dave and this course he's going to take. She tells me her Tom was reading something about that metal framing.

Alexander says, "Framing." And we praise him for the eighth wonder of the world.

We sit in Jan's yard with the sheer rock that's out there casting a deep shade. There's a cool comes off of it. Felt good that hot afternoon. Alexander, he was sitting naked in his plastic pool, in the shadow of the tall rock, scooping up water and pouring it over his little pink knees.

I tell Jan about what just happened to Sally. Jan listens careful, keeping one part of her brain on Alexander, but listening to me too, the way good mothers can do.

My sister Sandra could never do that. She wanted to think about anything? She'd yell at Jenny to sit still and shut up. She can't seem to divide herself into two, the way Jan here's doing.

Jan says she might know some way to work things out for my friend if she wants to live up here. "Taa-taa not in your mouth," she says. "You know we're worried about Dave's dad. We don't think he ought to be up there in the winter alone. He's a funny old soul, but he wouldn't hurt a flea and he's not hard to get along with. Mind you, you'd have to work it sneaky. Let him think it was his own idea."

I walked around town, wondering, and then it was time to go back for Sally.

"Sally," I says, as soon as she gets in the car, "are you crazy?"

"I don't know," she says, happy, gunning the T-Bird, ponytail flying out the window in the breeze. She wants to see the town. "Tips weren't bad. Jinping and Hong are great. Grandma's a sweetheart. I'm learning Mandarin."

Well, we parked in town and Sally run to the hardware store. Starts peeking in the glass door.

"There he is! I bet that's him!"

She's hurting my arm.

He ain't even that cute, to my way of thinking. She's blocking the door. Nobody can get in to buy their nails.

"Josie said!" is all she can get out of her mouth, so I take and sit her on a bench. If she's going to live around here, she better watch she don't get a reputation for a nut case.

"Shhh! Sally! Act normal!" I'm saying, looking over my shoulder to see if anybody's staring. They already think I'm crazy.

Josie told her she seen a hardware man taking something out of a box, and she seen Sally pregnant.

That's what Sally wants more than anything, really, eh. But she's never been able since she lost her little daughter. The men line up, of course. Sally's so pretty and so sweet-natured. But she runs away. Scared she'll have a baby and it will die.

"Now look here," I'm trying to say, but I could've saved my breath to cool my porridge.

Sally was up off the bench tearing all over, squealing and staring, finding her town.

Sally was not kidding. She snowed Dave's dad without half trying, had him coming up with the offer of his whole upstairs and year-round indoor plumbing before we had our peppermint tea drunk after dinner. They shook hands on it.

So there's Sally on Tuesday night, at Group, giving her notice. Thank you very much. Goodbye. Everybody's struck dumb.

Meredith fools around with her charm bracelet. "Well, this is sudden, Sally! Can you tell us about what led you to make these decisions?"

You can see Meredith thinking, same as I did, what? Are you crazy? (Poor Meredith. Here's another one getting ahead of the program. Getting ahead of Meredith herself too, I'd say, looking back.)

You just know, eh, that you can't tell a starry-eyed notion like about Josie's town to Meredith. So we have to let her suffer.

Out in the smoking area, we had the real meeting.

"Rose's got something to tell yous," Sally says, and she sits Marg, Darlene, and Tammy down on the bench there, in a row. Being Sally, she's got to mother them. "Brace yourself. This will surprise yous. Marg? No more of them palpitations lately?"

When she's through, I say, "Okay, my friends. The thing is, we have found *the lake* and *the town*!"

So of course the next weekend we've got Marg's Chev full

of Tammy and her kids and Darlene, and Josie's dog. Me and Sally and Jenny are with Dave in the truck, and we're all heading north.

Me and Sally are trying to explain what all this is about.

I tell Jenny it's a place our friend Josie seen in her dreams. Sally says it's like make-believe. It's a play place that we've pretended about, to make ourself feel better when we were sad.

That makes sense to Jenny. She nods her head, looking satisfied, as if, why wouldn't you go and play in a magic place if you know one?

But Dave, he's still having trouble. "Did they offer you better wages?"

Sally's beaming. She says, "Not as good."

Dave keeps his eyes on the road.

He really had to wonder when he seen us all loose in the town. We stand there looking at a lawn swing in the furniture guy's front yard. How often, going through the hard stuff, did I daydream about that lawn swing? I remember doodling a picture of Tammy's kids on it, little Meghan's hair flying out free in the breeze.

We're holding each other by the arms, patting each other on the backs, blowing our noses. Dave and the three kids and the dog, they all snuck off and played in the park, letting on they didn't know us.

That was a day to remember, that first summer day, us all walking on air. You couldn't have took us to no place, not if you flew us to the most famous place, or inside a movie star's mansion, or what's the name of that castle they got in India a king built for his dead queen and covered it in jewels? You couldn't have took us anywhere on the face of this earth that would've meant what that little washed-out town meant to us, walking through it all together like that, with the sparkles from the pink rock flashing around our sandals.

We seen a chicken running loose, and we made such a racket that we scared it under a hedge.

I showed them the pie woman's house and the pie sign hanging on her picket fence. And they read it out to each other like a poem. "Homemade pies. Ah."

"Fresh local blueberries."

Marg touched it with her little pudgy pink fingertips.

We went and stood on the corner, looking at the gas station.

Tammy, she keeps saying, "It's another world! It's another world!"

Part of my head keeps thinking, oh bull. It's the most regular place I was ever in. But I sure knew what she meant.

Sally just beams and says that the good Lord works in mysterious ways.

Darlene says she wishes she lived here.

Marg says, "Hard to believe it's real."

Tammy, she nods, looking all around. Happiest look on her.

20.

WHEN WE GOT BACK home I made myself a new stepping stone. I got a pink piece of paper to be like the rock back north. I wrote *I can dream*. I smeared it with glue and shook out silver sparkles all over it.

Dave, he sits at the kitchen table, eating Shreddies, watching me there with the magic markers, glue, glitter, and kid scissors that I keep for Jenny.

"You got the whole thing there," he says. "Rock, paper, scissors."

I'm down on my knees, setting out all my stepping stones in a row, leaving a good space between them so they'll come closer to reaching all the way across the room, door to stove, so I can marry Dave soon. He laughs at this rule I've made, that we can't get married until my stepping stones go all the way across the room. But he gets it. He knows I want him to marry a healed-up person. And I want to be a healed-up person when I make them big promises to him.

"Dave?" I says. "Do you ever think of moving back north?"

Dave makes a low, wanting sound, right from his chest. I expect him to grab my ass. But it's not that kind of wanting. He's staring out the window. What he's wanting is home. He wants the north, his own folks, the way they live back there. He could've talked all day and never told me plainer than what he said there, just with that *Mmmm*.

"Group are talking about trying to move up there," I says.

Dave's eyes light up for a flash. Then he says, "Well but how could we? What about Jenny? And we got our jobs here. And Josie."

That was always the worst of Josie. She's what you might call a big picture person. Never hands you none of the little hows and what abouts. It was a jigsaw puzzle, that big picture of hers. Sometimes parts of it would snap together sudden, like what happened there with Sally and the waitress job and Dave's dad. That all fit together nice. But then we're looking at a dozen other bits and pieces of all this, wondering.

Now, Sally might have put her hand to the plough, but she had not cleaned out her apartment. And you know Sally. She collects stuff. We started out considerate.

By the second week of trying to help her pack, we're giving her junk away behind her back.

"Think she'd ever miss this?" Marg's holding up something with hooks on it, out of the back of the hall closet.

"What is it?" Tammy says.

They didn't have a clue so they give it to the mission.

Whenever Sally raised a fuss, Marg told her she'd feel better for it after. "It's like taking a good dump," Marg says. "Your place here is bound right up. Go on back to them jam jars."

Sally has been squirreling stuff in jam jars since the world began. You can't take and toss the whole shit load of them because the odd one's got something in it that matters. Nobody can sort those but her.

She turned out one of them jars and it had a toy animal in it, the kind they used to give out free in tea, years ago. It's covered in that greasy dust you get in a kitchen. Marg's laughing, "How many times have you moved this treasure? Look, the tail's even broke off of it."

I'm about to laugh too.

I stop. I'm looking at the thing. I says, "What is that? A cow?"

Sally says, "Yeah, looks like it." She can't remember where

she got it. A funny feeling that I know pretty well by now comes over me. I tell them Josie's talked about a broken toy cow. Something to do with Meredith.

So then we all stand there looking at the little dusty cow in the palm of Sally's long narrow hand. Are we supposed to take it for some kind of a sign?

"Maybe Josie would want us to bring Meredith in on everything?" That's Tammy. Her eyes get big.

"We could use somebody with an education," Marg says.

"Yeah," I says, "maybe. But then again maybe this tea bags cow don't mean blank all."

We can't have Sally getting the idea she can't throw nothing out. If every little stupid thing she ever kept in a jar is some omen, we'll be standing here till we're old ladies.

"You're the one told us," Darlene says to me. She's mad because she wants somebody to tell her if this cow is nothing or something. She don't like the question hanging there.

I says, "Josie never knows what nothing means, half the time, neither. She just sees things. Keeps in mind what she sees. Sometimes things add up. Okay, so we've saw the cow here. Let's keep it in mind and keep on going."

And I thought to myself, if this means something, we'll see it again.

I felt like I was starting to get the hang of living from picture to picture, always knowing that the world was bigger than me, that there was lots I could figure out and lots I couldn't.

Marg, she had the most trouble that way. She didn't do too good with the jar that had either a piece of junk or some big clue about Meredith in it.

She keeps on coming back to it all afternoon. "Do you think we're supposed to tell Meredith all about the hotel? That could be what's meant."

Now, I have a lot of time for Marg. Out of all them, she grates on my nerves about the least. But I'm telling you, at one point there, I finally drop a stack of magazines on the table, so brisk the dust flies up out of them. I look at Marg and I tell her, pretty short, "We don't know, okay?" Of course, I'm sorry right after.

"It's all right Rose," Marg says. "We're all trying to think like Josie, now we don't have her with us. That's just more of a stretch for some of us than what it is for others."

"Josie's still with us."

"Not the same."

The next jar had a blonde curl in it, from Sally's little girl that drowned. Marg hands her a clean tea towel. We all stand there and watch her wrap up that jar to bring with her.

Moving can only do so much, eh. There's stuff you're going to carry with you.

It done Sally good to get pried loose from some of the most useless crap she'd been holding onto. But she wouldn't let us throw out nothing that had to do with the hotel. Dave, he tramped up and down her four flights of stairs there, carrying all them boxes of *Do Not Disturb* signs and "tell us how we done" forms. She had to take her pink paint and her little tin cans full of plants she's been starting in the windowsill. Those were going to grow into flowers, for to plant on the terrace of the hotel. Never mind that we don't have no terrace, not to mention no hotel.

Faith, according to Sally, will move mountains.

Dave took off his ball cap and wiped the sweat off his forehead with his shirt sleeve. Said it wasn't faith that was moving this mountain. Her tablecloths and napkins was in a pile halfway to the roof. We packed them up in garbage bags and Dave found room for them all in the truck.

Dave don't like a lot of junk around. He's cheerful over the throw-out pile. "A couple of moves," he says, "are as good as a fire."

So anyways, we finally got Sally moved.

Then there was the rest of us left looking at each other, waiting for a sign.

No sign come along during Brent's trial.

Josie, she was still in the hospital, laying there, saying pretty near nothing. Nobody seemed to be able to tell us what was going to happen to her. We'd go and take turns sitting with her.

We were all she had, too. Her mother was ashamed of her because she got her name in the paper, and her brother called her a bitch for bringing the cops into it.

I said to Josie's brother, the only time I ever talked to him, I says, "She never called the cops. It was the hospital done it. She crawled into the hall and the neighbour called the ambulance."

"She shouldn't have made Brent mad at her. Then he wouldn't have hit her." That was his frigging opinion.

By the time our part in the court business was over, the whole next fall and winter had been used up.

I was burned out. My head was full of pictures nobody needs. How exactly he done it with the kitchen chair, clobbering her over the left side of her face and then, when she'd fell, over the back, smashing in her ribs, puncturing her right lung, crushing her kidney. Trauma to this and injury to that. That was all we'd been listening to. Fractures. Complex fractures. Impact. Damage to the elbow. Permanent impairment of quality of life. Severe concussion. Blow to the skull. Repeated, brutal blows to the back. Damage to the spine. Oh my God! What a time. I'm not even going to tell yous about it.

We were all sick that fall and winter. We kept catching cold. We'd sit there on Tuesday nights, the ones that was left, blowing our nose, listening to Meredith try to help us. I didn't get one stepping stone in all them months. Nothing shifted.

And on top of that, there was poor little Jenny. She was crying every time I left her. I thought maybe that was some kind of progress. Better than staring out after me, too stunned to cry, like she always done at first. But, God, it was hard to leave her with strangers and her crying her heart out! The foster family was good people, as far as I could see. But Jenny, she kept saying that Timothy (the rabbit) wanted to come with me.

When I think back, I think, Jesus, why did I leave her there all that winter? But, at that time, I didn't see I had a choice. I was working. Who would look after her at my place? I went to see her as much as I could, and took her out places.

The first nice Saturday in March, when our part in the court case was over and done with, me and Dave got Jenny and walked down to see the ducks coming through on their way north.

This was our second spring doing that. Jenny was about to turn six. She said that looking at ducks in the spring was our tradition.

She's got binoculars dragging down her neck that Dave's Uncle Pete had in the navy. They weigh a ton and hang down to her knees. She likes them though. Won't let us carry them.

"So now them three over there, are they greater scaup or lesser scaup?" Dave's teaching her how to know that by the shape of the ducks' heads, even if the light's not good enough to see the colour.

"Silly!" she sets him straight. "They're mergansers."

"Dave's got to get up earlier in the morning if he wants to fool you, don't he, eh?" Dave says. He thinks she's the smartest kid.

She is real smart. Mind you, she likes Dave's jokes.

"How do you get down off a horse?" he says to her.

She smiles up at him. "I don't know."

"You don't," he says. "You get down off a duck."

She wants to laugh, but he has to explain to her about eiderdown, that you get off a duck. Then she laughs.

Dave will shoot duck in the fall. But he has a feeling for them too. That might seem funny to any of yous that ain't familiar with hunting. I know Meredith had a hard time with it. But them guys that are outdoors a lot, right from when they were young, some of them seems to fit into things just right. Same as wolves do and other hunters.

Anyways, I watch the two of them, Jenny with her pigtails flying in the March wind. Him and Jenny climbing down to the shore for a closer look.

It's the first time in ages I had any thoughts of cavemen. I think, Dave's like man was to start with. He ain't out of place in the world.

I watched them ducks, the way they pop their rear ends up and disappear.

I thought, we're going to duck! I seen us like a bunch of little ducks, mooning and making a dive. Out of harm's way. Diving down to the bottom of the lake, where our lost gold was laying on the sand.

That's the type of thoughts I was thinking—picturing more than real thinking—while I watched Dave and Jenny go down to the water. It was bright blue and boy did it sparkle! Them floating birds was all out there, hundreds of them, playing in it, bobbing like corks, paddling with their rubber feet.

I don't get how they can swim around in that ice water, but Dave says they don't mind.

"Lord love them!" I said. It just come out that way. I was thinking of how froze you'd think their feet would be.

But of course Dave and Jenny, they die laughing. Lord love a duck! I'll never hear the end of that.

Sunday morning me and Jenny are making pancakes. Dave's reading a book about some people that are crossing Africa on foot. He tells us whenever anything happens. "They're at this swamp place, and you got to watch you don't sink down. You got to step on the mossy knolls."

"What's a knoll?" That's me.

Him and Jenny already know. They looked it up another time. "Near as we can make out, it's a bump."

"Why don't they say 'bump'?" I crack an egg.

Jenny's got no patience with the way I am about fancy words. She loves them.

She's got the wooden spoon there, stirring up the batter. I tell her, "It don't matter if you leave a few knolls in that."

Her and Dave laugh at me.

I think about what talk is and how it matters. Jenny, she's

picking up a whole new way of talking. Living with them foster family people, she sounds the way they sound. That's going to make her whole life different. It's going to let her do things nobody'd hire me for, the way I talk.

Me and Dave, we took Jenny back to the foster home on Sunday night.

Dave was sitting in the front room at our place, after. Looking at the wall. He hates prying her little hands off his arm when it's time to go. Hates to hear her cry. It's getting worse the more she loves him. And the more he loves her.

I says, "Are you going to see what they're doing in Africa there, whether they step on whatever it was?"

He says, "She don't want me to read ahead."

I go sit beside him, put my arms around him.

He says, "That shithead fooling with her!"

"It's not like it hurt her once," I says, "and was over and done with. It keeps right on hurting her every day. It'll hurt her when she's my age!"

Dave, he had no idea how common this was. Thought a sex offender was like some weirdo you read about in a huge big city where nobody's got any morals. He thought this Ian prize of my sister's was the worst criminal in the province. Couldn't believe he'd been right here where we lived. He ought to be electrocuted and then hanged, to suit Dave, and then have a truck drove over him backwards and forwards, and buried head down in a dump.

"Well," I says, "but it ain't rare. I know."

"What?"

"It happens, Dave."

"It's the most sickest thing I ever heard of, messing with a little wee girl! I hope I never meet that fucker when I've got a gun!" Then he looks at me. "What do you mean, you know?"

I was thinking of telling him about myself. Dave, he knew we was all going to Group for to get help. He knew it was on account of troubles in the past and the present time. But that's alls he knew. I hadn't ever said what exact same trouble was at the root of it for every one of us. I wasn't at that bright yellow *Don't Keep No Secrets* stepping stone yet. Lost my nerve. "Well it does happen. Not infrequent," was alls I said.

"What? In like Los Angeles?"

"Here, too."

"No, it don't."

"Yeah."

"What are you telling me? There's a lot of guys around here go doing a thing like that?"

I know it already bust Dave's world that Brent, who he'd grew up with, would beat a woman half to death with a kitchen chair.

He kept shaking his head, all winter, saying, "I never thought he'd turn around and act just like his old man."

"That's how it works, Dave."

"He never would've wanted to turn out like his old man."

I told him that our own town and every town was full of people like my sister Sandra's boyfriend, Ian, that will take advantage of little kids to get their rocks off. I hedged around telling him exactly how I happened to know that.

Poor Dave. It was like I was trying to tell him the town was half things from outer space that only look like people.

I says, "That's the facts, Dave. I'm sorry."

"Sorry?" he says. "You in the public works department?"

"I'm not apologizing. I just feel bad telling you this shit."

Dave, he took care of himself his own way. "There can't be many will beat up women and go after kids," he said. And that's what he kept on thinking.

21.

NOW HERE WE WERE in spring again. Josie'd been laid up for ten months, four in the hospital and then in the home where they moved her to. I went up to see her on a sunny Saturday afternoon late in March. Wheeled her down to the sunroom.

Josie still don't say much, but she's perking up some and you can see she likes to hear about all our friends and what's new. I tell her, "Marg got kicked out of AA."

Well Josie, she chuckled. First one out of her in all this time.

"Yeah," I says. "I guess somebody let it out that she don't drink nothing but chocolate milk."

"Tammy's young Meghan got two *A*s and three *B*s. Used to be failing. Meredith says she's got more emotional stability now."

Josie smiled.

"Darlene says your dog says you're getting better."

Josie smiles again. This is a good visit.

"You're going to have to fight to get that dog back from her now, you know. She's like in love. Says she don't need the internet guy, or even pills, long as she's got your hound."

It's a bit hard to keep talking to Josie when she don't say hardly nothing herself, but she's sitting up looking at me. Different to when she was just laying there with her eyes shut and I'd ramble on like talking to myself. I don't know if I should talk to her about the bigger stuff now. I don't know if anybody told her that Brent got ten years.

I don't know if she wants to hear the things I used to tell her before, the worries that are on my mind, like how Jenny's doing. And my sister's fucking wedding in two months. I don't know if I should tell her that Dave's cousin-in-law, Tom, has offered Dave a job.

We're trying to make up our minds on that one. It's Dave's dream offer, to move back north and work with his cousin there, doing this building he took the course on. But then there's Jenny to think of. And my job. And of course I wouldn't say it, but there's Josie herself too.

I says, "Are you eating?" She looks like a thread. She don't answer.

"Josie?"

She looks at me. I can see she's in there.

I says, "Want me to read you Sally's letter that just come?"

Josie's eyes brighten up.

Sally writes a good old-school actual letter. Sends us all the dirt on what's new up north. I got her pink envelope out of my purse. Sally's big round writing on it. I start reading.

> *Dave's dad witches water. He told these Walmart people they were going to hit a big aquifer if they dug where they were planning on. So they don't pay no attention, eh, and they dig this great big excavation. No water. Think the old man's a crackpot. Well, the crew gets there the next morning to pour the footings and what they got is an Olympic size swimming pool. I told him it was the Lord's doing, as He don't hold with Walmart.*

I look up from the letter and I says to Josie, "Sally figures she knows the exact opinions of God Almighty on any topic you can name."

Josie says, "Hardware man?"

I looked at Josie severe.

I says, "Sally is buying more shelf brackets and sandpaper than what ten people need in their life. And it's your fault, talking to her so wild about that hardware man. She gets dressed up to buy a bag of nails."

Josie just sits and smiles. She looks out the window. I can see her watching the shapes of the clouds. They're running through the air today, up in the wind.

"What do you see up there?"

Her eyes are bright.

"Do you see your hotel?"

Josie makes a little move with her hands. I think she wants me to keep on, so I try. This is not what I do easy, but I look up at the clouds with her and I says, "Wow, there's your hotel up there! Look, it's painted up a nice bright white. There's the blue lake shining behind it! I see they got all the white sheets hung out flapping on the line. Won't they smell nice! Oh, and there's sailboats in the lake, having a brisk ride today, ain't they?"

Josie sits there with her face to the sky. She says, "Pie lady." We talk about which cloud is the lady and where's this pie in the sky.

Josie's different now. But on the other hand, she's no different. The basic her is right there. And nothing else.

It's like when they take and melt down ore for gold.

"God is like a refiner's fire," according to Sally. She'll say that when things get rough.

Struck me, and I couldn't help thinking about the fire in a refinery. Metal works, steam pouring out the stacks. Glory hole of the furnace, raging hot white-orange centre of it blazing like the sun. I could hear the way a roaring hot fire sounds. Smell the smoke. And the ore getting melted in that awful heat was our brains. We were going to come out solid gold because the hottest centre of that fire was God. Weird idea, but I remember it made a certain amount of sense, during the trial.

Me and Jenny seen a thing on TV, too. How the stars get formed, in almighty heat and commotion.

22.

I WAS THINKING ABOUT THAT, as a matter of fact. I was at my desk at work, staring into space. My mind had went to the fire and explosions up in the universe and how God must be in them, or whatever you like to call It that makes the stars. The heat that goes into making anything new, that's what I was thinking about. Getting your niece or your friend or yourself a new chance, a new habit, a new way, a new thought—anything new at all—is hot work. You feel like you've fell into a vat and got smelted.

Dirk walked in.

"It's part of your journey, Rose. It's very common for people with your background of abuse. The key is to understand it and to learn from it, not to berate yourself."

That's what Meredith said, after everything had happened with Dirk.

Frances told me that she had struggled with the same problem herself in the past.

Marg just said, "Oh no!"

And Sally, she brought Dave's dad all the way down from Strone in her T-Bird to set me straight.

I'm getting ahead here. Trying to skip over what happened with Dirk. Avoidance. I wish I didn't have to out with that. I feel so bad about it. Wish I hadn't went through that particular fire or dragged Dave through it.

Poor Dave, he didn't deserve to get smelted.

I wound up kicking Dave out.

"What?" Yous are saying, "What for?"

Well, there's two ways to look at that. The way I was looking at it at the time, I had my reasons. I said I was sick of his socks on the floor. I said the fizz was gone out of it.

Of course, the way I see it now, that's all bull. You can step over a lot of socks, or even pick them up and wash them, and still be getting a good bargain, with a man as kind and close as what Dave had been to me. Wasn't like he was getting no free ride. He was doing his share other ways. And what the hell is fizz anyways? Nothing but adrenaline.

And the guy I met.

Okay, here I go. I have to tell yous about Dirk. He was what Dirk rhymes with, as it didn't take my friends long to tell me.

Dirk, he was good-looking if you like muscle. He had shiny black hair and big shoulders. He come into the office at McIlveen's Plumbing and Heating and told me I was cute.

Now, take even that right there, eh? That should've told me something.

Dave, he said things like I'm a good aunt. But somebody that says I'm cute has got to be either hard up, blind, or else just lying to get some, quick.

Now, Dirk, he was never hard up, on account of all the women that like pipes. And he wasn't carrying no white cane.

He starts coming into the office, paying attention to me that old way. Not the way I'd knew lately, where you pay attention to the actual person, see if they're a good aunt or what they are. Nothing like that. Just the old shit I was used to before.

But that right there is my weak spot, eh. It's the bent key that just fits right into my bent lock.

Dirk, he knows a bent lock a mile off.

I'm sitting there with somebody's bill for their new drain pipe of their laundry tub in my hand, thinking about the almighty heat at the centre of things, and sort of calling it God the way Sally does.

"Behold, I make all things new." That's what God says, according to Sally.

I come back to planet earth, and there was a man with his shoulders pretty well filling up the door frame.

He asks me how old I am. Says I look a lot younger. He would have never guessed thirty-four.

And then he waits a day or two, eh. You can tell them operators because they're not in a hurry. He just takes his work order form, gives me a look, and trots his firm ass out to van number three.

Then he strolls in another time and tells me I got a rich woman's type of a nose. I'm so stupid listening to that baloney, but I can't seem to help it.

Couple of days later, I've got pretty fingers. I look at them, after he walks out, holding an invoice for a shower installation. They ain't pretty, but they sure are shaking.

The other fellows, when they come in, they all just say, "G'day, Rosie. How's she going?" They hand me their paperwork, tell me about their last stupid customer.

"If this clay pots woman calls again, tell her we've went out of business."

(That's a pottery teacher and the kids she teaches. They keep getting clay down the sink. Can't remember to wash their hands in a bucket, eh, and dump it in the garden. Stick their hands in the sink. Clay runs down and hardens up somewheres halfway to the sewer.)

"I'm going to take and throw a stick of dynamite down there the next time," Fred says.

I can laugh with these guys. I can feel what it is to talk normal friendly to a man. I tell myself that's good and the other is bad. I try to hold on to the good way.

But I'm starting to watch out the window for van number three. I'm waiting for the way the air feels different soon as he walks in. There's a charge to it. What Meredith calls "heightened intensity."

It's a shot of pure adrenaline, is what it is. And I'm the old junkie, back-sliding into loving that high.

"Everyone in this group was raised in a charged atmosphere. You must recognize that you will miss that heightened intensity. You will be tempted to get into situations of heightened intensity again."

Meredith used to say that all the time, back when I was in my ripping magazines and throwing mouthwash phase, when I couldn't stand peace and quiet.

I said to myself, "Dirk's just looking for some, quick. He don't give a shit about me. Dave, he really does." But the way my gut seized whenever Dirk come through that door! I ate his stupid compliments.

I did try. It's true. I went for long walks by myself, trying to get sorted out. I knew I was getting sucked in. I knew it was worse than stupid. I knew it was mean to Dave and wrong for myself and bad for Jenny. I knew.

But then Dirk would be back there, filling the door again.

Of course Dave didn't make my heart pound like that. He never did. And anyway, your heart don't keep doing that once you know somebody.

By the time Dirk's up to telling me I've got the tits of a young teenager, I'm beat.

He asks me to meet him, secret, at his place. And I nod.

The old rush is right there. I listen to him tell me I'm the hottest little thing. Feeling special, feeling the buzz. There is something about a secret sex life. The way it pulls you in. It's exciting. Once you're creeping up the side stairs, there is no amount of good ideas or decent feeling that can stop you. It's as bad as drinking. It'd been over a year for me, since I felt that high.

I'm going past all the beat-up doors in Dirk's building. My knees are weak, the world's lit up odd. It's quite a feeling. It is. There's no two ways about it. A secret date with somebody new, somebody good-looking who don't care what he says, to the point where he calls me cute, that's quite a feeling.

I thought back to when I first met Dave, how it was just good to get a hug. Now I convinced myself that that with Dave wasn't the real thing. No fizz to it. This here with Dirk had the old buzz, all right.

Dirk was in there waiting for me in his boxers, with a beer in his hand. I will say for Dirk that he did have quite the chest and arms on him. He peeled my stuff off slow.

For about thirty minutes, I felt like a movie star.

Then, of course, I felt like a piece of shit. Crawling home, telling Dave I'd went to see Josie.

Then the whole week after. Not going near Josie for fear of them eyes of hers looking at me. Feeling like garbage in the can again. Not being able to stand what Dave would think of me if he knew. Doing it again anyways, like I'm an addict. It went on like that for a month.

I kicked Dave out so he wouldn't find out. I couldn't stand him to know what a piece of crap I really was. I told him to go ahead and take that job back north.

That was a sorry scene. Dave asking me what he could do different. Me telling him he should've picked his damn socks off the floor, knowing all the time that it ain't socks-related.

It's all about my twisted insides. I know that, even when I'm yelling he don't like to go out enough. I know it's all besides the point. I know I'm the point. I know and I say them things anyways, and I'm so ashamed I'm sick.

Last thing he says to me, standing in the door with his boots in his hand, he says, "What are you going to tell Jenny?"

Boy, was that the Question of the Week! How was I going to answer to them blonde question marks? I could see her running into my place expecting to find him.

I didn't go to see her that week.

The one and only thing I done right that month was I went to Group.

I drag myself upstairs, the Tuesday after Dave left, and I'm feeling lower than slobber. Every stair step I climb is telling me: I've screwed up again. I've screwed up again. Just when it looked like I might've learned something and grew, I screwed up again.

Meredith, she said all that stuff about it's not uncommon for people of my background.

Now, if you remember, I seen a sour look on her face a number of times, when you might've thought she'd be pleased. The opposite thing happened this night here. I told Meredith I screwed up my relationship. I'd made a mess of my life again. I'd lost everything that I thought I had gained. Forgot everything I thought I'd learned. I told her I felt like a piece of garbage stinking in the can. And this little bit of a smile went acrost her face!

She looked at me more that night than she ever done before. She smiled at me way more.

Marg had her mouth shut tight during break. Darlene had hers working. Tammy sat and looked at me like I'd just fell off a train and my head was missing.

I says, "What are you looking at?"

Tammy says, "Nothing." Picks up a magazine. Keeps on looking at me.

Darlene, she's saying Dave was such a nice man. Give her and Tammy and Marg and Sally a duck each last fall, all cleaned nice. Sat in the courtroom with us. Was good to Jenny, working steady, had a truck that wasn't that old.

I says, "I don't want to talk about it!"

Tammy finally says, "If I could find a man like Dave, I wouldn't be going back to Peter."

23.

I THOUGHT THAT PARTICULAR TUESDAY couldn't be any worse than what it was until I heard that. "WHAT!"

Sitting in her wheelchair, Josie sometimes said, "There's hope." But you really had to wonder. When Tammy let out that she was going back to Asshole, I felt like there was zero hope for anything.

There's no hope for an idiot who will turn around and walk right back into a mess like that, and there's no hope for her boy or for her girl. That's what I thought, sitting on the plastic chair there during break that night. There is no hope for stupid Tammy or for stupid me, or for Jenny or her children's children until God Almighty gets fed up enough to end the frigging world.

"Ah, Tammy, you're not!" Marg says.

And then you know what Darlene done? She says, "Tammy, don't do it! I'll give you the dog."

Now, of course, Tammy can't take the dog in the apartment she's in. But she stopped and looked at Darlene.

"We'll trade," Darlene says. "You come and live in my place. You walk the dog regular, every day, morning, and night. Meghan and Matthew can hold the leash. You got to feed the cat up on the counter so the dog don't eat his kibble. Or you can stay where you are and we'll say he's your dog and you and the kids got to look after him, only he sleeps at my place."

Tammy sort of hesitated there a minute.

Marg seen her chance and jumped in. She said, "What if I come over and stay with you? I'm sleeping on the couch right now anyhow. There'd be no law against having a big fat pet like me in your building, would there?"

Tammy says, "They want me to fill out a tax form."

Marg says, "You can do that, Tammy."

Tammy says, "Peter always done it."

"Assho—Peter ain't the only person on earth can fill out a tax form."

Tammy says, "I wouldn't know where to start."

Marg says, "Tammy," she says, "we'll take a look at her, together, at your kitchen table."

Eventually Tammy said all right, she'd try.

I sat and looked at her. She'd said all right. All right, she wasn't going back to Asshole! She was willing to hold on and keep trying the new way, hard as it was.

I thought, if I'd have only told these guys what stupid thing I was planning on, and let them talk me out of it...! But no, I had to keep it secret. I had to walk right into it.

That's when I started to think about what keeping secrets will do to you.

It was so lonesome and quiet to come home. No Dave there to ask me nothing about Group. No new progress on the dollhouse. Nobody dying of thirst in a desert to hear about. No big boots on the mat. No arms of nobody that loves me for having kind hands or being a good aunt.

I put the kitchen light on, hung my coat up on the giraffe coat hanger Dave put up for Jenny.

And I went and got out paper and scissors. I spent a while figuring out what colour I wanted.

Yellow. I picked yellow for to write *No More Secrets* on. A new stepping stone.

Wished to God I'd got to that step a few weeks sooner. Told them about Dirk instead of keeping it a frigging secret, keeping the big buzz in it to make me act foolish.

How I got to sleep that night was thinking about Josie. Curled up in my bed in the dark, thinking of the way Josie is, a real nice comfort come over me. Josie looks up at the sky and feels us floating through space. Breathing in and breathing out. My own warm breath under the blanket. The pink air in the evening. Josie looking up at it. The dark blue night clouds, hanging in folds like the curtains of an angel's house.

24.

IT WAS A GOOD THING Marg went to stay with Tammy right away. Marg was telling me on the phone the next day. I guess Asshole's been after Tammy. Phoning.

But he picked the wrong night to try going any farther with it.

Poor Marg, she's laying on Tammy's couch looking at TV, last night, she says, along about eleven-thirty. She's got the sound way down, and she's just dozing off. She reaches for the remote and, Jesus, the door's moving! Just jiggling a bit, moving in its frame, like somebody's working at the lock.

Marg says, "You never seen a fat woman move so fast!"

I guess she was up off that couch and hit the floor running. Tammy hadn't bothered to put the chain on the door.

Now, you've got to wonder why. But, see, this is the thing with people that are what Meredith calls "self-destructive," like Tammy. You learn how to treat yourself from how your parents treat you when you're young.

Did yous know that? That's a big thing I learned. Let me repeat that for yous. You learn how to treat yourself from how your parents treat you. So, you see, if your parents hadn't no regard for your safety or your well-being, you won't grow up to have no regard for your own safety or well-being. You might be apt to leave the safety chain undid, when anybody with a normal notion of self-care would fasten it.

Anyhow, Tammy's was not on.

Marg, she felt bad that she never thought about it neither.

Somebody'd got past the downstairs locks. And the door was just quietly jiggling in the frame.

Marg says she did zero to sixty in one half-second, making for the chain.

"Them two kids of Tammy's have only been just starting to sleep good. Last thing they need is Asshole busting the door down in the middle of the night!"

That's Marg. Doing the fat lady world record half-second sprint, nightgown flapping. Nothing in her head but keeping them kids from any more bad dreams.

I guess she rammed that chain home just before the lock give. Then she's dialing the cops.

They done all right, too. Got there right quick, blocked all the downstairs exits before they made a sound. Searched the building. Caught old Asshole in the janitor's closet, down in the laundry room.

Marg give a shudder. She says, "What is it with laundry rooms?"

I'm thinking, and janitors' closets.

Marg had been getting so she could go down there and run a load sometimes, overcoming her old memories. Now she's back washing her things upstairs in a bucket.

Anyways, that looked good on Asshole. He got charged with illegal entry and some stuff to do with his restraining order.

Marg says she never wanted to be a frigging security guard; she wanted to be a nurse.

I says, "You're doing the best out of all of us."

"Nah," she says, "Sally is."

"Next to Sally."

"You were doing great too, Rose," Marg tells me.

"Well, I sure screwed that up."

"Dave might give you another chance."

"Why should he?"

"He loves you."

I says, "Why should he?"

Then Marg says, "There's lots of good reasons anybody can love you, Rose. You're a good person. You got a great drive in you, to work for a better life. But I don't think it's about the reasons, so much. People just feel love or they don't. Dave, he happens to love you."

"Marg, I'm a piece of shit. I cheated on him."

"That type of thing always was your downfall," she says, "just the same as double chocolate doughnuts with sprinkles always was mine. I went out and snuck two, day before yesterday. We're going to both have to keep working on things."

I pour it all out to good old Marg. I tell her I was trying so hard and everything was really and truly deep down better, and me and Dave was closer than I ever thought could be. And he's the sweetest man alive, and I miss him a hundred times a day. I can't even look at his giraffe coat hook on the wall or his fish Jell-O mould in the drawer, or his roses wallpaper border in the bedroom that he put up because of Rose being my ... I break down bawling. Kleenex is out, and alls I can see to grab for my running nose is one of the napkins that Sally give me.

"Look," Marg says, she says, "Dave knows that you got issues. You got to tell him your issues are to do with sex, Rose," she says. "You been doing good for a year. You screwed up once. You're real sorry. You're going to try harder from now on."

I stood there, hunched over, wrecking the napkin with blowing my nose in it and bawled in Marg's ear.

"Oh Marg! It's a lot frigging worse than sneaking doughnuts."

She says, "He loves you. You talk to him. Tell him you're awful sorry."

"How could he ever forgive me?"

"Well maybe he can and maybe he can't. But, if you want my advice, I think you better tell him and see."

So then of course, Marg got on the phone to Sally. Told her me and Dave had had a fight.

25.

I GET UP SATURDAY MORNING and there's feet in the downstairs hall. I look down and there's the grey top of Dave's dad steaming up the stairs. Blonde top of Sally marching right behind him. I shut the door quiet and quick. I know that the two of them's here to set me straight. Just the way they clump up them stairs. They've been driving since dawn. They don't want no bullshit. If you don't think somebody can say all that by just the way they stomp up a set of stairs, you should've heard them two.

I ran and hid in the bathroom. Combed my hair. Thought about what a low bag of scum I have been to this good man's good son. Listened to them knocking.

"Rose!" Sally shouts, like she's my mother. "Open this door!"

I dab cold water on my eyes. Then I crawl out and let them in.

"Could yous use a coffee?"

I thought everybody in Strone would know the whole thing by now, and what a whore I was. But it turned out Marg hadn't said nothing about that part.

Dave was back there staying with Jan and Tom, working in the construction, letting on nothing hadn't happened. Dave's dad and Sally didn't know nothing about me being the town tramp. They didn't even know me and Dave'd had a fight until Marg told them.

"So now what's all this about?" Dave's dad, he goes right for the point.

"I'm not fit," I says, "for as fine a man as your son."

"Pretty hard on yourself, ain't you?"

Sally busts in with some of her church talk. "All we, like sheep, have gone astray," she says.

I'm getting out cookies. "What did yous want? I got windmill cookies a guy at work's selling for the Dutch Reformed. Or could yous eat a meal?"

They didn't eat breakfast yet! The big sweet idiots drove all the way down here to me without even stopping for breakfast. So I fry eggs while I'm trying to give a rough idea of just how far astray this particular sheep has went.

Dave's dad wipes the toast crumbs off the corner of his mouth. He says, "I figure you and Dave'll be all right."

"No!" I yell that at the two of them.

"Faith, hope, and love remain," Sally tells me, through her mouthful.

I yell at her nothing at all remains. I'm a goddamn whore.

Dave's dad stands up. He ain't used to people screaming that word over the eggs and coffee.

But Sally, she's one of us, of course, and she's used to you-name-it. So she don't even quit spreading her jam. She says, "You're not a whore, Rose. You're the survivor of childhood sex abuse, which can work out looking similar, but ain't."

"Why not if it acts the same?"

"Because," Sally says, "it's a thing that was done to you. Sit down, Al. It was done to you when you were a poor little girl like Tammy's Meghan, there, and Jenny. You think it's going to be their fault if they got some stuff to work through later on? Well, do you? It's going to be all their own fault if they screw up sometimes, when they're first trying to get their life straightened out? So, there you go."

"I can act any way I want and just blame it on somebody else a long time ago, is that it?"

"Course not. You got to try your damnedest."

"I was trying!"

"That's alls you can do."

"I made all these stupid stepping stones." I grabbed them out of the kitchen drawer and threw them all over the floor. I'm crying. I says, "What's the use? I'm just that kind. I'm a slut, for which there's no help."

Sally keeps trying to tell me what comfortable words St. Paul saith, that to all who are heartily sorry for their transgressions....

I start yelling about Dirk the jerk, how I don't know enough to keep off his back stairs because I crave the adrenaline rush and the secret sex.

Dave's dad, he's like at a skeet shoot, with all this flying by and blowing up. His ears are hanging out like this is more about the seamy side than what he heard in his thirty winters at a lumber camp.

Finally I says, "Look," I says, "I gotta go get Jenny. We'll take her to the park."

Sally drove me over in the T-Bird. Dave's dad, he stayed at the apartment. Said he'd clean up. (Looking for a rest.)

On the way to my place, Jenny says, "I want to phone Dave."

"I don't know the number, honey."

Al was washing dishes with his back to the door when we come in.

I'm just starting to tell Jenny, "There's a man here who is..."

But she caught sight of the plaid shirt, drowned me out with a shout, made a running leap for Dave's dad.

Then she jumps back and stares at him.

Al says, "Hi there. Did you think I was Dave?" He says, "I'm not him but I know him real good. He's been telling me all about you."

Dave's dad was a hit at the park. He knew how to teach somebody to skip a stone (which ain't the same thing as just knowing how to do it yourself). Me and Sally sat on a bench and looked at the wrist-flicking lessons there, while she tried to tell me that the Lord forgave me. My throat was burning to cry.

Then Sally went and played with Jenny. Dave's dad took a turn at me. "Back in my day," he says, "if a woman done like what you done, that'd be the end of her, far as any man was concerned."

I hung my head. I wasn't going to be able to hold back from bawling much longer.

"But," Al says, "times are changing."

Head still low, I looked at him out of the corner of my eye.

"Times are opened up nowadays. People talk about things they never used to. That's all to the good," he says, "because life ain't clear cut. A person can get all turned around and do a fool thing. A wrong thing. But that don't mean there's no good in that person or no chance of them getting themself straightened out. Used to be, women who strayed was automatically wrote right off. Not so much now."

I don't know if yous have been up real early, when it's still dark? Did yous notice, long time before the sun really rises, it already ain't so dark? That's about where I was. Sort of a lighter grey starting to dawn on me there, with Al hinting I might not have to be automatically wrote right off of Dave's good books.

Soon as we get back to my place, the phone rings. It's a nurse at the home. "I have somebody here who would like to talk to you."

"Josie? Are you phoning me, Josie? Hey! Wow! That's great that you can phone now! How are you? Sorry I haven't gotten in to see you lately. I been kind of busy. Some stuff going on here. Listen, guess who's here today? Sally come to visit! She'll say 'Hi' to you."

Josie cuts through this crap, and she says, "Man at the door with a lucky ticket." That's all I can get out of her.

Sally talks to her for a while. Tells her all about how things are going back north. Tells her the Good Luck Restaurant's brightened up since they're using her tablecloths. Bought a bunch of them off her.

All them tablecloths Sally made on faith, a year ago last winter, is coming into use, apparently. Not at a hotel of our own. But still, they ain't sitting in a bag under Sally's bed neither. And Sally, she's not laying in bed.

"She's got my barn half full of yard sale beds," Dave's dad, in the background, tells me.

Oh boy. Sally with an empty barn to fill! There's a thought. I say, "Put a stop to her, Al. I'm not kidding you. She'll fill available space like a gas vapour."

Josie wants me again. Sally hands me the phone.

I hear Josie's little voice. "A man at the door. With a lucky ticket."

I says, "You sound like a fortune cookie."

She didn't say nothing. Sat there waiting.

I says, "Okay, Josie." I says, "I hear you."

Still waiting.

Finally, I says, "What do you want me to say? I'll try. Okay? I'll try again!"

That was alls she wanted, I guess, because she just gently hung up.

Dave's dad "just happened to have," in his shirt pocket, Jan and Tom's number, where I could call Dave.

Jenny was colouring with Sally, kneeling up to the coffee table in the front room. I didn't think she heard. But Jenny don't miss much. She knows we got the number now to call Dave. And I'm not going to hear the last of it until I call him.

I start for the kitchen. Sal gets up and follows me. Wants to know how everybody's doing. I told her about what happened at Tammy's place.

I say, "Can you believe that Tammy was all set to go right back to the way things was before? Just because of her tax form!" I says. "She didn't know how to fill it in, so she was right ready to waltz back to Asshole."

Sally, she's standing there leaning her back against the broom closet, just looking at me. I remember I've did worse than

Tammy. She was just thinking of going right back into her old mess. I've went and really did it.

I let out a big sigh.

"It's like we're on a rope," I says to Sally, "and it's tied to a centre post of misery so alls we can do is go in circles. The more we try to break free, the more we go in misery circles."

Sally hangs her head and shakes it. "I know," she says. "Sometimes I still give up and sleep all day. Still!"

Dave's dad had came in, in time to hear the part about going in circles. He says, "You know, there's been times in my life I thought I was going in circles. But when you come to look back on it, you see it wasn't circles you was going in. It's more like a set of spiral stairs."

He goes and borrows Jenny's blue crayon, and he draws us a picture on the bottom of my shopping list. I can see his big old hand yet, that worked in lumber all them years—rough, arthritis knuckles—holding that little crayon and drawing us a picture of the set of spiral stairs that everybody's on.

"See, we start here." He moves his finger, tracing up the spiral he'd drew. "Now see here where it loops back around. Looked at one way, you'd say we was right back where we started, eh. We're back here on this here side of the circle. But are we in the same place?"

On a spiral, of course, going around didn't bring you to the same spot you started from.

Sally says, "Higher up."

"That's right," he says. "And look here, if you keep going"— he showed us with his finger following the blue line—"you're going to feel like you're looping right back around again here. And here again. But the fact is you're not, eh. You're never going to be in the same place twice. It can feel like it. But you never are. You're higher up every time because you've learned things. Long as you're learning," he says, "you're going up."

When I'm kissing Jenny goodbye at the foster home, she makes me promise to call Dave. "Before sleep."

"Okay, honey."
"And make him come back."
"I'll try."
"Make him."
"I'll try my very best. But I don't know if he will."
God, between her and all the rest of them—!
So I go home and there's Sally and Dave's dad still parked in my front room, looking at me.
"I'll call," I says.
They sit there waiting.
"Not while the two of yous are gawping."
So they finally leave.
I dial the number and croak out to Jan that it's me and I want to talk to Dave if he's not busy.
Dave comes on. Of course, with all of them after me, I haven't had no time to think of what I'm going to say to him. "Oh Dave," was as smart as I come out with.
We fixed it up that he was coming to see me next weekend.
Afterwards I called Marg all excited and brung her up to date and cried. She said she was real glad.
Marg's for being optimistic. She says look at how good things are going. She says, "The bad guys is pretty near all cleaned off the streets."
Marg's dad, Josie's Brent, and now Tammy's Asshole was all in jail.
"We're in a different place to where we were this time last year!" she says. I hear the words echo.
Learning, eh. Learning's like that. You hear a new thing once and you're going to hear it again soon. Have yous noticed that?

I finally got myself over to see Josie. Sunday afternoon. She's sitting in the sunroom. It's one of them pretty, green days in April with sun and clouds. Josie's looking at a green patch of the lawn there, lit up with sunshine. There's red and pink tulips out in bloom.

"You always say there's hope for the world. Looks it today."

Josie turns her head. She's something now! When she looks at you? The eyes on her! Big and strange in her little white face. You feel like you should bless yourself or take your hat off.

Her thin little see-through fingers was resting on the dark green arm of the wheelchair there. I took and lifted her hand. It was cool and dry like a small, smooth stone.

I said, "Thank you, Josie! Thanks for calling me!"

"You climbed the stairs."

I said, "No, I took the eleva—oh." Them stairs. "Yeah."

I sat and told her how I treated Dave and that he was coming in five days to see me anyways. How Jenny loves him and I hoped to God there was some way to patch it up, for her sake as much as my own.

Josie sat there, smiling sort of faint, like the statue of a saint, looking at sunshine and shadows moving over the grass.

26.

MONDAY MORNING, Dirk comes into the office. I says, "We're through." He gives me a sour look, as if to say it don't break his heart. He shrugs, picks up his work orders, and takes his athletic rump out the door. The only thing bugging him is he wishes he'd have dumped me first.

He revs the McIlveen's plumbing van number three like a man that ain't used to being the one dumped. Roars on out of there. I figure it'll take him ten minutes to get over it.

Tuesday, he give it one more try, just to see if he could get me going again and then be the one to dump. He's standing there telling me in a low voice that I'm one hot lay and he misses my little wet hole.

I push a work order across the desk to him. I says, "You know what, Dirk?" I says. "You better get on over to this address here. They got green water standing in the basement drain. That's a wet hole."

Me and Dirk, we were on what Meredith calls a "professional basis" from there on. (Last I heard he was after both the girls at the dry cleaners.)

So anyways, that Tuesday, I went to Group. Marg, Darlene, and Tammy was there.

Marg's still staying with Tammy, helping with the kids. Gives Marg something to do, eh. She'll pack school lunches. Help them with their spelling. Pays for her own food and helps plan. "Okay, Tammy, how much have you got till your cheque comes? All right, so we've got to get four more family suppers and ten more school lunches out of forty-two bucks."

"And we don't feed them crap neither, do we?" Tammy looks proud.

Some health nurse give Tammy a piece of paper about how many fruits and how many grams of skim milk cheese and all that you're supposed to eat. Tammy, she's took it right to heart.

"Green and orange is the best so you don't get cancer," Tammy tells me. Her and Marg look over all the sale vegetables careful to find ones that are still good.

We're in a huddle, with our heads all leaned in close, and I'm telling them what was the only wet hole Dirk got today, when Meredith walks in. We shut up, but we were still grinning. I saw one of them looks on Meredith there for a second. *What's the matter with her now? Mad she's not in on the joke?*

Meredith smoothed out her raspberry-coloured skirt behind her before she sat on it. She pulled the two sides of her purple jacket, with a raspberry weave through it, together across her big front. I guess they must pay her pretty good for working on us.

She tells Marg, Darlene, and Tammy that they're "doing very well" in that kindergarten-teacher voice which grates on me so bad.

Tammy, she never drew a breath the last eighteen years of her life without Asshole telling her to. She never had a bank account. Never paid a bill. Never went to a store by herself. Never cooked a meal somebody didn't tell her to. She never answered a phone call. Asshole wouldn't let her. Let him or the machine take the calls. She never even knew till last year that her own favourite colour was blue.

I sit there, pissed off, listening to Meredith tell her "Very good, Tammy" in that voice. Tammy is doing great. Really. You got to say it in a straightforward voice: Tammy is doing excellent.

And so is Marg. The kid with the hole in her heart, who couldn't run and play like other kids. Stuck at home all the time with her frigging father who kicked her mother out and made Marg take her place in the bed. Beat her when she tried to run away to her mom.

Only nice safe place, when Marg was a kid, was the hospital. Her heart would act up. She couldn't get her breath. When she was turning blue, he'd finally take her in. The hospital was heaven full of healing angels in their white dresses, with a kind touch, calm voices, and a mask that let her breathe.

Tammy and Marg are not kids that did a neat job colouring! These are full-grown people, wrestling, hand to hand, with what I call the rockslide and Sally calls the devil.

My opinion is Meredith ought to see that and treat them respectful.

When it come my turn, I said Dirk was done and Dave was coming to see me on the weekend.

Meredith starts in about me taking some time out from men until at least next summer. "It would be healthier to take some time for yourself before you begin to date again, Rose."

"Date?" I says. "This is Dave."

Sally called on Thursday. "Dave's all excited about going to see you," she says. "He's got a surprise for you."

I says, "Oh Sally." I says, "I'm so scared."

"It's going to be all right."

I didn't say nothing.

"Wear your fuzzy sweater," Sally says

"You and your pink."

"It lights you up real nice."

"It ain't going to be about my sweater."

"It's going to be all right." Sally said that again.

"Do you think..." It was hard to get the words out. "Do you think I better tell him?"

"About Jerk?"

"Yeah."

There was some quiet while Sally done her thinking on that one. "I think so," she says finally.

"I can't! I'm not going to."

"So what did you ask me for?"

Marg called Friday morning while I was eating my toast. "I won't keep you, Rose. Just called to wish yous luck for this weekend."

"Thanks, Marg."

"Mind you tell him everything, so you don't have nothing dragging on your conscience after."

"Sally said the same."

"You going to?"

"No! I don't know. Maybe."

"Well, best of luck, girl." Then she adds on, "You should tell him."

On the way to work, waiting to cross a street, I shut my eyes.

I says, "Oh, Josie, what do you see in them shadows on the grass? What's coming next? What's going to happen?"

I stand there on the curb like a blind person, eh, with my eyes shut, hearing the cars roar by, straining to see like Josie sees, beyond eyesight, into tonight and tomorrow.

What come to mind real strong was the colour yellow. To me it meant the yellow stepping stone. No secrets. Tell Dave.

"Josie, tell me the future! Are we going to be able to patch it up?" I opened my eyes.

Across the road, where the sun was shooting through the clouds, there was like a hundred welding torches roaring up out of the ground, blazing yellow. Yellow tulips.

I had to go and look in them, see their purple centres, with thin stripes of red, and their sex parts. Wish ours was beautiful and sweet smelling like that. I remembered Dave telling me that he liked a woman's smell.

I was all the way to work before it hit me to wonder if Josie had anything to do with me seeing them yellow flowers in that blast of yellow light, just when I'd been thinking that yellow meant: *no secrets from Dave.*

I sat down at my desk and opened up the appointments

book. Get a grip, Rose, before you go as nuts as what Josie is herself! How would she have anything to do with where the town council horticulture committee seen fit to put in a flowerbed or where the sun seen fit to shine?

Dirk, he was the first man come into the office that morning. Picked up his day sheet fairly civil and went on out.

Once the adrenaline's gone, you can see straight, eh. I look at the back of him leaving and I think, all this trouble over what? That ass?

27.

I WENT TO SEE JENNY Friday night after work. Took her a chocolate egg. Didn't have the heart to tell her Dave was due in an hour. Me and him had to talk. I told her he'd be here in the morning and we'd come see her.

"Right after this sleep?"

"Yes, sweetheart."

"As soon as I wake up?"

"Don't wake yourself up extra early. We can't come get you until nine o'clock."

Nine is the rule at the foster home. She'll sit and wait, watch the big hand crawling all the way around its circle. We were five minutes late once, and Jenny was in a cold sweat. Pure white. Terrified. Jumped for me like a drowning person. Clung on all day. Cried like a baby if I left the room.

Meredith says that would be from fear of abandonment. I think it's like if yous stepped into your kitchen one day and the floor give way. Landed yous right in the basement. After that yous wouldn't step so confident.

Something like that happened to Jenny. The floor of her little world had gave way, and here she was dropped in this strange home. Me and Dave being there when we say we will, that's alls she's got to stand on.

Her mom's wedding was five weeks from that Saturday. The social workers warned my sister, Sandra. They said that's it. If she marries this Ian treasure, she's giving up Jenny for good.

Sandra still says she's marrying him.

Me and her had a big fight on the phone a month or so ago, when Dave was still here.

"Bastards!" she says. "Taking my own kid away from me! They think their shit don't stink. It's your fault, Rose! For getting those dickheads into it. You couldn't let me handle it."

I says, "You weren't going to handle it!"

She says, "You seen me slap her for it."

"How is slapping her going to stop him?"

"She leads him on."

"She's a little child."

"She's a little flirt."

"She's a kid that wants a hug. She don't have a dad. She wants to be loved. She don't know about being a flirt or nothing like that."

"She'll spread her legs for him."

"How do you know?"

"Ian told me."

"You want to marry a guy that teaches your baby daughter to do that and then turns around and blames it on her?"

We wind up screaming at each other, but it don't do no good. The next week she's on the phone again, expecting me to show up at the wedding. She wants me for a bridesmaid, if you can believe it. She just don't get it that no amount of wedding is going to change what this Ian is.

I ain't going.

I says, "You think I'm going to throw confetti on yous? I'll tell you what I'd like to throw on him," I says. "I don't know why they even let him out of jail."

"All right, Rose," she says. "You don't have to get rude."

"Rude?" I says. "What do you think? Child abuse is polite? You go and marry the fucking creep who—"

She hung up on me.

Good riddance.

I told Dave when I got off the phone that time, I says, "I

can't see where her and me can have much to say to each other after this. She's my own sister," I says, "my only near relation outside of Jenny."

Dave he said, "Yeah, but..."

I put my face against Dave. And he said to me, he said, "You're going to have other relatives soon."

He was talking about me marrying him and belonging to all those folks of his. All them decent people who would hurl at the thoughts of a stunt like what Ian there gets up to. They'd be warning him off their land with twenty-twos. Not frigging baking him a wedding cake.

So now Dave was coming back to me in one hour, for to give me a second chance, please God, to belong with him and his decent people.

Walking home, I tried to think. I could start in with, "It really wasn't nothing about your socks."

The question is—I think to myself as I'm going around the break in the sidewalk to my place—the question is: should I tell Dave about Dirk?

When I got in, I threw my jacket and purse on the chair and phoned Marg.

I says to her, I says, "I'm just as bad as what Tammy's Asshole is. I'm all right for a while and then all of a sudden I act like a maniac. That running after Dirk was like what a maniac would go and do. Maybe Asshole looks at young Matthew bleeding out of the side of his head and can't believe he done that, neither, after. Maybe he goes through a time where he thinks he could never do that again. And then he turns around and does it again!"

Marg said, "I'll tell you the difference between you and Tammy's Asshole. You're working on your problem, and you're making headway. Asshole ain't. He's just going around in circles, the way we all used to."

"What makes you think I'm making headway?"

"What you got with Dave is a million times better than what

you ever had with any man before. True or false?"

"True till I screwed it up."

"And your job is way better. Plus, you know a lot more. And you got a bunch of true friends who know your whole story. You can figure things out better. If that ain't all progress—" She pauses. "Look, you slipped this once. But you're going to handle yourself better from now on. You're bound and bent. You got the tools. You're going to do better. You're not screwing up no more. That's what you got to tell Dave. Level with him. Tell him what you're up against. Swear to God you can do better. You can!"

Sally calls again to say God bless us.

Tammy calls. Says I'm not like Peter the least bit.

I'm so wound up by this point, I can't think who the hell Peter is.

Marg's in the background calling, "Tell her you mean Asshole. She won't know who the hell Peter is."

By the time I was finally done on the phone, I didn't have time to eat or nothing. I just ran and took a bath, shaved my legs, done what I could with my hair. Jenny says my hair is "independent" (The words she comes out with!). Did put on my pink sweater.

I was sitting on the edge of the bed pulling my second sock on when I heard him on the stairs. I sit there, froze, eh? Sock hanging off of my toes. Trying to hear what kind of a way he's walking up them stairs.

He ain't in a hurry.

He taps on the door, quiet. Figures he has to knock, now, on our own door!

I hopped out there, whipped that door open, and grabbed him in my arms like the end of the world. I told him everything before I even fixed my sock. Door standing open. Chilly spring evening air from the stairwell on my half-bare foot. Me talking into the front of Dave's jacket, telling stuff I would have never thought I could tell a man.

Just right out with it. No lead-up, nothing. How would you anyways? How would you lead up to telling your boyfriend that your one little fault happens to be you're awful apt to sleep around?

Dave, he just stands there in the mud room.

I'm talking to his third jacket-dome, telling it I'm so frigging sorry and I'm going to work sixteen times as hard and do what the shrinks say and whatever it takes to be a decent woman for his and Jenny's sake and my own sake too and I can, I can, I know I can, if he can only forgive me, which why would he?

After that, I didn't have the nerve to raise my eyes up and look him in the face.

He just stands there, eh. I don't know what he's thinking. I'm too scared to look up. His arms are limp, hanging down at his sides. Them arms were always so quick to hug me, before.

My foot's cold. There's a robin singing.

He'll turn around now without a word and go. Or maybe he'll say some word first, that'll burn. I've done it now. I've threw away my lucky ticket.

Finally Dave says, "So it wasn't my fault?"

His fault?

I said, "You in the public works department?"

When I hear a snort of a laugh, I glance up at his face. Dave's nice eyes. Full of pain. That I've caused him.

He says, "Are we going to spend the weekend in this mud room?"

So I thought to let him in. We sat down at the kitchen table.

I could never part with this table afterwards. I'm sitting at it now. Got my computer on it. It's an ugly old table. Legs made out of chrome. Top's a pale turquoise plastic with a design of like black doodle marks. But there's so much has went on at this table! Gingerbread princesses with silver buttons. Jell-O fish. All them Monday nights trying to fill in my homework sheets (What am I guilty of? What am I responsible for?). The morning after Josie got hurt, Marg sitting here with a notepad, making like a shopping list of what we had to do (Get boxes. Take shovels. Dig out plants. Hide plants. Call cops.). Dave's dad and Sally eating their eggs at this table while I whipped my stepping stones at the four walls, screaming.

Me and Dave sat. He says, "So you been fooling around on me?"

I look down.

"And you're telling me it's part of your trouble, that you're working on?"

I give a couple of little wee nods. I'm studying the table leg, where there's two metal parts that join to the rim of the tabletop.

I tell him in a low voice, "It's like I fell off the wagon."

"And your group there is supposed to help with this?"

"Well, this and all kinds of troubles. They're coping mechanisms. Whether you drink, or sleep all day, do drugs, hide in the house, or like what I done. It's from before."

"Before what?"

So that's when I finally tell Dave I was a childhood sex abuse survivor.

Dave's a long time taking it in. Asks questions and then just sits there, tracing around the doodle pattern in the table with his big finger.

He can't believe it. Albert, my father, that he had a beer with on Christmas! Seemed like a regular old man!

"It's dirt common, Dave. There's millions of them abusers walking around looking regular."

He didn't say nothing more for a long time.

I'm with this red-hot anxiety feeling in my chest. What does he think of me now? Can he ever feel the same? It never even entered my head to hope that he could understand about the buzz. Me backsliding into being addicted to the adrenaline rush buzz. If he could ever understand that, he'd see that it hadn't been nothing personal against him.

Finally he says, "So you're just like Jenny?"

I can't look at him. Kitchen window's a square of purple blue behind his shoulder. Robins out there singing as the dark comes on. Working overtime to raise up their next generation to fly.

"Rose?"

"Yeah?"

"I was saying you're in the same boat as what Jenny is."

"Was, when I was a kid."

"Why didn't you never tell me this before?"

I says, "Didn't want to make you sad about how the world is, Dave. Didn't want you looking at every kid you seen and wondering if they were going through hell."

"You got no business to try and look after how I see the world! That ain't up to you. You got to just level with me."

I heard like an echo. Rose, can you give us an example of something that is not your responsibility?

So I done my best to level with him. We spent a long time there talking about Dad and Mom and me and Sandra. I didn't hold back nothing.

I was thinking, what the hell. This is the last time I'll ever see him anyways.

Then Dave, he jumped in with a different topic. Started telling me the whole nine yards on his drug dealing days.

Me and Dave in the kitchen, screwed up humans, putting all our faults and our shame on the table. We didn't turn the light on.

Dave said there was something about the quick buck you can get for weed, eh. He said he's working steady with Tom now. Likes the work. Pay is fine. Everything's going good. And yet, he says, a guy he used to know come up to him sideways the other day after work, offered to let him in on something.

I looked at Dave, sharp. Not that it was my place to say nothing. If he was going to tell me he was backsliding, selling dope again, what was I going to say? Tsk, tsk?

Dave said he didn't go for it.

"You're better than me," I says.

Now, what he was wondering, he says, is whether the way

he felt dealing would be anything along the lines of the way I felt sleeping around.

I can't believe this man. He's trying to understand! That's what he's talking about this for! He's trying to understand where I'm coming from, what could've made me go and be unfaithful to him. He's not hitting me over the head with a kitchen chair like maybe I deserve. He's thinking of how he's not perfect himself, and he's trying to get a feel for what made me do what I done!

I tell him there's nobody else like him in the world. I tell him I love him dearer than I do another human being outside of Jenny. I tell him he's the kindest person, even to try and think how to understand, after what I've did!

We sit there listening to the birds' music.

"Wanting to sell dope, eh, it's not even for the money anymore," he says. He looks down, sheepish, and he says, so quiet I can hardly hear him, "It's for—I get sort of a buzz."

"Yeah!" I says. "Like the air changes?"

He looks up quick.

"That's a way to put it."

"Everything's sharper? Your heart's pounding?"

Dave nods, eager. "Yeah. Yeah."

"Meredith our group leader calls it 'heightened intensity.' Says it's from adrenaline."

It's pretty near dark. We're these two shapes, and our two voices are coming out in bursts. Naming what it feels like to get a rush off something bad.

"It feels real, real good for a minute!"

"Oh yeah! But then you feel like shit for months."

"That's the truth."

We talk about that we want to make good lives. If it's nothing but adrenaline, some chemical in our blood, that makes us act bad, we don't want that. We can do without them couple of high minutes. We agree there's ways to feel good for a long, long time. Like loving each other and Jenny. Regular decent life don't give us a buzz, but it adds up to a damn sight more in the long run.

My anxiety red-hot chest is turning hot pink and tingly with hope bubbles. Dave puts his hand on mine.

I look up, and there's three stars framed in the window.

The night Dave got to know the worst about me and still liked me anyways!

Three stars in the window! Me, him, and Jenny.

Them stars seemed to come back to me like the chorus of a song because of the three stars Josie showed me, so long ago now, in her picture of her precious town.

Nine o'clock in the morning, nothing would hold Jenny. She got one look at Dave's truck out there waiting for her. Bust out the front door like the bronco out of the chute. I'm trying to hang on to her while the foster care lady's saying goodbye.

"See yous around five!" I call to her over my shoulder while Jenny's dragging me down the front steps.

Dave jumps out of the truck.

The two of them make a run for each other. It would have did anybody's heart good to see. He catches her up into the air, with her little yellow sneakers waving. She clamps her arms around his neck fit to choke him.

He'd have choked to death, cheerful, sooner than loosen her off.

28.

So that's how me and Dave got back. I told him a thousand times how I was sorry and wasn't never going to do nothing like that again. He told me he was sorry for the dealing and wasn't never going to do that again. We said we could help each other.

We had a good morning down by the bay with Jenny. She showed Dave how she could skip stones now. He told her he learned from the same old man that taught her. She stood there with her feet planted, looking up at big Dave and trying to take in the idea that he had once been a little kid like her. And old Al was his father!

When she was tired out playing on the shore, we went home and made pancakes. Dave and Jenny were settling down to read their story. She had to remind him what had been happening when they left off three weeks ago.

He says, "There was a flood coming, wasn't there?"

"No," she tells him, like he's slow, "it's the Australian outback. What's coming must be a fire."

"Oh, fire, yeah," he says, and he winks at me over her head, as much as to say, so smart!

He read to her a long time. She fell asleep with her head against him, there on the couch. Fire out of control on three sides and a mountain behind, but she's safe with Dave. We let her nap.

We had a lot of patching up to do.

Dave was awful pissed at Dirk. Wanted to go punch his lights out.

I says, "There's no use blaming him any more than we need to be blaming anybody who bought what you were selling. This problem here is between my own two ears. It's me, Dave," I says. "I can control this. And if I don't, it's my own fault."

I told Dave alls I could about it after we'd took Jenny back that night. We went for a long walk. I told him I figured I could handle this type of thing now, if he could give me another chance. I told him I was getting sorted out.

It felt good to finally find something that was my own fault. My childhood was not my fault. But the thing with Dirk, that was. And I could do better. It was up to me.

Sunday night come too quick, and Dave was back out in the mud room, sticking his feet into his boots. Took us a half hour to say goodbye. He said he'd come back Friday.

"You know, eh Rosie, that you've hurt me bad."

I'm crying. I mumble about being ashamed.

He says, "My mom and dad always told me there was no harm in being ashamed of what I done wrong. They said that's how people learn. If you do something that ain't fit for a good person to do and feel real ashamed of it, that's how you come to do better next time."

"That's like what Meredith tells us at Group. We're not to be ashamed of ourselves, only of our wrong actions."

Dave says, "That's right. Nobody says you need to be ashamed of yourself here, honey. Just of what you done wrong."

"Oh, Dave!"

"Same as me. After we had that close one with Brent there and yous had to help me cover it up quick and I lost all that money and could've gotten sent to jail… I was so ashamed of that mess! I finally smartened up. I thought, fuck this, I thought, this has came damn close to wrecking my whole life. What if I got sent to jail? What about Rose and Jenny and Dad? I thought, I'm done with this!"

I hugged him and kissed him, thanking my stars he wasn't going to be in no jail.

He says, "I guess you're still going to that Tuesday night group?"

"You bet."

"Keep on," he says. "They'll get yous sorted out."

I watched him clump down the stairs, his camo hunting jacket and his ballcap there. He looked back up at me from the downstairs door.

How could he love me? But it was plain to see he did. My lucky, lucky ticket!

It was the grace of God, according to Sally on the phone. It was the merciful kindness of the everlasting Father.

I says, "So, Sally," I says, "where was this merciful God when we was kids?" We had a long argument on the phone about the mercy of God, which don't always come when it would do the most good, seems to me.

Sally, she tells me I ask the wrong questions. She says I'd be farther ahead to accept the goodness that's coming my way now and thank the Lord for it.

"I'll take it," I says. "And I'm glad of it. But if I thank anybody, it's more likely Dave and you and Josie, Dave's dad, Marg, Frances, Meredith, more than God."

"Well, who do you figure sends you all them people to love you and help you out and show you the way?"

"Same place that sends me all the ones that screw me up."

"You're living in outer darkness there, Rose, where there's going to be wailing and gnashing of teeth," Sally tells me. But she don't sound like it bothers her. She's so glad me and Dave are back on the rails.

I can hear Dave's dad in the background, asking questions. Sally tells him that everything's blessed peachy.

The rest of them all called too, and I was on the phone half the night, telling my good news.

I went to see Josie. There she is, in her wheelchair by the window. She turns to me. Smile on her like noon sun on a chrome bumper.

Give her a hug. No need to tell her nothing. She knows. I just take a seat beside her and sit there, the both of us grinning.

"Josie?" I says, after a while. "Friday morning, about seven-thirty, I was so worked up about the weekend coming and scared what was going to happen with Dave, I shut my eyes and tried to talk to you. Did you, by any chance, like pick that up...?"

She reaches down into a carry sack she's got hanging on her chair there. Takes a snapshot out of a pink envelope. The Strone town fountain in spring with a bed of yellow tulips!

Between her and Sally, they can just about talk me into seeing the everlasting arms of mercy holding up the world.

She goes fishing in her bag again. Comes up with a smooth stone. I sat quiet, watching her rub her see-through thumb on the stone.

Now, how in the world could she know about the tulips? I wondered over it for a few minutes. Then I just give a shrug, the way Josie does herself.

Her thumb was still running over the smooth stone. In my mind, I started to see bright gold, flickering wave patterns and criss-cross patterns, like light playing on the bottom of a lake. I bet she was doing that to my brain. Few months ago I would've jumped out of the chair and shook myself to get rid of the weird feeling, told her to quit messing with my head. But, by this point, so many weird things had happened that I sort of give up.

I relaxed there, breathed deep, let my body go limp, my arms heavy on the chair arms, watched Josie's thumb rub the stone, looked at the bright ripples it was casting on the back of my mind, thinking, okay. Don't care if it's weird. Don't care if I understand how or why. Josie was with me some way when I was looking at yellow tulips last Friday, praying for Dave to still love me. Josie's showing me the bright lake rippling over the gold sand.

A story Sally likes to tell come floating through my mind. Suffering person come up to Jesus Christ once, begging to get healed. JC's weird question was, "Do you want to be healed?"

Such an odd question. And what's it got to do with Josie's thumb and the tulips and the lake ripples?

Didn't know. Didn't care. Sat there letting the bright little waves wash over me, thinking, okay. There's bad in the world, but there is also good. There's friendship and there's luck and there's love. Ain't my job to figure it all out. Just have to let it be. Okay. I want to be healed. I want to be healed.

I tried to talk to Dave, before, about what would happen if my sister Sandra went ahead and married Ian. Dave, he never could take it serious. Always said Sandra was going to wake up any minute and call off the wedding. The wedding was getting close now, though. And no signs of her waking up.

"Call her again," Dave says, the next weekend. "Set her straight."

"I already talked myself blue in the face."

"She can't be really going to."

I says, "She is really going to!"

"No way."

"She is, Dave."

"You got to tell her not to."

"What do you think I been telling her for the last six months?"

"Talk her out of it."

"I can't."

"But, if she marries the prick, they'll never let her take Jenny back."

"No, they won't."

"It don't hurt to try again," he says.

Well it did hurt, as a matter of fact. But I tried. Saturday morning. Dave was standing in the kitchen, in his bare feet, backing me up. Sandra's phone was ringing. I says to Dave, "I said it all fifty times."

"Hello?"

"Sandra," I says. "Listen, could we meet someplace?"

She agreed to that so I went down to the coffee place. No Sandra. Waited half an hour, playing with a spoon. I pushed on the bowl end and made the stem end go up and down.

I'm wasting my precious weekend afternoon. Dave's hanging around the apartment and here I am sitting here, eh. I'm just about fed up when she shows up. I don't waste no more time. I start right in and tell her she's got to leave Ian.

"What would I have in the world if I left Ian?"

I says, "You'd be ten times happier, for one thing."

"I'd have nothing," she says.

"Your daughter is nothing?"

"I mean," she says, "that I'd have no love in my life, nothing to live for."

"Sandra, he's not the only man on the planet earth. And even if he was, a man is not the only thing you can live for."

"He wants to marry me."

"Another one could want to marry you."

"Ha!" she says. "Sure."

See? That's the whole thing right there, the way I'm starting to look at it. Self-worth, they call it at Group. Sandra's got a bad case of low self-worth.

I sat there staring at my coffee mug. I know every stinking detail of how her self-worth got to be what it is. I looked at her mouth, the way she was chewing on her lip. I could see our old man's hairy dick shoving into that mouth when she was no bigger than Jenny (bad sights list). Her gagging (bad sounds list). The smell of Dad's ass (bad smells list). I reached across and tried to take her hand, but she shook me off.

I was trying to take away the best thing in her life, the way she was looking at it. I was trying to screw up her one chance at happiness.

There's other stuff to live for, besides a relationship. I tried saying that again.

"There's no point to nothing if I'm not with him. He makes me feel alive."

That alive feeling. The buzz. What a person will do to get that! I tried to give her some idea what they do for you at Group.

Sandra, she said I seemed more lighthearted before I started in with the damn Group.

"Lighthearted? I was just never talking about nothing serious. I was Minimizing my problems."

"Alls that group's did for you, Rose," she says, "is it's made you a pain in the butt. Now you think you know it all and you want to tell everybody else how to run their life."

Sandra was mad at me, but she wanted to cry too.

"You used to just be there for me!" she says.

"Look," I says, "I could be home with Dave. He's got to leave this aft. But I'm sitting here with you."

"You won't even come to my wedding!"

"I'll come to your wedding—"

She looked up quick, but I wasn't done my sentence.

"I'll come to your wedding the day you find yourself a decent man to marry. Not a pervert like what our father was!"

People was starting to turn around and look at us. I didn't give a shit. I was started.

I says, "There's a woman called Pam at the shelter."

Sandra looked at me. She quit chewing her lip.

I prayed.

There was this space of time. The sound and the smell of coffee brewing. Clinking of cups and spoons. Sandra looked like her mind could be opening a crack. I'm sitting there trying to haul some kind of mercy into that little space, get some kind of a foot in the door that looked to be opening.

I didn't want to say a word for fear it would be the wrong word. I just sat there looking into her scared eyes, praying to Sally's merciful God.

If Sandra would please oh please come to her senses, throw Ian out, and take Jenny home, she'd be in a group, doing her sheets and figuring stuff out. We'd be here having coffee, talking about the time she almost married a child molester, shaking our heads over it. She'd find lots to live for, get a hobby, some friends, a job, raise up her beautiful little one the way the robins does, singing.

I wanted that for her so bad I could taste it.

Sandra says, "You're better than me."

I told her it wasn't a dog show. Nobody better than the next person. We're all just in here trying. Anybody can make up their mind to try. If she'd just please try—

Sandra grabbed her bag. Said she was trying for a new life. Her own frigging sister wouldn't even be her frigging bridesmaid. Stomped out. Left me to pay.

When I got home, Dave was right at the door to see how things had went.

I shook my head. Hadn't been the day for no amazing grace.

Dave banged his fist on the mud room wall. Busted the drywall.

I stood there looking at the insulation, thinking about what kind of a wall I always hit with Sandra, what kind of insulation.

29.

SO THEN, FINALLY, Dave seen that Jenny wasn't never going home. I wanted me and him to adopt her. I never dared to say it yet, though. I could see there was a lot of stepping stones between here and there.

Me and Dave were only just starting to patch things up between us. I still had to show that I could act right, myself. Jenny was better off where she was than she would be with me if I was going to run after creeps. Dave had to make sure that he was done with the drug dealing. We had to figure out if we were moving back north. If so, I'd need to find a job up there. And, before we could do anything, we had to, as Meredith says, rebuild trust.

"It's interesting, ain't it, eh?" Dave says one afternoon. "Josie and her second sight."

"Yeah. It's something."

"That's what got Sally living back north, looking after Dad."

I told Dave about the picture of the yellow tulips.

Dave says, "And she pictured me as the handyman, remember? You were just telling me about that when the landlord called me up and offered me my first paid handyman work. I felt like Josie opened the door. Alls I had to do was walk through it."

"Tammy and Sally are still always talking about that hotel thing. Even Marg. She don't much believe in it. But she'll mention it when she needs a pick-me-up."

It was after that talk, on Sunday night just when Dave was

packing up to leave, that I got my nerve up to finally tell him I had a picture of my own. I told him I could picture me and him adopting Jenny.

Dave, he stopped with his shirt half-folded. This was only our second weekend back together after all that had went on. Dave looked at the red plaid shirt in his hands. "Well," he said, "maybe someday." Said he thought we had a ways to go before we could make plans like that.

He had every right to say it, so I didn't cry till after he'd went.

He'd be down next weekend. We'd talk it over some more, he said. He give me a pat on the shoulder.

I said that would be fine.

He went.

Then I ran around the apartment and screamed. *Why did I do that with Dirk? Why did I go and do that?* Now everything was different between me and Dave. No telling when or if he could ever feel the same again.

I started cleaning stuff. There was me with the floor mop, bawling, punishing the grey vinyl peel-and-stick floor tiles in the entryway. I'm scrubbing back and forth. Can't believe I screwed Dirk. Can't believe I was such a frigging weak useless piece of crap. Pretty near took the finish off them tiles.

Lunchtime on Monday, Marg come over to bring me a doughnut, since she was out sneaking one herself. (Said not to tell Tammy.)

"I've went and wrecked it all," I says to her. "Now he don't trust me. How could he?"

"Give him time, Rose," Marg says, licking her fingers. "You just got to show him you're not going to do nothing like that again. It's going to take some time. You'll just have to treat him right, keep on getting yourself fixed up and wait patient."

Patient, eh? When I got home that night, I made myself a new stepping stone: *Patience*. I stood on it. Stood on one foot and the other, watching the sky out the window go from pink to mauve to that dark blue.

Patient. Okay. Patient as a stump, that's me, I'm telling myself. But I can tell yous, I was none too patient inside. If everything could just be back to how it was before! If Dave could just forget this ever happened! If he could just hurry up and trust me again!

Leaned my elbows on the kitchen counter. Wondered how long it would take. Next weekend? Four more weekends? I was fighting off a feeling that trust could be an awful slow-growing type of a plant.

To practise being patient, I decided I was going to stand there till I could see a star.

I never watched a star appear before. It took so frigging long to come, but it was nice when it finally showed. Silver tip of a needle, sewing one bright stitch into the dark.

When I was over to see Jenny, we took the rocking chair out on the porch to wait for a star. I told her it takes patience, waiting and watching for good things to come. (There's me, eh, talking like I'm this wise old aunt. Half the things I tell Jenny, I only just found out myself the day before.)

Jenny pointed to the dark. "That's like me."

I looked where she was pointing. Couldn't see nothing. I says, "Is there a star there somewheres?"

"No."

I held her to me. Her hair smelled good. Her head was buried just under my chin. "Are you telling me you're like the dark?"

She nods. "Nobody should see me."

"Why shouldn't nobody see you?"

"Anybody, Ann Toes."

"Okay. That," I says. "Why is that?"

"Because I should be ashamed of myself."

"Who told you that?" I'm thinking, fuck, if they're telling her that here, I'm going to kidnap her!

Into my collar, she whispers, "Mommy."

I talked to the social worker (Mrs. B., Jenny called her, and that's as much name as I ever had for her). She was all right.

She told me that, yes, Sandra had been over to see Jenny this weekend. No, nobody in the foster home would be telling Jenny that she ought to be ashamed. And, yes, she'd have a word with Sandra about it.

I said, "Look," I said, "my sister is so screwed up. You really got to keep an eye on her with Jenny."

They sure didn't, though.

Couple of weeks later was the long weekend in May. The weekend of the wedding. Dave said the sign out in front of the hall should read *Congratulations, Sandra and Dickhead*.

"*Congratulations, Dickhead and Stupid*," I says. Because, the way I see it, she's just about as bad as him.

I was to take Jenny with me on the bus to Strone. We were going to spend that weekend with the folks back north. Dave, he'd found a turtle Jell-O mould. Told Jenny he had a surprise for her.

Which reminded me, I heard Dave had a surprise for me too, a while back. Hadn't saw it yet. When I asked him about that on the phone, he got quiet. So I dropped it.

I show up to get Jenny on Saturday morning.

Foster woman says, "Come on in, Rose. Jenny's in the sun room. She's been happy all morning just with a blanket and the chairs in there. She made a blanket fort and crawled in under it with her rabbit. I haven't heard another peep out of her. Jenny! Look who's here!"

No answer.

The woman winks at me. She puts on a voice and says, "Now I wonder where Jenny and Timothy Rabbit are!"

I play along. "I bet they're in the fridge." I open it. "Nope. I guessed wrong."

We play like that for a while, look a few more foolish places to let Jenny think we can't guess where she is. But me and Jenny got a bus to catch so I say, "Hey! I wonder if she's in the blanket fort!"

No answer.

"Okay, Jenny. Come on out now, honey. We got to get going. We're going to see Dave."

No answer.

I look in the blanket fort and laugh because we've been playing this game by ourself. Nobody in there.

Foster woman says, "I dropped that fern and spilled the dirt. On the cream carpet, of course. Jenny must have gone up to her room when I had the vacuum on and I couldn't hear her. Or maybe she's in the den."

We looked those places and met each other back in the kitchen. We'd quit laughing.

Woman hurried down to the basement playroom. I checked all the bedrooms. I looked in the upstairs bathroom. In the closets. Behind the shower curtains. We searched the house. We started running. We looked in the garage. I searched the backyard, under the bushes, around between the house and the garden shed, up the ladder in the playhouse, under the porch, while the foster woman was doing the same out front. When we'd looked everywhere, we come running back into the kitchen, panting, and stared at each other.

She starts calling the police, and I take off.

I got a feeling I know where to look. She's been told ten times that it ain't happening, but Sandra's been going on and on about having her heart set on Jenny for a flower girl at her frigging wedding.

I run the five blocks to Sandra's. I pound up the stairs. I knock. No answer. Still have a key. Use it.

Sure enough, there's a fancy dress hanging in the kitchen. Jenny-sized but grown-woman style. Silver, slinky, shiny. (Sandra hasn't got the first clue about kids, eh—that a little girl ain't a woman.) I'm just about to holler for Sandra. Something stops me. The bedroom door's shut.

Why would that be?

I kept quiet. Went along the hall. Nobody in the bathroom

or the front room. If Sandra and Ian were here with Jenny, what would they be doing in the bedroom with the door shut?

Then I heard a sound off my bad sounds list.

I'm standing there in Sandra's kitchen, looking at that little adult dress, thinking, if I ever do one right thing in my life, let me do it now. If Jenny really is in there, don't let me scare her. Don't shame her. Walk into that bedroom and do the right thing, whatever that is.

That sound. I felt like I knew that sound. I felt like Ian was in there with Jenny.

Oh god, and my sister was probably out getting her toenails painted or something.

Ian's a fair-sized man. Me, I'm only five foot four.

I give myself that half-second breather. For a person that don't specially believe in anything, I seem to pray a lot.

I put my hand on the bedroom doorknob. It was locked.

What now?

I picked up the kitchen phone and I dialled 9. I stopped. If I dialled 9-1-1, what would happen to Jenny? I didn't want no siren scaring her, no police making her feel like a criminal. I thought it would be better to get her out of there myself, gentle and quiet, if I could.

With the phone in my hand, I walked back over and stood near the outside door. I called out "Hello?" like I'd just came in the house and didn't suspect nothing. I'm thinking, I'll give him three seconds to get up and open that bedroom door. If he don't, I'll make the call.

Silence.

"Anybody home?"

Nothing. Why don't Jenny answer?

"Ian?"

A man's voice. "Who's there?"

I said it was me and I come to shake hands with him on his wedding day, wish him all the best. Oh thanks, he says, but he's just out of the shower. Could I wait a minute? He said, cool as you please, for me to take a chair.

The old adrenaline was cranked up full. My head had went clear. I could see real plain, hear real sharp. There's a pair of orange flowered oven mitts laying on the stove. I'm staring at them like I never seen an oven mitt. The thumbs is dirty and one's burnt.

I could hear Ian getting something off a coat hanger. Some other little sound I don't know what it would be, like a sort of a muffled door closing sound and some funny shuffling around. Why don't I hear Jenny, if she's here?

Then there's the groom strolling into the kitchen in his bathrobe. He don't look to me like he just got out of no shower. There's a cobweb hanging on his hair.

He went to shake hands.

I wasn't touching him. "Where's Jenny?"

"Jenny? Oh, she's not here."

I shot past him into the bedroom, phone in my sweating hand. There's nobody in the bedroom.

I can hear him from the kitchen, asking what I'm doing. "Sandra's out," he says. "And what would Jenny be doing here?"

He sounds so casual I have one flash where I wonder if I'm wrong.

The white duvet is messed up. Purple sheets ain't. Looks like the bed's been made once today. Just the cover's been used. Ian's standing in the doorway. He's tall, a bit overweight. He's got fair, thin hair and a red face.

I hear a sound like a mouse makes in a wall. One tiny little scratch. But it wasn't no mouse. That was all the proof I needed.

Adrenaline's got its place. I heard that scratch, knew it was Jenny, knew what I had to do and done it, all in one flash. I flew out of that bedroom, ran past Ian, shouting to him that I was going to puke. Ran down the hall. Locked myself in the bathroom. Made a loud retching noise while I dialled. Flushed the toilet to cover while I whispered the address. Told them to send police quick.

Then I strolled back down the hall, and I sat in the kitchen with Ian, my heart pounding. Said I had a touch of flu. Felt okay now.

"So, what kind of finger foods you planning on serving this afternoon?" I says to him.

He looks me up and down. His eyes are narrow.

"Little toast things," he says.

"Oh, yeah? Those are always nice," I says, and I can see he's starting to relax.

"With like cheese on them," he says. "And pickles."

"Pickles too, eh?"

"There's a woman makes up these trays," he says.

"Whereabouts does she work out of?"

I feel like I been sitting there about a year. What the hell else can you say about cheese things and pickles? What's Jenny doing? Is she hiding under the bed? In the closet? What has he told her to make her so she won't call out even to me? She must be able to hear my voice. Did he threaten her or what? I asked if there was going to be devilled eggs. Where was them cops?

I heard the siren across town.

"So, Ian," I says, "got a new suit?"

Ian, he told me about his Salvation Army store three-piece suit, good as new for twenty bucks. Fits him like tailor-made, he says. I'm nodding, asking him what colour and listening to the siren turning up Maplewood.

"Fine blue stripe, eh? That'll look sharp."

Said he got some two-dollar shoes from the same place. I told him to make sure he took the two-dollar sticker off the bottom of them before he went and kneeled down at the front of the church.

Stupid the way your head works at a time like that. A picture flashed into my mind: Sally's God Almighty zapping him right through between the shoulder blades with a zig-zag cartoon bolt of yellow lightning. I let out one hysterical sort of a laugh.

Cops had the brains to shut the siren off before they turned on to this street. Ian's telling me how many cases of beer he's got in. When I hear the cops' boots on the stairs, I stand up and run.

I look in the bedroom closet. The scratch I heard sounded like that direction. Nobody there.

The cops are in the kitchen, asking who called. Ian's busy telling them we never called. So I run back out there and say, "Yes. I did." Because this here man is a child molester who I just caught with my little niece that he must have stole out of her foster care, I don't know how.

So then they're blocking the door, and they want to know where is the little girl. I run back to the bedroom. Now I can shout for her.

Nothing.

We looked high and low, the one cop and me. "Jenny!"

I checked again. Nobody in the closet. Nobody behind the curtains.

"Jenny?"

Nobody in the big dresser drawers. Nobody in the cedar chest—the hope chest, as poor Sandra always called it. Nobody in the bedding.

The cop says, "You sure there's a child here?"

"Shhh."

I thought I heard it again, the little scratch. It was coming from the closet. That's what I thought before.

"Over here!"

"We already looked in the—"

I whipped open the closet door, and then I could really hear it from up above.

Jesus! In the walk-in closet off that bedroom, there's a trap door to the attic. We pushed it up and we found her, naked, tied, gagged, stuffed up there, laying in the insulation.

I stood on a box, holding up the trap door while the cop chinned up and looked.

I thought how Sandra'd be dumping all them trays of cheese

things. The waste. I was froze stupid, thinking of that who-cares thing, while the cop lifted her down.

Then I got my brain working and grabbed a sweater of Sandra's to wrap her in. I didn't want that blanket off the bed. I didn't want that to touch her.

She'd been tied up with two belts. Sandra's green scarf was the gag. We got her loose, and I bundled her to me. She was like a rag doll, except that she turned her face and hid it against me.

My arm was getting wet.

The cop said, "She's bleeding."

30.

I PHONED DAVE from the hospital. Dave was for roaring down here to murder Ian. I says, "Drive careful, darlin'. We'll be at the hospital all night. Leave the gun."

The doctor said Jenny was tore down there, but they'd get her fixed up. He stitched her up and give her something for the pain.

Late in the afternoon, when Jenny was sleeping, I called Marg. She rushed right over.

Marg, she bent her head and put it against mine. We cried like that, with our foreheads together, hanging on to each other's heads. Marg's felt cool on mine.

"How does merciful God sit there in heaven and look at what happens on this earth?"

I could feel Marg shaking her head. We sat on the two chairs there at the foot of Jenny's bed, and Marg put her arm around me.

I looked at the pattern in the hospital floor. Hate terrazzo floors. All I'd been working for, trying to learn and grow and help Jenny, had come to this. There was no way to help her.

"This will make a mental case out of her!"

Marg says, "No. You'll help her. You and Dave and his folks. And us all. She'll get through it. Same as we done ourselves."

I let out a moan.

Marg says, "No. Okay. Not the same as us. Better than us. Way better. We come through it alone. She's got people to help her. That's going to make all the difference. You'll see. It will, Rose."

Jenny whimpered in her sleep.

Dave got there after supper. He was beside himself. I took him out in the hall to try to talk to him.

I was just laying my hand on his arm when the elevator opens and out walks Sandra. The bride, in her jeans, carrying a tray of food. Her hair's all glued up fancy. Must've been at the beauty parlour this morning.

Of course, there hasn't been no wedding. The groom's over town in a cell.

Dave stares at her with his eyes bugging out. Vein jumping in the side of his head. She walks past us into the room where Jenny is. Dave right behind her. He says, like he's choking, "You left her alone with him?"

Jenny moans and turns over in her sleep. She don't quite close her lips. Dave, he stifles himself.

Sandra holds the cheese things out to Marg.

"Well," Marg says, in the dead silence, "don't those look nice."

Dave's hands clench. He wants to send that food to the roof. He don't want to wake Jenny, though, so he holds on.

Sandra set the tray on the night stand. She looked at Marg and glanced sideways at me. She wouldn't look at Dave.

She hadn't even looked at the little soul laying there hooked to the IV bag with her hair spread out on the pillow. Jenny's hair is fine as fine. Josie used to tell her it's what the elfs knit their sweaters with, light little threads of gold and air. "You wear your air in pigtails," Josie used to say.

Dave's staring at Sandra like she's something which the health inspector had gave the thumbs down. If Dave had saw Ian right now, there'd have been bloodshed. And, to his way of thinking, Sandra's pretty near as much to blame. The muscles twitch across his shoulders and in his big hands.

I'm thinking, that's all we need is Dave to deck my sister. I put my hand on his shoulder.

Jenny opens her eyes. We jump over to her.

I says to her, "Jenny. Mommy's here."

Jenny looks past Sandra. She says, "Dave!" Dave, he leaned over her. She fell back asleep with him stroking her head.

I watched his working-man's hand smoothing them threads of air hair. I could've bawled just from how much I loved that man right then. Even if I didn't have a half dozen better reasons than that for bawling.

Jenny kept sleeping.

That night went on and on. We hung around. Tension in the room was working up to explosion level.

Dave, he kept glaring at Sandra.

She wouldn't look at him. Wouldn't look at me neither. Letting on she was reading some magazine.

Thank God for Marg sitting there like a concrete lion!

Sandra was holding up the magazine tight, looking over it at her shoes. Dave was twitching and pacing. Fiddling with the string on the window blind. Sitting down. Standing up. I didn't know how much longer he was going to be able to be there in that room with Sandra.

How could she let this happen? What was she? Mental? Was she evil? Did she not give a fart about her own child? I could see him dying to just shake it out of her. *The jerk was a proved pervert! How could she leave him with Jenny? How could she even stand the sight of him? Marry him? What kind of sick, shithead notion? Where was her brain? What the fuck was the matter with her?*

Dave started rubbing his right fist in his left hand.

I asked Sandra if she could use a coffee.

There weren't many people in the hospital cafeteria at that hour. We took a table in the back corner. First words out of Sandra's mouth, before I had even sat down, was, "You think it's my fault."

I took my time sitting down. Had a swallow of the coffee. Bitter and too hot. Tried putting some more sugar in it and stirred it around more than what it needed. Then I started in.

I give my sister the long version of what I think about fault. Let her have my whole frigging rockslide theory. We sat there till midnight, and I told Sandra more than she ever wanted to know about whose fault was what, in my opinion.

Sandra kept trying to interrupt me. But I wouldn't shut up for nothing.

I made pictures on a napkin. Circles for the generations. Arrows for trouble. Arrows from circle to circle. Down the generations. Circle for Grandma and Grandpa's day. Arrows raining down from them on to Dad and Mom in their day. I wrote *Sandra* in the next circle down. I showed arrows shooting down on her. I made *Jenny* in the next circle down and showed the same shit arrows shooting down on her.

I grabbed another napkin. "Take cows, for instance…"

I'm there, doing my damnedest, trying to draw cows. They take their right turns, in their day, standing watch over their little ones, faithful, while the earth rolls on from age to age.

Sandra's fed up. "What are you talking about? Are you calling me a cow?"

"No," I says. I pound my fist on the cow picture. "The cow watches what the frig is going on with her baby! The cow gives a care!"

I should have never said that. But Jesus Christ you'd think she never heard one word I said!

"I've did my best to be a good mother!" she says.

"You have not!"

"You don't have a clue what it's like being a mother."

"And our father and mother? I guess you think they done their best for us?"

"Don't keep dragging them into it! Poor Mom was a saint, and you're awful hard on Dad. He always kept a roof over our head." Sandra dug down in her purse for a Kleenex. "I was supposed to get married today, in case you forgot! Jenny was going to be our flower girl. I got the smartest little dress for her, and she didn't even want to wear it."

"What planet are you on, Sandra? Mrs. B. told you. You knew Jenny wasn't even supposed to be at the wedding because she is not safe anywheres near that frigging creep you want to marry!"

Sandra cried, and I sat and looked at her. She was crying over her ruined wedding day, a dress that never got put on, a garbage can full of cheese things and pickles. Herself, in other words. Not Jenny.

"Why did you leave Jenny with Ian?"

"I never thought she'd do that to me on my wedding day."

I says, "So, according to you, what happened today was not Ian's fault or your own fault? It was a child's fault? She's the one in charge?"

"She likes it."

"She likes getting tore open, gagged and threw, naked, into the mouse shit in a filthy attic?"

"She goes looking for Ian to touch her dirty. She'll slide right up to him and stand there, pushing against him. But I thought that, on my wedding day—"

"Ian is old enough to know what's right and wrong. Jenny ain't."

"So you are saying it's my fault!"

"I never said nothing about you at all."

"That's what you're thinking."

"I'm not thinking about you!"

Sandra can't get that. She says, "But you think it's my fault."

I shoved my chair back and stood up. "Alls I know is: grown people have to look after kids."

What was the use of trying to talk to her? I went to take my cup back. I wasn't going to drink that lousy coffee. Cold now anyways.

Sandra follows me. She says, "I'm not letting a kid run my life!"

I just look at her.

She says, "I got a chance to get a husband."

"And you don't give a fart what kind of a human being he is?"

"If it wasn't for her, he'd be perfect. He's fun. He's good-looking. He loves me.... You don't care about me, Rose. Alls you care about is her."

I says, "There's nothing I can do for you."

"What's that supposed to mean?"

I says, "The day you decide to work on your own life, that's the day you're going to know what I mean."

"You want me to go to one of them whiners' groups and tell some shrink my life story."

"Yes, I do."

"What the hell for?"

"So you won't be so frigging screwed up! I can't explain it. They build you up inside, so you're not so needy."

"You talk so weird now."

"I've got some new words. It makes me so I can figure this kind of stuff out better."

Sandra says, "I'm going to the hall to take down the bells and streamers. Will you come and give me a hand?"

I said I was going to stay here.

"She's got Dave and Marg both sitting there. Jeeze, it's just a few stitches."

I said I was staying here.

Sandra stomped off. Mad because she was going to have to take down the white paper bells by herself. She was having such a bad day. I wasn't supporting her.

31.

THE NEXT FEW MONTHS there, after Jenny got hurt, it's like everything changed gears. The days and nights we spent watching with her, after she got her fever....

Okay, let me slow down long enough to tell yous. Jenny got an infection. They couldn't get it to settle down. Fever went sky high.

Marg and Tammy took turns sitting with her in the daytime. I hardly ever went home. Right after work, I'd grab a bun or something from the grocery store on the way to the hospital. Dave was there every minute he could be. Twice, he drove down after work, sat up with her all night and drove all the way back to Strone in time to go to work in the morning. His cousin-in-law, Tom, who Dave works for, he found out about that. Said for Chrissake. And give him some days off with pay.

Jenny lay in the white sheets there. Her skin was dry and burning. She wasn't herself. Talked crazy. Kept saying something about a zipper between her legs. Begging me to do up her zipper.

I told the girls not to say nothing about it to Josie. No good upsetting her. But of course Josie don't need telling.

One day Marg went to see Josie and she said, "Talk about the lake."

Took Marg a while, trying to talk to Josie about the lake and Josie shaking her head.

Josie finally said, "For the fever."

So we done that. We talked to Jenny about ripples washing along the edges of Lost Gold Lake. Marg would tell her how clear and cool it is, how good to jump into. I told her about the fresh, watery smell of the breeze, the splashing sounds of the water by the shore. We like washed her hot skin with them thoughts, and she'd go limp and listen. "Are you seeing it, honey? Can you see like bright ripples in water?"

I wished the old Josie was there. She was so good at getting people to picture things. I tried to talk like her, the way she used to, putting in about the bands of bright and shadow rippling over the sand. I told Jenny to picture the deep green, the blue, the sparkle, and the shine, the fish moving through the green shadows of the trees.

Jenny opened her cracked lips. She whispered, "Underwater birds." So I knew she was right there.

Sally, of course, she was praying up a storm. She come down with Dave the second weekend.

I said, "The north climate there must suit you, Sal." She was looking just great.

Dave says her and his dad have got a vegetable patch planted, enough for an army. Sally says she's going to can and pickle, save them money next winter.

"Oh and Dave's dad has picked out the site for our hotel," she tells me.

"Has he picked out who's going to give us the money?"

"One thing at a time," Sally says. "Al's found a real good aquifer. He's got a marker drove in right where we should dig the well. Up on Macaulay's Point."

Me and Dave had to smile.

"It's too bad you can't pickle some of that attitude of yours," I says.

"Hope and faith by the jar," Dave says.

"So you got Dave's dad daydreaming about the hotel."

"Not but what Macaulay's Point would make a fine site for a lodge or something like that, if old man Macaulay would ever sell, which he won't," Dave says. "It's a beautiful place up there, ain't it, Sally Ann?"

"Oh, gorgeous! Water on three sides." Sally, she leaned forward in the hospital room chair, while Jenny was sleeping, and told us in this low voice (but eager, like a kid) all about what her and Dave's dad have been doing towards the hotel.

They're not fooling. They really think they're going to make it happen. See, Sally'd been buying beds and dressers at yard sales, for the hotel. Dave's dad got a new tractor, and he wanted Sally's trash furniture collection out of his barn. Dave's cousin Jan took a look at the stuff one day and got all excited. Said it was right in style. "Shabby chic," she said. Worth something. "Old junkers" is what Al called the paint-missing bits and pieces. Said they should have a bonfire. But anyhow, Jan got hold of some city lady, and Sally sold the stuff to her. Cleaned up. Opened a separate bank account for the money. Calls it the hotel account.

And then, when the Walmart site flooded, there, the way Al said it would, it was good for Al's water-witching business. He was putting the proceeds of that in the hotel account.

Now they're working on Dave's cousins. People are starting to chip in, Sally says.

Dave told me private, later, that they're thinking of it more as tipping Sally for looking after their Uncle Al. She's making it so he can stay on at home and they don't have to worry. But they say, "Here's a bit for your hotel, Sally."

That give me a shock.

"All them people know about the hotel?"

"Why not?"

"It was a secret."

"Can't get no place keeping it a secret," Dave says. "Tom's interested in the idea. He might even back it. A lodge, like. Somewheres by the lake. Tom's doing good, eh. If he decides to go for it, yous will get your hotel, all right."

"What?"

I woke Jenny up.

"What's wrong?"

"Nothing's wrong, sweetheart. Something's good. I'm happy."

"Oh." She drifted back off with a smile.

"If Tom comes in on it, it'll really happen?" I says.

"Can't see why not," Dave says. "He could likely round up the money."

"Does he seem real interested?"

"Can't never tell with Tom. He's got the poker face and he'll think things over careful, look at all the ins and outs before he says much. But my guess is, yeah, he's real interested."

So, anyways, we changed gears. Soon as Jenny's fever broke and the doctor said she was going to be fine, we went into action.

What happened to Jenny was a wake-up call. Shook some sense into me and Dave. We felt like we had to get our act together. Fix things for Jenny. It was plain to see nobody else was going to do it.

We told the Children's Aid that we wanted to adopt her.

They said they were prepared to start the process. There would be interviews and assessments. We said fine.

First weekend Jenny was good enough to travel, I took her back north. Dave met our bus.

He says to Jenny, when we're walking to the truck, he says, "Here's one for you to try on Grandpa Al. Ask him how the letter *A* can help a deaf lady."

Jenny's bobbing along beside Dave. She grins up at him, waiting on the answer.

Dave writes in the dust on the truck. Shows Jenny how the letter *A* can make *her hear*.

Riding in the truck, I was thinking too bad there wasn't no kind of a magic like that where my sister was concerned, no way to make her hear.

It was a business trip this time. Me and Dave were looking for a house, and I was looking for a job.

I hadn't been up there in a long time. I drove by the fountain where I made my wishes last year. Thought of Al's picture of the spiral staircase. Here we were coming around to the same place, but boy, was it different from last time!

The town was a real town, this time around. Mind you, it still had just enough of Josie's daydream in the air that I wasn't too surprised to see a *Help Wanted* sign in the window of the plumbing place.

"You're the one goes with Al's boy!"

That, and my experience and a good reference from work, was how I got the job.

Sally and Jenny had lunch going, when I come dancing back. They were making a picnic to eat on the dock.

Me and Dave looked at eight different houses that weekend.

"The third one there wasn't bad, with the workshop," Dave said when we were laying in bed under an old quilt at his dad's place that night. I always think of the cottage smell of that house when I look back on them days. It was sort of a damp smell, old wood and old fires in the fireplace.

That place didn't feel like *it*, though. It sat, bare naked, up on a hill. I didn't care for that. Looked lonesome and cold.

Dave grunted, but he didn't argue.

I never seen myself buying a house before.

"If you rent, you're just throwing her down the drain," Dave says. "We're better off to buy."

All this was brand new to me. Just the thoughts of having my own house!

I went to see Josie the next week, finally. I hadn't saw her the whole time Jenny was sick.

"Josie?" I says. I was feeling a bit cautious, not wanting to say she was a fortune teller, which pisses her off. But I had to ask her. "Is the hotel and everything ... is it really going to come true?"

Josie, she raised her chin like a wild horse, like as if she could smell our luck starting to change. Didn't look pissed off.

"It is, isn't it? It's going to come true!"

Josie nodded, but she looked sad.

But that was so great! Why would she be sad?

"Do you think we're leaving you? Of course, we wouldn't leave you here, Josie! We'll take you along with us. I'm planning to look for someplace up there for you."

That might be the only time I ever seen Josie surprised. Them eyes widened up.

"Some fortune teller you are!" I says. "You don't know shit about the future if you think we're ever going to leave you behind!"

She reached out her arms and we hugged, her sitting forward in the wheelchair. The bones of her spine sticking out.

I told her I'd look into chronic care homes where they could look after her, near to me and Dave. I told her we were looking for a house to buy.

"In a valley," was alls she said.

Dave got cranky, traipsing all over, turning down perfectly all right houses because they weren't in valleys. I knew enough by now, though, to wait.

"All things come to them who waits," according to Sally. We have to wait for God to answer our prayers. (Mind you, she don't give Him no peace until He does.) Josie, I don't know whether she prays, or what you'd call it, but she's sure got some type of a hotline to Whatever. She never gives up neither. Both of them two girls are full, to the hairline, with hope. Josie gazing at her pictures till she can see the times to come. Sally sewing, planting, collecting stuff, starting a hotel bank account, saying her prayers.

Sally don't just wait and pray. She hops into action. She "puts her hand to the plough," as she says.

I hadn't said nothing yet to Marg or the others.

Tammy was in a panic the next week, over the vice principal wanting to talk to her. Asshole was out of jail by this point, and Tammy, she figured she'd better call him up and get him to talk to the vice principal. Marg's over there holding Tammy's hand while Tammy phones the school. They say the vice principal is in a meeting, ask can he call her back. So Marg spends the whole day walking up and down in Tammy's apartment, waiting for the phone to ring, convincing her, forty times, not to call Asshole in on it.

"Turns out Matthew shoved some other kid in the schoolyard," Marg told me. "Nobody even got hurt. They give him a detention, and that was alls there was to it."

Me and Marg were sitting at the Times Square Restaurant. I invited her there. To tell her about us moving. Was not looking forwards to it.

Marg, she was busy catching me up on our friends, and I sat and listened, wondering what I was going to do without her.

"Darlene's met some prize over the internet again. This one's trying to get her to fly to Cancun."

"Oh, Jesus. Good thing she can't afford to."

"Yeah. Hey did you hear she won the fridge?"

"She did? Still got the fridge draw at the Pig, do they?"

How was I going to lead up to telling Marg? Finally just bust out with it. Said we were moving.

Marg looked at the cream mixing into her coffee. "Wish I was going too," she says.

I grabbed her hand. I says, "Why not? That would be so great! This will make it perfect!"

Marg looks into her mug. The cream in the coffee looked like them pictures you see of outer space, swirls of worlds. Marg said Tammy and Darlene would fall apart the minute she turned her back on them.

Marg got a deluxe sundae with peanuts and caramel sauce. She smiled at me over the top of Mount Whipped Cream there. "Tammy'd kill me if she seen this."

"Tammy still the calorie police?"

"Can't you tell? I'm fading to a shadow." Marg give her belly a pat. She's still a big fat woman. But definitely not so much as before. Marg gobbled down a few big mouthfuls. "I know this ain't doing me no good," she says. She looks at the sundae, sad. "I know it's a bad Coping Mechanism. It's what I done for comfort when I was an abused kid. I know it'll only make me ashamed of myself later. I know and yet I'm eating it."

Marg said she had to find some healthy Coping Mechanisms.

We were learning that in Group. Meredith said you got to find some good way to get comfort. It ain't rocket science. But, frig, it was news to us at that time. "Healthy Coping," Meredith calls it. We were to take notice of anything we liked to do that was not damaging and could give us a feeling of comfort. It was crucial to our ongoing mental health, Meredith said, that we find healthy sources of comfort to replace our old, damaging coping mechanisms. I made a *Healthy Coping* stepping stone that night.

I made it a turquoise colour because a comfort I'd took notice of was walking beside water. I noticed that lakes and streams, the colours and the motion of them, could comfort me any time.

I notice that I get comfort, now, out of working on writing this, too. I like trying to write stuff down. Time goes by, eh, and I'm sitting here, lost in space, trying to get yous to see what I'm seeing in my mind's eye. All them pictures, so bright and so dark. And the voices too, loud and soft, out of the past. Telling yous about the Times Square Restaurant there, I could smell the grilled cheese. Kind of fun. Maybe I'll even write about something else after I'm done telling this.

Whatever works for yous, eh. Long as it don't hurt nobody else, leave yous worse off after you've did it, jam your arteries, poison your liver, kill off your brain cells, blow up your love life, get yous arrested or beat to pulp, or make fat pigs out of yous.

Some people, it's model trains. Make theirself a little wee world they can handle. Some people, it's scrapbooks. Fight off death, so it don't wipe out all memory of theirself. Whatever gives yous a bit of comfort. Make sure yous find something like that.

32.

THE FOSTER HOME was in deep shit for losing track of Jenny that day. Not that they meant to. Sandra must have peered in the window and beckoned Jenny out or something like that, but it looked like the people might not get to be foster caregivers no more.

Jenny was at this other place now, for the time being, while me and Dave were scrambling to put together a real home for her. She hated the second foster home.

We had forms to fill in about how we were planning to provide for her, where she would be living, who was going to look after her while I was working and all that.

Too bad the good Lord don't make people fill in this type of information before He hands out the kids in the first place.

The Children's Aid had a lot of questions about Dave. I could see why. They got to watch they don't send Jenny into another abuse situation.

"They want a police check on you," I says to him one night on the phone.

There was this long silence. Finally he says, "There's nothing on paper."

"What's that supposed to mean?"

"Well, there's cops around that town that pretty well knew, eh, what I was into, before. They took me in a few times. But they never pinned nothing on me."

I started breathing again. "That'll be okay then, likely."

"Think so? They won't ask around?"

"I imagine they'd have to stick with what they've got in their computer or whatever." I hoped to God I was right.

Alls Dave can think of is we got to get Jenny out of here, get her where she's safe, before something else happens. He don't trust foster people to look after her. And why should he?

He keeps saying, "We got to get her out! We got to get her out!"

The foster home, they're not bad people. But there's always things that go through your mind, eh. You think, what if the foster woman turns her back and Ian jumps out and grabs Jenny? You remind yourself: Ian's in jail. Well, but what if some other jerk grabs her?

What if it's sort of true what Sandra said about Jenny looking for it? We learned in Group that kids do get conditioned to sex.

(I remember we all had that Question to Think About one night: how did your abuser condition you to accept sex? We were joking about it on the stairs, Josie calling out, "Don't forget to think about what kind of conditioner you use.")

I kept phoning the foster woman to ask her if she was being careful at the store, careful with any uncles that come to visit, careful, careful of our sunshine.

I went over there as much as I could. Jenny was miserable, missing the first foster people, not sure of nothing. Her mother wasn't coming to see her no more.

I told Meredith in Group once about the way Jenny first showed me a picture of what Ian was doing. Jenny couldn't say it. She didn't even know a word for it. But she could draw me a picture. Meredith told me about this whole line of shrink work that's about getting people to draw pictures. Not just kids, neither. Art Therapy, they call that.

The adoption people were talking about lining up a shrink to work with Jenny in our new place. Jenny really likes doing art. I suggested how about an art therapist.

It's funny, eh, the way they stare at a person like me if I

come out with anything like that. Like the way they'd stare at Josie's dog if he lifted his nose off the floor and said to get Jenny an art therapist.

Well, they did get her an art therapist. And maybe I got a couple of brownie points for thinking of it.

Anyways they told me everything for the adoption was coming along. I'd did good on the assessment.

Sandra signed her release papers. She was waiting for Ian to get out of jail, she said. She still wanted to marry him.

Dave did good on his assessment.

I went back north the next weekend to house hunt and talk to the people at the plumbing place. They wanted me to start in about a month's time. Dave, he'd been working on the baby-sitting angle. Lined up his cousin Jan, if that was okay with me. I was real happy with that but surprised. I wouldn't have thought to ask Jan. Why would she have to babysit, with Tom doing so good?

She don't have to, Dave tells me. She'd like to. She thinks it would be nice to have Jenny around, and little Alexander would like Jenny to play with.

The way these people think, eh. It blows me away. People that would take on an extra kid when they didn't have to! Jan would like to have Jenny!

Kids was a pain in the ass. That was the idea you grew up with in our family.

We had to write on the form where Jenny would be living. We needed a place quick. The "house in a valley" thing was getting past a joke.

Dave was in a mood after I turned up my nose at the fourth house that was good except that it was built on rising ground.

We went into the Chinese place for lunch.

Sally's waiting tables. There's old Elmer that's always sitting in the corner. He yells out, "David! You look so miserable anybody'd take you for a married man!"

Dave, he managed a smile. He was still pissed off, though.

Uncle Elmer there, he won't quit. He moves over to our table. "What's eating you, son?" he says.

Dave says, "House huntin'."

I was looking at the vinegar bottle, thinking back on the first time I ever come here, how John who makes the furniture had took hold of the vinegar and used it to stand for the church. And I was in a dream land, finding Josie's town.

And now here we were, coming here for real.

Real was different than dream. But I wasn't ready to throw dreams away. Dreaming's what's got us this far. We'd be fools to let go of it now.

"She's got this notion." Dave lets out a sigh. "She wants a house in a valley."

Elmer, he looks at me. They've wondered about me, right from the start, eh, because I knew what kind of pies there was here that day, and a couple of other things. Them stories ain't lost nothing, I'll bet, in a year's worth of telling.

"In a valley!" Elmer says, looking at me strange. "Got the second sight, have you?"

"Me, no," I says. "But we got this friend, she does. I never knew her wrong yet. She says pick a house in a valley."

"Well then," Elmer says, "I take that for a sign! You're meant to buy my place!" He gives us a big yellow, teeth-missing grin.

After lunch, we're bumping along a gravel road with Elmer, going to look at his place. Elmer's getting up in years. He's been thinking it's about time to sell. Says he can't find a woman who wants to move in with him and chop the wood for his stove. At least he won't have to move far, he tells us. There's a nice place right across the road.

The goosebumps come over me like I'd ran through a sprinkler. Josie! That's what you're up to!

"What kind of a nice place is right across the road?" I said that but I was pretty sure I knew.

I could see Dave's jaw relax. He was guessing too.

"Oh," Elmer says, "like a nursing home. You can have your

own apartment in the one end of it. Or if you need more doctoring, you can move into a room on the other side. County runs it."

We come over a hill and there they are below us, down in the valley, a little house looking cosy under the trees at the end of a long lane. And, right across the road from that, a nursing home.

The house was what the real estate people like to call "a handyman special." Elmer, he hadn't took a hammer and nail or a paint brush to her since his shoulder give out.

"Well, it's in a valley," Dave whispers to me, as if that was all you could say for it.

"How long you been having the shoulder trouble?" Dave says, standing in the hallway, wiggling the stair rail.

Uncle Elmer says, "I was shovelling out around the hen house door and something give, right in there." Elmer puts his left hand on his right shoulder joint. "Which year was that we had the big snow in April?"

We walk through to the kitchen.

"A while back, I guess, eh?" Dave says, looking around.

There was a tin pie pan on the floor in one corner Elmer had been using to spit in. Didn't always hit.

"If I'd knew you was coming," Elmer says, "I'd have did the dishes."

"Generally just do them up Saturday night while the water's hot?" Dave asks him.

Elmer give a nod.

"I see the hydro goes by here," Dave says. "You never got her hooked up, though?"

Uncle Elmer said, long as there was a sun in the sky, he wasn't going to pay nobody for light. And he had two good oil lamps, upstairs and down, for when the sun was down.

The best thing about Elmer's place was it was right on the lake.

There was an old screen door with a spring. Water pump by the porch. Upstairs had two rooms. I was standing in one looking out at the apple tree just outside the window, thinking that Jenny would like to wake up and see that. It was all out in blossom, white and pink. The buds is dark pink on the outside. They open up pure white. Made me think of hope and Sally.

A robin flew up with a dew worm, folded, tidy, in its beak. That's how they'll carry a worm to their babies. That parent bird flew up to a branch four feet in front of my face. They've got a little bright spark of a black eye, eh, and I'm telling you, it looked at me special.

You get a little nuts once you're started with this "seeing signs" business. Oh well. Don't cut off any type of seeing that you can do, I'd say. See alls you can. See signs and wonders. Look at a pink bud and see hope. Why not? Listen to the birds in the trees if they're telling you something.

Dave, he was in the other bedroom, shaking his head at the condition of the floor boards. Elmer had took and sawed a square right through them for the stove pipe.

"I suppose you like this dump?" Dave whispers.

I was lit up like one of Elmer's oil lamps.

Dave put his arm around me. "He better not want much for it." But I could see he liked it too. Against his own better judgement. He liked it.

We went away to think about it. Come back a second time. Took Jenny with us. First thing she done was she stood there inside the front door with her eyes shut, smile on her, right about from one pigtail to the other. She took a great big breath.

She says, "It smells like Grandpa Al's house!"

That hunt camp damp, the water nearby, mouse, wood going soft, ferns by the door.

I says, "We'll get her cleaned up and aired out. That's what we'll do this summer, eh, honey? You can help me and Dave."

"We have to be careful not to destroy the good smells," she says. "Can we please paint it all shades of yellow?"

"If we buy it, you can pick whatever colour you want for your room."

"How about this room here, Jenny wren?" Dave's looking around the front hall, which is no colour exactly and stained with wood smoke.

I can see we're likely going to buy this piece of crap, and I'm all bubbling happy.

I asked Elmer if I could take Jenny upstairs and show her around. She scampered up like a chipmunk. By the time I got there she'd already found the robins' nest.

"They're sleeping!"

Being little, she could see right in under there where the nest was tucked. I squatted down with her and we looked at the two fat babies, resting their beaks—big red-edged wedges like two pieces of cherry pie—on the side of the nest. We could see the little birds breathing.

"Two kids in the nest, eh?" I'm thinking to myself on the way downstairs. "Did I take my pill this morning?"

This seeing signs thing is getting ridiculous.

Me and Jenny went outside and played in the laneway, looking at the wild pear and cherry in blossom while Dave dickered with Elmer. We seen a vole and Jenny said he was wearing a teeny little velvet track suit. When we got back, I could see by the satisfied way Elmer was spitting off the porch and the dizzy look on Dave that we were homeowners.

33.

MONDAY MORNING I'm at work doing inventory when Marg calls. Tells me Asshole's out on bail, which I knew, but she says Tammy's having coffee with him today and, plus, Darlene's went and flew to Cancun!

I stopped at Marg's on the way home from work. Had it figured out what I wanted to say to her.

"If they want to be that frigging hopeless, Marg," I'm saying to her in my head as I walk up the street to her building, "if the two of them is that bound and bent on screwing up, there is nothing you can do about it. You might just as well move to Strone with us and leave them to it."

Why they keep letting these jerks out of jail is more than I know. Every time I think we've got the worst of them rounded up, they let one go and we're back where we started.

Marg had Tammy's two kids with her, so we didn't get to have a serious talk. What I did find out is how attached her and them kids has got. Marg's been over there half the time this year, you know.

So there's young Matthew. He's ten now. Him and Marg are trying to make a paper kite the way they seen on some TV show. Meghan, she's twelve and she's spread all over Marg's bedroom floor with her scrapbook stuff, cutting and gluing.

Matthew was giving out instructions like a supervisor. And Marg, she was putting her thumb where he told her, to hold the two sticks, and she was folding along the line he'd drew, and then she was hunting in the back of the drawer for more string.

Meghan, she come looking for a magazine she could cut up for pictures. Said she wanted nice pictures of pretty things for her scrapbook.

"You know, Meghan," I says, "you can have a section for things you don't like, too, that maybe ain't so pretty."

Marg took a glance at me.

"You could cut out pictures of scary things," I says, winking at Marg.

Marg joined in, "Things that are sad."

"Things that make you mad."

"Things you are ashamed of that are not your fault."

"Things you are not responsible for."

Meghan looked back and forth at me and Marg. Kids always know when there's more to the story. What were these two old ladies smiling like that for, with sad eyes, and telling her to cut weird stuff out of the magazines, instead of just nice stuff?

"Meghan, honey," Marg says to her, "me and Rose here, we've cut up a lot of magazines in our time, eh, Rose?"

"Oh yeah!"

"And that's one of the main ways we've learned how to tell our ass from our elbow."

The kid stared at us. How did we learn anything in a magazine?

"You try that," I says to her. "Start with: think of things that scare you," I says.

"I don't want to."

"Best thing you can ever do," I says.

I went in the other room with young Meghan, sat down with her, and I levelled with her. I told her something about the bad stuff that had happened to me, and I told her what had started me on the way to where I am now, feeling a lot better, getting my life going right.

Meghan's "no way" had turned into a "maybe." But she sat there looking at the magazines like she wasn't sure what to do.

"Did you need any help to get started, Meghan?"

She said that what scared her wasn't going to be in no magazine.

I took and flipped a magazine open, let the pictures float in front of her, the way Frances done for me, way back in the beginning. Meghan stopped one of the pages.

"You don't have to know why you're choosing any of them," I says. "Just if you see one and it looks like it's about fear for you, cut it out and paste it on."

Meghan, she stayed in Marg's room with a stack of magazines. I went out and me and Marg, we patted each other's shoulder.

Marg, she said to me, she said, "You're such a good person, Rose."

I didn't necessarily think *bullshit* so much that time.

Matthew, he was fed up with the talking. Wanted to take his kite out to the hill.

Marg took him. I stayed there and made macaroni and cheese for us all. Didn't hear a peep out of Meghan the whole hour. She was in there cutting and ripping. I peeked in and saw her paper stuck with fists, sheets and blankets and hearts, all torn and torn again.

Dave won't believe it how common this is, this way of tearing up kids. He's got to think it's real unusual what happened to our Jenny and to me.

When I was getting ready to leave, Tammy still hadn't called. She'd been "having coffee" with Asshole since ten o'clock this morning.

Marg stepped into the hall with me and shut the door behind her. She whispered, "What should I do if Tammy comes back here with him?"

"Lock your door and call the cops." I said it firm. I'd learned my lesson by now. You don't fool around with these abusers. "He's not to come near them kids. There's a court order."

"But what about Tammy?" Marg says.

I says, "I don't know. Want me to stay?"

"No, no, Rose, you're busy this week, what with moving.

You've been more than kind here tonight."

"Are you going to be okay?"

"I've locked that bugger out and called the cops on him before now." Marg put her chubby chin up.

I give her a hug. Marg, she always has a nice baby powder smell to her, and she's soft as a pillow.

I told her I love her.

"You too." She pats my arm.

We were at the start of the month of June. It was a beautiful night, still light after supper. Air was sweet. I come across a big lilac bush in a vacant lot and picked an armful.

Josie was propped up in bed, looking at her curtain moving in the breeze. She put her face in the lilacs, breathed them in.

To this day, when I smell lilacs, I can feel that hour. How it was, after my long day, to sit there on the edge of Josie's smooth, white bed and tell her that we'd found our valley.

34.

TUESDAY COME and I had to go to Group for the last time. Now, you know, me and Meredith, we'd never saw quite eye to eye. But what I learned from her is most of the most important stuff I ever learned in my life. So I was ready to thank her very much. I had a card for her and a little present, wrapped up. I go to hand them to her.

She don't take them. "You're making a mistake, Rose," she says.

I went cold. Everybody looked at her. Silence.

Was this Meredith? Meredith, who was always there with her questions? Do you think it's appropriate for Asshole to bust the dog's teeth, Tammy? Whose fault do you think it is, Marg, that your father's in jail? Darlene, do you think it's really the best idea to marry somebody you never saw in your life? Always them professional little questions. Never no statements, no judging.

But now all of a sudden, there's Meredith, out of the blue, judging me in black and white: *You are making a mistake, Rose.*

I'll tell you, it stopped me dead. I'm one of these people who tend to think, if I don't agree with somebody, that they could be right. At that time, I was more like that than I am today.

I look around at the rest of them.

Everybody was gawping at Meredith. Frances, the helper, looked like the boss was losing it.

Meredith says, "You haven't completed your therapy."

I said I planned to go for therapy in my new place. That was part of my deal with Dave, I said.

"You'll have to pay for it, you know. This is one of very few areas where this service is available free of charge."

"I know that. But it's important. If I have to pay, I will."

"But you know how unstable you are, Rose."

She was white as a sheet, breathing quick. I didn't know what to make of it. She's the one looked unstable to me. "You will go back to your old behaviour patterns."

"I'll be tempted, likely," I says, "but I know what to do now."

"What will you do?" she asks me. And I wish yous could've heard the voice on her. It's like I'm below human intelligence. Like, *what will you do, you moron?*

Me and Dave had it planned. If he got tempted by the drug scene or if I got tempted by some guy, we were going to run straight and tell somebody. Get help. No secrets. We'd broke through on secrets. We knew, now, why them things had a hold over us. It was the secret buzz. Now that me and Dave were teamed up to beat it, I felt good about our chances.

Or I did until Meredith says to me, she says, "You need to be in this group, Rose."

"Wouldn't another group do me?"

Meredith says, "I am the one who has become familiar with your history."

That brought me up short, I can tell you. Could that be right? She's the only one could help me? There was no other type of help that would do me? I felt scared. Would I have to start all over again?

Frances looked like she was busting to say something.

I says, "My history?" I says. I'm thinking, isn't that just about the same as the history of half the frigging world? Wouldn't any shrink pick up the gist of it pretty quick?

"I have worked with you for approximately eighteen months."

I don't know what to say. I'm confused. Is she telling me I'm going to fall apart without her? Could that be true? Did it have to be her and no other shrink? Jeeze. Maybe it was true! She was making me wonder. I had counted on going to Group every Tuesday. Meredith had steered me right.

And then she said to me, she said, "Rose, you are in no position, at this time, to adopt a child."

Trickles of sweat run down my sides, under my shirt.

"You are a victim of childhood sexual abuse. You have a number of unresolved issues. Your behaviour is unpredictable. The problem will be passed on, through you, to the child."

"There's just the one problem that's cropped up lately," I says. My voice is shaky as my hands.

"Just one, you call it!"

Meredith puffs herself up. She looks even bigger. What is that in her voice? It's like she wants to scare me. It's working. She is scaring me.

"I'm not fit to adopt Jenny?" My throat is tight.

"I would certainly not advise it!"

I want to ask her why not. But I'm scared of what she'll say. I look at a scratch on the table, trying not to cry.

Meredith's voice is still going. I can hear her telling me that I involved myself with a man again recently and might do so again at any time and that men like that are very dangerous to children like Jenny and that I am statistically unlikely to protect her. She's amazed the adoption has been approved.

I'm stammering that I'm hoping for better things.

Meredith tells me that my chances are very slim.

Frances stands up.

She says, "Dr. Debenham!"

Meredith gives her a stare, cold as a dead fish. "Yes, Frances?"

Frances's busting to say something.

Meredith, she's daring her to go ahead and try saying it.

Frances said that her feeling was that this decision was up to Rose. But then she sunk back down. She had her job to think of. Couldn't lip off to Meredith too much.

By the time Meredith got done with me, I felt about as much

self-worth as a puddle. I didn't hear much else that went on there that night. I barely even heard the rest of them out in the hallway afterwards, trying to tell me that Meredith was full of shit.

Got home. Phoned Dave.

There was nothing he could say to me.

"She's a professional. She must know." That's alls I could choke out.

I told him we should forget the whole thing. I wasn't fit for a mother or a wife. I told him I'd better keep working here, since I need this shrink. No other shrink would do. We'd better not buy the house. I said I was going to call Children's Aid and say forget about the adoption.

35.

DAVE, HE WAS BEGGING ME, "Give yourself some time! What the hell's happened? Think it over!"

The next day at work I'm stunned. I don't know how I got through that day.

I was shrunk to nothing. I was no good for a mother to Jenny. I was unpredictable. I was a victim. I was never going to be no different. Meredith said. Meredith had went to university. Meredith must know. I needed Meredith. She was the only one could help me. Better stay here with her and let go of all the crazy dreams.

Just when I'm finishing for the day, there's a car load pulls up in front of McIlveen's Plumbing and Heating.

Out piles Marg, Tammy, and Tammy's kids. They troop in and stand there while I sort out somebody's hot water heater that was rusted through and the water was pouring out the bottom while the pump was overheating trying to keep the tank filled. They look at me while I turn off the lights, lock the door. Then they frog march me to Marg's car.

They took me to Josie.

Josie was sitting on the veranda. The kids, they spotted a good climbing tree by the porch and was up it like monkeys. Tammy went hurrying after them, fussing. I walked across the grass with Marg.

Josie, she watched us coming to her. Never took her eyes off me. Watched me climbing the steps to her.

Soon as we're on the porch, Tammy and Marg, they let loose yapping, trying to tell Josie what the problem is. They're flapping and clucking.

"Meredith told her she's not fit!"

"She says she's not going to marry Dave now!"

"You tell her, Josie. She won't listen to us!"

"She wants to give up on adopting little Jenny!"

"She is so fit for that, ain't she, Josie?"

They sounded like kill day in the hen yard, as Al would say.

I was sitting beside Josie, on a low stool, not saying nothing. If I wasn't fit, I wasn't. If I was screwed up permanent, that was that.

A child of my own and I was going to save her? Our family had been dysfunctional since cave days. I was going to make it right?

I was never going to screw around no more? Looking at a lake was going to help me? A cripple across the road? Some big business plan? I was going to be in on it? Help run it? A loser like me?

I'm no good. Never will be. What the hell use is it to struggle and try to learn? You'll be right back here anyways. Dreams is for kids. The whole world might as well be paved right over in a solid sheet of concrete.

Tammy told her kids not to climb so high.

Marg says, "Oh, they're all right."

"There's no reason Rose can't be a fine mother, is there, Josie? Meredith's got a hold of the wrong end, there, I'm sure," Tammy says.

I was thinking how, when you're a kid, it all depends on what the adults are telling you. Are they saying you can climb high or are they telling you you can't?

Josie, she just sat there until the worker come to get her for her supper.

Then there was this quiet. They seen that she hadn't had no chance to say nothing. She was being pulled backwards, away from us, in her wheelchair. Made me think of a wave rolling out. She said, "I see the toy cow."

The things Josie says, eh, they'll hang there in the air. One car went by. Josie rolled away.

Tammy says, "Rose likely gets it, don't you, Rose?"

I says, "What she's talking about is Meredith. That's all I know."

We headed back to my place to make dinner. In the car, I talked about the last time Meredith bawled me out in Group. It was a long time ago now, before Josie got hurt. Meredith had been yelling at me that no man was going to rescue me. I had to do the work for myself, as if I didn't know it.

"And that's the same thing Josie said back then. She seen a broken toy cow."

"But what the frig is it supposed to mean?" Marg says.

"I don't know. Something. Meredith's messed up or something?"

We stopped and picked up Jenny.

I was quiet and there was a big cloud at the back of my mind, but it was okay with them all jammed into my place, cooking. Tammy's Meghan kneeling up to the coffee table, drawing and colouring with Jenny. Matthew found one of Dave's adventure books laying around.

When they left, the weight had shifted a bit inside me, but I still wouldn't promise nothing.

Sally phoned. Marg had told her.

"We shall mount up with the wings of eagles," she says.

"Okay, Sal."

"You're going to be all right now, Rose?" she keeps on at me.

"Oh, I don't know."

"You think about what Josie said. You figure out what that broke goat means."

"Cow."

"I bet it means you're as fit as can be for Jenny's mother and Dave's wife."

"How's it supposed to mean that?"

"Well, but I bet it does. We can tell Dave not to worry, right?" she says.

"Look, Sally, I don't know. I don't know nothing. I feel like a truck hit me."

"Things won't look so bad in the morning," Sally said. "The mercy of God is new, every morning."

Dave's dad, Al, come on the line. "How come you got cold feet all of a sudden?"

I told him Meredith, our group leader, says I'm never going to be able to look after Jenny.

He says, "Them people with the big education can be wrong, same as the next person. Look at that Frank fellow comes up here. He makes the big bucks. Must be smart some way, but for fixing ordinary everyday problems, I never seen a man stupider."

Jenny was staying over with me. I went and sat on the side of the bed and looked at her sleeping. Her soft little hand was curled. Fleck of yellow crayon under her thumbnail.

I tucked the blanket up around her and got ready for bed. Cuddled in beside her.

I used to argue with Sally about this mercy of God she talks about. My point was: why don't He just fix the world up so's we're not all crouching down here, moaning for mercy? Wouldn't that be more use than leaving us how we are and taking pity on us once in a while?

But who knows? Maybe there is something you could call "new mercy" in the morning time because, when I woke up, things didn't look so bad. I felt better.

Moods, eh? It's funny. Things can look dark as hell one day and a whole lot brighter the next. For no particular reason.

I just laid there looking at the summer morning light on the wall, listening to Jenny. She was kneeling on the covers, happy, talking about our new home, where Dave was going to build her a playhouse with a portcullis.

"A which?" I says.

"Portcullis, Ann Toes, to keep out enemies and let in the breeze."

I knew we were going to go ahead after all.

I give notice to my landlord, said goodbye to Bertie, downstairs, and to McIlveen's. Me and Dave signed the purchase and sale agreement with old Elmer there.

Marg and Tammy come over to help me pack. "Good job you're not such a frigging pack rat as what Sally is," Tammy says. "Remember when we moved her?"

"Oh jeeze!" Marg laughed her shook-milk-jug laugh. "Poor Dave lugging all them gallons of pink paint!"

Tammy's laughing too. "Her and her lima beans! How many cases of them did we lug?"

I says, "And about a thousand sprouts and seedlings in tin cans, and her fussing in case we might break one!"

"Hey, did you hear, Rose?" Tammy says. "Sally's let down because it turns out the only single hardware man, there, he don't like women!"

Marg says, "She's been at the hardware more than church! Got Al's drive shed crammed with new rakes and shovels, all for a gay guy!" Marg's trying to wrap my dishes in newspaper, but she keeps having to rest them on her knee to laugh.

I laughed at that about the hardware man too. But there was like this little edge of my mind that wondered. I was so used to Josie knowing pretty well everything. It was weird she was wrong about Sally and the hardware guy. Well I guessed she was allowed to be wrong once.

We had a lot of fun that weekend. Marg stayed over with me. We kept one pot out of the packing to boil our tea water in, and we lived off a jumbo box of soda crackers and a jar of almond butter Tammy brought over. She said it had more something than peanut butter.

Sunday morning, we're eating almond cracker sandwiches

for breakfast. I ask, "Darlene still in Cancun?"

"Due back Wednesday," Marg says.

"And?"

"Alls I know is she sent the dog a postcard," Marg says, half choking herself chuckling through her cracker. "Said it was sunny and not to chew the orange flowered chair."

Tammy and the kids has been over there every day, looking after the dog. According to Tammy's kids, the dog knows that Darlene's not doing so good.

"Idiot," I says. "She must've spent her whole cheque on the plane ticket. What's she think she's going to live on for the rest of the month? She'll have nothing to put in her new fridge."

"Good luck's wasted on her," Marg says.

"Jesus," I says, "I wished she'd level off. She's either where she won't put her nose out of her apartment or she's flying to frigging Cancun!"

"That's Darlene. She's down or she's up."

"She's better off down. So we can sit on her." I says, "Anything could happen to her out there. She hasn't got no judgement."

Marg heaved herself up off of the box there with a big sigh. She started working on my kitchen drawer, taking stuff out, piling it on the counter for me to go through. "What've we got here?" she says. She's got my stack of stepping stones in her hand. So I explained and showed them. I set the stepping stones down, one at a time, across the floor. I hadn't put them all out for a long time. Had quite a few new ones since the last time. They made a long path now, twisting around the boxes, all the way from hot red pain to pale blue patience. Then there was never giving up hope. Trusting my own judgement.

"There should be one more," I says. "It's turquoise. Here."

"Healthy Coping." Marg, she leaned on the stove to set the piece of paper down at the end of the trail.

"This is telling me something," she says, patting the stove.

It was striking her the way *Healthy Coping* was right by the stove, since a lot of her problems have to do with food.

That's what that little omen meant to Marg. It hit me way different. The piece of paper just fit right in there perfect, next to the stove. My stepping stones reached right across the whole floor now, all the way from the door to the stove. I wondered if Dave would remember what we always said we'd do, once the stepping stones reached all the way across the room.

When Dave come with his truck to help me move, there they were, the different coloured stepping stones, all the way. He took one look at that. "Huh!" he says.

I wasn't sure if he remembered. Seemed like maybe he did, the way he said "Huh."

He didn't say nothing else, though. Just took my end table down to the truck.

I stand there wondering. *Does Dave remember? I bet he does. But maybe he don't want to get married to me anymore. We're going to live together and have our Jenny with us. So I guess it don't matter.*

What's a wedding anyways? I'm trying to say to myself. Just a big waste of money. We're better to put it into fixing up that old place.

That's what I'm trying to think, but I can feel the tears wanting to come. *Dave don't want to bother with a wedding. He don't know but what I'll turn around and be unfaithful to him anyhow. He don't think I'm worth going through a wedding for. And let's face it, I'm not. What right have I got to dress up like a bride? As if I'm something special any man would want?*

That's how fast I can fall down one of the big holes in my ego. By the time Dave come back up from the truck I was lower than a shoe.

He had something in his hand. Said it was a surprise. He put it behind his back and made me guess which hand, teasing, smiling at me.

I come sailing back up out of my low spot there, and I made a grab for his big left hand. I pried his fingers open. There was a little, blue jewellery store box, kind of beat-up looking, like it had been in the glove box of the truck a while.

"How long you been carting this around?"

"You said you wouldn't marry me till your papers there got all the way across the room," he says, "and then you quit making them for a long time. I thought maybe you didn't want to."

He thought maybe I didn't want to!

"Anyways," he says, when I let him come up for air, "took you so long I got her pretty near paid off. Ain't you going to look? If you don't care for this one, we can trade it for something else," he says, watching me open it.

Now, you wouldn't think a guy like Dave would be so hot at picking out the right ring for a woman's hand, would you, or guessing what type of things a particular woman might like. Don't seem like a talent he'd have, does it?

But you just never know what talents a person has got.

36.

WELL, WE DONE HER ALL. We moved back north. I went to work for Dodd's Plumbing and Heating in Strone. We got Josie moved into the rest home across the road. Dave's police check come through, and we could go ahead and adopt Jenny.

She finished her kindergarten year, said goodbye to her second foster home, there, that she never liked, and come with us, permanent, on July the nineteenth. We picked her up in the truck and put her between us.

I'll never forget that. Putting Jenny between the two of us and driving off. Anybody tried to hurt this girl again, it would be over our two dead bodies.

The first summer up there we spent fumigating Elmer's old place, fixing everything that had broke since the year it snowed so bad at Easter and Elmer had put his shoulder out. We found nice pine boards under the kitchen linoleum there and a child's button shoe in the wall with an 1872 penny in the heel.

Al said you'll find them in a lot of old places. They used to put them in for luck when they'd build the walls. Luck for the children.

We put that in Jenny's room on a special shelf.

This is still Elmer's place, to people up here. "I hear yous are living up at Elmer's, eh?" That's what everybody said when they come in to pay their bill at the plumbing place I was working at now.

Sally, she got a boyfriend that summer. The brother of Jinping and Hong, there at the Chinese restaurant. He only come up to her shoulder. Sure seemed like the guy for Sally, though. Always thinking about the condition of his spirit and the balance of his character. He helped at the restaurant some. But he was also opening up a kind of a factory outlet wholesaling work clothes that his relatives back in China were turning out. But he still made time, somehow, to stand on the bridge with Sally and fish and smile and argue about what unseen forces are behind the universe.

Me and Sally kept on trying to talk Marg and Tammy into moving up closer to the rest of us. We could see they were starting to lean towards it.

They didn't know what would become of Darlene. She was back hiding in the house again now, wouldn't even walk the dog, wouldn't tell them nothing about Cancun. Wouldn't talk about moving. Wouldn't go to Group.

Marg, she said her and Tammy didn't know what to do about the dog. They can't have it at their buildings. Tammy's kids are attached to it. Darlene's quit looking after it.

"But she loves that dog!"

"Not no more. She's on some pill now where she don't feel nothing. Not one emotion at all."

I said to Marg on the phone, I said, "Well then, she's got what she always wanted. Come up here and bring the dog with yous."

Marg, she was wavering. "But..." she says.

I said, "Darlene is never going to change because Darlene won't try! She won't even take step one and face her pain. There is nothing yous can do about a person if they will not face their pain."

Marg, she sighed. "She was doing pretty good after she took in that dog of Josie's. If she had of just held steady there, not re-traumatized herself..."

Re-traumatized is right. That's what she must have went

and did. "It helps to have a few words for the stupid things we do, don't it!" I says.

"Thanks to Meredith," Marg says.

I don't know what to say. It's true. If it wasn't for Meredith, I wouldn't have what I have today. I'd be sitting back in the Women's Shelter, black and blue from jerk number a hundred and sixty, looking at the stepping stone poster on the wall. Then again, it was Meredith tried to take it all away from me again at the last minute. Sally calls her a "mixed blessing."

"That psychiatry woman" is what Al calls her. "That psychiatry woman can't be no good because yous are all still crazy," he says. Thinks he's funny. He's had no use for Meredith since she told me I wasn't fit to adopt Jenny.

The social worker looking after the adoption, she put us in touch with the counsellor up here for Jenny. Marion, the art therapist. We walk into her office. Jenny's got a tight hold on my hand. I look at this woman, and I do a thing I'm learning. I pay attention to see if I'm getting any hunches.

Her shoulders looked easy and loose. Hands quiet. Feet comfortable and still. She looked at us pleasant and normal. Like Frances. My hunch was she was okay.

I told Josie about it, sitting on the porch at our place, looking over the lake. "I think this shrink they got for Jenny is all right."

Josie, she nodded.

To the south of us, about a half mile along the shore, there's a point sticks out into the lake. That's this Macaulay's Point they talk about. Old guy lived out there in a falling-down house (worse than ours, even). That shack was sitting on the prettiest lot on earth. Lost Gold Lake sparkling on all sides.

"That's the place Al and Sally always talk about putting the hotel, eh Josie?" I says.

"Near the caves," she says.

Which I didn't know what she was talking about, except that she always used to say our hotel was going to be by some caves.

Sally and her boyfriend come around the point in Al's duck

boat. "There's one you got wrong, Jos."

Josie, she didn't say nothing, just kept on smiling, watching them drift and cast their lines, out in the sparkling water.

I wish I could tell yous all to live by water. At least go stare at water if you get the chance. I don't know why it's such a comfort to me. Meredith told me once that it has to do with the watery sounds in the womb before we're born. I don't know. But I'm telling you, sitting on that new porch of ours, looking at the water, listening to them sounds of comfort, that was a good part of how I got where I am today.

I looked at that water with the pink mist lifting off it in the morning. I looked at it silver and black in the moonlight. I watched the thunderstorms roll over it and the rain pour into it, grey and wild. I heard it lap and ripple. I heard it roar and crash. It sparkled, shone, glowed, and sang, different every hour of the day. Always good. I felt like it was washing and washing my wounds. The notion I got was it was making new patterns of wavy light, right in my brain, in place of the old, dark patterns.

Marg and Tammy, they made the move! Found theirself two apartments in an old clapboard house in town, right on the main street. Moved up to Strone.

Josie's dog, he come to live at our place. Jenny was happy about that. Josie too. Her and that dog. I swear they can talk to each other. You should've saw them the day they got back together, after so long!

Tammy's daughter Meghan, Jenny thinks she's the cat's pyjamas. She is a real nice girl, too. She'll let Jenny tag after her. They walk the dog together.

Young Matthew there, Tammy's lad, him and Josie took a shine to each other. He started going over to see her. Took her outside her building in the wheelchair. She'd sit in a back corner of the parking lot and watch him do his skateboard tricks by the hour. Clap for him when he done good.

Al, he always has a lot of time for Josie. He's got the idea that crossword puzzles are good for your brain, eh. So he'll sit with Josie. Try to get her to think of a seven-letter word for "salubrious" or whatever he's got to fill in. Once in a while, she'll just come right out with an answer. Might be the only thing she says all day. Anyhow, she likes the company and so does he.

I was walking along the main street in town, one day about that time, heading for the post office. Tammy's up on a stepladder inside the front window of her new place there. Her blue drapes that Sally made for the other place are up. Seem to fit good.

I stop.

Take a wild guess what Tammy's got dripping from her fingers? She's lifting them out of a pail of wash water. Stars! She's hanging up a sun-catcher decoration. Little crystal stars, dangling on pieces of fishing line. She's drying them in a cloth, then lifting them up, glittering. I stand there looking at the clear plastic suction thing. Tammy's pink fingers pressing it to the window glass.

I went to the door. Told her these stars had been in the picture of the town that Josie had, way back at the start!

Tammy said she found them in the back of a cupboard, all covered in dust.

"They cleaned up nice, eh?" she says, looking at them sparkling there in the window, new-washed, throwing rainbows across the room.

Dave, when I run home to tell him, he didn't see nothing particular in it. Just said, "People before must've had them hanging there when the picture was took."

"But the curtains too!" I says.

"There's more than one set of blue drapes on earth, Rosie."

"But I seen them in the sky, too!"

Dave's getting a kick out of me, here. I'm so excited over Tammy's front window. He thinks I'm cracked.

I told him where to go, and I went galloping to Josie. She didn't say nothing. But she sure smiled.

Well, Marg and Tammy, they started in, trying to raise money for the hotel. Tom, he still hadn't made his mind up. Wouldn't say nothing about it yet. But that never slowed down Tammy and Marg.

Marg had her first bake sale. Sweated in the kitchen for a month, loading Jan's freezer. And then she brought all the baking out and loaded a table, the day of the fishing derby. Marg bakes beautiful. Sold out. Put the money in the hotel account. Come to more than I would've thought, too.

"My days of undercharging are through," Marg says, putting her chin up. "This is high-quality baking. Nobody blinked an eyelash at my prices, neither."

Tammy, she went to work cleaning houses. She was going to charge way too low but Marg helped her find out the going rate. Couldn't talk her into charging that much. But she come up closer to it. Still had her disability to live on. So she put the cleaning money in for the hotel.

It made me nervous. But Dave said, "Let them. It makes them happy. Gives them something to shoot for."

I kept track of everybody's contributions, separate, in a ledger book. Seen it like a savings account for each one.

In the fall, when the air was fresh and the woods was shining into the lake, making red and orange and yellow fires in the water, I got Sally to sew me a new dress.

She cut my hair and put stuff in it.

I said, "He's not marrying me for my looks. I don't know what he's doing it for, but it sure ain't that."

Sally had a hairpin in her mouth, but she said, "Watch your negative self-talk."

She helped me on with the dress. Then she put her arm around my shoulders and took me to the full-length mirror.

"Oh!" I says.

"You look real nice, Rose."

"Will it keep if I breathe?"

She said I could do hand springs.

It was the first minute that it ever occurred to me I might be sort of pretty in the right light.

I says, "Must be a trick mirror."

Shift in self-image. There'd be a stepping stone in that. I'll have a path of them a hundred miles long before I'm through.

Jenny, she was twirling around the house in a fluffy yellow dress. She told Sally she wanted to look "as much as possible like a magic princess."

"She wants a pointy hat, Rose," Sally had told me, back in the summer. "I guess that wouldn't be right for the wedding?"

Dave, of course, he says, "No harm in a princess hat." Then he told his joke about what the priests wear. He says, "How come they call him Father and dress him like Mother?"

When we got to church, Dave's dad was just pulling up in the old T-Bird with Sally. "Look at you! You look just beau-dee-ful!" He hollered that across the church lawn.

"You don't have to sound so surprised."

Sally must have been after Al with the bleach and the iron. She even had his hair trimmed.

Walking across the grass, through the bright, crunching leaves, to the church, I thought of my mother, who'd been dead ten years at that time. I wondered what had been in her mind on her wedding day. Did she ever have the feeling that Dad was a good idea?

I thought of my father. I thought, God help him. All twisted up.

I thought of Dave's mother. Wondered if she'd be okay with giving her boy to me, if she had lived to see this day. I thanked her in my heart. *You must've been a good mother.* I thought how glad she'd be that Al was going to have a little grandchild now to swing on a tire.

I took Al's arm, the dad I wished I'd had.

We all climbed them sparkling pink stone stairs together.

Jenny went skipping ahead, holding Marg's hand, waving her magic wand. I think she liked the sound her new patent leather shoes was making, smart little pats on the stones.

My one foot and then the other stepping from stone to stone as we climbed them steps, like I was in that old poster at the shelter. Felt like I had crossed the river. And here I was, all in a bright, happy shimmer, climbing up on to the sunny shore. The music swelled up. Our friends and family stood with a sound like a gust of wind.

If you were ever at a cottage, you can picture the way water will throw a lot of wiggling reflections up all over the walls and ceilings, eh? In that church, the water reflections play through stained glass windows. Jell-O jiggling bunch of jewels—emeralds, sapphires, rubies, gold—glimmering all over.

"It was made by my fairy princess rainbow spell," Jenny told us after.

Down at the front, with his cousin for best man, there was Dave. My lucky ticket, ready to get cashed in.

Dave was cleaned up real nice. And the way he watched me walking down to him! You'd have thought he was the lucky one. He was standing, as it happened, in a rippling patch of strong gold lake-light. Glowing like the blessing that he is.

That was a sweet walk, I can tell yous, down that aisle! Love on both sides of me. Tammy's eyes streaming. Her and young Meghan dressed up in hats. Matthew staring around like he's in Aladdin's cave. Jan's little Alexander, shined up adorable in a wee little bowtie, standing on the church pew, waving to Jenny.

Do yous want to find a man? Look for one that hasn't got his brains too handicapped by his father or mother. That's my advice.

Men tend to be like parking spaces, eh? Have yous heard that joke? Jan told it to me. Why are men like parking spaces? The good ones are taken and the rest are all handicapped.

Yeah, well Dave, my husband, he's the exception. Mind you, sorry girls, he's taken.

Sally, she got up and read out of the Bible where it says that love "endures all things, forgives all things, hopes all things." She reads where the saint there, that wrote it a long time ago, says that even if he had've knew everything and talked with the tongues of angels, if he had no love, he would not be worth a fart.

Everybody from Group bawled.

Jenny was worried. Marg bent down and whispered to her. She says, "It's all right, honey. Us and Auntie Rose are real happy, is all."

"But you're crying!"

"We're happier than happy."

"Dave's going to cry too!"

Marg was whispering to Jenny, telling her, "Dave's just real happy too."

We could barely croak out our promises. But, by God, we promised.

And it was just the very next spring after that, we built the hotel.

37.

BUT WAIT TILL I TELL YOUS. Tom made his mind up. Come over one night in November. Sat down with a cup of coffee at the kitchen table. Told me and Dave he'd looked into it. Seemed to him a lodge up here would be a good idea. He was ready to back it. He figured he could round up enough investors. His construction company would build it. We were to run it.

I sat there stunned. Looking at the steam curling up off my coffee. The hotel was really going to happen? Really? In this world here where we live and breathe? Not in no fantasy world?

By the very next week, Dave and Tom and Al were starting to talk location, numbers, timeframe, backers. It was starting to really happen. I couldn't believe it.

I kept saying to Dave, "I can't believe it!"

"You're funny. Long as something's insane and hopeless, you believe it's going to come true. Soon as it's sensible and it is coming true, you don't believe it."

Josie, she just sat and smiled. I was in a fog all through them first three weeks, trying to get my head around what was going on. We were going to build the hotel! Really and truly, on this here planet. With what we had all saved and what Tom was willing to put in, and what some other people were lined up to invest, they figured there was enough to get it going. Planned to turn the sod by spring.

Dave, he took Elmer's old woodstove out of the house and put in a new one that fall. Wasn't so sure the old one was safe.

That's what he said. But he didn't fool nobody. He took her out because she was a kind where you couldn't see the fire. And Jenny wanted to watch the fire.

I says, "You're spoiling her rotten."

I didn't mean nothing. But Dave says, "I don't know how come people use that word *spoil*." He says, "Brent's old man there, he spoiled his son. Spoiled his whole life for him. And your father, what he done to your sister and you. You don't spoil a kid with treating her kind."

So anyways, we got this new woodstove. Josie and Jenny are in the front room one night after dinner, looking into the fire. It's around about the end of November. Dave's at the arena playing hockey. Snow's swirling into the black lake outside. Wind roaring through the woods. Jenny's telling Josie what shapes she can see in the burning logs.

"A beautiful, big new castle," she says, "in place of a little old house that burned down."

Josie, she's listening, nodding the way she does, like she knows exactly what that's all about.

It give me the creeps. I put down my knitting. Went and drew the drapes shut.

We were supposed to get the hydro hook-up before now. But, by this time, we weren't so sure we wanted it. Liked Elmer's oil lamps. Jenny said that ordinary lighting would ruin our dream house. Me and Dave felt something like that too. It had been like camping there that first summer and fall.

Mind you, it could be a bit spooky at night, when the hallway was dark and even the front room was full of shadows, late in the fall there. Especially when Josie and Jenny would get that look on them, gazing into the fire.

Jenny's concentrating on a log that's well burned and glowing bright orange. She says, "There's a doorway."

And Josie says to Jenny, she says, "The man with the lucky ticket is at the door."

I wasn't paying much attention. Counting my knitting row.

Wasn't like I never heard that one before. But we did hear her say it, right at that moment. I'll swear to that. So will Jenny. And then there really was somebody at the door.

Jenny jumped up.

"It's the man with the lucky ticket!" she says.

I went cold. Give Josie a sharp look. She just smiled at me, nodding. Wind gusted around the house. That weird dog, he didn't bark, the way he normally does when somebody comes to the door. Just raised his nose up off the floor and looked at Josie, like they both knew something.

Jenny, she's tugging on my hand. She wants to go see.

I struck a match and lit a candle. I'll admit I felt weird.

I says to Josie, "What's going on here?"

Josie didn't say nothing. Turned to us and sat there smiling, with the firelight glowing gold, on one side of her face.

I pulled myself together, went and opened the door, holding up the candle to see who it was. Jenny behind me, peeking around. The flame jumped in the wind, and I cupped my hand to keep it from blowing out.

It's Dave's dad, with a funny look on his face and the snow falling on his ball hat.

I says, "Something wrong?"

He stood there, looking at us. The strangest look. He's breathing heavy.

Jenny says to him, she says, "Do you have a lucky ticket?"

Now Al, he stared at her, strange, for a second or two, his eyes getting wider and wider. He's breathing funny. I set the candle on the counter and reached for Al. Pulled him in out of the storm.

"What's the matter? Something wrong? Shut the door, Jenny."

Jenny pushed the door shut against the wind. Candlelight quit flapping and burned steady.

"Are you the man at the door with a lucky ticket?" Jenny asks him again.

Al give out at the knees and pitched forwards. I had hold of him. Eased him onto the floor. I was on my knees fanning Al with a tea towel. Sent Jenny running for a damp wash cloth. When Al come to, he looks at Jenny, squatting there wiping his forehead with the cloth.

I'm saying, "Are you all right? What's the matter? I'm going to call the ambulance."

But Al, he waves me off. "No. No. I'm all right," he says. He's looking at Jenny, and he says, "How did you ever know?"

Jenny tells him, "Aunt Josie said."

"Oh," he says, "I see."

The two of them looked satisfied now, like they had her all explained. Al rested his head back on my arm.

Dave come in, pretty near fell over us. Wondered what in the world. Picked up his dad and lay him on the couch by the fire. I went and pumped fresh water. We got his coat and boots off of him, propped him up comfortable, tucked him in a red blanket.

Josie, she's just there rocking in her chair, smiling. Dog's tail is thumping on the floor.

When all the flap was died down, and the colour come back into Al's face, he told us he just won two point four million dollars. "So that will help with that lodge yous wanted," he says. "Jenny knocked the wind out of me there, asking about the lucky ticket," he says, "when that was right what I'd came here to tell yous."

Now me and Dave are the ones that need fanning.

You never know what'll go through you at a time like that.

I remember the first words out of my mouth. I said, "But we don't need it now! We're building the hotel ourself anyhow."

Yous won't believe me, but the truth is I felt like crying. Like little Alexander there if you take something out of his hands that he can do by himself and you do it for him. He'll cry.

"Own self can do it!" he says.

Al says, "I know, Rose," he says. "Yous were going to do it anyways. It's not like you couldn't have did without this money. Now, if yous want, you can keep it in the family a bit more, is all. This'll just give yous a nice boost, and yous won't need to get so many outside backers. What this is is it's just the road rising up to meet yous and the wind at your back."

Al looked into the fire. "I've saw luck work this way before," he says. "Seems to come when people don't specially need it. After they've made their own luck."

Al's himself again. Sitting up. Him and Jenny and Josie, they're all just smiling peaceful.

"Yup, that seems to be how luck works. How was the game?" he says to Dave.

Dave's standing there, stunned.

"We won," he says. I don't think he knows if he's talking about the hockey or the lottery.

"Now then, Miss, you give me quite a turn," Al says to Jenny. "So, Aunt Josie told you I had that lucky ticket, did she?"

Jenny's got her pigtails jumping as she nods. "Aunt Josie can see things that are in future time," she explains. "She has first and second sight."

Josie was wrapped up in a blanket, rocking, peaceful, looking at us all. Them sky-coloured eyes that can see through the wall of time shining in the firelight.

Dave says, "Dad! Are you sure?"

The phone rung.

"That'll be my mother," Al says. That's what he's taken to calling Sally. Sure enough, it was Sally, just home from work, checking up on him.

Her T-Bird was soon bumping up our lane. Marg's old getaway car wasn't far behind. They were all jammed into our little place, celebrating on low fat crackers and soya cheese from Tammy. Sitting in a circle, faces lit up, talking about how we were going to build a fancier hotel now. Better have a fireplace in the lobby, seeing as we're millionaires.

Just like old times! Us all in a huddle, happy, talking crazy. I'm leaning in, shivering, saying that we ought to build it out of pinkish, sparkling stone. The kids had went limp, leaning against the adults, watching our faces.

    Dave was right. I'm funny this way. I believed less in the hotel that winter night, when it was a sure thing, than I ever done in the waiting room at Group, when it was a crazy idea. Seemed like we were all just carried away with Josie's picture, dreaming in the firelight while the snow swirled into the lake.

38.

I'M ASHAMED TO TELL YOUS the very next thing that happened. Better not leave it out, though. I'm forcing myself. I hope yous appreciate me coming out with it like this. Facing it's how we haul our poor asses out from under, get ourselves up there, stepping on the stones, instead of laying under the rockslide.

A lot of us is left with sex problems after childhood sex abuse, and it don't just disappear because you want it to. I got thinking of another man. Jack, he was one of the carpenters. Stopped by our place one day to get some lumber Dave had stored in the shed.

Cold, sunny Saturday in January. I was out shovelling the path to the driveway. Jack, he walked out of the shed with a plank on his shoulder, and me and him, we took a look at each other. I blink. It's awful bright out, but I'm not wrong. Jack's got his eyes on me. That way. Shoots through me like hot brandy.

Jack starts finding reasons he needs to stop by our place. Can't live without a set of hinges he thinks he seen once in the back of Elmer's driveshed. Would I mind holding the flashlight for him while he dicks around, taking his time, chatting me up, and pretending to look for them? I'm standing there like a moron holding the frigging flashlight as if he couldn't set it on a shelf.

I'd look out the window for Jack's black truck, waiting for

that hit of hot adrenaline. I'm saying to myself, There's no harm in this. Just peps up my day. We're not doing nothing. Knew better, of course. But that's what I was spineless enough to be telling myself.

When it got worse, I told myself I was a piece of garbage, that Dave and Jenny would be better off without me. I'd never be no different. Didn't matter what happened. I was never going to be able to get over craving this old buzz. I'm thinking, yes, I am different. I'm higher up the stairs now. I can do better. Yes, I can. No, I can't. Damned if I can't beat this. Damned if I can.

This gone on for a month. Hadn't really done nothing wrong. But I was driving by the building site for a glimpse of Jack. Listening for the sound of his truck in our lane. Laying awake beside Dave.

Married to my Dave. Mothering Jenny. Money sitting in the bank. All our dreams coming true. And that's what I was doing.

Of course, I steered clear of Josie for as long as I could. Felt lousy about that too.

Finally stopped in on her one day. She's sitting looking at a picture she's holding in her hands.

I says, "Hi, Jos, I'm going into town. Did you need anything?"

She looks at me.

I says, "Did you want anything in town?"

She holds out the picture for me to see. It's her picture of yellow tulips. I told her I'd bring her some flowers from the store. Brighten up her room.

"We can use a look at flowers in February, can't we?" I says, and I'm halfways to town before it hits me.

The yellow tulips!

I turned around in a farm lane and drove right back there to her. I shut the door of her room behind me. "Okay, you know, don't you?"

She looks at me, steady.

"What do you want me to do?"

She keeps looking at me.

"Damn it, Josie! I can't help it!"

She keeps looking at me.

"It's the way I am. It's my weak spot."

She don't say nothing.

"Good luck is wasted on me!"

Josie wants to show me the tulips picture again, holding it out to me, looking at me with them eyes.

I'm ashamed to say that I took a swipe at the picture. Knocked it onto the floor and steamed out.

Dave's asleep that Friday night. I'm laying there sweating for Jack and worrying over treating Josie like that. In the dark, I can see yellow tulips.

Last time she showed me them bright flowers, Josie was trying to get me to be honest with Dave about Dirk. No secrets. That's what she was up to again now. It was her little code. She was pushing me to tell somebody.

Well I tossed and turned. I fretted and fumed. I got all tangled up trying to think my way around it. Couldn't think straight.

Then I stopped. I didn't have to think! Just use the plan.

Now, see, this is important. Plan ahead for what you're going to do the next time your spiral stairs loops back around. No use saying they won't. You need a plan. When you're on the sane side of your circle, whatever it may be, you got to make up a plan for what you're going to do next time you're insane.

I had the plan me and Dave had worked out when we got back together. You get tempted, you tell somebody.

Last thing I wanted to do, mind you, was tell anybody. So frigging embarrassing. I would've rather been shown on TV picking my nose.

Jack was still at the dropping by stage. Paying compliments. And I was still in the "cream your drawers" stage. So private. Nobody's business.

But I got up the next morning. Didn't pay no attention to my own feeling. Didn't pay no attention to the worming-out thoughts in my brain. Just got dressed, drove into town, marched right straight up to Marg's, and banged on the door.

I'm sitting at her kitchen table fooling with a piece of paper, folding it and unfolding it.

"I met Jan up street," Marg says. "She tells me Jenny seems to be coming along pretty good."

"Yeah," I says. "She's doing awesome."

There was this big long silence. I'm making a fan out of the piece of paper.

Marg says, "I got a new bedspread. Tammy don't like the pattern. Puts her in mind of fried eggs."

I'm not getting up to go look at the eggs bedspread. I'm sitting there flattening out my fan, folding it a different way.

Marg says, "Rose," she says, "what's the matter?"

God, I hated to say! Me and some guy again. Marg won't believe I am this bad, this stupid! Maybe I won't tell her. Maybe I can get through it on my own. Nothing's really happened yet. Maybe I'll just be on my way.

No! No thinking! I'm not fit for thinking right now. Just do the plan like I promised I'd do if I ever got into this type of a mess again.

I looked at my foot in a brown sock, rubbed it around on Marg's floor. And I come out with the facts.

Then I hear the famous, calm, Marg emergency voice, saying, "You're doing good to tell."

Never said I was bad or stupid. Just helped me plan out the next move.

Next time Jack come bumping up our lane in his truck, I was to just nod to him through the window. Show him I was on the phone. Point for him to go ahead and get whatever he needed out of the shed. Let on I was real busy with the phone.

That's what I done, too. I was on the phone because I dialled it the minute that black truck turned into our lane. What I was talking about was him. Telling Marg, one minute at a time, just what I was going through.

"Okay, here he comes. I can hear his truck in the lane."
Marg was saying, "Good girl!"
This is what we'd fixed up to do. She was my help line.
"He's parking by the pump. Oh, Marg, I'm weak in the knees. I'm weak, Marg! He's waving to me...."
"Give him a little wave back, same as you would anybody," Marg says. "You're not so weak, Rose. Think back on all the strong things you've did. Tell me about them."
"I found a decent job and quit Ken?"
"Yes, you did."
He's hanging around waiting for me to finish. I tell Marg when he signals to me to come outside.
"I can't do this, Marg. I got to go. Bye."
"Wait. Hold on. Keep talking to me. Tell me more strong things you done."
"I want to go out."
"Tell me what you done when you caught that guy with Jenny."
"Got the police."
"And you kept him there talking until they come. I always think how strong you were, Rose, to sit there talking with him till the cops come. Now, you're in that good house, that you're fixing up there with Dave. That's your home. Right? That's what you really want. Your married home with your good man. Your little girl. If you're strong enough to talk about cheese and pickles with a child molester to keep him busy till the police come, you're strong enough to stand there now and talk to me and let this Jack be a mistake that you don't make."
I stood there listening to Marg. And looking at Jack.
When I didn't go out, he come to the door.
"He's knocking! I can't stand here and leave him knocking!"
Marg tells me that what they had her do, in the hospital, when she was a little girl that couldn't breathe right, was they had her count her breaths.
"I can hear this one nice nurse yet. 'You're going to keep

breathing, Margie. Count your breaths, Margie. One, two, three, four.'"

So Marg gets me counting the knocks on my door, thinking of her in her favourite place when she was little, where they didn't beat her or screw her but stood by her through her panic times and kept her breathing.

That's how we got the Marg we love today, standing by, so kind and calm, in panic times.

"Eighteen," I says to her when he's finally pissed off and marching to his truck.

Marg, she babysat me like that every step of the way. When I wanted to go looking for him, I went to Marg's instead. Whenever he come by, I got on the phone to Marg.

I moaned to her that I was just as hopeless a idiot as ever and nothing hadn't did me no good or taught me nothing.

But Marg says to me, "Nope." She says, "You've broke the abuse pattern now. You're not keeping things a secret, the way you had to do with your dad and you always done, from then on, with every Tom's Harry Dick."

It was true. The pattern was broke. Just the fact of not keeping it secret made enough of a crack in it, let enough steam out, so that, in a while, I cooled down!

Jack buggered off. Nothing had happened. It was all over.

Nice bright Saturday morning around that time, I dropped off Jenny at a little friend's house for a birthday party. Driving back home, new snow glowing white on all the trees, I was singing in the car. So proud I hadn't caved. So glad and relieved and grateful and proud! Got home. Headed for my special drawer. Something had sure shifted. Figured I'd make a new stepping stone. Sun fell on the piece of Tammy's blue curtain material that was in there with my stepping stones. Picked it up and run it through my fingers. Put it in my pocket.

I'm thinking, thank God! I'm better now! I done it! I beat that old pattern! Thank God! I got nothing to be ashamed of this time. Haven't screwed up! I was trying to figure out what the new stepping stone would be. Couldn't sit still. Went dancing back outdoors. Drove back out the driveway. It's so nice, eh, when there's a fresh snow and the sun comes out. Didn't know where I was going. Turned left on the township road. Me all by myself there, rolling along, singing. Even singing, I still felt bottled up. More wanted out of me. I'm thinking, oh thank God I didn't screw up! Thank God!

Wound up at the church. Reverend Watters come out of his office. Hadn't saw him since the wedding. I asked if I could go upstairs and thank God.

Ministers must be like Pam at the shelter, eh, trained not to faint. He just smiled and said, "By all means."

I open the door to the holy room there and peek in. With the lake froze, the colours from the windows are laying still, pools of coloured light on the floor. Red, blue, green, gold. I creep in, creaking the door. It shuts behind me with a soft kind of a thud. Nice old smell in there, wood and hymn books.

I was busting to talk to Whatever it is that brings us around and around, gives us another new day and another new day. You screw up fifty times, and yet there it comes, sure as morning: chance number fifty-one.

Sally calls it grace. Me, I wouldn't know what to call it.

Alls I know is my heart was straining at the seams. All the times I'd screwed up! How weak and shameful and stunned I had acted! And yet I had been gave another chance! And this time I'd won! I'd did it!

I was getting choked up. Put my hand in my pocket for a tissue and come across my swatch of violet blue. Took it out. Unfolded it.

Squatted down and lay it in a pool of yellow gold light. Smoothed it out on the red carpet. Boy, in that light, did that deep blue ever glow rich! New stepping stone. Never wrote nothing on it, though. I don't know the word for what that is.

But I know the feeling. I stood on the new stone in the patch of gold with my feet lit up. Felt like my full heart busted open with like a squirt of relief and what gushed out was some church thing of Sally's. I said to the quietness in that place, I said, "Mercy is new every morning!"

39.

NEVER TOLD SALLY I done that. She'd have been all over me, trying to pry me away from my pancakes on Sundays and win me for the Lord. Whatever may be between me and Whatever, I figure it's none of Sally's business.

She's got enough to do, working on her boyfriend, Tao. She's trying to win him for the Lord. He just smiles at her so you couldn't guess what he's thinking, and tells her he's a Taoist, like forty generations of his folks before him.

Well, we were on track for to build the hotel. We were up a couple of million bucks. And I had done good with a temptation instead of doing bad. Which one of them things do you think I was happiest for?

Let's put it this way. If I hadn't of managed to control my stupid self, none of the rest of what was going on wouldn't have did me much good, would it?

Josie smiled at me when I come in to see her. Give me the old high beams. I took the wrapper off a pot of yellow tulips I brought her, set it in her windowsill.

The only remark she said that day, she said, "The hardware man."

I says, "Not now, Josie. I told you."

I put two new white cotton undershirts into her dresser drawer (Josie has trouble keeping warm). I says, "That guy don't like women. Sally's got her little Chinese fellow. You know that. They sit and play cards now the water's froze.

Argue over what kind of a hand it is that moves the hands of time. They're two peas in a pod."

Josie, she didn't say nothing, just smiled at me, at the tulips, at the snow falling on the pine trees and tall rocks outside.

Three guesses who had the most to say about the plans we got into that winter. I says to Dave, I says, "You can't let a six-year-old design a hotel."

But Dave, he grins. He says she's got more good ideas than the architect.

I says, "It don't need a turret."

But Dave says, "Where else is a princess going to stand and look out over the lake from, and watch her ships come in, if she don't have a turret, eh Jenny wren?"

"And let's make a drawbridge," she says.

They played at this hotel thing like it was another one of their Jell-O projects. I couldn't always tell when they were pulling my leg.

Dave and Al even tried to buy Macaulay's Point for a building lot because Jenny said it was the right place for her castle. Old Macaulay wouldn't sell. Liked his shack. Said his great-great-grandfather built her, in the year of confederation.

They offered him way high.

I says, "For frig's sakes, that's a waste of money. Another lot will do as well."

Anyways, he still wouldn't sell. So they give up and started dickering for another piece, pretty near as nice, further along the shore.

You never seen a kid change like what Jenny done in that first year with us. From the lost little soul with the white face, standing there watching me leave her at the foster home, to this here spunky little item she was most of the time now. For me and Dave, and Al too, she was the point and the joy of just about everything we done.

Of course she had her low times.

Her shrink told us that there'd be lasting effects from Jenny's traumas. We weren't to look for miracles. A child that has went through what happened to Jenny is going to have a lot of healing to do.

I knew that by now, if I knew anything. But knowing it did not make it easy to watch.

Dave, he wanted her happy all the time. Couldn't stand it when she'd sit in the rocking chair staring. Or when she'd crouch on the stairs with her stuffed rabbit, weird look in her eyes, pulling its long ears through her fingers, over and over and over.

Dave wanted to go cheer her up.

But I says, "Leave her be. She's grieving her losses."

Timothy, the stuffed rabbit, he was a help. Jenny talked for him. Got him to tell me things.

The rabbit told me, "Jenny's extremely sad."

"Did she say what's on her mind?"

"Jenny wants to see her mommy immediately."

"You tell Jenny that's the same as anybody would feel, in her shoes. You tell her she wouldn't be a normal human person if she didn't never miss her mommy."

I told the rabbit to tell Jenny she couldn't see her mommy and I knew that hurt.

I got out my red *I can stand pain* stepping stone and let Jenny stand on it. She hunched over, held her stomach, and she started to scream.

I stand there, helpless, wondering, should I call Sandra? Or should I call Marion, the shrink? Tell her how bad Jenny's missing her mom? I know what she'd say. Her and the case worker already told me Jenny was not to see Sandra. Not until after she'd fully attached to me and Dave, made the break with her past. It would retraumatize her, they said.

I'm trying to hang on and remember: she's just feeling the pain. She needs to feel that pain. The first stepping stone. The worst one. Pain.

Too bad the worst one is first. But that's what I'm here to tell yous. It gets easier. Stand the pain. Just put up with it and don't run away from it and don't do nothing to blank it out and you are on your way, pretty soon, to better times ahead.

Jenny is in pain, and Dave comes running in the house to see who's getting murdered. Jenny's bent over screaming like torture.

He tries to hold her. She yanks away, screaming. Terrible.

Dave takes a fit. Starts yelling. My sister and her bleeping boyfriend should have to stand here and see what they've did to this child.

I give him a look, as much as to say, yeah, I know, honey, but shut up.

He starts banging around the house, fit to be tied. She's clutching at her little gut, these like knife-edge screams after screams tearing her open. He's slamming doors, growling. Don't know what to do with himself.

I yell at him, "Dave!" I says, "For God's sakes!"

So he goes storming out of the house. Cuts down the red maple, working like ten men. (It was shading out the garden anyways.) Chops up Sandra and her frigging dickhead boyfriend into stove lengths.

Jenny, she screamed so I thought she'd turn herself inside out. Drowning out the noise of the chainsaw. Then she's just crying. Puts her face against me. After a while, we went and sat in the chair and I rocked her.

"I want my mommy. I want to go home."

"I know, sweetheart. You can't go home. I know it hurts."

Soon as she was feeling better, the sun bust through for Dave too.

She went through some rough times. She felt her pain, and she grieved. Later on, she raged. Pounded the stuffing out of good old Timothy rabbit there, a few times, threw him down the stairs, flailed him with a skipping rope, told him he was a mean, mean mommy.

I watched her, step by step. Sewed the rabbit back together. Was I ever glad I knew them steps! Knew each step was okay. Kept telling her it was okay.

It's okay to feel pain. Okay to feel anger at the ones that have did you wrong. Okay to be sad for what's lost and gone. Okay to scream and cry and get it all out.

Sooner or later I'd always see her, pigtails jumping, riding by the window on Dave's shoulders. Or she'd be bumping along in the truck with him, heading off someplace, with a happy face. Or running after him up the lane or out to the shed. And Dave, he'd be looking relieved as if somebody finally just moved a truck that had been parked on his foot.

I said to him, "Davey, she's doing good. The first few steps is the hard ones. She'll be on to the happier stepping stones pretty soon."

We loved her the best we knew how, good days and bad. And, on the whole, I could see it was going all right.

"This being parents ain't so hard, is it?" I says to Dave one day. "It's a wonder so many people can't seem to do it worth a shit."

"Oh, I think most people do it good enough," Dave says. "Except for two certain ones I could mention."

You can't convince Dave that there's more than about two people on the earth like what Sandra and Ian are. He just wouldn't be able to take in that there's this frigging avalanche, little kids bent double, all over the place, with this same pain.

And grown people hobbling around in circles, drinking or sleeping around or taking drugs or whatever to numb the pain.

Marg, you know, she never believed in the hotel before. But, now that it was coming true, she was so matter-of-fact about it. Like the lights were turned green. Time to drive on ahead. She was busy checking out wholesalers. Housekeeping carts, towels, fire alarm systems, hair dryers that hook to the wall.

Tammy, she was trying. Putting in her kind of ideas. Let's

hand out mace spray with the shampoo and shower hats. She didn't seem to know enough to be too flabbergasted with the fact we were really doing this.

Sally, of course, was not surprised the least bit. Faith could move mountains.

Al, he grumbled that, to hear Sally tell it, you'd think it was going to be the Lord writing the cheques.

Josie, of course, she wasn't surprised neither. Just nodded and smiled.

Seemed like I was the only one amazed and worked up. Running around like a chicken with its head cut off.

I says to Al, I says, "That's your money. You don't have to do this with it."

"Oh, I thought I had to."

"But now, serious, Dad, is this what you would want to do with it? Maybe there was something you'd always wanted to do, yourself?"

"Well," he says, "I will be wanting to hold back some of my capital for a project I got in mind." He says, "Out there on the island in front of my place, I think it's about time we invested in about fifty foot of new rope for to put up tire swings again. How would that be, princess? Grandpa will put up a bunch of swings this summer, eh, for yous to swing on and jump in the lake."

"Can Matthew and Meghan and Brett and Julie and Alexander play too?" (Tammy's kids and some of the cousins there.)

This is just normal life, far as Dave knows. A father backing a son and daughter-in-law's venture. A grandpa putting up swings for to make kids happy. Dave gets a kick out of the way things like that still make me cry.

The next thing that happened was the old Macaulay place burnt down. "The house that burned down before the castle came!" Jenny said.

I turned around and looked at her.

"Remember? The night Grandpa Al fell on the floor."

"Jenny can see," Josie says.

"In the fire," Jenny tells me. "I saw it in the fire. A house burned down and then, out of the ashes, a beautiful castle arose."

Josie says it again, "Jenny can see."

So, of course, nothing would do Al and Dave but they had to switch plans and start talking to Macaulay again, see if he'd change his mind and sell them the land now his shack was gone.

Al said it was a better place anyhow. That was where he was voting for all along. There was a real good aquifer up there.

I said to Dave, "You don't let a kid pick out a building lot based on what she thinks she seen in a fire."

Dave says, "Look," he says, "yous all moved up here to this town because of a wrinkled-up, five-by-seven picture of it Josie cut out of some old magazine once. True or false?"

"Oh, come on. It wasn't that simple! A lot of things went on and we wound up..."

"Nope," Dave says. "That's the long and the short of it. You might just as well admit it. And this piece of shit house here, why did we buy this?"

"Well, but we like it. It has a good feeling to it. It's on the lake...."

"Yeah and we passed up a dozen better houses. Why? Because they weren't down in a valley, the way the picture was in Josie's little nuts head. Correct?"

"Okay, Dave, but..."

"And this here hotel idea. This is based on what?"

"But..."

"Are we a crazy bunch of dreamers or ain't we?"

"I'm not used to thinking of myself like that. I always thought I was more the practical type."

But then I got this echo of Meredith: "We have to live in the real world now that we're grown up, Rose. We can't live in a dream."

I never bought that, did I? Hung right on to the dream, in

spite of her. Scratched *fantasy* off the bad list.

I put my face against Dave, my arms around him. He's strong. Feels like tire rubber.

"Anyways," he says, talking into my hair, "what's wrong with Macaulay's Point? Not like it's impractical. You can see the lake on three sides. Old man seems to want to sell, now."

I told him Macaulay's Point was my dream place for to put the hotel and also a sensible place for it. I told him I didn't know why I was arguing.

"And if Jenny can see like Josie can, that'll be a good thing, won't it?" he says. "It'll come in handy."

I didn't say nothing. What's the use? The world's a way weirder than what I ever used to think. Real and dream is more mixed together.

I looked out the window after supper and there's Sally's T-Bird bumping up our dark driveway.

"Can I talk to you, Rose?"

I put my coat on, and we walked in the lane. The winter stars back north are bright as diamonds. She didn't say nothing for the longest time.

So I finally asked her, I says, "What's on your mind?"

"Tao asked me to marry him."

"Well! Did you want to marry him?"

"Yes." Her voice was like she was going to cry.

"What's the matter, Sal?"

It was a real cold night. I stamped my feet to make sure they weren't froze as we crunched along.

"It's too dumb to say."

I said, "Not because he's Chinese?"

"Oh, no."

"And his side don't mind?"

"No, no. His grandma told him I'd have lucky children from now on."

"Is it your old fears? Because of what happened when your daughter—"

"No. I think I've worked through that. I really want to try again. I'd love to get married to Tao and have children. That's what I've prayed for, but..."

I thought, oh shit! I bet I know what's the matter.

I said, "Is it because of what Josie says?"

I could hear her sniffing. Sally don't cry very often. I scrounged in my pocket for a Kleenex.

I had to smile. I says, "Ah, come on. If you want to marry Tao and he wants to marry you, you go ahead. Never mind Josie."

Sally says, "But she's never wrong."

"The only unmarried guy at the hardware store," I says, "he lives with Art Petty, who frames houses for Jan's Tom."

"I know, I know."

We talked it over for a long time that night, walking up and down in the cold. I tried to convince Sally to go ahead. Told her sometimes Josie's pictures didn't mean what you'd think. Reminded her about Josie's lucky ticket vision, how I thought Dave was the lucky ticket.

"It's a damn good thing I did marry Dave, see, Sal, but it turns out it was nothing to do with Josie and her pictures. I only thought it was. What if I'd gone and did something I didn't want to do because of her? Or not did something I wanted to do? Maybe it'll come clear some other time what Josie's talking about. That's how we got to use this second sight or whatever it is. Along with our own brain and our own feelings. Just for a hint. Not for the gospel truth."

I could see, by the time she left, she still wasn't sure what to do. She was scared. Sally, you know, she needs a gospel truth.

40.

OKAY, SO, BY SPRING, we had our site and we had our blueprint. Dave and his cousin, Tom, had their construction crew over there soon as the ground dried out enough to get the machinery on the land. Dave's dad, he was right in his glory, sitting on a stump, supervising.

Jenny, of course, she always wanted to be tailing after him, to watch Dave build her castle. She had her own little hard hat and work boots. Al would meet her school bus at the end of the lane when she come home and take her over to the site.

I wasn't one bit keen on her being over there. I says to her, "You stay out of the road of them trucks. Stay with Grandpa Al. Hang right on his hand. Don't you go wandering off in the woods, or down by the shore there. You could fall in the lake and drown and nobody'd hear you for the uproar, what with the machines and all the sawing and drilling and hammering. And look out you don't step on a nail."

And I says to Dave, when we were alone, I says, "You tell your dad to watch her. I don't like all them workmen around her."

"You worry too much."

"I worry the correct amount I need to worry based on what the hell this world is like."

"Dad'll look after her."

"How's he supposed to watch her and watch yous pour the footings at the same time? I know what men is evolved for ever since cave days. Yous are evolved to hold your breath, watching for a turkey to shoot, thinking of nothing but what's in front of your eyes. Your brains thinks of one thing at a time."

Dave said she'd be fine. She was sitting on a stump with Al, way out of the road. It was an education for her, he said, to see how a building went up.

"Yous weren't evolved to nurse a baby in one arm, stir the pot with the other hand, chew the fat, keep one eye on the toddler and the other on the fire, and teach the older girl to sew, all at the same time, the way us women was."

Dave always thinks things are going to be great. And me, I always think there's disaster coming. The truth is normally someplace in the middle, so we balance out all right.

Dave was after me to quit work at the plumbing and heating place. Said millionaires generally don't have to listen to nobody yelling at them about sludge shooting out of the shitter.

Tammy stopped by one day. I made the comment that I might quit work.

She got this sad look on her. "I wish I could get your job after you. But I get all bent out of shape over every little thing. That's what Matthew tells me every day. Says the lights are on but there's nobody home. Says I'm no good for nothing. Guess he's about right."

Chill went over me. What was young Matthew doing talking like that to his mother?

I went and got Josie to let her sit on our porch the next Saturday. It was getting to be nice weather again, but the bugs wasn't out yet. Gee, it was good to see the open water again! Josie watched the breeze sweep patches of sparkle over it.

I picked up Dave's binoculars, the ones that his uncle had in the navy. Scanned Macaulay's Point. Good job Al's got that orange plaid coat. I could always spot him. Jenny was right beside him. Little yellow hard hat. Pigtails sticking out from under the sides of it. Cute overalls tucked in the tops of her boots. Al was pointing at something, and she was gazing up.

I made up my mind to quit worrying for a few minutes. Put down the field glasses. Took a swig of tea.

I said, "Listen here, Josie. You got to tell Sally she can go ahead and get married."

Josie never said nothing.

"It's getting past a joke," I said. I said, "Josie, are you listening?"

I'd been after her for months now. She didn't give me no answer. You can't drag nothing out of that girl.

We could hear the sounds of the hammering, sharp, across the water.

"Can you believe it? They're over there building your dream hotel, Josie! Never thought for a minute we'd really live to see it. Do you remember how you used to build that thing for us in the air, when we hadn't nothing else?"

Josie smiled. She knew what I was saying. She looked over at the point. She understands everything, same as you or me. And more. Only she sure don't talk much.

I let out a sigh.

"Young Matthew's been badmouthing his mother."

There's not so much of a trick, sometimes, to seeing how the future could go. Josie looked out over the lake and said, "Matthew."

"What are we going to do about that kid? He's starting to sound like his frigging father."

Nothing else was said for a while.

Then I said, "I sure hope the hotel winds up being a good idea. Hope people want to come up here. And what about the people like us that we were always going to help? What happened to that part of it? What are we supposed to do about that?"

Josie's eyes seemed to focus different. I watched her careful.

"What is it?" I says. "Did you see something?"

"Cave," she says.

"Cave, eh?"

Josie nodded.

Could she see red fire jumping on rock walls? Caveman, wrong in the head, his twisted face? The long, long shadow of his raised-up arm?

Al, he was getting a kick out of how rich he was. Kept trying to think of what a rich man would do. Not that he ever done nothing to his tarpaper house or bought a truck from any decade in living memory or nothing, like most people would've. He still was traipsing out to his backhouse in all weather and grousing about Sally using indoors when it was nice out. He had two pairs of pants, one for working and one for good. Sally was after him to buy new ones. He just asked why he would want more pants. Said he already had twice as many pants as arses. Wouldn't buy tea now the mint was coming up. Grew and shot most of his own food, and Sally still canned it.

Sally, she loved making all them shelves and shelves of jams and tomato sauce and fruit and jellies in jars. Born homebody. That's Sal.

But she was still wrestling with what to do. Just couldn't bring herself to forget about this thing Josie said to her years ago. A box opening. Something about a hardware man. That's who she was to marry. She wouldn't give Tao an answer. She was praying for a sign.

Marg was fed up.

Them two get along, eh. But they're different as chalk and cheese. Sally tall, pretty, gentle, and all wide-eyes belief in every kind of magic. Marg short and four square, both feet flat on the ground, sturdy and practical. She said, "Oh for frig's sakes, Sally. Go ahead and marry Tao. It's what the two of yous both want. There's no sensible reason on the earth why not to."

Now, Al's idea of spending large was he phoned me at work one day and says, "Don't go home and cook, Rosie. I'm taking yous out for supper."

We went to the Chinese place. Sally was working.

Elmer was there and four of his cronies, sitting in the corner with coffees, having a good laugh. One of them's Charlie. I know him from the plumbing business. It's spring, so they got a bunch of new Frank, the Toronto guy, jokes.

This Frank, lawyer fellow, when he comes up north every spring to open his summer place, first thing he does, every year, is he finds out his pipes is busted.

They tell him every fall. You got to drain out all the pipes real good, eh, Frank. If you leave any water in them, it's going to freeze and burst the pipes. Frank, he figures he's got them drained. How hard can that be, if these clowns can do it? Won't hire nobody to do it for him. Gets mad if you say something. He can handle her. He's smarter than this bunch. Nobody can tell him nothing. He's the big shot. These here are the lowlifes.

Then, of course, May two-four, regular as clockwork, there's Frank on the phone. He can't imagine how it happened.

Charlie does an imitation of the Frank guy's high-pitched voice: "It's a complete fluke!"

Elmer slaps the table, laughing. "Exact same complete frigging fluke every year!"

Al says experience is overrated. You can do the same thing wrong for thirty years.

Sally sat with us when she wasn't waiting on nobody.

Dave calls and nods to the Chinese grandma, sitting at the till there. He says, "Goodnight, ma'am."

Grandma likes Dave. She talks away to him, putting her hand on her back and making faces.

Jinping tells us that her grandma's talking about her sore back that just started acting up this morning.

Al goes through some pointing and nodding with her. Says, "Sounds like sciatica. Tell her to lay on her back and draw her knees up. One and then the other." He draws his knees up, where he's sitting, showing what he means.

Jenny went out to play in the yard when she was done eating. We could see her squatting down feeding grass through the cage to Hong's rabbits. Al always teases Hong about them. No matter what he's eating, he says, "Good rabbit." Orders sweet and sour rabbit balls.

Hong, she gets him back today. "For you, Mr. Al. Flied labbit."

Sally's boyfriend, Tao, come racing in, all excited. He's got something in a fair-sized box that he's wound up to show Sally and us. Looks real proud. Sets the box on the corner of the table. He has to tell us all about it before he will open it. His company used to be called China Importation Enterprise. What I gathered was, somebody in Hoi Nan figured out that there was room for improvement on that name, in terms of letting anybody know what the frig they were selling. So what they done was they put Tao here in charge of cooking up a new name in English.

"Words to express high durability of clothing," Tao says.

He makes quite a production out of leading up to showing us the new letterhead that he's got there with the new name on it that he's made up himself. He's been looking at some computer website where you can put in a word and get a list of all the other words that mean about the same. He's got it printed off. Reads it out.

"For adjective, I consider: *Strong, Tough, Solid, Hard, Durable, Long-lasting, Everlasting,* and *Immortal.* For noun, I consider: *Clothing, Clothes, Garments, Wear, Outfit, Fashion,* and *Togs.*"

Elmer and his buddies are all sitting there, eh, listening to this. Tao opens up his box.

And Sally, she shoots for the roof like fireworks. Grabs her orange apron over her mouth, bunching it in her fists. She hoots and howls. Her eyes are squeezed shut. Tears. You can't tell whether she's crying or laughing.

What's the matter with her? I peek in the box.

There it is at the top of four thousand sheets of paper: *Zhou Tao, R.R. #1, Strone, Sales Representative...* and in big letters, his brand new, made it up himself, company name: *HARD WEAR.*

They were all clambering to know what it was. Dave, he looked in the box and read it out loud.

Charlie says, "I would've thought you might get some confusion with a name like that."

But Sally, she's pretty near cutting off Tao's air, crying, thanking her heavenly Father. And I'm laughing, trying to hug the both of them at the same time.

Elmer says, "Women seems to like it."

"That's what you're after, selling clothes."

"Ellen always bought my overalls."

Dave and Al, they're sitting there, the way they're getting used to by now, waiting to find out what in the world just happened.

Tao, he's one of the family now. Because that's the same thing he's doing too. His eyes are round, for him, and he's looking from one to another, blinking out through me and Sally's hugs and kisses, wondering what in the world.

I don't know why he never run it past some of us that talks good English before he went and got all them sheets printed off. But, then again, if he had've, Sally maybe would have never braided the pink satin ribbon into her long blonde hair. And we wouldn't have had their wedding reception for the first event at our brand new hotel.

It wasn't open yet. We weren't done drywalling. But we planned on filling up the gaps with flowers.

"We won't need to buy them," Sally told me, waving her hand around Al's.

She had plants growing in buckets and barrels all over the place on Al's porch and windowsills, all up his driveway. She had flowers growing out of his old tin bath tub. (She makes him sit in a real bath once a week now.) She had gardens full of flowers. She had flowering vines all over his rusty harrows and ploughs in the yard.

"All from the seeds I planted," she tells me, with a shining face.

I remember so clear the day she moved up here, the first out of all of us. Her and her baby plants that were going to grow up to be flowers on the porch of our hotel, dumb as that sure seemed at the time.

When we're sweating, unloading the second trailer load of buckets full of blooming plants out on to the hotel porch and it was a solid wall of pink flowers from end to end, and you couldn't turn around for pink geraniums in the washrooms or see anybody behind the reception desk for more pink flowers, Dave wondered whether we maybe had pretty near enough flowers.

I told him what we were looking at was not just flowers. "What we're looking at is Sally's hope."

41.

THE YEAR AFTER Sally and Tao got married was another big year for the bunch of us. According to Sal, God moves in mysterious ways. Tao, he says that the way down is the way up. Whatever. Alls I know is the world is weird, the way things work out sometimes.

That first summer at the lodge, it was a lot like the way we'd had it pictured. But different, of course, because real life is full of stuff that you don't exactly picture beforehand. Little wee details like the green pens we got and the type of phones, the smell of new wood. It was all actual stuff.

I set up my new desk at an angle so I could look out to my right and see a strip of the sparkling lake and also keep an eye, over the other way, on the front desk.

Sally, she was getting set up to run the dining room. We had her in charge of the decorating in there. She was having a fight with the design fellow over the colour. Him threatening to jump off a bridge if she went and painted the walls of this wood, stone, and glass dining room the colour she wanted, which she said was like the inside of a shell and he said was like bubble gum. What they come down to ended up looking good to me. It was a subtle clay tone, according to the designer guy, that picked up a shade in the stone.

Dave comes in the office and he says, "You sure that ain't pink?"

I got my bifocals that year, so I could read him the paint

chip. "Says here it's *Pre-dawn.*"

Anyhow, with the view out them windows—the lake on three sides, blue at breakfast, green mirror for trees at lunch, silver with the moon at dinner—that couldn't help being one gorgeous place to sit and eat. We built the star-gazing patio, put a see-through roof on her, like we always said. We got the deck chairs and the red lights. We done her all.

There was the hotel, standing on solid rock in the real world, not nobody's fantasy. Stone on stone.

John, the furniture guy, he made us handsome log furniture for the lobby. We set it up in front of the big fieldstone fireplace.

I put my hand on the smooth wood. Run my fingers over the cool, rough stones.

Sally seen me. She says, "Blessed are they that have not seen, and yet have believed." I'm a Doubting Thomas, she says.

Her Tao says all that we have ever seen in the mind, exists in some dimension.

Anyways, I seen the lodge standing there in broad daylight with the Canada maple leaf flapping from the flagpole in the morning sun. I could hear it snapping in the wind and the gear jingling against the pole. I sat in the chairs. I seen the new landscaping with cedar chips. I walked on the flagstone path up to the door. I smelled the paint and the new wood. Helped to clean the windows.

I guess I didn't quite believe it was ours, though, till they hoisted the banner of Princess Jenny. Dave got Sally to sew that for her. A yellow flag with a big *J*. Rigged that up and flew it right under the maple leaf. When I seen that waving in the breeze off the lake, I went and turned in my notice at the plumbing place.

Me and Marg went to work, full steam ahead, me in the hotel office and her on the desk.

Tammy, she was there all the time too, once we got going, helping with the housekeeping. It done all our hearts good to see the changes in Tammy. If she could take her time, she could think things through good enough. Made her so proud.

"Remember how she used to diddle over every little thing?" Marg says. "Couldn't never make up her mind or get going on nothing?"

We figure it was being so upset and nervous all the time, used to make her seem stupider than what she is.

Marg done great on the desk, right from day one. The general public, it can't come up with nothing more outrageous, ruder, more of a disaster or nothing, than what a sex abuse survivor has been used to. Marg, she can hold steady through anything. I can hear her out there.

To one person, she's saying, "Sorry to hear that."

"Well, thank you very much," she's saying to the next one.

And to somebody else, all in the same steady Marg tone of voice, "We'll get your father an ambulance."

Business was on the slow side. I was sick worrying that we'd made a big mistake. Put Al's money into a dumb idea. Who was ever going to find out about a place way up here? We done some advertising. It cost a lot. Didn't seem to do much.

Dave's dad, he started renting out boats and doing sightseeing trips. Dave tried to convince him he didn't have to do nothing. But Al said he was weak in the knees from how much money he'd laid out lately and he'd be happier bringing some in again. Anyways, if he sat idle, he said, he'd get old.

Young Matthew started helping him.

And that'll be the making of Matthew. Tagging after Al, learning all about boats, motors, repairs, ropes, fishing, birds, weather, and how to live. You could pretty near stand and watch that kid grow that summer, grow and heal and straighten up.

Jenny, she was having a grand old time too, tagging after Dave, swimming or boat-riding with Al, helping Meghan around the hotel, playing with the cousins over at Jan's. She had a lot of freedom. I was always nervous, but I tried not to let that cramp her style too much.

Josie, she'd sit on the veranda. Jenny'd go sit beside her.

That's what she usually done in her sad times now.

I could get a glimpse out my office window, Jenny staring or hugging her rabbit and Josie watching her, nodding.

I'd have rather saw Jenny swinging on the tires all the time, jumping into the lake, laughing with the kids, or running around after Al or Dave, like she didn't have a care. She did them things. But then she'd be sitting in the shadow of the wall with Josie, gazing, serious, out at the sparkle and shine of Lost Gold Lake.

That was Jenny's nature. You could see it more and more. A thoughtful, deep little soul, with lots of happy times and also a wide streak of sadness.

Town of Strone got an almighty kick out of having its very own millionaire. Local paper run a story, pretty near every week for a while there, on Al winning the lottery. What Al was thinking of doing with his money. Tom's construction firm using a new type of beams. Al witching for the well. New resort lodge coming along on schedule. New resort lodge being named The Sunny Shore. We was always news.

Of course, relatives Al never even heard of started getting in touch.

"They get a warm family feeling for me," he said. "Comes over them sudden when they read about the money."

We never did find out who told the newspaper about Group.

Alls I know is I was sitting by the woodstove at home, one Wednesday night, with my feet up, for once, reading the paper. And I read that millionaire Al Smith's daughter-in-law, Rose (née Underhill), who many of us know from Dodd's Plumbing and Heating, was a survivor of childhood physical and sexual abuse.

I hopped out of my chair like it had bust into flames, called Tammy and screamed at her. But she swore it wasn't her. Said she never told nobody nothing.

I was ready to sue that damn paper.

Two days later, Marg steams in waving another newspaper

clipping. Her aunt in Toronto sent it to her. And, holy shit, if we aren't wrote up in there too!

The human interest story that I'm telling yous here, the drift of it anyways, is right there in the paper! This group of low socio-economic sex abuse victims without a thin dime is now sitting pretty, aided by a backwoods millionaire lottery winner. *Real-life Cinderella story*, it says.

We were mad as wet hens. Blamed it on Darlene. I bet it was her. Talked and fumed about getting a lawyer.

But we never got around to that. Because, man, was that Toronto article good for business! The phone just started and it never quit. Online bookings filling in. Hotel caught on.

And more than that, too. The day come when Marg called me out to the desk and introduced me to a guest.

"This is Natasha," Marg says. "She's one of us."

So that's how that all got started. Without us doing nothing to reach out to them, people, as Meredith would say, "from backgrounds like ours" just started showing up and talking to us.

You'd see Sally sit down at a corner table with a guest. Or you'd see Marg walk around the desk and shake hands with somebody, looking her or him in the eye a certain way. I'd bring a person into my office, open up the bottom drawer of my filebox, and get out one or another of my stepping stones. The first one, usually: that old, red *I can stand pain* stepping stone. That first step. My red piece of paper was getting pretty tattered by then, but you could still make out the block letters I'd printed on it in black crayon: *I CAN STAND PAIN*.

Tammy, she'd be out on the veranda, making this slicing down gesture, the right hand coming down on the left, in no uncertain terms. And we knew she was telling somebody to make the break, cut the asshole clean out of their life and don't take them back for nothing, no matter what.

It wasn't just women, neither. We sure found that out. Lots of little boys have came in for the same shit. Mixes them up something awful because they've got the gay question to think about on top of everything else.

We heard every kind of a story there is. Heard them over and over. It was quickly getting past what we could handle. I went and talked to Jenny's shrink, Marion. Got her in on it. She started setting up retreats and weekends at the hotel.

One day a telemarketer called. I got a soft spot for them people, eh. I know what the frig it's like doing that job. I got talking to her. Wound up telling her to get to a shelter.

Held the line while she looked up the number for it. Made her promise to go there straight from work.

"And you don't have to work where you're working," I says. I told her to look at the job listings. And, when she called for a new job, to tell the people what her strengths are.

She didn't know she had any.

I says, "Sure you do." I told her the strengths she must have had to survive this far and be working at all.

Marg heard me preaching there. She had to laugh. She says, "You're worse than what Sally is," she says. "You're like born again."

I says, "What?" I says, "Am I supposed to leave somebody sitting there with her background taking shit and say nothing? She's a bright one. She's only got to take that first step. and she'll be on her way."

Marg smiles, pats my shoulder. She says, "Go, girl!"

As Al said, the road was rising up to meet us and the wind was at our back.

42.

WE HAD A WHOLE YEAR like that. And it wasn't until the summer when Jenny was eight that she come running in one day when I was opening the mail. "Guess what I saw! A cave!"

I set a handful of letters down.

"It's big and special," she says, "and full of pictures!"

"Did Josie say something to you about a cave?"

"No."

"You sure?"

Jenny nods.

I says, "Are you fooling me? Is it a pretend cave?"

Jenny said, "No. It's real."

I says, "Take me to it."

But she wouldn't agree to that. It was a secret. It was magic. Nobody could find it. I questioned her on that until I got to be pretty sure that the cave wasn't a real cave. Seemed like it was some fantasy play place of her own. I asked her again if Josie had put it into her head.

No.

But where else would she have got an idea about a cave around here?

When she'd been going on about it for a day or two, I went and talked to Josie. "I guess you and Jenny been talking about the old caves idea, eh?"

Josie looked at me blank.

"Did you say something to her about that? You must have. She keeps telling me about a cave."

I have hardly ever saw Josie looking like she didn't know what I was talking about. But that's the look on her now. She frowned and shook her head.

I asked the rest of them. Everybody claimed they hadn't said nothing to Jenny about a cave.

It got so Jenny would tell me every night, when I was tucking her in, about what she seen that day in the cave. I'd sit on the edge of her little bed there and look out at the apple tree in the last light of them summer days. Little green apples forming. Robins flown.

She told me there was a man in the cave. Then one night she whispered to me the man was like Ian. It give me the creeps.

"A man?" I says. "You're pretending, right honey? The cave is make-believe? And the caveman?"

Jenny said no. She said it was real.

"Are you talking to some stranger out there?"

No. Not a stranger. She said she knew the man in the cave from long ago, when she was little. He was at mommy's house.

I said, "You are going to have to show me and Dave this cave tomorrow."

Morning come. Jenny said she couldn't show us.

I says, "Why not?"

She didn't say nothing. So I said, "The cave's pretend, really. Ain't it, Jenny?"

She didn't say nothing.

"Jenny? Is this all fantasy?"

She shook her head.

"Well then, I want to know where this cave is and who this man is!"

I couldn't get her to agree on showing me the place. I told her she was not to go there by herself. She was not to talk to no man out there in the bush.

I called the shrink.

She said Jenny was finding a way to talk about what had happened to her. That was why Jenny was telling us that the man was no stranger. She was revisiting her past. It was positive, she said. To Jenny, it was not pretend because it was about something very real in her own mind. I should let her keep taking her little walks and communing with nature. I should just listen to her stories of what she was finding.

I says, "But there's no real cave, right? There's not some man out in the bush?"

Marion said some more shrink stuff that meant no, it was pretend.

I listened, night after night, sitting there in the summer dusk, getting the chills. Jenny, she'd curl her little body tight up against me and squeeze on my hand and tell me what the man in the cave showed her today.

I was stalling on telling Dave. Knew it would drive him nuts.

When I finally told him, it did. "Fuckhead Ian must've got out of jail! He's hiding out back somewheres." Dave's heading for his gun locker.

I says, "Hold on. I bet we can check if Ian's still in jail."

We checked. He was.

Dave says, "I shouldn't have read her all them adventure stories."

"For crying out loud, it's not your fault!" I says.

"I'm going out there and find this cave."

"There is no cave."

"I'm looking anyhow."

He might just as well go and look for a cave. Give him something to feel like he was doing about it.

The shrink said to listen. But it was no piece of cake, listening to this stuff, I'll tell you. Jenny, she whispered to me every night about the cave man. The cave man showed her the hidden entrance. The cave man showed her the rabbit man. The rabbit man told her how the world began. The cave man was old.

Maybe, to her, Ian was old.

The shrink, Marion, got her drawing pictures of this cave and the man in it.

One day, when I'd went to pick up Jenny, Marion asks me into her office. She says, "Jenny seems to be working through her abuse experiences. But what has me stumped is that the details she's drawing are authentic-looking, like actual cave paintings." Marion looked at me. She was creeped out. Said she'd like to show us the pictures.

Me and Dave went by ourself to see them. Jenny's strange pictures were spread out on the long table in the art therapy room. The shrink, she had four library books spread out alongside of them.

"It's details like this that really make me wonder!" Marion was pointing to a picture in the top right corner of one of Jenny's papers.

I like this shrink Marion, eh. She's just a human being, leaning over the table with a puzzled look on her. (Not on any high throne like what Meredith always used to be.)

The picture she's pointing out is a thing kind of like a rabbit, red, with long ears sticking up. It struck me odd Jenny wanting to draw with that rust red colour so much. Wasn't a colour she normally picked out.

I said I'd took that animal for Timothy, Jenny's stuffed rabbit. Mind you, Timothy, he's yellow. But there was a picture in the library book looked a lot more like it than Timothy.

The shrink says, "Have you ever taken Jenny to see any petroglyphs?"

Me and Dave look at each other.

"Rock paintings done by First Nations people? Natives?" Marion says.

We shook our heads.

Spent a long time in there, leafing through the books and Jenny's drawings, feeling weirder and weirder. We found six different drawings Jenny done that looked like ones in the books.

The shrink, she come up with the idea of showing this stuff to somebody that would know. That's how we met Cheryl, the petroglyph expert, who's a First Nations person. Cheryl's a good friend of mine now. We go for walks or we take a canoe out and we talk about everything under the sun.

Nothing weird about Josie seeing the future, as far as Cheryl's concerned. Says there's some like Josie in every generation. They're sent to us kindly by the Great Spirit to show us the way.

How she talks strikes me a lot like the way Sally and Tao talks. We're sons and daughters of the earth and sky, the way Cheryl puts it. Sally says we're children of the light. Tao will tell you you're connected to every strand in the web of all.

For sure, if yous keep on learning about yourself, you're going to come to the night-blue stepping stone that I don't know a name for. I just call it the mystery stone. The spirit stone.

That first day we met Cheryl, we took a folder full of Jenny's pictures and drove up to her place at the far end of the lake.

Sitting in Cheryl's front room, you look down the long shore of Lost Gold Lake towards our place. Macaulay's Point is way off, floating in a blue mist. Water's real quiet and green today. Somebody has a canoe out. Looks like it's sitting on a mirror. Just like back in the days when Cheryl's people was the only ones here.

We opened up the folder. Cheryl, she took one look at them pictures. "Has your daughter ever been to the place that you folks call Macaulay's Point, that peninsula down there?"

We told her we owned it.

Cheryl, she got a funny look on her. We might just as well have told her we owned the northern lights.

Anyways, sure, we said Jenny'd been around Macaulay's Point all the time the last year and a half. Told Cheryl we were the ones just built the lodge there.

Cheryl, she watched the red canoe slipping along in the green shadows, near shore. Looked at Jenny's pictures again, careful. I could see her making up her mind whether to tell us something. She decides to. She says, "There are hints in stories about a cave near here."

Dave shoots up out of his chair. "There is a real cave?"

"People have searched for one, because the oral tradition seems to suggest that there may be one; but, if there is, it has not been found. There are four vision pits in that area, but they are not caves. There are paintings on the rock face but they can only be seen from the water."

Cheryl was excited. She tells us that Jenny's pictures remind her of certain Anishinaabe petroglyphs, but they are not the specific ones known to exist in this area.

Who the hell's this cave man? That's what me and Dave wanted to know.

Marion, the shrink, she thought that Jenny was making up that part, even if there was some real rock pictures out there somewheres.

"Shrink says Jenny's telling them tales to help herself work through what happened with Ian," I told Dave. "She says Jenny's probably weaving a fantasy around some powerful pictures that she's found. It's important to her to have the place be a secret. It's her private healing place. We shouldn't intrude into it."

That's what I said to Dave, passing on what Marion, the shrink, was telling me. But I was none too comfortable. And I never seen Dave so restless. He's a busy man these days, with all he's got to see to. But he still found the time to worry himself ragged.

He was in my office every half an hour. "Where's Jenny?"

"Out in the boat with your dad and Matthew."

"No. They come in."

"Then she's likely in the kitchen with Sally."

"No. I checked."

"Then she'll be just out back."

He'd go look. He had to see her every second.

Jenny, she missed her freedom. Dave didn't want her outdoors without somebody watching her. He was turning into a bigger worrywart than me.

Finally she come right out and told him she wanted to go to the cave. Dave, he said fine but he was going with her. "I want to go by myself," she told him.

"Look," he says, "you got to tell me. Are you talking about a real cave?"

Jenny, she looked at the floor, wiggled her toe around.

"Jenny!" he says. "I'm asking you a question."

She wouldn't say nothing.

Dave got mad. Started yelling at her that this wasn't funny. He had to know. "Is there a man out there?"

She wouldn't say nothing.

I says, "I wonder if maybe she don't know, Dave."

"How could she not know?"

"Well, like Josie. She don't always know if she seen something or dreamed it."

Dave, he was going crazy. He says, "Listen here, my girl," he says. "You are not to be off in the bush by yourself. You hear?"

Jenny, she keeps on looking at the floor.

So then we run into our first real trouble with raising Jenny. She started sneaking off.

Me and Dave got frantic more than once. We'd be out searching for her. She'd come wandering back, dirty. Secret look on her face.

Dave was out in the bush at all hours, trying to find out if there was really a cave anywhere out there. Or a man.

Josie, she got restless, which I never seen before. Didn't want to sit and look at the lake. Didn't want to sit in her rocking chair. She was always hugging herself, squirming. She wanted to go from one place to another all the time. Her dog would pace around and whine.

I'd yell at it to lay down.

Tammy was always wheeling Josie somewheres. The guests, ones that knew her story, they were nice to her. Matthew, he'd walk on his hands, bring her his lizard. Sally would be fussing around, trying to make her comfortable. Nothing seemed to quiet Josie's mind. Whenever I'd sit beside her a minute, she'd grab my hand. Eyes wild. "The cave man!" she'd say. Or, "The cave father!"

One time she said, "The grandfather!" And she looks at me with this look on her face like she's begging me.

I says, "Jos," I says, "what?"

She hung on to me with both her hands, like she could tell me through the grip of her fingers. You should've saw her eyes!

What could be eating her? The cave grandfather? Josie sure didn't look to me like she was thinking over some old theory of ours. She was trying to tell me something. I couldn't get what it was.

We were all trying.

The men, they were going to fix things, eh, the way men will try to do, lord love them. Sally's Tao, he went and moved everything around in Josie's room. Said she had the garbage pail on the wrong wall and the bed facing away from the door. That explained her, as far as he was concerned. That'd unbalance anybody, to have their garbage can over there.

Dave, he thought Josie was on the wrong medicine. Went and talked to them at the home. Made them call the doctor.

Al, he tried to get her to do crossword puzzles. If you don't do enough crossword puzzles, your brain will seize up, according to him. It was pitiful to see him sitting there trying to get her to think of a seven-letter word for highly strung. And her staring at him, urgent, squirming in her wheelchair.

Us women, we were all talking about it, the way women will. I said to Sally, "I guess you're on this?"

Sal knew I meant praying. "Oh, you bet," she said. "And the Lord is merciful, abounding in steadfast love."

For me, eh, there's times when it's not so hard to believe something like that, and times when it's pretty well impossible. But good old Sally. Through thick and thin, she keeps on saying, "All things works together for good."

Tom's whole construction crew and a bunch of friends of Cheryl's come down one Sunday, and they went over Macaulay's Point, every stick and stone of it, hunting for a cave. Couldn't find nothing.

Dave still wasn't satisfied. "Bush is so thick back there," he says, "you'd never know if you missed some crack in the rock someplace with brush hanging over it that a person could slide into."

We'd all help keeping track of Jenny. We'd mention, "Jenny's with Meghan." Or, "I just seen Jenny. She's right there on the dock with Al." Or, "Jenny's in the kitchen. They're hulling berries."

It was like there was a storm coming.

The shrink still said that Jenny was using the cave stories to work through her issues. But nobody could think where she was getting them pictures from. And me, I was sure that we were in for something. Just even to look at that dog of Josie's pacing around.

"For frig's sakes, lay down!" And he'd lay down for a half second.

Jenny kept drawing pictures. She would not stay home.

Dave says, "What are we going to do? We can't tie her up."

We tried grounding her. Taking away treats. Yelling at her. Reasoning with her. We explained to her what all could happen to a little girl by herself out in the bush. Sent her to her room. Locked her in once and she got out on the shed roof and climbed down the apple tree. Nothing worked. The kid kept sneaking off.

Then the storm broke. The day come when we could not find Jenny. Nobody'd saw her for a half hour. Not with Meghan? Not with Al? Not with Dave? Jan?

We hunted high and low. We shouted ourself hoarse. No answer. Everybody helped. We run along all the paths back and forth to our place and the boathouse and the dock and everywheres. Guests started helping. Al went all along the shore in a boat. No Jenny.

I don't know if yous have ever lost a kid? Oh my God! You feel your stomach drop, eh, and your heart's just banging. Your mind's racing. *She's drowned. She's kidnapped. She's run over on the highway. She's lost in the woods.* You don't know which way to run.

When we'd looked everywheres, we called the police. They brought dogs.

Back north here, that's a mean kind of bush to try and run through. It's all great big rocks that are right in front of you, ten, twenty foot high, like cliffs. There's blackberry canes that'll tear your skin like fish hooks. There's deer flies, mosquitoes thick as smoke. The ground's all roots and bumps. You trip and you get bit and you've got to scramble and climb and hunt for a way around or over or through. There's swamps. There's bears.

So there's me, sweat running off me. I'm filthy, panting, cut, my shirt's got a big rip I'm holding shut, pushing on the pain in my side, as I run through the bush with this one policeman. I get whipped in the face with a branch. The bloodhound, he's pulling out ahead on his leash, nose to the ground.

Adrenaline is quite the drug, eh? I'm sailing over logs. I'm climbing over rocks. And I still got wind for yelling. Yelling and yelling, "Jenny! Jenny!"

Dog took off faster. Me and the cop puffing behind.

We come to the edge of a swamp. The cop, he stood there looking around. Swatted a bug on his neck. Dog was flummoxed. We were puffing and panting.

In the one direction, the swamp opened out into a big beaver pond. The other way was a solid wall of bush.

I yelled for Jenny. There was a bit of echo. Then quiet.

We seen, stepping out of the bush, my father.

43.

YOU KNOW, I have worked awful hard on knowing real from not real. I'd have to say that that there particular minute was the hardest to tell. Seemed like a bad dream, but there was Dad. Dad was standing there, knee deep in weeds, holding Jenny's rabbit by the ears.

The dog, he took a leap, run right past the old man, dove into the tall brush. Me and the cop went scrambling after the dog, and it brought us straight to Jenny. I grabbed her to me. Relief pouring over me like out of a busted pipe.

I started to call Dave on the cell. Couldn't. "Dial Dave." I held the phone out to Jenny.

She was that awful calm. I hear her regular voice. "Yeah. I'm okay."

Him, loud with a question. "In the cave," she says, "with the cave man."

A cave man holding a rabbit by the ears.

I grabbed the phone. "She was with my—"

Then it really hit me. *My father!*

"With who?" Dave's voice is coming out of the phone.

Dave's asking questions. Cop is talking to Dad. Dad's standing there, large as life, with his lumpy chin. Jenny's talking to me.

There's a crow sitting still in the air, but the ground is sailing under it. The trees are sliding away from the crow.

I sit down on the ground. The ground is moving. I put my head between my knees. Have to hurl. Stick my face in a bush.

The cop and Dad are standing over me.

"Are you all right, ma'am?"

The cop's got a hold of Dad, by one arm. The rabbit's still hanging there from his other hand.

Wipe my mouth on a leaf. Sit there, holding on to a root. Sky still sliding, with them two men in front of it. Throat burning. I'm moving away from them, riding on the ground.

Jenny's busy talking to Dave on the phone.

Dad looks like a bum. I don't like him standing up in the sky like that. The way Josie said. The cave man in the sky with the rabbit.

So I try to stand up, but the ground sails off at an angle, like a circus ride. I give up on the standing. Sit back down in the scratchy weeds. Mosquito and my heart in my ear.

"Ma'am?" The cop's trying to get through to me.

The old man hasn't said one word.

My head buzzing in circles with a deer fly.

"Can you identify this man?"

I look at him. I wish I would say something.

Don't know what all happened after that. Cop must've called the other cops. I just sat there, stupid. I remember looking at a big blue dragonfly, seeing what beautiful green glass eyes it had on it.

Jenny, she curled up beside me. She kept patting my forearm with her soft fingers.

If yous had asked me right then, I would've told yous there was zero hope on this planet. Nobody couldn't escape nothing. Didn't matter what I'd did. Didn't matter how far I'd went or what I'd tried for. Here was the very exact same goddamned old man, hanging over us! Might just as well have left Jenny right where she was, let Sandra raise her. She wouldn't have did nothing to keep her from getting screwed by her grandfather. I hadn't neither. For all the good it had did to bring her here! All our luck. All our work. He found us just the same. It was like Jenny's fate found her, just as sure as sure. And if that's the way she goes, what is the frigging use of ever getting up in the morning?

That's what I thought, sitting in the rough weeds, looking in the glass green eye of a bug.

Dave showed up, running. Sally right behind him. They squatted down, grabbed us. My face went looking for Dave's dent in the chest. I felt the ground slow down.

Dave and Sally helped us up. I'm clutching Jenny.

So there we are, standing in the bush.

I thought, Jesus. I thought, I wish it was a million years ago and we were starting over, right here. We could take and put that old man out of his misery. Smack him over the head with a rock big enough to make a clean job.

Sally is on the phone to Marg and Tammy. The cop over there somewheres, faint voice asking me whether I can identify this man. And, "Do you want to press charges?"

Dave said we sure as hell did.

Jenny was took to the hospital and my old man to jail. Police wanted to hold the old man, and we sure wanted them to. But nobody knew what to charge him with.

Doctor couldn't find no injuries on Jenny or traces of fluids on either one of them.

Jenny wouldn't say nothing. Police child worker talked to her. Nobody could get her to say nothing but that he showed her the cave. The rabbit man knows about the fires that are under the lake and the way to the world above.

Dave talked to her. I talked to her. Marg took a try. Nothing.

"The beaver people take kids' baby teeth for luck." That's all she'd say. Legend stuff. Nothing about Dad.

"Did he do with you like what Ian done? Jenny, did he touch you inappropriate?"

"There are three layers of worlds, Ann Toes. Did you know that?"

We were at our wits' end.

The shrink, Marion, tried to get Jenny to draw what happened. Couldn't get nothing but more cave pictures.

Marion said, "I think she found the images in the cave so powerful that she could dissociate from her body very easily in there. She seems to have gone into the pictures and blocked out all other memory of whatever happened."

"Like our friend Sally. She used to go into a radio. Be with the people in the radio. Blanked out Mr. Mullen in the back room of the garage."

Police said they couldn't hold Dad without no evidence.

Dave's life, at that time, was nothing else but pleading with Jenny. "You got to tell us, sweetheart! Please tell somebody. Tell Ann Toes or Marion. Or tell Dave, if you want. What happened, Jenny? What went on in that cave?"

She clenched her arms around his neck and cried.

I says, "Dave, she don't know. She's blanked it out."

Dave went to the lawyer in town. Lawyer said this wasn't his line. "You want to talk to Frank Wilson," he said.

Dave says, "Lawyer Frank!" he says. "He don't know c'mere from sic 'em. Can't drain a tap."

"He's no plumber. But he knows his own stuff. He's got a reputation for this type of cases."

Al says, "Them big city lawyers are slippery as deer guts on a door knob."

But Dave calls Frank. Next I know I'm sitting in Frank's screen porch, looking at the big view from up there, sipping iced tea. And take a guess what he's asking me? He seemed to recall that he read something in the newspaper to the effect that I was a survivor myself. You'd have thought, by now, I'd be used to everybody knowing this. I might just as well be wearing a T-shirt printed *I Done It With My Dad*.

"Could we talk about the present time?" I says, polite as I could manage.

Frank, he says that the problem with Jenny's case is the lack of evidence. He says, in my own case, we'd have something to go on.

"My own case?" I says. "That's thirty years ago!"

"That would not exclude the possibility of pressing charges."

"You mean we could fight him on Rosie's behalf?" Dave's getting fired up with a new thought here.

I'm sitting, looking at the wicker furniture, thinking about Pam at the shelter, who told me that the past don't go away.

At first, I said no. Jesus. No! Last thing I want is to go to court in front of the whole world and talk about the most embarrassing, painful, dirty thing that ever happened to me.

But what were the choices? We could either let Dad go scot-free or we could do the way Frank here was saying.

What the hell. Everybody and their aunt already knew my frigging story anyhow. If this is what it would take to shut down that old menace. I said okay.

Dave told about my sister Sandra. "He done it with her too."

Frank's all happy about that. More evidence. He's going to contact Sandra.

"Dad got a number of kids at the school where he works, too."

Frank was keen to get them all in on it.

I said, "How would you ever find them people? They've all grown up and lots moved away. Most of them probably never told a soul in their life. Half them likely blanked it out and don't even remember."

Frank, he says that he'll consider possible ways to locate people that may be able to testify concerning my father's abuse. In any case, we'll have my sister's testimony to back mine.

I warn him she's nuts and no help.

He asks me if I have ever been in treatment with any mental health professionals.

I tell him just a woman named Meredith Debenham. He says he'll call her for our expert witness.

"Oh no!" I says. "Leave her out of it!" I don't ever want to lay eyes on Meredith again.

But Frank and Dave, they go on at me. "Your psychologist's evidence would be material to the success of the action, particularly if we're not able to contact any other witnesses. Her expert opinion could be critical to the outcome."

"You'd let the old fuckhead go! Let him run loose screwing little kids, maybe getting Jenny again, just for some idea you don't want to see Meredith...?"

"Okay," I said. "Okay. Okay."

That night, me and Sally were standing on the hotel porch, watching a storm come in. The wind was up, roaring through the trees, lifting out Sally's hair. We held on to our coats, to keep them shut at the neck.

She says, "Dark is His path on the wings of the storm!" She give my arm a squeeze. "But there is joy in the morning. Things will get better," she says.

I says, "Sally," I says, "I'm fresh out of patience with God."

I could feel her go tense.

I kept on. "It's like Something wants to torture me and mine! We can never get away."

Sally told me Saint Somebody said we had to run, with patience, the race which is set before us.

In my mind, I seen Jenny running up endless stairs, trouble at every turn.

Blew up and yelled at Sally. We're standing out in that storm. Belting rain breaks loose. Wind to knock the breath out of you. Woods and lake roaring. And I'm out there screaming at Sally not to talk to me no more about frigging God.

"I hate the thoughts of Him! He tortures innocent kids!"

"It's nothing to do with God," Dave says when we're in bed. "Your dad read the newspaper, that's all."

Everybody'd read about us in the paper. Why wouldn't the old man? He must've saw I was rich and headed up here to see what he could get off us. Wandered around out back, checking things out and come across that cave, and Jenny.

Poor Dave. He looks so miserable.

I says, "Darling, I'm sorry."

"What are you sorry for now that ain't your fault?"

"I've brought you so much pain."

"What did you do? Phone the old fuckhead and ask him to come sleep in our cave? I wish you wouldn't have did that," he says. He's pulling me in close to him.

I dreamed my stepping stones were getting pelted with rain, blew around like litter, wrecked in the storm, flying off into the woods and lake. I was running after them, trying to catch them and stuff them under my coat while they flapped and tore in the wind and fell apart, wet, with the words all running and blurred. My red pain stone was plastered to the flag pole. The blue cloth stone, it was soaked too but, when I picked it up, it didn't fall apart. I set it in a patch of gold light. But when I tried to stand on it, I fell off. Fell down and down.

If the old man didn't go to jail, we were going to have to sell the hotel and move. Try to find somewheres to hide from him. Maybe we could go to a different country.

In my dreams that fall, no matter where we'd ran to, he always come after us. The shadow of his lumpy chin would pass along the walls of foreign cities. I dreamed he was coming across a desert after me on an evil, grinning camel. I went into an igloo and crawled under a fur blanket to hide. But he was under there too, reaching for me.

44.

I WALKED INTO A BACK ROOM we got at the hotel, one Saturday afternoon in November, and there's Tammy's Meghan with Jenny. Meghan's a teenager now. Pretty girl. Dark hair. She's come out of herself a lot in the last few years. Her and Jenny got magazines spread all over the table. Scissors and glue.

"Look, Aunt Rose. We're making fear collages," Meghan says.

Fear collages!

I looked at her. "Your mom tell you about those?"

"No! You did!"

"Me?"

"When we were kids. The night you came to Auntie Marg's and made good macaroni. Matthew made a kite? You showed me about cutting out pictures of things that scared me? Remember? We were sitting on the orange shag carpet in Auntie Marg's bedroom."

"You got quite the memory."

"I'll never forget that," Meghan says, looking up at me from where she's sitting there with Jenny, all the pictures spread out in front of them. Jenny's cut out a bed with purple sheets. A closet. Door glued on the ceiling of it.

She was right into it, cutting off the top of a little girl's head. I watched her glue a green scarf over the mouth.

I said, "Meghan, thank you!"

Told Sally what the two girls were up to. She said it was a blessing. Well, really what she said was that I was a blessing.

I sowed the seed of loving kindness, years ago, passing on to Meghan what I'd did in Group. And here was the fruits, she said.

Of course there was no such a thing as private life for any of us now. First Nations people, they were wound up about their legendary cave getting found and pissed off about the idea of dirty things going on in it. Of course, with a mythic cave and sex both together, the news people were having orgasms. Cheryl, the cave picture specialist, was on TV. Al was on the radio.

Hotel was full. We were all hurrying like a herd of turtles. Trying to keep up, feeling heavy.

Me and Dave made a decision to tell Jenny what was going on. We were charging the old man from the cave, her grandfather. To keep her safe. So he would never bother her again.

Jenny said, "How can they put him in jail when I don't remember if he did anything wrong?"

I levelled with her. Told her he done wrong to me and her mom, too. Long, long time ago. And that's what he was going to get in trouble for now.

She said maybe her mom didn't remember.

We sat quiet.

Jenny was thinking, nodding to herself, looking into the fire.

I said to Cheryl, the cave pictures expert, who was getting to be a friend of mine by then, I said, "I wouldn't be surprised if we got us another one along the lines of Josie. Our young Jenny sees stuff in the fire. Like she seen the Macaulay place burn down. She looks at the phone just before it rings. Okay and here's an example too. She woke up last Wednesday. She says, 'Let's go to Grandpa Al's.' I said later, after school. But no. Not later. Nothing would do but we had to go straight over there before breakfast. And it was a good job we did. He'd went out to that frigging outhouse of his before dawn, tripped over a root. When we get there, he's sitting on the ground. Needs a hand up. It's like Jenny must have knew!"

"A young seer," Cheryl says. According to Cheryl, it was whatever happened in the cave that done it.

When she gets talking about her religion, Cheryl quits making much sense to me. Just like Sally or Tao on either one of theirs. On a good day, I can go along with the basic feelings of any of them. But when somebody gets busy explaining why there's air and bugs and us and everything, or exactly how come somebody's a saint or a seer, they lose me.

Dave's the only one always makes sense on the religion topic. He says, "Who the hell knows?" Says his favourite author on the mystery of the universe is Howard I. Know.

Dave says life's like beer. It's not in you very long. Only difference is, he says, with life, you got a choice whether or not you're just going to piss it away.

Jenny quit running off. Soon as we found the cave and the old man, that seemed to break the secret spell or whatever it was. So thank God we didn't have that to worry about no more. Somebody was with her all the time, and she didn't make no objection.

There was a foot of ice on the lake, by this time. Al, he took a snow plough out there. Cleaned off a great big skating rink for the kids.

"You'd never guess, to look at her, would you," I says to Marg one day when we were looking out the window. Jenny was a blur of sunshine out there in her bright yellow coat. Blue hat and mitts. Stripy scarf flying. She was chasing after Matthew, trying to steal his red toque.

Marg, she smiled. "You wouldn't guess, to look at us now, neither. Running this place, doing good. I never used to do nothing but worry and eat double-chocolate doughnuts. Sally was snoring all day. Tammy trying to run back to what's-his-face. And you, Rose—!"

With all that had been going on, I hadn't thought about any of that in a long while. "You got to keep that in mind," Marg says. She says, "That's what shows you how far we've came."

I leaned on the windowsill, watching them skate. Josie was by the lobby fireplace.

"Come and see the kids," Marg says to her and wheels her over.

Josie looked at them kids, nodding, the way she does, and smiling.

"What do you see, Josie?" Marg asks her. "Can you see how the kids are going to do, in the times to come?"

"No!" I says. "I don't want to hear!" I clamped my hands over my ears.

I seen them eyes of Josie's following Jenny, watching her fall and get up. The ice, it was striped blue with the shadows of the trees at the edge, and the colourful kids sailed in and out of shadow and bright.

Josie watched our Jenny getting up again after another fall. She watched how Jenny brushed the snow off her knees. Josie nodded. You'd almost think the minutes couldn't flow unless Josie give them the nod.

Tammy come along with a housekeeping cart.

Marg says, "Look at that, Tammy. Look at them kids of yours, growing up here with us all for family and nobody beating the shit out of them."

45.

NOW THE HOTEL WAS FULL of people that knew our story. Marion the shrink, and a fellow, Ed, who was also a shrink, they were running retreats and weekends and whatnot for groups. Everybody that had ever got abused, and had any money, seemed to know about our place. (We said we'd have to figure out a way to help the poor ones, too, which we've did now, with a fund. If you bought this book here, you've chipped in.) Somebody was always putting out their hand, wanting to greet us as their sister.

I took a break and went and whined to Josie one day about Meredith coming up here for the trial. Told her I had this firewall in my head about Meredith. Felt like I could not face seeing her.

"There's something wrong about Meredith. Remember you used to say she'd missed the patch of light like that leaf you seen? Landed in the dark. She's like she wants to drag me into the dark too. She pretty near kept me from marrying Dave and adopting Jenny. She like undermines me. I don't have a leg to stand on around her. Feel like I'm just sinking down, helpless. Floor turns to chewing gum. I got to let her come. They say we need her for the case. I know I'm being a baby. I don't even have to talk to her. But I feel like all my strength will be gone if she's there. I won't be able to give my own evidence or answer the lawyers or the judge. I'll screw up. We'll lose. If Meredith's there."

Josie, she's got this bag that hangs on her wheelchair, you know. She keeps it full of her pictures that she likes and little weird stuff that means something to her. Josie fished in that bag and she brought out a jar. If it wasn't that same mason jar Sally had in her apartment, way back when, the one with the little red-brown, china cow!

See, Tao, he won't put up with clutter in the house, eh. Says it's bad chi. So Al's barn and Marg's spare room, and even Josie's bag, were storing crap that Sally couldn't part with.

I unscrewed the lid. Dumped the cow into my hand.

Josie's dog tilted his head and looked at it.

Josie, she reached out and took hold of the ends of my fingers, pulled my hand towards her. I knew that, for Josie, this little cow was tied in with Meredith. Josie looked close at the way the cow was laying in the palm of my hand. She took and traced along the lines in my skin with her see-through finger, studying my hand and the little broken toy that was laying there across the lines of my life and heart and wealth and children and whatever else them lines in your hand are supposed to be.

I says to her, I says, "You got no business taking offence when people call you a fortune teller."

Josie frowned. But she was showing me that this Meredith woman was in my fate or fortune or whatever you want to call that. Part of what Meredith herself would call the "pattern."

I'd drew the Meredith card again. No way out of it. That's what Josie was telling me, just with the light little tickle of her finger tracing the lines in my hand.

We all had bad dreams, in them weeks. Dave would cry out. I'd reach for him. "It's okay, Davey. Wake up, love. It's all right."

We go back to sleep and the next thing, I've hollered out and Dave's rocking me.

And Jenny, half the time, she was in bed with us too, curled up against me.

"It's okay, Jenny. It's going to be okay, sweetheart."

I had so much I wished I could ask Josie. What was going to

happen now? Would we ever bust out of the curse that seemed like it was out to get us, in spite of all our love and luck? Was all this heat and noise what Sally calls it, a refiner's fire, baking us to solid gold? Or were we just plain getting burned?

Now, lawyer Frank, there, he keeps fishing disgusting details out of me about what happened with Dad years ago. Writes it all down.

Dave says, "He's going to make your old man pay for what he done to you and your sister too."

"That's not the way I'm looking at it."

Dave got hold of the wrong end of the stick. Started going on about that's the trouble with me. I don't think I matter. I only care about Jenny. I don't see that I was a poor little girl once, too, same as her.

"Honey," I says to him, "it won't help me for that old man to suffer."

"He's got to pay."

"The kind of a cost we're talking, nobody can pay it."

Dave said, "How can you feel sorry for him, after what he done?"

I said, "Do you want to know how his jaw got to be like it is? His father, my grandfather, kicked him in the face when he was seven years old. Shoved him down on the floor and kicked his face in."

Oh God. I just wanted it over.

I moaned to good old Marg all the time. She knew. She's been through a court case.

"If only Meredith wasn't going to be there!"

"Meredith won't bite you."

"She's bit me before."

Lawyer Frank, he got hold of my sister. Explained things. Asked her, polite, if she would be willing to take part. Told her it was to benefit Jenny. Jenny was not safe while this man was at large. For her sake and for the sake of all other children who might come into contact with him, it was a matter of great importance. There was only one other witness so far. And it might come down to my word against our father's. Sandra's evidence was going to be crucial.

She said to fuck off, so he subpoenaed her.

I'm in the back room dumping on Marg again one day in the spring. She's trying to pry out of me what I'm so scared of about Meredith coming.

I'm pretty near crying. "I don't know what of!"

Young Meghan walks in and says, "Aunt Rose," she says, "sometimes it helps to cut out pictures of the things that can scare us."

I look at the kid. The bright eyes on her. Her and Marg take a glance at each other. Meghan grabs a stack of magazines, plunks a pair of scissors on the top of it, holds it out to me.

Don't matter how often I do this kind of thing. It always starts out feeling like a dumb waste of time. I always have what the shrinks call Resistance. Feel foolish. Think there's not going to be, in no magazine, a picture of what I need to look at.

"Do you need help, Rose?" I could just hear Meredith asking me that.

No. Dammit. Not your help, I don't. You pretty near wrecked my frigging life, Meredith.

Then, of course, there's the picture that I need. My thumb stops the pages. I open the magazine out flat. Milk ad. Cow. And of course, the page, it just happened to be tore right across. Only word left under that tail-less cow was *Good*.

"Seek and ye shall find," the way Sally puts it. "Knock and the door shall be opened unto you."

Cheryl, my First Nations friend, she'll tell you life's all about the spirit's quest. Go looking. Whether you look at the stones under your feet or the clouds over your head. Apparently, the pictures in the magazines, the lines in your hand, will do. Long as you're looking and seeking with your heart wide open.

It's all universe. And Tao, he'll tell you that the universe is nothing but patterns of meaning.

(That philosopher dog of Josie's, eh, he raised his head when Tao come out with that. Got this intelligent look on him. You'd have swore he was getting ready to give his own opinion.)

Anyways, there I am, cutting out the ripped cow. *Good*, it says. If I ever seen a frigging omen, that was it.

Who knows, eh? Maybe something bigger than any of us was leading me by the hand, there, helping me along. Maybe we all got good parents, if we look for them. Look up at the sky and call it our Father. Look at the earth and call it our Mother. Maybe it's true. Howard I. Know?

Alls I know is that you've got to quit struggling like a drowning person and find a way to trust that you can float.

46.

HOTEL WAS DOING FAMOUSLY. Al was over at our place one night and we showed him the books. Good thing he was sitting down. He nearly passed out (Al's one to faint, eh). Melted right back on the couch cushions.

Dave was laughing at him. "Never thought you'd see that kind of a number for our bottom line, did you Dad?"

Al takes a swig of water. Wipes his mouth on his sleeve. He says, "I'd have took that for a long distance phone number."

Dave sits and chuckles.

We still have our same place, eh, that we bought off of old Elmer. Still no hydro. Heat with the wood stove. We stay over at the lodge a lot. But we like to get away and come home here. Specially in nice weather. Be ourselves. Relax. Kind of like having a cottage that you can walk to.

Jenny's laying on the floor with her arm around Josie's dog, both of them, for all I know, reading the future in the fire.

When Jenny was going to bed, she said, "Ann Toes? You always say that I'm a good person."

"You are."

"Well, then, why did I go to the cave?"

"Good people can do wrong things."

(Like me sneaking up the back stairs to that jerk Dirk's place. The pull of that, eh. Going after the adrenaline rush.)

"There's a pull to certain things, Jenny."

She says, "Not just for me?"

"Oh, no. Heck no. Lots of people feel a pull towards all kinds of things that can make their heart thump faster. I've been there myself."

"And that's not bad?"

"Well, feeling the pull ain't bad. Nobody can help what they feel. Going with it, though, that's what can lead to trouble. We got a choice about whether or not we do things. Got to use our brains."

"But it's such a strong pull!"

I says, "Where you went wrong was keeping it secret, not letting nobody help you."

"I told you about it."

I says, "No, you didn't. You wouldn't tell us what was going on or what you were feeling or nothing. You cut us off. You can't pull back against them bad things all on your own."

(I thought of how hard Marg pulled for me that time I had the crush on the carpenter.)

I says, "Jenny," I says, "it's like a tug of war. You get some other people pulling with you, and that's how you win."

"But," she says, "I was on both sides."

She's so smart.

She cuddled up to me. I stroked her pretty hair.

47.

THE COURT CASE COME ON. Getting dressed to go, I was worked up into a panic. "What are we going to do if we lose? We'll never get away from him! We'll be jumping at shadows all our life!"

Dave's trying to remember how to tie a tie.

They had my father sitting there. Poor old bugger. Looked like the rockslide had just brained him. He's blinking out from under.

Marg's on the one side of me and Dave on the other. Al next to him. Sally, with Tao's grandma, holding hands, in the row beside us (Sally's long, white fingers and grandma Zhou's old veiny yellow ones squeezing together there).

Plus, you know, eh, all of Dave's aunts and uncles that are retired. Jan was home with the kids, but Tom was there. A good amount of Strone squeezed in at the back. John, the furniture maker. Old Elmer and his buddies. The hardware guy and his partner (Sally used to be in there so much, eh, they're pretty near family). Josie didn't seem to want to come. Alls she said was something about a flat tire.

I looked around and I thought of what me and Jenny were talking about, how it helps to have people pulling for you.

I hadn't saw my sister Sandra since the night at the hospital. There she was. Looked about the same. Sitting fiddling with her purse strap. Enough makeup for ten whores, as Al would say. High heels. Tight sweater.

Hurt my heart to look at her. God, I wished she would get some help! Dig herself out of the rockslide.

I wondered what she'd say here today. *Please God, let her do this one thing for Jenny! Just this once. Let her tell the hard facts. Let her see that's the only thing that helps. Just face it. Tell her story, plain and true. Put up with the pain.*

I didn't see Meredith no place.

I'm in my numb state that I go into, which has its time and place, I'm telling yous. It's like what they shoot into your jaw at the dentist. I'm like one big fat froze face.

There's a Legal Aid lawyer up there getting paid to say that my father's an inoffensive senior citizen. Under the freezing, I can feel this lawyer's talk drilling into me.

The old man sits and blinks. You have to feel sorry for him, the way he looks.

They get him up and he tells the court his daughter Rose is a liar. I'm rich and he's poor. I never lifted a finger to help him. Left him living in a cave. What kind of a daughter is that? And now I just want to get him put away so I don't have to share nothing with him or look after him in his last years.

The Legal Aid fellow asks him if I ever invited him into my home or even shared a meal with him.

"No, she never did. My younger daughter Sandra will have me over for a meal. But Rose, there, she always treated me like a leper."

The Legal Aid fellow quits jabbering, and our lawyer Frank gets to start. He's got all them words, same as Meredith. "Incest, childhood sexual abuse, misuse of authority, cruel, violent, inappropriate..."

He worked up to finish his opening talk with a splash, talking about the long-term impact on the quality of life of these two women present, Albert Underhill's daughters, Sandra and Rose.

I see Frank sneak a look at his watch, and I figure he's thinking, like I am, where the hell is Meredith?

Well, the thing dragged on. Frank, he tried to trick the old man into letting something slip. "When were you last in contact with your daughter Rose?"

"She run off with some young buck when she was fifteen. Broke her poor mother's heart. Since that, I only ever seen her at Sandra's, the odd time."

"And you never attempted to contact her, at any time, until you learned that her father-in-law, Mr. Allan Smith, had won the provincial lottery. Is that correct?"

"First I heard was I seen it in the paper. I wasn't even asked to the wedding."

"Did the newspaper that you saw publish a picture of your daughter?"

"No. Her husband's father. That looks like him over there."

"Mr. Underhill, how did you know that the person referred to in the newspaper was in fact your daughter?"

"Seen her name."

"Your daughter now goes by her married name. In an internet search, I discovered over two thousand women by the name of Rose Smith. And I asked myself, Mr. Underhill, how did you know that the Rose Smith referred to in the news was in fact your daughter?"

Dad said it was just a hunch, but lawyer Frank kept on at him about it.

He said, "Her picture has not been published, but the life story of the Rose Smith present here today has been widely publicized. It has been reported in the media that the Rose Smith present in this court has a history of severe sexual and physical abuse by her father. Details have been revealed. I believe that you recognized those details. Did you know that story because you were a part of that story? Mr. Underhill, were you, in fact, the villain of that horrific story?"

I thought Frank was going pretty good there, but the Legal Aid fellow, he stood up and whined some objection. So the old man never had to answer that question.

Then they get Sandra up.

"Ms. Underhill, going back to your memories of childhood, would you tell the court what was the nature of your relationship to your father?"

Sandra, she stands there, eh, blinking, like the old man. She don't know what to say. Never breathed a word to nobody about the horrible, dirty secret thing of her childhood. Thinks she'll crumble into dust if she ever does tell that she done it with her father. It's awful hard to come out with, even when you got lots of support.

But, in a place like this, with a big judge up there looking down at you, and your sister (who you're not speaking to), and everybody your sister knows, gawping at you—!

There's me, praying again. *God Almighty, if you are merciful like Sally claims, let my sister come out with it!*

Frank, he worked on Sandra with a crowbar.

No. She didn't remember nothing about her childhood.

Not a thing. Nope. Sorry.

Could she call to mind her home life as a teenager?

No.

What was the earliest time she was able to recall?

She didn't know.

Could she describe the dwelling place where she lived as a child?

Old green clapboard house on Ferry Street.

Did it have a basement?

Yes.

Did she have any memories associated with that basement?

No.

Her father was a janitor at the public school she and her sister attended. Was that correct?

Yes.

Did she have any memories associated with the janitor's mop closet, in particular, or the boiler room?

The other lawyer objected. But the judge, he let the question stand.

But Sandra just lied and said no.

Did she have any memories associated with school?

No.

Did she have any impression as to whether her upbringing had been happy or otherwise?

None at all. No.

When was the last time she saw her father?

Finally my sister told Frank, "Look," she said, "lots of people has worse problems than what we ever had. If you don't believe that," she said, raising her voice, "just go take a look around Sick Kids' Hospital!"

I'm thinking, Sandra, if you got a flat tire, you got a flat tire. Nobody says it's the worst problem in the world. But you better stop and take a look at it. What else are you going to do? Drive on the rim the rest of your life?

That's what I'm saying to all of yous, that have got flat tires, eh. Pull over. Get yourself jacked up. Undo the bolts. Find the leak. Get her patched and pumped up. As Dave says, there's no use in yapping about somebody else that's blew a head gasket. That don't fix your tire.

The judge, he needs bifocals and won't admit it yet. Spends his life putting his glasses off and on, sliding them up and down his nose. He don't look too impressed with nothing he's heard so far. It was plain to see lawyer Frank wasn't doing so good now. I could hear Al bitching in Dave's ear about the money we were paying him to stand up there and accomplish blank all, by the hour.

So then they got me up. It's a good thing I'm froze solid. I tell the dirty old story like it's somebody else's. None too convincing, likely. I sound like a robot. Can't help it.

Did I remember my childhood?

"Yes, sir."

Could I tell the court about it?

My voice wouldn't come out very good. "My father there done it to me."

"Could you clarify that for the record? What did he do to you?"

We dragged through the whole nine yards, the stuff that nobody wants to hear. The metal thing he shoved up me.

What was the metal thing?

I didn't know. Round at one end. Shiny.

I had to tell that room full of my neighbours that, when I was a little girl, it always hurt me to pee. I told about the times I got burnt, what, exactly, he done to Sandra in the cellar. The both of us in the closet. The boiler room.

When it was done, I sat back down beside Dave. He whispered that I done good. I wasn't even shaking yet. I was thinking, thank God Meredith wasn't here. Then I'm thinking, but she should be. We need her.

Frank, he called a doctor up, and the doctor said yes, she had examined my scars. Yes, it was possible that those in my genital area were caused by the means described in my testimony. It would be difficult to account for them otherwise. No, she could not be certain. Yes, the scars on my back were the result of burns, probably sustained in childhood. Yes, it was reasonable to believe that I could have been thrust and held against an object such as a boiler pipe.

Thanks very much, doctor.

Where's frigging Meredith?

Frank's stalling around, and that's what he's thinking, I'm sure. We need Meredith to show up and say what she knows about me and my long-term suffering.

Otherwise it's coming down to my word against the old man's.

I sit there wondering, like I've been wondering over and over all year, how we're going to be able to keep Jenny safe from him if they don't put him away. Are we always going to be worried about her like we were last summer? Jumping out of our skin every time she's out of sight? What are we going to have to do? Sell the hotel and move? Change our name? Hide? Will we be able to hide, the way the papers love us?

And, even if we can get Jenny away from him, how many other kids has he got time to fuck up before he dies? Plus, I'll have my work cut out just to keep Dave from murdering him.

Frank sounds like he's running out of filler. Meredith better come soon, and, please God, make it good. She's about the only gleam of hope.

Finally we hear a little commotion at the back. There's Meredith. Smaller than I remember. She's apologizing to the judge for being late. Says she had car trouble.

Frank calls her, and she's on the stand.

She was halfway through her first words, telling the court she had been working with me in her role of psychologist for the Family Services Alliance during the period of—

She glanced at the people sitting there. And then she seen my father. Well, the colour Meredith turned! Same shade as the tasteless redecorating at that place where Josie and Sally used to work. Sick grey. She leaned forwards, fingers white on the brown wood.

The court police guy, he come speedwalking.

Town of Strone quit breathing.

"Are you unwell, Dr. Debenham?" That's Frank.

The judge, he's chiming in too, asking if an ambulance is needed.

"That chin!" she says.

She wasn't loud, but they heard it in the back row. Some said, afterwards, that what she said was, "That's him."

I don't know. I heard "chin." Same difference.

There was some quick, quiet talking back and forth. Frank, he said the witness was not ill, but he asked for a recess. Something about new evidence. Judge stood up. Everybody stood up. Judge walked out. Whole room bust out in hubbub. Lot of kind hands and faces as we passed through the room.

I remember the door opening. Blue sky.

We went home for a break. Sally tried to make us eat lunch. Al kept saying, "What in the name of wonder?"

Two o'clock we're all back in there. Meredith's in the stand. Frank, he told the judge that his witness was here in two capacities. He would ask her some questions about my psychological history. It had also come to light most unexpectedly, he said, that this witness had personal knowledge of the defendant, which would have a great bearing on this case.

The judge, he come to life. Tried looking at Meredith both ways, with and without his glasses.

Meredith has her hair combed, but she's still the colour of month-old pastry. Eyes and nose red.

Frank starts in with the psychology.

I can't listen to Meredith tell about me. I'm waiting for the other part.

It's not always such a bad thing to be able to fake good, eh. She was up there, shoulders back, answering questions like a pro. Held herself together, never turned her face left or right, never looked at the old man or nobody else neither. Give her answers clear and strong.

When they were through talking about me, Meredith's own time come. And that's how she finally took, for herself, that "important early step in healing" that she was always getting other people to take. Up there in the witness box, Meredith was face to face with her own childhood trauma.

I felt sorry for her, eh. She didn't have no Marg's arm around her. No Josie's hand to squeeze under the table, like what I had when I told.

Meredith, she took it like a soldier, though. Up there, all alone. Told her story to the top of the dark brown door frame at the back of that court room.

She quit using big words. Told it simple as a kid would.

"I had made a little farm in a shoe box," poor Meredith said. "I had gone to a lot of trouble with it. I made a little red barn out of folded construction paper and stuck cotton batting clouds in the sky behind it. I coloured fields, green and brown and golden-yellow, and I made little toothpick fences.

I had some small plastic animals. I had a pig and a goat and a horse. But I didn't have a cow. Until that day. In my mother's new box of tea, there was a perfect little china cow, just the right size for my field.

"It seemed like a wish come true," she said, in her shaky, new, human voice. "It was just what I was looking for. It seemed magical. As if somebody had known exactly what I needed! A perfect little red-brown cow to look over my fence."

The judge give up on his glasses. Plunked them on his desk. Wanted to know if this was relevant.

Frank shuts him up. "Directly relevant."

"I carefully picked my project up off the windowsill of my classroom and I went down the stairs with it, after school, being so very careful not to damage it. I remember very clearly going down those worn, black stairs, carrying my shoe box farm. I was afraid that the glue on the toothpicks might not hold...."

I got in this soft mood, sitting there listening to Meredith, thinking how you couldn't begin to make life up one half as weird as what it really is. Meredith and my old man! Not only was she screwed up just like me, the exact same frigging old man had screwed up the both of us. No way! What were the odds? But there it was. Ferry Street Public School. Meredith in knee socks, going down to see the janitor because he promised to show her something. Something to help with her little farm, which got dropped in the boiler room—scattered her little fences, broke her tiny, magical, new, china cow.

I could just picture Jenny doing a school project like that. She'd spend so much time on it. Glue one toothpick to another for a little fence. Stand the little animals, so careful, on their coloured fields.

Meredith was right back there in days gone by, talking about the model farm as if it getting damaged was the saddest part of the story. Saying it over again in a mournful voice. Her little cow, that was just the right size to look over her little fence and had came, like magic, in her mother's new box of tea, that very morning. I could see Meredith was dissociated from her pain now, just like she probably was at the time, concentrating on the toy farm. So she didn't have to think about what else was getting broke.

Just imagine what must've been going on, in the insides of her, all them times when she was pushing the rest of us to face what she couldn't face herself! Getting one person after another to come out with what was locked up tight as a drum inside herself! All the years she'd did that! Seeing people face their pain and move on. And herself never moving one bit. No wonder she didn't really want us to get acrost the river, when she couldn't! Oh my god. She was jealous of us. That was it.

I thought of Josie, at home. I bet she could see Meredith standing at the top of them worn, black public-school stairs right now. That's where Meredith had been standing all her life, eh? Too scared to take the first step back down and face what was at the bottom.

Just about nothing seems to surprise Josie. I figured the coincidence about my father wouldn't strike her much. Too weird, for anybody else, is just normal for Josie. That's the way she seems to think the world is, rolling in the great unknown, bringing us back around and back around. Another morning and another morning, in case we ever decide to face the day.

Wouldn't surprise me if Josie's dog was saying, "Well, finally, there's where the cow fits in!"

I think, when nobody's around, the both of them can talk just fine, Josie and her dog.

48.

Now, don't worry. I'm almost done talking. Just one more thing I gotta tell yous and it puts the icing on the cake.

After the trial and all that commotion, things settled down. Old Dad there was locked up. Meredith, she was on her way to dealing with her own shit. In time, she made a real good counsellor. Comes up here now and runs groups.

The only question left was the big one: Jenny. Same question we started with at the very first. Can we save this kid? Can we fix up her world for her? Will the damages be too much or will she be all right after all?

Few months after the trial, Marion started to sound cheerful on that. Said Jenny was coming along nice. Me and Dave, we thought so too. Spell was broke and she quit running off. She moped around for a while and then we could see her starting to take an interest in her normal stuff.

Nothing new blew up. We got some quiet years after that, for her to grow up in. Time slipped along, the way it does. We done our best and hoped our hardest. Jenny grew.

Any of yous that have raised kids will know that worry is a part of it. You're going to worry about them kids. Are they doing okay? Are they going to choose okay when they come to an age to make their own decisions? How's the world going to treat them? Are they ready for to handle it? For a kid like Jenny with all her traumas, you worry a hundred times more.

I says to Dave sometimes, "Do you think we've really did it? Have we saved her? Will she be okay?"

"So far, so good," Dave says.

And that was true. Jenny had a lot working in her favour. All of us there for her. She had her ups and downs. Not so many downs, as time went on. Her mood got more even. You could see her slumpy shame shoulders straightening up and all the sunshine that's in her starting to beam out more and more, as the years went by.

She joined the high school band. Trombone. (Dave said Al was lucky to be getting deaf.) She made good friends. Good marks. Loved her art courses. She was talking about being a Psychotherapist in Art Therapy, like Marion and Meghan. She was not just daydreaming neither. (Mind you, I'm the last person to laugh at daydreams.) But Jenny, she already had it researched where she wanted to go through for that kind of work, and what undergraduate study you do first, talked with her guidance counsellor at school, all that. If there ever was a youngster who looked like they had their act together, it was our Jenny.

But the fear still preyed on me. I done my best not to show it. But it was right there. I'd get awful flashbacks of what she had went through and I'd wonder if she could ever get healed. I'd think about the avalanche. The weight of all that, the power of it to crush anybody in its path. Rocks the size of destiny hanging over my sweetheart. Me and my little line of paper stones looked like a pitiful defence.

I used to talk to Josie about it, rocking by the fire in the winter, rocking on the porch in the summer. I would tell her the point of my life was to save that kid from the rockslide and I'd ask my deep-heart question. "Is it really working? Have we did it, Josie?"

Josie, she told me once, early on, she said, "Wait for a sign."

I couldn't get no more of an answer out of her. So that's what I done for years. I hung on, waiting for a sign, while we watched our Jenny growing into a fine young woman.

"What sign, Josie? How will I know if we've won or lost?"

I suppose there was plenty of signs but I'll tell yous the sign that hit me. It come along quiet and beautiful as the light of morning.

October. Me and Dave had took the day off for our anniversary. He was still asleep and I was laying there watching the early morning lake light play on our bedroom ceiling. I could hear Jenny moving around in the kitchen, getting ready for school. Then I heard her quick step on the stairs and her light tap on our door. She's got a pen and paper.

"Sign this, would you?" she whispers.

I'm reaching over to the night table, pawing for my glasses. "What am I signing?"

"Just a course change form. I'm changing out my art class."

"What for? Art's your favourite."

"I got Mr. Creepy this year."

I sit up like I'm on a spring. I hiss, "What? Why? What's going on?"

"You don't have to overreact. I've been going in at lunch to work on the dragon and he's been hanging around and I just don't feel comfortable, so I'm changing my course."

"Jenny, what did he do creepy? Why did you call him Mr. Creepy? Did he treat you inappropriate?"

"Relax, Ann Toes, it's just a feeling. Something about him. I'm out of there. Gotta hurry." She kissed the top of my head and blew a kiss in Dave's direction. She says, "Have a fun day off, you lucky ducks." Her feet skimmed down the stairs, the outside door tapped shut and that is when I got it. I seen what just happened. I seen good hope in it for all the years ahead.

I lay back, let the joy run over me. She changed her course. That and the course of history, I'm thinking. She felt something wrong, listened to herself, took her own action, all on her own, based on her own hunch. Our young bird, on her healed-up wings, was taking to the air.

We'd get Mr. Creepy looked into. But it wasn't him I was thinking of, right in that minute.

Alls I could feel was wonderful. What would possibly be the word for a feeling like this? What would be the stepping stone? If I could ever make such a thing, it would have to spring like a trampoline. It would have to be made out of sparkling lake light and I would jump high as the sky on it.

What's a word for when something is the point of your life and you work and work and work and then it has worked and you've did it? Triumph. That could be it. Triumph. Like, in my head, we're at the Olympics with gold medals on our necks and the music swelling up proud, crowds cheering.

Dave's rubbing his eyes, mumbling, "What's up?"

I was squeezing the breath out of him and wetting his chest with my tears. I'm telling him, "We've did it, Davey!"

ACKNOWLEDGEMENTS

I extend grateful acknowledgements to The Arts Group and The Vein of Gold Group. I wish to express particular appreciation for all the insights and specific knowledge offered by those members who are social workers and therapists, as well as for the friendship and encouragement of all who have offered feedback on this book during its development. Special thanks to Edward Hagedorn, MA, Psychotherapist, Art Therapy.

Huge thanks to my husband, Richard C. Hill, who has devoted countless hours to assisting and supporting me in the completion of this book and who is my lucky ticket.

Note: The English vernacular spoken by Rose and her friends is common in rural Ontario. It is carefully and faithfully represented in this book.

Laurie Ray Hill is best known in her area as a playwright. She has had plays produced and has won awards including selection of one play as Finalist in Theatre BC's Canadian National Playwrighting Competition and another as Eastern Ontario Drama League Best Original Script. She taught creative writing for many years with Loyalist College. Vision Loss Rehabilitation was a beloved career that took Laurie to homes and schools throughout a wide region, working with people who, like her own father, were blind or visually impaired, teaching specialized travel skills like street crossing with white cane or guide dog. All along, she has been secretly writing novels. Recently retired, she lives in Brighton, Ontario.